WHO'S WHO IN HELL

'Robert Chalmers is a master craftsman and the suavest man in England'
Hunter S. Thompson

'The best first novel I've read since *Catch-22*' Alan Bleasdale

'Well written, genuinely funny, yet thought provoking novel... Highly recommended' *Daily Express*

'Jolly funny' *Spectator*

'Very funny...The obits editor Chalmers creates is a glorious eccentric'
Daily Telegraph

'All the trademarks of Chalmers... an economy of style, a complete absence of flashiness and an acute sense of what makes people tick. It is also very witty' *GQ*

'[A] gifted first novelist... his invention rarely flags and the comic set pieces manage both gloom and laughter... his writing has an intelligence and dignity which makes him significantly superior to many of his coevals' *TLS*

'A witty, edgy and ironic look at modern living' *Sunday Telegraph*

'Its depictions of eccentric journalists at a major broadsheet are probably the best and funniest in fiction since Evelyn Waugh's *Scoop*'
Literary Review

'Pithy, witty and compellingly paced, Chalmers' highly impressive first novel is a bittersweet examination of love and loss, rich with precise dialogue, believable incident and memorable characters' *Big Issue*

'Chalmers reveals enough talent here to be as new and distinctive a voice in contemporary fiction as Nick Hornby' *City Life*

'Chalmers has much to say on love and death and has a fabulous, comic roving eye' *Metro*

'A fast and furious comedy of manners with a very human soul; and a romance that's reflective, wise and warm'
Hampstead & Highgate

Robert Chalmers was brought up in Manchester. He lives in London and this is his first book.

WHO'S WHO IN HELL

ROBERT CHALMERS

Atlantic Books
London

First published in Great Britain in 2002 by Atlantic Books, an imprint of Grove Atlantic Limited.

This paperback edition published in 2003.

The author and publisher wish to thank the following for permission to quote from copyrighted material: Patrick Creagh for 'What Made Him Do It?' from *Lament of the Border Guard*; Endomorph Music for 'Don't Trade Me in for a New Model' by Croker & Brooke; Bitter Sweet Music for 'The Devil is My Friend' by Patrick Huntrods; Plangent Visions Music Inc. for 'The Birds Will Still Be Singing' by Declan MacManus; EMI for for 'Five Hundred Miles' by Hedy West; Lucy Jones Music for 'Sweet Old World' by Lucinda Williams; Zevon Music for 'For My Next Trick I'll Need a Volunteer' by Warren Zevon.

10 9 8 7 6 5 4 3 2 1

A CIP catalogue record for this book is available from the British Library.

1 84354 028 2

Printed by Mackays of Chatham

Atlantic Books
An imprint of Grove Atlantic Ltd
Ormond House
26–27 Boswell Street
London WC1N 3JZ

'Not that you need making any better, miss,' Mrs Bowater assured me. 'Even a buttercup – or a retriever dog – being no fuller than it can hold of what it is, in a manner of speaking. But there's the next world to be accounted for, and hopes of reunion on another shore where, so I understand, mere size, body or station, will not be noticeable in the sight of the Lamb. Not that I hold with the notion that only the good so-called will be there.'

'Wherever I go, Mrs Bowater,' I replied, 'I shall not be happy unless you are there.'

Walter de la Mare *Memoirs of a Midget*

PART ONE

CHAPTER 1

He had noticed at an early age how everywhere looks all right on the map. Peel Park, a brutal wasteland where he had been headbutted, spat at and beaten almost to death, was, on the page of Daniel's Manchester *A to Z*, an inviting-looking green rectangle: the kind of place, a foreigner might have concluded – glancing idly at the book in the reference section of some distant library – where a man would linger over a glass of Sancerre before walking his lover back towards the city lights at dusk.

A few pages on in his street plan, Eastern Circle, where Daniel Linnell was born – a road which he had last seen weirdly illuminated by the torched remains of a heavy German car – had a precise, geometric form which suggested scrupulous order and decency. The map was one of life's more perverse deceptions and Daniel, as a boy, had even come to see it as a source of comfort. Shut up in his room in the wake of some minor beating, he would pick up the *A to Z*, locate the scene of his most recent torment, then stare silently at the street as it now appeared – unthreatening, timeless, and perfect. It would not be too much to say that in these moments, with his map in his hand, he found a sort of grace. Which made it all the more remarkable that every time he saw it, even on paper, his spirit was broken by Maple Street.

Remarkable too, because – in a balanced inventory of his setbacks in Maple Street, London W1 – incidents involving major violence, terror, and sexual humiliation (among the things which had driven Daniel most swiftly to his map cupboard) were almost entirely absent. But balanced, in Daniel's experience, was never quite the word for Maple Street.

He had gone there to work at Resolve, a private therapy practice, where he was completing his probationary year as a counsellor. The centre offered a well-intentioned, if expensive, service which, because many clients contacted it over the phone, was unkindly described by one of Daniel's colleagues as 'the Samaritans with a swipe machine'.

Resolve occupied the entire ground floor of a Maple Street office block. There were four consulting rooms; each had a door leading off a large reception area, where there would generally be one or two clients creaking anxiously in the cane armchairs. Waiting customers could choose between reading style magazines from the transparent coffee table (current issues bought by the practice, not old, donated copies – a sure sign, Daniel said to himself when he first saw them, of shadiness) or staring at the two angel fish who gaped vacantly back at them from the aquarium. Guy Montgomery, Resolve's founder and director, had installed the large fish tank in the hope it would inject a feeling of medical expertise, because dentists had them.

And to work at Resolve – Linnell still cringed every time he heard that name – you didn't need medical expertise. Daniel, who had taught English to business students in Limoges for a year, then drifted in and out of temporary jobs for five years after leaving college, had been surprised and delighted to learn that his degree in French and a Certificate in Humanistic Counselling from a six-month course of evening classes, which he had taken out of boredom as much as anything else, was enough to get him a start as a mental health professional.

And now, as Daniel neared the end of his probationary period, Montgomery and his two partners agreed he was good – even brilliant – at dealing with intense cases of emotional damage. He had an unusual combination of attributes: a keen, if unfocused, desire to assist humanity and a capacity for detachment from other people's pain. He might have been a GP, a news photographer, or an executioner. He was their kind of man.

Guy Montgomery himself had been a repertory actor until he had a nervous breakdown in the mid-eighties. It came on suddenly, according to the version that circulated in the Resolve staff room, when he first burst into tears, then lit a cigarette, while on stage in Sheffield playing Hotspur in *Henry IV*. Even then, so the rumour went, it was only when the sprinkler system went off over the stage that the conscript audience of fifteen-year-olds noticed that anything was up. When Montgomery recovered, he took a degree in psychotherapy. After a year's service with another London counselling centre, he set up Resolve with the encouragement of his less fragile wife Linda, who was in charge of the books.

The perfect elocution Montgomery had retained from his theatrical training made him sound insincere – which, for the most part, he wasn't – and, though he had never set foot on a London stage, he was prone, especially at social events, to indulge in small, outdated gestures of Metropolitan flamboyance, such as panatella cigars or hats. His real Christian name was Colin.

'If he knows so much,' said Deborah, one of Daniel's fellow probationers, when she heard Linnell defending him, 'why does he wear that cravat?'

Resolve clients were referred to by their first name only, like saints. For the benefit of customers who were desperate, or abroad, there were four soundproofed booths at the end of a short corridor, each of which contained a telephone and a small desk. The booths were staffed twenty-four hours a day, and were charged to a caller's credit card by the minute. On the phone, as in one-to-one consultations, Daniel had been taught to remain silent for the most part and, when he did speak, to steer the client towards their own solution or, as Montgomery preferred to term it, 'resolve'. It was a technique that went down well with most callers who were not, on the whole, great listeners.

'It sometimes occurs to me,' said Lynne, one of the senior therapists, 'that if I just left the phone on the table and nipped out for a dhansak, when I got back they'd be sorted.'

Such irreverence in the private conversations of the staff, like the 'sin per minute' league table Daniel had posted on his locker door, would have horrified the customers, but did not necessarily denote a lack of compassion; it was just one way of not going mad. The dangerous gulf in tone between the robust talk in the staff room and the hushed, measured exchanges in the consulting areas had been brought grotesquely into focus a couple of years before Daniel arrived, when a therapist who was on the telephone in reception fixing up a new appointment for a middle-aged psychotic with deviant tendencies, noticed that his fellow counsellors were preparing to leave for the pub. Reaching for the privacy button on the switchboard, he called out, 'I'll see you in a minute, I'm tied up with the sheepshagger' but hit speakerphone by accident, so that he and his colleagues remained frozen in a horrified tableau, as the client's voice called out his terrible response: 'I heard that pal.'

Montgomery initially tried to deny that the incident had ever happened, then found he couldn't, and began to address it directly in his introductory staff seminars. On the front of his plywood clipboard, which was generally hidden by his patient's notes, Daniel had written the sheep man's words, as a warning to himself, in red felt pen.

Serious psychiatric cases were rare, though Daniel did see one, Elliot King, on a regular basis. King, who was in his late-fifties, was an American saxophonist. At the height of his success, in the seventies, he'd led his own band in the States, where he enjoyed a cult reputation among fans of contemporary jazz. As his appeal had faded, he'd worked increasingly in Europe, and settled permanently in London in the eighties. Even now, Daniel knew, there was a rack of King's records in the Oxford Street music stores and, when he was well, he could still fill the Festival Hall.

Daniel's own attitude to modern jazz – dominated by loathing and ignorance – turned out to be no obstacle, as King never spoke about his career, except in his very early years in Birmingham Alabama, when his parents had trained him to tap dance. 'I can still do that, you know,' he once told Linnell, getting to his feet and circling the room, each foot gently tapping out three beats as he walked. It was an effortless movement, and he did it without ever breaking his stride. Sometimes he'd do it when he was waiting in reception, to let Daniel know he'd arrived. 'When you hear that tap man,' he said, 'you know I'm out here for you. You hear that, you get that last damn maniac out of there.'

Elliot had spent periods as an in-patient in psychiatric wards. 'I don't ever want to go back there,' he told Daniel. 'Here I get you. There, there's the doctors always messing with me.'

'Here,' Daniel said, 'you pay.'

'There,' Elliot said, 'you get robbed. I got all my music robbed there. And my cigarettes. And my telephone money.'

He tended to view his counselling sessions less as the solution to his problems, more as a diversion from them. He was softly spoken and, unlike many musicians, his hearing had survived unimpaired. He used to complain if Daniel spoke too loud to him. 'Hey,' King would say. 'Easy. My ears are still OK – God knows how. It's my mind that's gone.'

Elliot had built up an encyclopaedic knowledge of the hundreds of small towns he had visited in his years on the road. From time to time, without warning, Daniel would fire a place name at him – Lubbock, say, or Duluth, or Des Moines – and Elliot would have to supply three points of information, like area code, population, or most famous former inhabitant. It had become a game between them. In his darkest moods, which were rare but very frightening, the musician was also a religious obsessive, whose nine-inch kitchen knife ('Mike') had been urging him to commit murder. In desperation, Daniel had finally advised Elliot, who was six foot two and weighed two hundred pounds, to bury the knife in the back garden, a proposal that appeared to put an end to the trouble.

If a threatening incident did arise, counsellors were taught to inform reception that there was a 'Code Six'. Montgomery had got the idea after witnessing an incident at his local supermarket, where store detectives had spotted a man shoplifting. There was a request on the tannoy for 'Customer Service Eleven' which, Montgomery explained, was the cue for all the biggest men from the meat counter to sprint out, wrestle the suspect to the ground, and sit on him.

But the majority of Resolve's clients, especially the telephone callers, were bored, drunk or vengeful rather than clinically disturbed. Daniel, being single, frequently found himself working the phone lines at night. Often, as he struggled past the morning commuters, down into Tottenham Court Road tube station, and back to his small flat in a tower block by Clapham Junction overground station, it would occur to him that he had far more to complain about than most of his callers.

Most, but not all. One of his regulars was Richard, a young pianist from Oxford, who had been pushed backwards over the balcony at the Café Fitzrovia in London by his male lover. Richard fell twenty feet into the main restaurant area, where his landing was broken by a twenty-one-year-old woman who was celebrating her forthcoming wedding. Sitting with her, and not injured, were her fiancé, his mother, and her parents.

'Her name was Sara Allen,' Richard told him. 'She broke her back, and fractured her skull, and she died in hospital two days later.'

Richard, who was in tears, had told him the story at least a dozen times before, and there were no signs that repetition was therapeutic. The only shift in the emotional balance since his first call, Daniel noticed, was that now their conversations were bringing him dangerously close to tears as well.

'She's dead,' Richard told him, as he always did. 'I had two broken legs and a fractured cheekbone, and I was out of hospital in three weeks.'

'Every day,' Daniel said to him, sounding, to his horror, like some MGM padre, 'is a new day.'

'Every day,' Richard said, 'when I wake up, the memory of it comes to me, as if it was the first time. There's not a day goes by when I don't wish she'd been anywhere on earth but in that chair.'

'Because,' said Daniel, quietly, 'she'd still be here.'

'No,' said Richard. 'Because I wouldn't.'

So it was hardly surprising if occasionally, in the bar after a day shift, Daniel would betray the confidences of Nigel, a fifty-two-year-old sexual compulsive with manic-depressive tendencies who had recently been experimenting with Viagra. 'He's the last person in the world,' Daniel told his colleagues, 'who needs it. It's like tossing kerosene into a live volcano.'

'I took it,' Nigel had told him, 'then I sat on my own, downstairs in the kitchen for about half an hour with my Cindy Crawford pictures. Nothing. So I made a cup of tea and went out to lock up the greenhouse. When I came in again I started to read the share prices in the *Sunday Telegraph* and – berdoing!'

But it wasn't Nigel or Elliot, or even Sara Allen that had uniquely marked the name of Maple Street in Daniel's mind. Those memories he could live with. It was something else. It was in Maple Street, one evening just after Easter, that he met Laura.

The first thing he noticed about her were her eyes, which were – though it was not a category of iris allowed by the passport office – jet black. Otherwise she was an unlikely femme fatale, with shoulder-length, straight black hair and an underdeveloped, boyish figure that had caused her agonies in her adolescence at school, when she still cared what anyone thought of her. She smoked heavily, and she had the obstinate strength and the accent of her American father. 'Impervious' would have been a good word for her; nothing Daniel, or anybody else, ever said or did would ruffle her aberrant view of the world. She went off in his life like a bomb.

He met her in the Café Leon, a wine bar three doors up from Resolve, on a Monday at the beginning of April, a few weeks before his final assessments began. Daniel had gone down there around eight in the evening with a group of ten or so, mainly recent recruits to Resolve like himself. She was on the other side of the table with her boyfriend Robin, who acted as a consultant to the company. He was a practising psychotherapist – a real one, who helped detectives construct profiles of suspects. Robin spoke, with a quiet authority, about his police work. The great weakness about hardened criminal organisations, he said, was that their behaviour patterns were, to a certain extent, predictable.

'There are some professions, such as that of gangster,' he said, 'which naturally attract the psychopath. Fighter pilots,' he added, 'not airline pilots. Deep sea divers. Mercenaries. Coal miners...'

By this point, Daniel wasn't listening. Everything about her, from her torn canvas trousers to the way she smoked cigarettes, curled back into her palm like a football hooligan, semaphored the quality that Daniel found most captivating in a woman – the knowledge that his parents would have despised her.

On his left was Andrew, a softly-spoken young landlord with psychiatric ambitions; on his right, Deborah, who had attended Cheltenham Ladies' College and come to Resolve for something to do. Deborah was talking to her friend Maria about her recent liaison with a tennis professional.

'...and he's from Argentina,' Deborah was saying, 'and he's twenty-four, and he's called Santos, and of course he wants sex.'

'And?' Maria asked.

'And,' Deborah replied, 'I don't. You know...' she paused. 'I sometimes think I never really do.'

Daniel stared down at his almost-empty glass of lager. Andrew, he noticed, was pretending to watch the football, which was impossible to make out from this distance, on the television set which was fixed high on the wall in another room across the bar.

'He must be in tremendous shape,' ventured Maria.

'It's amazing actually,' said Deborah. 'He's got these incredible shoulder muscles, and he runs eight miles every morning.'

'And I would imagine,' a woman's American voice interrupted, 'that he has quite a remarkable cock as well.'

Daniel raised the line of his gaze to follow Andrew's, still fixed on the opposite wall, where he found that suddenly he too had no difficulty at all in making out Aston Villa. 'Whoops,' said Laura.

On another evening, in another group – with just one person to make some second, irreverent sort of a comment – Laura's remark might have simply broken the ice. As it was, it lingered in the atmosphere like poison.

It bonded them together as strangers, but not in a good way. Deborah was seething. Her friends, who did not include Daniel, felt like Underground passengers who had just witnessed a minor assault and done nothing to intervene.

Curiously it was Robin who appeared most disturbed by this exchange and he was the first to leave, closely followed by Deborah and Maria who, as she was getting up, told Laura she was going to pray for her. By half ten, the last of the group drifted away, leaving Daniel alone with Laura. Normally, for decency's sake, he would have made some token gesture of getting up to go himself, but he was with her now.

'Drink?' she said.

'Could do,' said Daniel.

You know that woman was right actually,' said Laura.

'Woman?'

'The prayer woman. The lady preacher.'

She got up, leaving him alone at the table and returned a couple of minutes later with a bottle of fierce Spanish red. 'She was right,' she told him, 'because I am bad.'

'You mean I was bad,' Daniel told her. 'Or I have been bad.'

She picked up the wine, ignoring the two delicate tulip glasses on the table, and pouring it into the large water tumblers.

Halfway through the second bottle, Daniel, whose upbringing had left him with strong traces of Puritanism and gentility, began to worry about her boyfriend. 'How did you meet Robin?' he asked.

'He asked me out,' she said. 'So I went. You see the thing is, I'm easy. The thing is, I'm a pushover.'

She'd been in England since she was thirteen; her parents, she told Daniel, had since moved back to the small Kansas town where she was born. She started to talk about her father. 'Robin,' she told him, 'says I'm his fault.' He was a technical adviser to an oil company and he had never forgiven her, she said, after she had an affair with a gardener named André. 'He was from Port-au-Prince,' Laura told him. Daniel looked puzzled. 'That's in Haiti. My father went crazy. He thought André was an asshole. As a matter of fact, he was right about André. Even your father can't be wrong all his life.'

Daniel noticed to his surprise that she was drinking almost as fast as he was, though with some incredible finesse which meant that he never seemed to catch her with the glass to her lips. He swallowed his own wine like a Labrador. She told him how she was born in Bedford Kansas and he noticed how the name already had a dizzying charm, even though he had no clear idea where Kansas was. She was twenty-eight, like he was, although she looked younger. Her mother was originally from Wales. When her father was first posted to Britain, the family moved to a house in St John's Wood. Laura was sent to Freshfields, a progressive boarding school in Oxfordshire. Before she came to England, her father's work had meant that Laura and her brother Paul had also attended schools in Houston and Bahrain.

She talked easily about herself. It was a quality he'd found to be rare in English people who weren't very drunk or suicidal, though on a normal day at Resolve Daniel listened to plenty of both. He wondered if that meant she was flirting, and decided it didn't. It was the American in her. Quite why Americans ever needed to drink was a mystery to him, since most of the ones he had met behaved as if they'd just had three large brandy and ports.

After Freshfields, she'd been to Bristol University. But it was school, she explained, that had confirmed her revulsion for everything her father stood for. 'The headmaster was this creepy ex-monk,' she told Daniel. 'When I was seventeen he wrote me these passionate love letters. This is a man of fifty. This is my headmaster. So anyway, when he wouldn't stop I sent them to the editor of the local paper. This guy turned out to be his son-in-law, and he drove round and handed them back to him. That kind of cooled his desire. He's a therapist now,' she said. 'Like Robin. Like you.'

'What do you do?' he asked her, desperate to change the subject.

'Do? You mean for work?'

Bugger, thought Daniel, who would have preferred to be damned as a therapist than bracketed with the millions of his compatriots who had been led to believe that a person had no worth if they weren't in paid employment. He nodded.

'I run a bar,' she said. 'It's just up the road.'

'A bar like this one?'

'Not exactly,' she said. 'It's called The Owl. It's a little weird, if you want to know the truth. And I take pictures,' she added.

'Of people?'

'Of dogs,' she told him. 'I like dogs. Dogs don't give themselves up easily.' Not, she was thinking, like me.

She fumbled in her bag and pulled out a Saturday supplement and began leafing through the perfume adverts. She had slender, elegant hands. 'Look at her,' she said, opening it at a picture of a half-naked woman leaning back on a bed, staring up expectantly at the reader. 'Look at her eyes. Bold and submissive at the same time. That's easy.' Daniel smiled. 'You're laughing,' she said, 'but you try and take a good dog. Elliott Erwitt spent fifteen years on his dog book.'

She'd been to places like Beirut and Vera Cruz. Her memories of her past consisted of a stream of foreign city names – each, no doubt, harbouring its own kind of trouble, each with its own consoling street plan. Curiously, he noticed, it wasn't the places she spoke of with great enthusiasm, so much as the journeys between them, especially by air. She'd been to school in five different countries by the time she was fourteen.

'Is there anywhere you haven't lived?' he asked her. The only significant upheaval he could have mentioned if he'd wanted to boast about his own early years, which he didn't, was his move to university in Liverpool when he was eighteen. And that was a journey – down the M62, a road that seemed permanently shrouded in rain or low, grey cloud – that didn't give anybody much to write home about. His father had worked as a surveyor on the motorway. His earliest memories were of being taken out to watch the road being cut out of the clay by the yellow earth-moving trucks with their huge pneumatic tyres. If one exploded, one of the excavator drivers had told him, it could kill a man. He remembered almost nothing from those very early years of his life, but he could recall every feature of the driver – his sallow skin, his muscular build, his dark features; even the unfiltered cigarette that he kept in his mouth as he spoke – and those words had stayed with him like a curse.

The year after the road was completed, his father, coming home one November evening, was struck from behind by a speeding mail van which forced his car under the wheels of the heavy goods vehicle in front, killing him instantly. The crash happened when Daniel was seven, in the years before the British had adopted the continental habit of laying flowers at the scene of an accident. Even so, he knew the place well: the central lane on the eastbound carriageway near Warrington, close to a strange-looking water tower. Every time he looked at the building after the accident, it had held out the threat of some new catastrophe which was never quite delivered, until one day he was driven back from college by his uncle, to visit his mother, who had been suffering from cancer, in secret, for two years. When they drew up outside the hospital's main entrance, Daniel's aunt, never the most tactful of people, walked up to the car. He'd wound down the window, letting in the steady drizzle, to hear her say with affected stoicism, 'She's dead then.'

He turned to look at Laura again and noticed she was staring at him, clearly expecting a response to something she'd said and that he'd missed.

'Pardon?' said Daniel.

'I said, where are you from?'

He told her.

'Salford,' she repeated. 'Well I've never lived in Salford.' The way she said it, Salford sounded exotic, almost thrilling. With Laura in it, he thought, Salford would be capable of anything.

She went off to use the phone. God, thought Daniel, who's she calling? Robin? A cab? He watched her, standing there at the payphone at the other end of the bar. She hooked her thumb into one of the belt loops on her canvas jeans, a habit that she had. He had to admit he was becoming – to borrow the sort of phrase he used to avoid the cloying language of sentimentality – rather keen.

The stereo was playing a mindless country song: 'If I fall, I'll take you down with me…' He found himself wondering if a song would become irreversibly linked with Laura in his mind, and hoping that it wouldn't be this one. He tried to think of a tune that she did remind him of, but all he could think of was a line from 'Paddy McGinty's Goat', a nonsense song he had heard on the radio as a child, about a billygoat who swallowed a case of dynamite. 'He sat down by the fireside, he didn't give a hang.'

'I had to call Brendan,' Laura said, as she sat down again. 'He's running the bar. I've locked myself out. Anyway, he says he's going to be up till three so that's OK.' Three, thought Daniel, looking at the wreckage of cigarette ends, old glasses and two wine bottles, one empty, one almost empty, on the table in front of them. It was just past midnight. By three, he'd be on a trolley in Accident and Emergency.

'Where do you live now?' he asked.

'I have a flat…' she began, but she was interrupted by a waiter who came with a new ashtray, placing a third, clean ashtray on top of the old one, an action which for some reason always commanded Daniel's entire attention, whatever else was happening around him. 'I have a flat,' she said again, 'in Crouch End.'

'It sounds nice,' said Daniel, lamely, his mind still reeling from that splendid singular pronoun.

'Yeah, that's right, Daniel,' she said. 'It sounds nice. It sounds so nice, I think there's a Stephen King story called Crouch End. It has a clock tower, and twenty-three Indian restaurants.' She paused and turned her black eyes on him. 'Like to see it?'

Her look said it was at that moment, in that sentence, that she had chosen him.

Daniel struggled to think of some reply that would show he had grasped the enormity of that dark look. 'OK,' he said.

'Shall we?' she said, mock English, mock-polite.

They walked out into driving rain on the Tottenham Court Road. The cold air hit him and, with it, the sobriety he had been shocked into was instantly extinguished. Laura flagged down a black cab. She had that easy way with waiters and cab drivers, an unmistakable sign of privilege. Daniel, like most of the people he knew, still couldn't order a coffee in McDonald's without wanting to apologise. On the Euston Road, when they stopped at some traffic lights, another cab ran into the back of them. Its owner started to rage furiously at their own smaller, older driver. They all got out and Daniel heard Laura say something half-audible to the other driver.

It had sounded like 'dickhead' – an impression that was confirmed when the larger driver began to walk towards Daniel with a look that suggested he, as her apparent escort, was the nearest legitimate person to punch; at which point the police arrived.

The cab pulled up outside the café where she worked. The front was all glass; tall, thin windows set in narrow wooden frames like an old greenhouse. Inside, he could see lighted candles and the occasional movement in the background, although all the tables looked unoccupied. In the café's front window there was a stuffed barn owl on a pedestal, delicately lit with small spotlights, as if it were an object of great value.

She went into the bar and collected the key, then led the way round to the back entrance, where they walked up the fire escape and across a flat roof, the approach to her own outside door. She let him in, then disappeared back down to the bar for some more cigarettes. The first thing he noticed was that all the lights and the coal-effect gas fire in the living room had been left on in sustained, futile defiance of her father, who was frugal in such matters. He wandered round the large living room to take his mind off the anxiety of whether, and how, he was going to make that formidable transition to intimacy, a journey that, in his life, always seemed to be marked by some moment of unforgettable awkwardness.

The kitchen was part of the large living room, though there was no sign that it had ever been used for cooking. The flat was not so much what you would call untidy as unattended to. On the couch, he noticed a CD of Elvis Costello's *The Juliet Letters*. He opened the case, and put it on. Her few other possessions were scattered around in a haphazard way, as if she was camping. On three shelves in an alcove she had piled her clothes: a few folded T-shirts, a couple of pairs of black jeans, two sweaters and a bright green dress.

He went to use the small bathroom, where he was more vigilant than usual because, he realised to his shame, he was furtively looking out for traces of Robin. There were none. He did notice, to his surprise, a collection of cosmetics, something he couldn't imagine her using, but which – in scarcely noticeable flesh-toned shades – she did. Prominently positioned on the bathroom shelf, in an amber-coloured container, was an aromatherapy tonic called 'Optimism and Focus'. Next to it, in a slightly smaller clear glass bottle, was a preparation the label described as 'Anti-Mating Oil – For Animal Use Only'; it was produced by Hatchwoods Limited of Apex Mills, Blackburn, and carried the brand name of 'Scram'.

He was sitting on a chair by the window, looking down into the street, when she reappeared – not from the front door as he'd expected, but through a trapdoor in the floor that led down to the bar by way of a fixed metal ladder. 'You know Deborah,' she said, as she approached him.

'Deborah?' he said.

She came and sat on his lap. 'Deborah. Well I'm not Deborah.'

She kissed him with a kiss that, he noticed, had none of the usual signs of tentativeness. Daniel slipped his thumb inside her belt loop, like she had, and she sat there until the CD had almost finished, her head on his shoulder. Below them, through the window, a huge yellow industrial refuse truck drew up to pick up the rubbish from outside the bar. It pulled up just as the CD player had reached the last track – a mournful, deeply evocative song called 'The Birds Will Still Be Singing'. It began with two pairs of rising triplets on a viola and even on her cheap machine they had a resonance that seemed to go straight to his soul.

'Summertime withers as the sun descends,' the song began. 'He wants to kiss you, will you condescend. Before you wake and find a chill within your bones; under a fine canopy of lover's dust and humerus bones...'

He felt himself taken over by an unusual mixture of exhilaration and great sadness. It was a moment he would carry with him for ever.

'Banish all dismay,' the chorus went, 'extinguish every sorrow. If I'm lost or I'm forgiven, the birds will still be singing.'

He'd heard this song before but never listened to it. In his mind, it bonded them like an exchange of blood. He looked down at the refuse truck. He could just make out the words 'Haringey Council' on the passenger door.

'Well, your cab's here,' said Laura. 'Are you going or not?' Daniel looked at her. 'Shall we?' she said.

Laura disappeared into the bathroom. Daniel went and sat on the edge of her bed – a double mattress on the floor. She'd left the bathroom door ajar. Glancing past it he noticed, to his alarm, that she was undressing in a matter-of-fact, practical way, as if for a medical examination. Daniel hadn't known her long, but he could hardly imagine she was the sort of woman who wore a nightdress. He still had his rain-soaked jacket on. In a panic, he tore it off, pulled his loose jersey and T-shirt over his head with the clumsy haste of a child and frantically wrenched off his boots. As the bathroom light clicked off he was still in his socks. He just had time to take them off and to lie down on the bed, on his back, in his boxer shorts, before Laura walked in. She was naked, but he hardly noticed. He was trying to look nonchalant, but his face had the frenzied, guilty look of a man who might just have committed a murder. She lay down next to him, on his left, lying on her side, facing him but not touching him. She put her left hand on his right shoulder and leaned her head on his left. It was hardly an intimate gesture, but Daniel felt as if he was going to blow up. She kissed him again. 'Like I told you,' she said, 'I'm easy.'

Laura was different from other women, and when she made love – as he would never tell anyone, anywhere, at any time in his life (though, as he would later reflect, he might as well have, enough of them must know) – she became delirious, like a ham actress feigning a fever. Passion – a devalued word used in its true sense – gripped her like madness, or death. She chattered in mumbled, half-formed sentences. 'Jesus,' said Daniel, 'Jesus.'

'You know,' she told him later, 'I don't have quite as much fun as I look as if I'm having.' She had her left hand on his right shoulder again and her head back on his left. He looked down at her and noticed for the first time a small scar, three-quarters of an inch long, above her right eye. He touched it, gently. 'I got that in Salina Kansas when I was five,' she told him. 'I got bitten in the face by Mr Noble's dog.'

'I love you,' he said.

She gave no sign that she'd heard him. He thought about saying it again, then didn't.

'I thought you were dead,' he told her. 'You know the Elizabethans used to say "die" for...'

'Orgasm,' Laura interrupted. 'You know, Robin – you do remember Robin, don't you.'

Daniel, who was unprepared for this, swallowed audibly, like a cartoon character.

'I see you do,' she said. 'Robin is my ex. So anyway, Robin is – was – a man who knows a lot of things. I used to tell him – all those words, all those long, therapist words are wasted on me. I used to tell him hey – don't forget – I have trouble remembering the meaning of any word with more than three syllables. Anyway, one of the things that Robin knows is the full range of meanings of the verb to die. He told me all about that. I said, "I died, Robin, but I didn't get to heaven."'

A brief new wave of guilt broke over Daniel. 'You know,' he told her, 'I'm pretty attached to monogamy.'

She got up without speaking and went to the bathroom; she pulled on a T-shirt and started brushing her teeth. Daniel watched her affectionately as she did it, with fast and deliberate up and down movements of the brush.

'You remind me of somebody,' he shouted, 'and I can't remember who.'

'Carole Lombard?' she called back, then spat toothpaste loudly into the bowl.

'No'.

'Ava Gardner?' She spat again.

'Oh dear,' he said. 'I think it's Top Cat.'

She laughed, a great, open, sonorous laugh. He lay back on her cheap pillows.

'Hey, Daniel,' she said. 'You know what I was saying about words of more than three syllables?'

'Yes.'

'What's monogamy again?'

CHAPTER 2

When he woke up it was light and he was alone. He sat up. On the pillow next to him there was a single yellow rose. He stared down at it. The stem still had its thorns and the petals, which were glistening with drops of rainwater, appeared to have been partly eaten by an insect. He looked around for a note, but didn't find one.

He pulled on his jeans. His leather jacket, still damp, was crumpled in the corner of the bedroom where he'd thrown it. He walked into the living room and looked on, and under, the telephone and answering machine for a number. There wasn't one. On the table there was a paperback book called *Fireworks* and, next to it, a large sheet of sketching paper, which he couldn't remember having seen the night before. Roughly daubed on it in huge letters, in red acrylic paint, he read: 'I remember when you kissed me, when I kissed you, in the Parc Montsouris which is in Paris; in Paris which is in France; in France which is on the earth. On the earth, which is a star.'

He opened a door he hadn't noticed before, opposite the bathroom. It led into another small room, which had been stuffed floor to ceiling with empty packing crates and suitcases.

Daniel left a note with his address in Clapham, where there was no phone, and his number at work. He left, closing the door after him, and walked across the flat roof, down the fire escape and out through a cluster of industrial waste bins.

He went round to the front of the building and into The Owl. Even though it was only eleven in the morning and the place was almost empty, the stereo was playing loud ranchero music and, once you were a few steps inside, it felt like midnight.

The main bar was long and narrow, with the counter and stools on your right as you came in. To your left, in this cramped passage, was a row of five small tables. Once you reached the end of the long zinc bar, the place opened out into a spacious dining area on bare floorboards. Daniel walked down to the far end of the bar and sat on a stool. The floor in this narrow part of The Owl was laid with rough stone flags, like a church, and the café's lighting came from dim electric bulbs hanging low over the dining tables.

The barman was more secular-looking: sallow, and in his late-thirties, his head had been shaved with a cut-throat razor, and his sleeves were rolled up to reveal muscular forearms tattooed with nautical motifs.

'Tea,' said Daniel.

The barman didn't seem to understand. '*Caffellatte*?' he asked, in a bizarre accent which Linnell, who had a GCSE in Italian, took to be some obscure dialect: Treviso, perhaps, or rural Sicily.

'Tea,' Daniel repeated.

'*Senza latte?*'

'Normal. Do you know,' he asked, enunciating with exaggerated clarity, 'where Laura is?'

'Laura?'

'*La ragazza*,' said Daniel, pointing up at the ceiling, '*al piano di sopra*.'

'No idea pal,' said the barman, in an accent that betrayed the origin of the exotic element in his Italian – Bradford. 'She was in a couple of hours ago; she just said she was going away. Want to leave a message?'

Daniel shook his head. He went home and changed.

His client that evening was John, a software designer from a Greek Cypriot family in North London. John had been at the wheel when his wife and young daughter had been killed in a car crash on the M40. The inquest had dismissed any lingering possibility that the accident might not have been his fault; he had been banned from driving for three years, then, as a final humiliation, a magistrate had fined him £350 for driving without due care and attention. When he had been wavering in his recent suicide attempt, John told him, it had been the thought of the £350 that had given him the courage to swallow the temazepam.

'Otherwise of course,' said John, his knuckles white as he twisted a set of worry beads – his grandfather's prescription for recovery – 'I'd have taken the £350 and gone out and spent it on petrol and got in my car and driven off to waste a few more innocent members of my family.' As he said this, the thin string of black leather holding the beads snapped and they flew out across the floor.

Both men got down to pick them up. The feeling of the acrylic carpet under his fingernails sent cold shivers down Daniel's spine. The sensation distracted him, and he found himself on his knees, staring down vacantly at the blue plastic beads in his cupped hands.

'What's up?' he heard John say.

'I met this girl,' Daniel replied without thinking, breaking every rule he'd been taught. He'd never even mentioned that his own father died in a car crash. 'And I don't know where she is.'

'What will you do,' said his client, 'if she doesn't come back?'

Daniel looked up at him. 'I don't know,' he said.

'You know there's only one thing anyone's ever said to me that has ever helped me at all,' said John. 'It was this guy who was in hospital with me; he was twenty-two, and he was a dancer, and he'd caught polio on a cruise ship in the Aegean. He was paralysed from the waist down and his fiancée had walked out on him. He'd lost his place at ballet school. He told me that to get better, you have to understand there are some things that you never get better from.' A bell sounded for the end of the hour's session. Daniel apologised for his unprofessional behaviour.

'You know what?' John said, as he was getting up to go. 'This is the first time I've seen you that I haven't left feeling worse.'

The rest of the week was quiet, until Friday afternoon, when he arrived to find Elliot King waiting for him. Elliot didn't have an appointment. He was sitting in Linnell's consulting room. Standing in reception, Daniel looked through the tall, thin glass panel, set in the door, above the handle, for observation. The American, who had just walked out on the band he was touring with, was fidgeting repetitively with the catches on a flight case of the kind DJs used for vinyl. He looked pale and agitated. Daniel knocked and went in.

'I am a servant of God,' Elliot told him, 'and yet I dwell among men of unrighteousness. They lay hands upon me; they cast stones against me. Men of great violence beset me.'

Daniel said nothing.

'Has my country not sinned?' asked Elliot. 'Have we not exported

Playboy to Europe? Have we not sent them *Hustler*?'

'Yes,' Daniel said, trying to think what further reply he could make to this. He stifled a suicidal impulse to say 'Thank you.'

'Help me,' Elliot said, suddenly.

'We are here,' said Daniel, 'to help you.'

'So help me,' Elliot said.

'Is it...,' Daniel found himself saying, 'is it the unrighteous man?'

'No,' said Elliot. 'It's Mike. He's out – and he's up to that evil stuff again.'

He opened the steel catches on the flight case and pulled out the nine-inch knife which he held clasped in his fist, close to him. He was hunched forward, and the tip of the blade was pressing hard into the underside of his chin. Daniel saw a small trickle of blood appear on the end of the knife and run down to the handle. He glanced into reception, where he could see two waiting neurotics. One of them was holding a men's style magazine. Its cover looked like precisely the kind of thing Elliot would disapprove of.

'Excuse me,' he said.

He left the room and walked over to the main desk where Sonia, the receptionist, was reading a book called *Staying Alive: A Common Sense Guide to Organics*. 'It's a Code Six,' he whispered.

'I'm sorry?' said Sonia.

'It's a Code Six,' he repeated. 'We have a Code Six.'

'What,' she asked him, 'is a Code Six?'

'We say Code Six,' he said, under his breath, 'because it sounds better than "Get somebody who knows what the fuck they are doing". In this case,' he added, 'the Metropolitan Police, then a clinical psychiatrist.' He looked up; one of the waiting patients met his eye, then looked away.

'I'll call Guy,' said Sonia.

'Fuck Guy,' said Daniel. He walked to one of the private booths down the corridor, and dialled 999.

He came back into the consulting room without speaking. Elliot was still in his seat; the knife was on the table, its bloodstained point facing Daniel.

'Bedford Kansas?' asked Daniel.

'Area Code 785,' said Elliot. 'I've never played Bedford. I've been through it, on the way to Topeka.'

'Industries?'

'Farming. That's what you see in the Kansas clubs. Farmers. They have these auctions, they're amazing. You know in the Midwest they have horses for everything; horses with roping blood, horses with cutting blood...'

Daniel heard the crackle of a police radio through the door. 'Elliot,' he said, 'I've just got to make a phone call. There are some police officers here. Could you see what they want?'

'Sure,' he replied.

Daniel walked into reception and motioned the uniformed constables towards the armed evangelist, then walked into the staff room, where Guy Montgomery was furtively simmering at the explicit presence of the emergency services.

'What the hell's going on?' demanded Montgomery, in a voice that was half-whisper, half-shriek.

'It's Elliot.'

'And?'

'And,' said Linnell, 'he's got Mike with him.'

'Ah,' said Montgomery. 'I see. Carry on.'

When Daniel walked out of the building twenty minutes later, Elliot was being escorted into a patrol car. 'I dwell among men of unrighteousness,' he was telling the two constables. 'They cast stones against me. Men of great violence beset me.'

'I see,' said one officer. 'Do you live in Peckham, sir?'

Daniel walked down to the Café Leon; it was five thirty, and the place was quiet. He sat on a stool at the bar. Pascual, the owner, who had become something of a confidant, gave him a glass of Torres Esmerelda, then poured a smaller measure of the aromatic white wine for himself.

'Are you sometimes visited, as I am,' asked Pascual, 'by the urge to board a train to Catalunya, knock on the door of Mr Torres, and shake him firmly by the hand?'

'I am,' said Daniel, half-heartedly. 'Buy two tickets.'

'Not today though,' said Pascual.

Daniel was about to look at the barman to see what he meant when, from behind him, two hands covered his eyes. He stretched his arms out backwards and put them round her waist, clasping his hands behind her back, with his palms facing out. He still couldn't see as she pulled his head back so his chair was tilted gently back, resting against her.

'If I fall,' she whispered to him, 'I'll take you down with me.'

They walked out to the Agra, an ancient Indian restaurant off Warren Street, where you needed a torch to see your way to your table. They sat down, and Daniel put his hand into his pocket, looking for his lighter; he pulled out a handful of blue worry beads and the thin leather thong, and dropped them on the table. They rolled towards her.

'You didn't miss me at all then?' said Laura. She was wearing a man's blue collarless shirt and black canvas trousers.

'Where were you?' he asked.

'I went down to see Robin,' she told him. 'He'd gone to his family's place in Kent. 'You know...I only met him at Christmas, and I didn't think he'd really care. But he lost it totally. He went berserk. You know what he said? He said' – she adopted a pompous, thoroughly English tone – '"This is the worst thing that has ever happened to me." So I said, "Yeah Robin, I always knew you'd had it easy."'

Daniel looked up, shocked.

'It's true. You're English. What would you call his accent?'

'Well,' Daniel said, 'I suppose it's sort of...Cockney.'

'Right,' she replied. 'Well, you should see that house. His father used to be ambassador to Hong Kong. Robin's idea of hard work is cocking an ear for the dinner gong.'

'What's the worst thing that's ever happened to you, Laura?' he asked her, feeling strangely defensive of Robin.

'When I was seventeen,' she told him, 'they caught four of us smoking grass at school. I was the only one that didn't get expelled, because I was the only one with a shoe box stuffed with scented letters from the Head. They suspended me for a week and my parents had to come down to pick me up. They hardly spoke a word in the car on the way back. The next day it was my dad's birthday; I talked to mom and I tried to do everything I could to make it up to him. We went out in the morning and we bought this cream linen dress with flowers woven into it.' She paused. 'My mom roasted him a chicken. I baked him a fucking cake. And then that evening I was sat round that table, with my hair up, with my grandparents and my brother Paul and my Aunt Laura from Priceville Alabama and everything and he pulled the wishbone with my mother, and I watched her let him win.

'And he held the wishbone up and he kept his eyes tight shut, for ages, like a kid. Then he opened them and he said, "It didn't work." And my mom said, "What do you mean?" and then he said it again, in this flat voice. "It didn't work. Laura's still here."'

*

In the weeks leading up to his final assessment, Daniel became less and less preoccupied with his work. Perhaps counselling had only been a way of deflecting his attention from his own anxieties, which seemed, for the moment at least, to have evaporated. For the first time, he started to worry about failing. As it turned out, his terminal point at Resolve occurred – Daniel, in common with most of his clients, was fond of 'occurred', because it was one of those precious words that made things sound less like your fault – earlier, and more horribly, than he had anticipated.

He was counselling by telephone, as he had been doing every day for the past three months. On this occasion, his performance was monitored by two external therapists who sat with Montgomery in an adjoining room. Monitored in sound only, which suited Daniel because he was not required to vary his preferred position for telephone counselling, sitting in one of Resolve's grey moulded plastic chairs, tipped back at an angle of forty-five degrees against the wall, a lighted Marlboro in his mouth. After a long preamble, 'E', a marketing consultant from Camberwell, finally got round – as Daniel had suspected he would – to the incest.

'For the last three years,' he said, 'I have been having sexual intercourse with both of my daughters.'

Daniel leaned forward to ash his cigarette at this point, and this movement allowed the back of his chair, pivoted against the wall, and now taking most of his weight without his back to brace it, to flex suddenly inwards. In the split second that followed, Daniel was plunged forwards. As his kneecaps shot up to meet his chin, he grabbed the underside of the desk in front of him, to save himself from slithering down the wall to the floor, and he tightened his stomach muscles. It was this last, involuntary movement that made him emit a sound like a man who has just been punched hard in the stomach; a sound which, as it was heard by his four listeners, an instant after E's confession, came over simply as 'Ooooffff.'

Shortly after that, more things occurred; things which, mercifully, were soon blurred by the passage of time, although he did remember that his departure from Resolve was hastened by the way that, interrogated afterwards by Montgomery, who liked him, he found himself retreating, as he had been taught, behind a comforting wall of silence. 'Sorry Guy,' was all he said, but he offered him no explanation.

A few days later, Linnell went back to Maple Street to drop off the case notes he had kept – contrary to instructions – at his flat. He was sitting with a coffee at the counter of the Café Leon, when he felt someone roughly grab his sleeve. He looked up. It was Robin. It was mid-morning, but he looked dishevelled, aggressive and drunk.

'Let me promise you a drink,' Robin said, in an ugly tone of mock congratulation. 'Let me promise you a whole fucking case of this year's port.' He fumbled in his pockets till he found a blank cheque, which he tore off dramatically and placed on the bar. Daniel noticed that Pascual had stopped stacking the shelves and was watching Robin out of the corner of his eye from the other end of the bar. 'Let me promise you a case of this year's port,' Robin said, 'to be collected on the day she leaves you. I don't think it'll break the bank,' he added. 'It won't be vintage.'

Daniel picked up the cheque and tried to hand it back to him. Robin refused to take it. Daniel tore it into six pieces and dropped it into an ashtray where, by chance, it fell so that the empty space for the signature was still visible. The name on the chequebook was R. Robinson. When he noticed this, Daniel glanced up at his bitter companion with a look that betrayed the beginnings of pity.

'You must have spent hours thinking that up,' said Daniel. 'Christ you must be desperate.'

'I did,' said Robin. Silence. 'I am.'

'She isn't unfaithful,' he continued, 'in the way most women are unfaithful. I am a therapist,' he added, 'and I know. With Laura, it's not some desperate reflex after years of suffering or loneliness. Laura is unfaithful by nature. Like...like a vampire.' Like a man, thought Daniel.

Linnell began to buy both of them brandies. Half an hour later, Robin was feeling better, and spiteful, again. 'She has this friend called Kate,' he said, 'who's even worse than she is. They slept with a whole rugby team. In Yorkshire,' he added, as though mention of the county would finally bring Daniel round to his way of thinking. 'You know...I think it's only fair to tell you something. Every woman has something she brings you that's unique. Laura's a woman who brings you surprises. Bad surprises. And it doesn't take much to win her over. A deserted beach, a crowded square. A dark night, a sunrise. The North' – he added, rambling now – 'the South. A good man,' he went on, 'somebody like you.'

At which point, to Daniel's horror, Robin started to sob, uncontrollably, there at the bar. Daniel found himself staring down the counter at Pascual, from a belief, he later realised, that the barman was from Leon, and consequently Spanish, and hence Latin, and so would know instinctively how to deal with a man in tears.

Pascual leaned round and pulled out a catering pack of paper napkins. He slammed it down in front of Robin. 'Let me know when those are finished,' he said.

CHAPTER 3

In these first few days, Daniel spent almost all his time in Crouch End. When he was back in Clapham, he took to writing the name Laura on loose scraps of paper, and hiding them in his books, to give himself the luxury of coming across them by chance many years later. When he did, he found that her Christian name – whatever its natural poetry, however great the achievements or pleasures it had provoked in the past – had become linked inextricably with catastrophe. He might as well have written Nagasaki.

The Owl, as much as its manager, had that irresistible quality of knowing exactly what it was. The character of the café – in marked contrast with the engineered uniformity of the theme bars that surrounded it – had evolved gradually in the two years it had been open, and its uniqueness derived not from some homogenised plan, but from small, unrelated things. The stone floor in the narrow bar area, where you could extinguish cigarettes underfoot, had been inspired by the irascible landlord of O'Malley's Fun Pub across the road. His natural impatience, and twenty years in a job where any man's tolerance would be easily exhausted, had engendered in him various symptoms, the most acute of which was a rabidly protective attitude to his emerald carpet. He had famously confronted the organiser of a funeral party who, in the confusion of bereavement, had somehow led thirty mourners directly from the crematorium to O'Malley's, without first reflecting that distressed pensioners in black ties were not a constituency that a Fun Pub was seeking to cultivate. Once there, blinded by grief, the man allowed the ash on his cigarette to reach an unacceptable length. 'Find an ashtray you bastard,' the landlord screamed at him, 'and empty it when you've finished.'

Laura had suggested the television set, installed on an aluminium arm, high on the wall opposite The Owl's zinc counter. 'I wasn't so worried about what you'd see on the screen,' she told Daniel.

'Why have it at all?' he asked her.

'It just stops the place looking...' She hesitated. 'I don't know...piss elegant.'

The set always showed some black and white film, like *The Thirty-Nine Steps*, or *Double Indemnity*, with the sound down. Each title would play for a day, uninterrupted except for the occasional evening when Doyle managed to switch channels. All The Owl's waitresses, whatever their age or country of origin, had a surprisingly broad knowledge of rugby league.

From eight thirty in the morning, when the staff arrived, the music was constant. You never knew quite what you'd hear: it could be the vibrant, tragic beat of Raï, or some aged Irish chanteuse; it could be Sam Cooke or the Alabama Three. In the main restaurant area at the back, where the natural light didn't reach, there were intricately woven North African wall-hangings, and a large poster, of the kind required by law in some American states, which explained, in discomforting detail, how to deal with a choking diner.

Laura and Brendan had both been hired by The Owl's owner, Jessica Lee, before the bar opened, two years earlier. Jessica was in her late fifties and, like Laura, had grown up in the United States. Her grey hair was cut in a rough shock and there was a permanent rasp in her voice. She'd had a traumatic divorce from a British civil servant, then thrown herself into a passionate affair with an Algerian, twenty years her junior, who had been shot in Oran. She'd retired to Devon and handed over the daily running of The Owl to Laura, who she looked upon as her adopted daughter. But Jessica would still drive up for a morning every fortnight or so, with Bella, her Newfoundland, and sit on a stool at the far end of the bar, the dog at her feet. She had a small office attached to the kitchen. A sign on the door said 'Knock Hard: Life is Deaf.' Jessica almost always wore black, and rarely drank. She appeared to derive a profound satisfaction from surrounding herself with younger people having a good time.

Brendan Doyle had arrived as a carpenter and had never gone away. The three of them had somehow managed to eliminate that particularly English atmosphere, as familiar in the cheapest corner café as in the Savoy, which encourages some diners to treat their waiters like bonded slaves and others to place their order as if confessing to homicide. The menu was dominated by North African dishes, freshly prepared, authentic and priced accordingly. At the same time you could always have egg and chips, and the ketchup bottles were permanently on the tables. The staff were paid a decent hourly rate, and shared eighteen per cent of the takings. Tips were returned to the giver.

Doyle and Laura shared the staff car – a battered black Saab 900 that Jessica had bought new in her married days. There were one or two other employees of long standing – Rachel, Laura's Ghanaian head waitress, had been there from the beginning – otherwise, the employees came and went.

The Owl had seemed alien, almost menacing, at first, and yet within a matter of a week or so Daniel found that he had imperceptibly become part of it. A few days later, he'd moved in. He started to work there on a casual basis, first as a waiter, then helping Brendan behind the bar.

'Let's not work too many shifts together, OK?' Laura told him. 'I've seen people…' – she used the word, he realised, so as not to say 'couples' – 'do that. They drive each other crazy.'

Contaminated by her own indifference to possessions, Daniel stored his books in his old flatmate's loft and dumped three cheap suitcases full of old photographs and clothes into a builder's skip in the Clapham High Road, an impulse which reduced the sum of his excess belongings to a holdall and an old grey and scarlet Bell's whisky case full of winter clothes, which he decided to sort through in a day or two when he had more time. He opened the door of the flat's small spare room, hoping to force it in among the empty suitcases, but couldn't. In the end he put his box on top of the small wardrobe in the bedroom, where it remained, forgotten and untouched. On a shelf inside the small bedside cupboard, he found a place for his *A to Zs* – three or four paperback volumes covering cities that he knew, which he still occasionally glanced through, from habit, before going to sleep.

He woke up one morning, a few days after he'd moved in, and she was leaning into him. She lay with her head on his shoulder. 'I need a coffee,' she said, 'and I don't want to move. Would you, er…' He was drifting between sleep and consciousness. 'Hey.' She prodded him gently in the ribs.

'Stop mithering,' he said, still half awake.

'Stop what?'

'Mithering.'

'What does that mean?'

'Mithering,' said Daniel. 'What do you think it means? It's English,' he paused. 'Isn't it?'

'In that case,' she said, 'I imagine it's to do with sex. With abandoning the core of your being in the dizzying grip of physical passion.' She smiled. 'I'll ask Brendan,' she said. 'It sounds like the sort of thing he'd know about.'

'He should do,' said Daniel. 'He's at it non-stop all day.'

'You know what?' she said. 'You suit me.'

This last phrase didn't strike him as the most significant of remarks at the time and yet, an hour later, walking down the traffic-bound streets to pick up a case of oranges from the local greengrocer, her words came back to him like a blessing. He became aware of an unfamiliar sensation, which he could only describe as a surge of pleasure at being alive. Struggling back into the bar with the box of fruit, he began to have an intoxicating sense of belonging, of the kind that some people experience when they pull on a uniform.

The bar work was exhausting, but it had an inconsequential urgency, like playing a video game, or doing a crossword, which was deeply calming. He lost himself in it. There were moments when he applied himself with the purpose and dedication he was meant to have sustained at Resolve. He eased the orange box down on to the bar counter. When he'd left twenty minutes earlier, Laura had been talking to Jessica in the office. Now, when he looked in to the small room, he saw the owner was alone, with Bella asleep at her feet. The dog half raised her head when she saw him, and there were a couple of dull thuds of tail on skirting board. He went in anyway and sat down. Jessica was sitting at her desk with her back to him, and she was on the phone. She waved at him, but didn't turn round. The dog rested its head, and one of its large paws, on his knee.

Jessica put the phone down.

'She has paws like paddles,' he said.

'Newfoundlands,' she told him, 'are born to be in the water. But you know all dogs can swim. Even the ones that look like they can't.'

He examined the large poster on the office wall, which he'd only glanced at before. It was a list of house rules, out of sight of the customers, roughly scrawled in various hands, in felt marker and biro. 'No Credit Cards. No Bartenders Juggling Bottles. No Walking Past Tables As If Wearing Blinkers. Nothing Served Or Not Served' – Daniel read the last item out loud – 'On The Grounds Of Fashion. What does that mean?'

'That means,' Jessica said, 'that if they order Bordeaux over ice or a gin and coke they get it. With a smile and...' She pulled away her handbag which had been obscuring a new addition at the bottom of the list, daubed in capitals, in red acrylic, in a hand he already knew well: 'No Mithering.' The paint, he noticed, was still wet and slightly smudged. Jessica smiled.

There was something about Jessica Lee. When she was growing up in Colorado, she once told Laura, she used to carry a small handgun in her make-up bag; a habit that, rumour had it, she had never abandoned. Even now, at fifty-eight, she was an object of desire for a number of young male regulars. By way of contrast with the militant diversity of the music in the bar, her own taste centred around Joni Mitchell and an American folk singer called Hedy West. When she arrived from Devon, which was always around 8.00 a.m., after she'd set off from Totnes before dawn, she'd let herself in to the bar and play her favourite, 'Five Hundred Miles'. They'd hear it as they lay in bed in the flat upstairs, and sometimes they'd wake up to it: a morose ballad that Jessica seemed to turn to for solace, like an incantation. Often, through the floorboards, they'd hear Hedy West sing that tune seven or eight times without a pause, sometimes more. It got to the point, Daniel told Laura one morning, after they'd been roused yet again by the song's first verse – 'If you miss the train I'm on, you will know that I am gone, you can hear the whistle blow a hundred miles' – that you couldn't believe she wasn't driven crazy by those opening lines.

'Yes,' said Laura. 'Well – maybe she was.'

Jessica had got the idea for The Owl from a café in San Francisco, across the road from the City Lights bookshop, which was a late-night bar that also contained a small naval museum. She'd originally planned to call it the Mermaid Café. It was a month or so before it was due to open that Brendan was clearing out the bins and found the stuffed owl, which had been thrown out by the previous owners. It had been placed on the rim of the skip and used for target practice by the son of one of the removal men, who had an air rifle. A pellet had blown out one eye altogether, and part of its beak had snapped off. Doyle picked it up and placed it, still on its pellet-scarred plinth, in a prominent spot inside the café's front window, its one good eye gazing out into the road.

As the renewal of the building had progressed, a small section of the window became a shrine to the abandoned ornament. Jessica came one day to find the bird had been mounted on a gold-painted oak branch, with fragments of bark and green silk ribbons for decoration. Then a piece of

A4 paper appeared next to the display, inscribed, in computer copperplate, with the words 'The Owl'. Doyle assembled the small spotlights which provided subtly flattering lighting for the battered bird.

It was only when Jessica saw the faces of her staff when the signwriters arrived, and were removing the display, that she relented. 'OK,' she said. 'Put it back. The damn bird's won.'

There were other matters on which Lee and her staff had not always been at one. Laura had agreed only grudgingly to the refusal of credit cards, because it meant more cash on the premises when they were closing up in the early hours. For some reason – it could have been Lee's large black hunting dog, the supposedly lethal contents of her cosmetic case, or the daunting figure of the head barman – The Owl never got robbed. There was rarely trouble of any kind. It was typical of his luck, Daniel told himself, that the first incident of real violence should have occurred in the second week he was working there.

It began on a Tuesday lunchtime, normally the quietest shift of the week. Daniel was helping Doyle behind the bar. They came in around eleven, a group of salesmen from a Japanese electronics firm who had just been awarded the contract to refit a nearby recording studio. There were six of them: four men in their late thirties, a woman, ten years or so younger, and a gaunt albino who looked as if he'd not long been out of college. Even before they opened their mouths, which wasn't long, Daniel could see that they were a very different group from The Owl's regulars. The men were in designer jackets with labels whose names were vaguely familiar even to him. The woman was wearing a scarlet suit which might have been tailored to set off her mean, pinched mouth. Each of them, he noticed, was wearing a wristwatch whose face was not concealed by their clothes.

Daniel went over to take the order, which was delivered by the most senior of the men. He was tall, with the heavy build of a former rugby player; he was greying at the temples and had the ability to reduce his table to instant deference with a scarcely perceptible movement. He called for a bottle of champagne, then, fifteen minutes later, inquired after, and flauntingly ordered, the most expensive bottle on the menu, a 1992 Australian red. Irritated that, by the terms of The Owl's licence, they had to buy food in order to be served alcohol, the group ordered a succession of side courses, like Merguez and guacamole. They ate greedily, and with their hands, each of them periodically half-cleansing themselves of the coagulated oil and pulped flesh of the fibrous fruit by sucking their fingers loudly, one by one. It was as if they were daring you to look at them, and it was hard not to: they were directly opposite the bar area, only a few feet away, and there was a bold exaggeration in their eating habits that Daniel had only previously seen attempted by mediocre Hollywood actors recreating a Mafia family lunch.

'We got it,' the senior manager said, 'because we didn't fall into the trap of that simple vision of the market as black and white.'

'Big-titted girls,' another man laughed, 'and small-titted girls.'

From that point on, every passing woman they noticed was smirkingly described as 'BTG' or 'STG'.

Their conversation was punctuated by outgoing calls on their tiny mobile phones, celebrating their achievement. By mid-afternoon, when Rachel and Laura arrived to organise the evening shift, they were still there, at their table in the narrow area opposite the bar. Twice they paid the bill and collected a receipt, each time complaining bitterly about not being able to use a credit card, at which point the most junior member of the party, the pale-skinned youth, who by now had acquired a look of haggard meekness worthy of a Dickensian orphan, was bullied into paying by cheque.

When they settled their account for the second time, at six fifteen, the mean-mouthed woman began trying to slide a crumpled ten-pound note under a saucer.

'We don't take tips,' said Laura.

The woman looked her up and down, and gave a lingering, scornful stare at the left leg of her jeans, which had worn through just above the knee. 'You keep it dear,' she said. 'You look like you could use it.'

Laura left the money where it was.

But then, as had happened the first time they paid, the group decided to have 'one last bottle', with the result that they were still there at seven thirty, when the evening bookings began to arrive.

Things took a turn for the worse shortly after eight, when the party paid their bill for the third time. It had been clear from the beginning that the albino apprentice was less accustomed to alcohol than his companions; now, his complexion had taken on a pallor which, set against his black suit, made him appear to exist only in monochrome, almost as if he had descended out of the television screen above his head where, for the sixth time since they'd arrived there, Robert Donat was locked in an embrace with Madeleine Carroll in a railway compartment in Fife. Emboldened by his share of eleven bottles of wine, the young man protested about having to pay every bill, and began to voice fears about non-reimbursement by the company's accounts department.

The senior manager produced a thick wallet of credit cards, and threw them, one by one, across the table, at Rachel, the Ghanaian waitress. 'BTG,' one of his employees sniggered, in a stage whisper. He began with various airline Executive Club cards, and ended with a gold American Express card. This last one skidded across the table, and landed on the floor. Laura went over, took Rachel gently by the shoulders, and steered her away, back towards the restaurant. She picked up the fallen card and handed it to the customer. 'You need to pay like you did before,' she said. 'You remember – by cheque.'

'I'm gonna report you,' he said.

'You are going to report me to American Express?'

'Yes,' he replied.

'For not taking American Express?'

He nodded.

Laura walked away. The group paid again, by cheque, then ordered more wine and, as they were obliged to do, another bowl of guacamole, which they sent back as having too much garlic. Laura took the dish away without speaking and the chef mixed a fresh, blander version. When she came back with the new bowl, the pale youth with the thin chequebook was slumped back in his chair, his eyes closed, with his head against a pillar, overcome either by alcohol or by the size of the latest authorised debit on his current account. As Laura put the food on the table, the woman in red with the mean mouth was talking.

'I read a funny thing about garlic,' she said. 'I read that if you have enough of it, eventually you stop reeking of it.'

'Yeah, that's right, honey,' said an American voice in her ear. 'Just like money.'

The salesmen had begun to disturb other customers, though the people at the table next to them – a tall man in his early thirties with curly fair hair and glasses, and a young Asian woman – had only just arrived and were, Linnell remarked to Brendan, far too engrossed in each other to start worrying about their graceless neighbours.

Among the five who were still conscious, Laura's last remark had engendered a smouldering vindictiveness. With their last order, they had finished the expensive Australian Shiraz, of which The Owl, which didn't stock a lot of fancy vintages, only kept a case.

The senior manager asked to see the wine list again. Looking at it, his senses temporarily restored by the energising power of malice, he noticed that there were ten-year-old cabernets from America and Australia, but only very recent, post-Mandela vintages, from South Africa. He called Rachel over and ordered a bottle of 1992 Californian Cabernet Sauvignon. He tasted it and beckoned her to come back. 'It seems corked,' he said. She went to take it away. He placed his hand on her wrist, to stop her. 'No, it's all right,' he said. 'We'll keep it. It may be me. It's a funny thing,' he added, 'but I prefer the South African cabernets from the early nineties.'

'We don't have any,' she said politely, not catching his meaning, 'of that age.' She was turning to go, but he kept an apparently light but actually unshakeable grip on her wrist, with his thumb and middle finger. 'I can understand that, love,' he said. 'All them black hands been all over them.'

Rachel turned and walked back to the kitchen. The grey-haired manager stood up, saying he had to get some cigarettes. Daniel, mentally prepared to play his dutiful role in the cataclysm he expected this incident to provoke, kept his eyes on Doyle, the figure he expected to precipitate it. He still had his eyes on him when, from the passage in front of the bar, he heard what sounded like the air brakes on a container lorry being released. When he looked ahead of him again, the senior manager had disappeared from view and the fair-haired man from the next table was standing by the bar looking unconcerned by the threat of retaliation from the executive, who he'd punched in the stomach with his full force and who was still doubled up on the stone floor by his feet. The stranger looked both barmen in the eye, but said nothing. His victim drew himself slowly to his feet, by holding on first to the legs, then to the back, of an adjacent stool. He staggered back to rejoin his colleagues. His two conscious male companions were on their feet, gesticulating and swearing. Brendan, his short sleeves revealing the full hideous range of his nautical tattoos, walked down the narrow corridor between bar and tables, to meet them. Linnell, a rather less intimidating figure, went with him.

'If you do want to do this,' Brendan said, 'I'd just like you to make sure that your mobiles are still charged. Because you're not using our phone when you need it.'

'Leave it Tony,' the manager said. His two lieutenants sat down again and began to make calls on their mobile phones.

A quarter of an hour later, two company cars arrived. On the faces of the chauffeurs, the same men who had brought the executives up from central London earlier in the day, perfunctory respect had given way first to veiled amusement, then dismay.

They carried the unconscious youth out first, then held open The Owl's front door for his superiors, who left without paying for the last two bottles. Daniel followed them, but he found Laura blocking his path and she put her arms round his neck in such a way that, if he'd kept walking, they'd both have fallen over. It was so breathtakingly disarming an action, and so perfectly executed that, at the same time as it melted him, he found himself wondering how often she'd done it before. The blond diner returned to his table. On the pavement outside, one of the businessmen turned and spat against the window.

Daniel took the young couple a bottle of champagne.

'It's kind of you,' the man said, 'but I don't need a reward.'

'It's not a reward,' said Daniel. 'It's an apology.'

Only two tables were still occupied at a quarter to midnight when, as they were cashing up, a small Nissan van pulled up outside The Owl. A hooded figure jumped out, heaved a heavy-based traffic cone through the largest pane in the front window, then leapt back in through the rear door as the vehicle set off again at speed. A group of five young women, on an antenatal group reunion outing, was fortunately placed at the far end of the room; the blond stranger and his girlfriend were also beyond the reach of the flying glass.

'What do you think?' Laura asked Brendan. 'Call the police, for the insurance?'

He shook his head. 'That's it done with,' he said. 'They won't be back.'

Daniel was clearing up behind the bar, watching the two workmen who'd arrived to board and secure the window, when he glanced to his right and saw the young couple standing at the end of the counter. It was almost one by now; he'd assumed that they'd paid and left long ago. The man was holding the bill, looking slightly flustered; delayed shock, Daniel imagined, from the events of the evening.

'It's not always like this,' he told them. 'It's never like this actually.'

'Your colleague...' the man gestured towards Rachel, who was sitting nearby, going through the till. Daniel found himself taken aback by this heartening return to civility on the other side of the bar. 'She just told me that you don't take credit cards. All I've got with me is a credit card. I could go to the cash machine...'

'It doesn't matter,' said Daniel. 'You don't have to pay.'

'They didn't,' interrupted Brendan, pointing at the broken window.

'No,' said the man. 'But I want to.'

'It's OK,' Daniel told him. 'But if you want to, bring it in when you can.'

'Shall I leave my credit card?' he asked. He put it on the bar.

Linnell picked it up and glanced at it. 'No,' he said, and added, as if to an old friend, 'Now you're being silly, Mr Peerless.'

'Steven,' the man said. 'And this is Jo.'

Daniel didn't reply; he began to feel distracted. Something about the situation had awoken a distant memory in him. Peerless asked about a rhythm and blues compilation from the Ace label that had been playing earlier in the evening. Doyle handed the CD to him. 'His name's Daniel,' he said. 'He's had a hard day. I'm Brendan. Take it. Bring it back when you like. Keep it.'

The money arrived a couple of days later, as Daniel was setting up the bar for the breakfast. It wasn't delivered in person, as he had expected, but by post. Peerless had taped the cheque to a black and white postcard of a man in dinner dress washing up in a restaurant kitchen and there were two CDs in the package: the Ace collection and another. He put the new album on. It was a raucous live reggae recording by a wild-sounding Armenian called Jo Corbeau.

'What the hell is that crap?' Doyle shouted at him. 'Turn it up.'

Steven Peerless took to coming in most days. His new girlfriend Joanna lived up the road; their visit to The Owl, he explained, had been their first date. 'God,' said Daniel, 'I'm sorry it got like that.'

In a curious way, Peerless said, they'd found that the poisonous ambience had somehow made their relationship easier to consolidate. When Daniel thanked him for the record, he explained that he'd got it for nothing; he was a music journalist.

Peerless took to wandering in at around eleven with a notebook; he'd disappear after lunch, sometimes coming back with Joanna, to eat in the evening. He was very unlike what Daniel had imagined a journalist to be. He was physically unremarkable. He was not, so far as Daniel could tell, especially arrogant or deceitful. The only journalists he'd ever seen had been on trains, barking self-vaunting phrases into their mobile phones.

'They always begin by saying the same thing,' he told Steven one day. 'I am on a train.'

'Ah,' Peerless said. 'That's the reporter in them.'

'I hate fucking mobile phones,' Daniel said.

Peerless reached into his pocket, and put his mobile on the counter, its thin aluminium casing almost camouflaged against the zinc. 'Only Jo has the number. Otherwise, it's for matters of life and death.'

'I imagine you need it most days then,' said Linnell, 'for all those album reviews.'

'It's not so much that,' Peerless replied. 'When I have time, I write obituaries.'

Daniel felt an instinct to recoil, as if he'd just learned he was with an undertaker, and yet, in the days that followed, when they talked about Steven's work, it was less about music, more about death notices. Obituaries were done, Peerless explained, not, as most people thought, in panic after the subject was dead or, as he had a tendency to say, 'gone'. They were prepared in advance, by freelance writers like him, who were paid on delivery.

'Christ,' said Daniel, 'don't you worry about hexing people – or hexing yourself?'

'I know I should,' said Peerless. 'The thing is that, in a manner of speaking, two dead men pay my rent every month.'

His unusual job did occasionally inspire moments of urgency. He came in one day with a sheaf of cuttings on Allan Edmunds, a disgraced football chairman who had been admitted to intensive care after suffering a heart attack on the Isle of Skye while he was leading a visit to a whisky producer on a club excursion. The ambulance had been called by a prostitute he'd taken up to his room. 'Dear God,' said Doyle, who knew the bleak island well. 'She must be the only hooker in Carbost.'

Edmunds, Steven said, was not expected to recover. He was perceived to have bled the once great club of its assets and this, combined with the circumstances of the onset of his illness, meant that the usual expressions of grief and sympathy had – even among his immediate family – been seriously attenuated. Peerless read Daniel his closing paragraph. A dry, understated indictment of Edmunds' personal and professional shortcomings, it implied, rather than stated, reckless alcohol abuse and an intense, unaccustomed level of physical exertion immediately prior to his attack. 'I don't like that ending,' he added. 'It's too literal. And it's too nice to him. He was pathetic. This is so absolutely the sort of thing you'd expect him to do.'

'Even if it does come close to proving,' said Daniel, 'that, contrary to popular opinion, he *was* capable of organising a piss-up in a brewery.'

'Bloody hell,' said Peerless. There was a radiant look about his face which, had the chairman been able to see it from his life-support machine, might have finished him there and then. 'Oh – hang on, I don't think we can say piss-up.'

'What about group tasting,' Daniel suggested, 'in a distillery?'

'You know,' Daniel said to Doyle, when Peerless had left. 'When he talks about his writing, I find myself...I have this really strange feeling in my blood, of excitement and irritation.'

'That's because you've been to college,' said Brendan. 'Us dumb fuckers just call it envy.'

In those first few weeks, the morning would sometimes begin with the arrival of a furious letter from Laura's ex-boyfriend, Robin Robinson. They were sometimes addressed to Daniel, sometimes to her. Whichever name was on the envelope, their obsessive tone was consistent. She pinned hers up on the bedroom wall for a week, 'to air them'.

In one letter she received, Robin described a night when Laura, delirious with fever and tossing her head from side to side, had called out his name. That, he said, had first surprised him, then moved him. It was two in the morning; there was a doctor in the room, a friend who'd been with him at medical school. When Laura called out Robin's name, the letter explained, the two men exchanged glances and smiled. But then came the other names: 'Peter...André...Stuart...Leo...Carlos...Derek.'

'Derek?' said Daniel. 'Have you...' She looked away. 'Derek?' he repeated. 'Oh my God.'

'I did it to make Robin pissed,' she said, her grasp of English phrasal verbs deserting her for once. 'I think it was something I saw in a film. I mean the names...OK...the names were real. You know you mustn't...' She paused. 'The thing is – I never tell anybody these things.'

'But you remember it all.'

'Yes,' she replied. 'Like I remember all the other bad stuff.'

Talking to Laura, Daniel – who had a natural tendency towards full and immediate disclosure – sometimes felt like a lifelong player of Snap who had been abruptly introduced to the world of poker. On an impulse – seeking perhaps to reciprocate Laura's unexpected admission – he told her about the death of his father and mother and the way his bereavement had become tied up with that dismal stretch of road.

'You know a small part of me envies you,' she told him.

'Pardon?'

'There's a part of me that says well – OK. That was terrible, but it's over with. That's one more sorrow that you won't have to face. It's over with,' she repeated, 'like a pulled tooth.'

'Except it isn't over,' he said. 'Because I remember it all.' He told her how he sometimes asked himself whether he would have formed any memory of the excavator driver's features, or the weather on that last time he'd driven over to see his mother in hospital, if the events hadn't been so intimately linked with tragedy.

'Are you crazy?' she said. 'Of course you wouldn't.'

A minute passed, in silence.

'Hey Daniel,' she said.

'Yes?'

'You ever look at a map of that highway?'

'Yes,' he said. 'How did you know?'

'Just a wild guess.'

The knowledge that he was her sole confidant concerning the more disturbing episodes from her own past was hardly reassuring. What Daniel knew of Laura's history filled him with an unease that could surface at the most improbable moments. He'd felt it, for instance, on the day they'd been visited by the drunken businessmen. There was just something about the way she spoke to them that had shaken him; a sort of excessive detachment, implying a ferocious, inextinguishable self-belief. If she could do that in those circumstances, he wondered, what might she do in others? It didn't matter. He was, as Steven Peerless might have said, gone.

The next time Linnell saw the obituarist, Peerless was on a stool at The Owl, talking into his mobile phone. He had a copy of the evening paper in front of him, with a large circle drawn in felt marker around a news item on one of the inside pages. From his side of the bar, Daniel tried to read the headline. It wasn't easy, because he had to be unobtrusive and the print was upside down. 'Suicide bid by Jazz…' was all that he could make out.

'There's nothing on him,' he heard Peerless saying. 'Nothing,' he repeated. 'What? Of course we do – he played with Miles Davis for Christ's sake.'

Daniel looked at the picture next to the article and he felt his heartbeat quicken. The man in the photograph was younger, slimmer, less anxious-looking and upside down, but still unmistakable. It was Elliot King. His first instinct was tremendous relief that the musician was somewhere where he would receive serious professional help. He thought about saying something to Peerless, then didn't.

He didn't see Steven the next day, or the next. But on the Monday, when Daniel had the morning off, he came into the bar for a coffee and noticed him at a table, alone, reading the paper. Daniel went over and joined him. 'Listen,' he said, 'you know…you know you were talking about Elliot King.'

'Oh God,' said Peerless. 'Don't remind me. I've got a week to find something out about him. A week that is…God willing.'

'The thing is…' said Daniel. 'I know him. I knew him.'

'Well?' said Peerless forcefully and with such abruptness that he took to it mean 'So what?'

'Well, I just thought you might be interested...' he began, doing his best not to sound offended.

'No,' said Peerless. 'I mean did you know him well?'

There was a forced patience in his voice now, but Linnell noticed that there was a harder certainty about him. 'I knew him, I'd say,' Daniel replied, 'as well as anyone.'

'Well why the fuck didn't you say so?'

'I thought – I think…Listen I was his therapist for Christ's sake. I thought that it would be a kind of…I don't know…A kind of treachery. It would.'

'First, you have to remember this is only going to come out once he's gone.'

'Dead.'

'Dead. And gone. And if you make it true, it won't be treason. True to his life, and true to his work.'

'I don't know anything about his work.'

'Find out.'

'What I was thinking was, I could talk to you,' said Daniel, 'and then you could...'

'Don't talk to me,' said Peerless. He stared to the side of him, like a vaudeville actor appealing to an audience for help with an idiot. 'Write it.'

'I'll think about it,' he said.

'That's right. You think about it. Then you write it.'

That afternoon, when he walked into the café, Daniel found Laura in the office with Jessica Lee, talking to Rachel about the waitress's son, Jordan. 'And you know he's three,' Rachel said. 'And he's started to ask for a dummy. He's never shown any interest in a dummy before.'

Jessica looked puzzled. 'A dummy?' she asked. She turned to Daniel. 'What's a child want with a dummy?'

'It's a pacifier,' Laura explained.

'Pacifier?' said Daniel. 'That sounds like something made by Smith and Wesson.' He glanced involuntarily at Jessica's handbag. To his great embarrassment, she caught him doing it. Rachel, as though it would help resolve the confusion, reached into her shopping bag and placed the dummy, still in its packaging, on Jessica's desk.

'Oh, for Christ's sake,' said Laura. She picked up the small plastic package and tossed it across the room to Daniel, who caught it. 'It's not complicated. It's a dummy,' she told him, 'you pacifier.'

They were interrupted by a motorcycle courier whose arrival was signalled by a furious barking from the bar area, where Bella was blocking the man's path. 'I'll go,' said Daniel. 'It'll be for Steven. He's the only one who ever gets biked letters.' He signed for the small package, and he was about to put it behind the bar when he noticed it had his name on it.

'Aren't you going to open it?' Laura said.

'No.'

'Why not?'

'Because I think I know what's in it.'

An hour or so later, alone in the flat, he pulled open the padded envelope which – as it was new, and not re-used, and had been delivered by hand, not posted – could only have come from one place. Inside he found a thick wad of cuttings on Elliot King, from newspapers and music magazines, and several CDs of his work. There was also a sheet of A4 paper. On it was scrawled, in large letters, *You Can Do This*.

He stuffed the things back in the envelope, and walked across the road to the bus stop. He'd arranged to meet Laura at Baker Street Underground station at seven. They often met there, in the old booking hall, ten feet below ground level. He was waiting in his usual spot, near a flight of steps that led down from the street. From here, the first you saw of an approaching figure was their feet. He found himself staring at the avalanche of shoes, almost hypnotised by the movement, wondering if the next pair he'd see would be hers and as he wondered, experiencing a little of the intense delight he knew would descend on him when her scuffed brown leather shoes appeared.

The steps were on his right. To his left, a drunk was urinating against a door marked 'This Area Is Under Constant Surveillance'. Directly in front of him there was a bank of public telephones. Through her, Baker Street, a place he had never regarded with any interest before, had become somehow enchanted. As long as he knew Laura it would never leave her: this ability to make a bland apartment special, a beaten-up old car attractive, or a tube station captivating. He went back to staring hard at the shoes and so was taken unawares when she put her hands over his eyes from behind, having come down the other entrance, the one she never used, to surprise him. He was glad he'd been early. He loved waiting for her.

They got a cab up to the Agra at Warren Street. They sat at a corner table faced by a black and white picture of Muhammad Ali, photographed at the Agra in the sixties, his huge hands placed affectionately on the heads of two of the waiting staff. Next to him, they looked like infants. Daniel had once talked to the current employees, he told Laura, and asked what became of the waiters in the picture. Each had come to an unfortunate end; one through sickness, the other through gambling. It was as though the big man's generous gesture, which looked like a blessing, had brought all of them, himself included, only calamity.

Emboldened by the restaurant's dim lighting and the image of the heavyweight fighter, he told her about Peerless and the package.

'So...what are you going to do?' she asked him.

'I don't know. I didn't like that note: "You can do it."'

'Why?'

'Because it isn't "can",' he told her. 'It's "should".'

If he'd had to confront the decision immediately, he'd never have done it. But they'd agreed to spend the next couple of days looking after Seti, one of Laura's friends who had flown over from the South of France. Seti was the sister of Jessica Lee's dead North African lover and she'd come for a short holiday with her husband, Michel. The Frenchman had a pencil moustache and the kind of raffish good looks and powerful build that might have brought him a career in Indian film. He was a social worker, he told Daniel, in project housing in Marseille. Their house was three hours' drive away in the Larzac, north of Montpellier, which meant that he could only get home at weekends. 'A *shame*,' Michel said, in barely comprehensible English. This was the only phrase, for some reason, that he had retained from a year of language classes and he never passed over a chance to use it. He spoke the words, as Brendan said later, with what was not so much an accent as an ongoing revenge for Waterloo. Michel reached into the pocket of his leather jacket and produced a picture of their farmhouse, a ramshackle property in what looked like an area of breathtaking natural beauty. Laura took Seti round the art galleries in the West End; Daniel reluctantly agreed to escort Michel who wanted to see the housing estates round Kennington and Stockwell.

The young Frenchman, who took endless photographs of the tenement blocks, turned out to be a likeable figure, bold yet self-deprecating. The visitors spent three nights sleeping on Laura's living-room floor. After they'd left, in the usual flurry of thanks and invitations to visit, Daniel told Laura how he felt ashamed at having prejudged the Frenchman, on the grounds of his looks and his job title. For him, like for most of his compatriots, he told her, the words 'social worker' had come to inspire an involuntary contempt, however hard they tried to fight it.

'Yeah, well, you should see where he works,' Laura said. 'He runs this terrifying estate of tower blocks outside Marseille. He holds that place together by the strength of his personality. And by his strength.'

After they'd left, Daniel went down to the bar and picked up the courier's package. He read the liner notes from the Elliot King CDs. Then, out of curiosity, he played one. Then he played another, then all of them. The early recordings were traditional jazz. On the recent ones, King was producing a sound more reminiscent, as Laura pointed out, of 'a big bird in pain'. Daniel laughed. 'I could use that,' he said and, saying it, knew that his mind was made up.

He wrote down everything he knew. He found that he'd spent so much time talking to Peerless about the journalist's own obituaries that the style came to him naturally. He wrote down everything because that was how he'd been taught to write patient profiles at Resolve. He imagined that he would edit the pages later, removing anything disrespectful to King's memory, though when it came to it he took nothing out. He wrote about King's lethal companion Mike, and his burial and disinterment, and about Elliot's habit of memorising facts and figures about American towns. 'King knew as well as any man,' he wrote, 'the spiritual solace latent in statistics.' He described, as best he could, the gift of a composer and performer in a field of music he didn't understand. King wrote one song, in the early seventies, called 'Life is Better on Cocaine', 'a philosophy,' Linnell wrote, 'that his own CV did little to confirm. The violent lack of control in his personal life,' he went on, 'was a disturbing but perhaps necessary corollary to his brilliant career as an improviser, in which he developed a reckless unpredictability that endeared him to two generations of enthusiasts.'

'One of the great jazz songwriters of his age,' he wrote in his final paragraph, 'Elliot King was a man who believed the pen was mightier than the sword, but didn't always have a pen to hand.' Once Daniel had picked up his biro and a notebook, it had only taken him two hours to write.

He sat down in front of the manual typewriter in Laura's room. A beautiful, weather-beaten black machine from the thirties, its carriage return was inscribed, in gold lettering, with the words: 'Remington – Made From American Parts with British Labour.' When he'd finished, he'd filled two sheets, typing – since he knew nothing of editorial convention – with single spacing between the lines and on both sides of the paper. Without bothering to take a photocopy of what he'd done, he put it in the post.

The following evening, Daniel was working behind the bar when Steven Peerless came in alone and ordered a bottle of champagne. Daniel, who was growing used to gestures of flamboyance, took one from the fridge. Peerless asked for two glasses. When Daniel handed him the bottle, the journalist filled both and, instead of moving to a table, stayed where he was at the bar.

'Is Jo coming down?' Daniel asked.

'No,' Peerless said. 'It's not for Jo. It's for us.'

'Oh,' said Daniel, without enthusiasm. He never drank when he was working. 'Good.'

'OK,' said Peerless. 'I gave it to Whittington, the obits editor, this morning. Two hours later, he was reading out the last paragraph – no, not reading it – he was reciting it, from memory, in conference.' He looked at

Linnell's face, expecting that its expression would reflect his own, which was one of real delight. It didn't.

'What's conference?' asked Daniel.

'Conference is…it's…it doesn't matter,' Peerless said. 'He loves it. He thinks it's brilliant. And,' he added, 'he wants to meet you.'

At this point Daniel, still showing no desire to celebrate, picked up his glass and drained it in one go. Peerless handed him a cheque for an amount that was more than a month's wages in bar shifts. Daniel stared at the figure in disbelief. Later, when he came to know more about the workings of a newspaper, he would realise that it wasn't the size of the fee that should really have struck him as miraculous, but its speed of issue.

He walked to the bank the next morning and paid the money in. Almost half was swallowed up by his overdraft. After a lengthy conversation with the under manager, they let him draw the rest out straight away. He put the cash in an envelope he'd addressed to King at his London hospital. He was in the queue at the post office when he remembered what the musician had once said to him about the level of security in mental wards. He walked out and caught a bus to Finsbury Park, then took the tube to Paddington, close to the hospital where he was detained. Daniel tried to leave the envelope at the main reception, but they insisted he take it to the ward.

When he got there, ill at ease in case he ran into King himself, he handed the envelope to the ward sister, a middle-aged woman who governed the front desk with a sternness that verged on caricature. 'Whom should I say called?' she asked.

Daniel, unpractised as yet in the arts of deception, and in no mood to prolong his visit by correcting her grammar, said nothing.

'Are you a friend of Mr King's?' the woman asked. She had raised her voice this time, perhaps assuming that Daniel couldn't hear. Deafness, he recalled Elliot saying, wasn't one of his problems. The ward was a small one and King couldn't be far away. He heard soft footsteps approaching from the far end of the corridor. One slippered foot – it may have been his imagination – seemed to be tapping gently, in a soft shoe routine, in triplets.

Daniel started to back away. The nurse sprinted round the desk, showing remarkable speed and agility, he thought, for her age. 'Any message?' she asked, defiantly. She was still holding the envelope which, it struck him horribly, and for the first time, contained thirty banknotes.

'No,' he said and left the ward. As he walked out of the building, he found himself in an emotional state of a kind he'd never experienced before, part elation, part self-loathing. It was a condition which his new career would do little to diminish. He walked the short distance back to Paddington Station, and his altered life.

CHAPTER 4

He loved to hear her talk about her home town. She told him about the Prospect Café in Main Street and how its owner, an ageing hippy called Sally, kept a large catfish called Jasper who was in his teens, and the way that, every day, she watched the British parliament on a small cable TV above the bar. In the Agra one night, Laura told him how, as a girl, she used to get up early and go down with Paul, her brother, to watch the early morning freight trains rolling in to Bedford from Denver or Kansas City. The railroad, she told him, ran straight through the middle of town.

'Why is that so breathtaking,' he said, 'when the tracks run by a road, or next to the sea?'

There was some deep, primeval connection, she said, laughing, between young children and freight trains.

'It's so sad,' he said, 'the way that magic wears off.'

She said nothing and looked preoccupied.

'What does Paul do?' he asked her, then added, quickly, 'for work?'

'You know, when Paul was twenty,' she said, 'he started to disappear after breakfast. He'd show up back at the house for dinner at night and he wouldn't say where he'd been. This went on for two or three weeks. In the end' – she paused – 'my dad had some guy follow him – I mean how fucked is that? – and anyhow it turned out that what he was doing was...'

The waiter arrived with the drinks and she fell silent. Daniel remembered some of the remarks that she had felt able to make in public and wondered what kind of revelation this new delicacy could herald.

'There's this big grain elevator in the centre of town,' she said, 'close to the railroad tracks, by the level crossing. That's where the trucks unload the wheat. They pick it up from the harvesters and they drop it at the elevator, where it's loaded on to the railroad trucks. And Paul was walking up there around nine every morning and climbing this metal ladder up the side of the grain silo. I mean it's just this bare, rusted iron emergency ladder, there's no safety platforms or anything. I went to look at it. It stops five feet short of the ground, because you're only ever supposed to be coming down, not up. And it runs up to the flat roof of the silo. It's got to be a hundred and fifty feet up. He was climbing that ladder and lying flat on his stomach, on the roof, all day. He'd take a pair of binoculars with him – he brought those home – and a litre bottle of Coke that he carried back empty.

'So my dad gets this creep to follow him and he delivers his report. Then one night we're all having dinner and my dad suddenly says, "Well, son, so you were up on the silo again today.' I thought he'd gone insane. And Paul says, "Yes, Dad", as if he was talking about going to a football game. And when he asked him why he went there, he said he was doing it because he wanted to see how the trains looked, down below. Now you've got to understand, he's spending eight, maybe nine, hours up there. He'd take the Coke bottle up there in his waistband, drink it during the day, then use yesterday's bottle to take a leak in and bring that one down with him at night, I guess so the workers wouldn't notice he was there.

'So then my dad talked to the guy that owned the elevator, because he knew him from the Elks Lodge. After that they let Paul climb up there any time he liked, except now he had to go up through the regular service stairs, which were inside the plant, not up the outside ladder. They even gave him a hard hat and overalls. What I couldn't understand was why my dad didn't go crazy then, when he first found out. He was just sort of "Oh yeah, well...he's a boy, you know." Anyway, Paul carried on going up the silo for a couple of weeks. Then one day I came in and my dad was in the kitchen and he looked worried sick. I said, "What is it? You look terrible." And he said, "Laura, you know Paul's climbing up there on the silo?" I said, "Yeah, I know." "And he's looking at the trains with his binoculars." "Yes." "And he's spending all day there." I said, "I know that too." "Well," he said, "I found out today that he's not writing down the numbers of those trains." She laughed. 'There was a pause and then he said, "You won't believe this, but" – she imitated the deep presidential timbre of her father's outrage – "he doesn't even have a notebook."'

She looked at Daniel. 'So what do you gather about a guy that does all that, and,' she said, going back into her dignified baritone, 'he doesn't even have a notebook?' He said nothing. 'And no,' she said quietly, 'he doesn't do anything for work.'

It was hardly the most delicate of confidences, but it brought them closer. And yet something from Robin's onslaught in the Café Leon still worried Daniel; there was one phrase that kept coming back to him, and wouldn't ever quite go away: 'She's a woman who'll give you surprises.'

Which meant he was especially taken aback when the following morning, a Friday, she told him she was going away the next day to make a parachute jump. She didn't even bother with a 'Didn't I tell you?'

'Why,' he asked her, 'didn't you say?'

She smiled, a little bewildered. 'I don't know.'

She kept her parachute, which she packed meticulously herself, behind the empty suitcases in the boxroom. By the time she met him, she'd made forty-eight jumps, the last twenty of them freefalls from ten thousand feet or more. She went up every couple of months or so, which was not unusually frequent. Unlike most skydivers, who tended to jump at their local airfield and socialise with a familiar group of parachutists, she seemed obsessively drawn to travelling.

'When?' he asked her.

'Twelve o'clock on Sunday.'

'Where?'

'Haverfordwest,' she said. 'It's near my Aunt Helen's house in St David's. You know,' she added, trying to change the subject, 'she lives in a road called Goat Street.'

'How high?'

'Twelve thousand feet.'

He'd slipped unthinkingly into the sort of question routine he used to repeat when he was a language teacher in Limoges.

'How much?'

'A hundred and fifty pounds.'

Laura stepped into the bathroom to take a shower. She was already in there when she noticed that she was still holding a lighted cigarette, which she extinguished in the toilet.

She turned on the shower and undressed, realising as she did so that she had forgotten to bring a change of clothes in with her. She could come back out in a robe, she decided, and get them later. She stepped under the shower. Jessica Lee had installed a secondary pump that transformed the feeble drizzle of English pressure into shocking, almost American, ferocity. Its power struck Laura more forcibly on this occasion than others because, in her haste, she'd climbed in while the water was still ice cold. But she stayed under, as though from some instinct for punishment, though for what she couldn't say.

She felt the water turning warm, and the muscles of her upper body relax. She glanced down at her left shoulder where she could just see the end of a strand of black hair; so black, she remembered someone saying to her once, in another shower, that you expected the water running off it to take on the colour of ebony ink.

It was just as the water was reaching her preferred temperature – hot, on the verge of painful – that she understood that she had been in some haste to get in there, and why. Listening to Daniel, she'd been reminded of how his abrupt questions had recalled her own, when she was first given the chance to make a jump. Then she applied herself to one that he hadn't asked, the next, most obvious inquiry about her dangerous recreation. She shut her eyes, raised her face to take the full force of the water and pondered the question she had anticipated, but that he'd never put to her – 'Why?'

CHAPTER 5

It would be nice, she thought, to say that she took to it by instinct; that it was no surprise that her gift for defiance should extend beyond such things as etiquette, school discipline and common sense, and embrace gravity itself. The truth was that, as with many things in her life, it had been a man. She had met him in the Broad Face, a cramped, spitefully local pub on the high street in Witney, while she was still at Freshfields School. Andy was blond and more than twice her age. He had a moustache. He was loyal to the flag in a straightforward way she'd grown used to at home in the United States, but had rarely seen in Britain, where patriotism had become redefined in her mind as a combination of jealousy, rage and vengefulness. He was not her type.

Andy had a habit of weighing his words carefully before speaking, which could make him appear dim. His looks were unremarkable. He was born fearless. All of these traits, Laura once told him, would have made him perfectly suited to a life of crime. 'What kind of crime?' he asked, after a pause that was slightly longer than usual.

'I don't know...*crime*,' she said. 'Joy riding. Drug running. Homicide.' But he had never known the terrible thrill of crashing at speed in a stranger's car, of collecting an illicit package, or ending another man's life. Andy didn't have to. He was an RAF parachute instructor.

She'd gone to the Broad Face with Ruth Lloyd, a girl who had the exaggerated angular features – and, in certain moods, the instincts – of a Disney witch. In their first few days together at Freshfields, Laura hadn't paid much attention to Ruth, whose manner was dominated by a feigned world-weariness of a kind which, Laura had observed, was cultivated by many pupils at Britain's more privileged private schools. But she soon started to notice her fellow student, for her surliness, and for the intimidating way she had of walking around the six-bed dormitory, naked and swearing.

She got to know her properly when they were both confined to quarters for a month, after they were caught, with a group of other girls, in the school's nearest pub, a large, soulless place called The Sun in September. The Sun had a dance-floor, and was licensed till midnight. The young landlord's relaxed attitude to under-age drinking and soft drugs meant that the pub was regularly raided. It was Laura's idea to try the Broad Face, whose dismal clientele was dominated by old men playing dominoes, on the grounds that Bernard, the landlord, was in his sixties and hence unlikely to be able to tell if a woman wearing make-up was sixteen or twenty-five.

'It's their age that does it,' said Laura. 'If you showed these old guys a woman of sixty-three, they could tell you how old she was down to the week. That's the beauty of Bernard. Every day he gets older. Every day he gets worse.'

They started to go to the Broad Face twice a week, and they sat in its long back room, where every table had a domino board and a wood and brass scoring block for cribbage. On the night Andy called in, they were talking about the more obscure games they'd played themselves, and Laura was telling Ruth about a pastime she and Paul had invented, called Oliver. To play it, she explained, you had to choose a person and the adjective least suited to them; it could be Hercules ('meek'), Kubla Khan ('frugal') or Little Richard ('retiring'). Then you told your opponent the adjective, not the name, and they had twenty questions, which had to be answered yes or no, to try to find out who it was. It didn't need to be a famous name, Laura explained; it could be someone from school, or your sister, or a shopkeeper from down the road. Each new round had to be introduced with the phrase: 'I'll give you an Oliver for Twenty'.

Twenty questions were never enough, Laura said, so generous-minded players might say, 'I'll give you an Oliver for Fifty'.

'Yes,' said Ruth, 'but how do you score? How do you win?'

Laura paused. There was no scoring. Nobody won. Oliver was one of those forms of communal madness that can evolve in families that spend long periods shut up together in tiny apartments or, as in the Jardines' case, hotel rooms and limousines. It was only now that she realised it. Here it sounded idiotic. She wished she'd never mentioned it.

'Why,' Ruth continued, moving in for the kill, 'is it called Oliver?'

'I don't know,' said Laura, glaring at her. 'I'll find out.'

'How?' asked Ruth.

And it was at this point, just as Laura felt she might start to blush for the first time in five years, that Andy walked over to their table and introduced himself. It was coming up to closing time on a Friday night. Although subtlety was not his strong point, Andy had accidentally arrived at the perfect moment both for Laura, who was desperate to seize on any distraction, and for Ruth, who was getting irritated and had run out of money. His initiative was watched with sidelong glances, first of amazement, then of envy, by the elderly regulars. It was about this time of night that, beneath the men's indifference, a gallon of the Broad Face's sweet, dark beer began to kindle furtive, hopeless yearnings. The physical origin of their curiosity was barely perceptible to the old men themselves, and these faint flickers of desire had no more chance of being noticed by the outside world than the minutest stirring of some torpid prehistoric fish, long believed extinct, as it lay, finally dying, among dim, icy rocks on the world's deepest ocean floor. Laura, being young, was oblivious to all this, but every time she and Ruth walked into the Broad Face, the bar's other customers might have been described, under the rules of Oliver, as 'indifferent'.

Andy sat down and asked if he could buy them a drink. Laura asked for her usual bottled lager. Ruth, hoping to score impressively on price and sophistication, asked for a large dry Martini. It was a drink that had not been served in living memory at the Broad Face, in any size, and which, when it was ordered, sparked a lively debate at the bar over what should go into it.

'Tart,' Laura told her, as she watched Andy standing, looking uncomfortable, in the middle of the ongoing conference.

'I *know* it has bloody cherries in it,' she heard one OAP shout. 'I fought in France.'

'What's your Oliver for him?' Ruth sneered, looking at Andy's jeans and ungainly biker boots, as he stood at the bar with his back to them.

'Coquettish,' Laura replied.

'Flamboyant,' said Ruth.

He came back carrying a tray. To avoid further argument among his posse of self-appointed advisers, Bernard had stood the drink – a double measure of Martini with a single shot each of gin and vodka, served in a straight half-pint beer glass – next to a stainless-steel pickle dish which he'd stacked with small piles of glacé cherries and lemon slices. Noticing that every eye in the room was watching to see whether Ruth would accept part, or all, of this garnish, and suspecting, rightly, that bets had been exchanged at the bar, Laura swept the lot in, and Ruth drained the Martini (as she believed etiquette required) in one go, to cheers. When the noise subsided, they had a few uneasy exchanges with Andy; the conversation was made more stilted by his habit of delaying every response by a couple of seconds.

'Talking to you,' Laura said, who had begun to feel sorry for him, 'is like making a transatlantic telephone call.'

Just after Bernard had called last orders, Andy unleashed what experience had taught him was his one interesting weapon: he dared them to make a parachute jump.

'I'll do it,' said Ruth, with the bogus zeal of a born deserter.

'When?' asked Laura.

'Tomorrow,' he said.

'How much?'

'Nothing. I've got a group of Oxford students doing a jump for charity.'

'Where?'

'Weston-on-the-Green.'

He had spare places, he said, because the two women in the party had dropped out. 'They called last night,' he said, 'to say they had a stomach infection.'

'OK,' said Laura, quietly. 'I'll come.'

A few minutes after ten the following morning, as Laura walked across the airfield at Weston-on-the-Green, Ruth was at a corner table in Peg's Pantry in Witney, licking hot chocolate off the back of a white plastic teaspoon. Laura could see the six male students from Christ Church College, sitting cross-legged on a patch of ground near the main entrance to the offices. They were talking among themselves and there were a couple of outbursts of uneasy laughter. Occasionally, she noticed, one of them would glance up at the sky. In the absence of strong winds or low cloud cover, novices would train in the morning and jump the same afternoon. As she drew level with the group, Andy appeared and led them into the building.

He took them into the gymnasium and handed out a form. The last section requested details of next of kin. As an American, Laura had to fill out an extra sheet confirming her identity. It asked for her passport number which, as she didn't have it with her, she invented.

'All OK?' Andy said, coming over to her.

'Yes,' she told him. She pointed to a box that said: Is this the name by which you are usually known? 'It is,' she said, 'but when things get intense I like to be called Samantha.'

They spent three hours in the gym, where they were raised to the top of a scaffolding tower in a hoist, then dropped on to mats. Andy and his senior instructor Chris taught them to bend their legs and fall sideways on to their shoulder, like a rider rolling off a motorbike.

'When you touch down,' Andy said, 'it should feel just like jumping off your kitchen table.'

There were, he added, 'certain scenarios', such as strong crosswinds, which could complicate landing, and that was where the roll was especially important, to avoid injuries to your legs or spine. Crosswinds could also result in a landing away from the target area. Weston-on-the-Green, he told them, to nervous laughter, was situated close to a sewage treatment plant.

'Everyone gets afraid,' Andy said. 'But fear isn't a big thing if you don't make it into one in your mind.'

Strapped in the harness, they took turns jumping off the scaffolding, counting out the seconds while they fell. They would be jumping from two thousand feet, attached to a fixed line which opened the canopy automatically, but they still needed to count, Andy told them, 'in case you get to twenty and nothing's happened'. That meant the main chute had failed, he explained, and they had to open the reserve for themselves. You had to shout out the seconds – 'thousand and one, thousand and two' – as loud as you could, as you fell in the harness, to the rest of the group. Laura could hear her voice echo off the gym walls. Down here, it felt foolish.

Over a canteen lunch few of them ate, Andy and Chris recited other mantras of the parachutist's faith, such as 'Altitude is safety' and 'Remember: you are not leaving the plane, you are entering the air.' The skies were clear, but the jump was delayed when one of the students (the son, Andy told her later, of the Commander of the Fleet Air Arm) was sick on his boots as they were about to board the small aircraft. This, she realised, as Andy rinsed his boots for him under an outside tap, was what she was most afraid of. It wasn't so much the jump itself; it was the way you didn't know how you were going to react when you were lined up by that open door: quiet and resolute; imperceptibly terrified; or screaming and quivering like a yellow rating in some black and white British war movie.

To some extent, she discovered later, this assessment had already been made. They were lined up to board the plane, though they were unaware of it at the time, in order of apparent nervousness: the Commander's son first, so he'd have less time to contemplate the void, Laura last. Once you'd boarded the plane, Andy said, you were committed to coming down, as he put it, 'the quick way'.

The plane was very small. Andy and Chris sat opposite each other on two sideways-facing seats at the front – to ensure, presumably, that none of their charges should make their suicidal leap prematurely. The trainees sat down the length of the cabin, hunched together facing the front, each person sitting on the boots of the one behind.

As the plane took off, Laura couldn't stop staring at the door which, to her surprise, was left open from the beginning. Looking more closely, she saw that there was no door. She closed her eyes and went through the routine again in her mind. They reached altitude. Andy leaned over to them and, shouting against the noise of the propellers, reminded them they would be going out at twenty-second intervals. He got to his feet; Chris stayed in his seat. She watched the Commander's son turn and stand in the doorway with his back to the drop, as they had been taught to do. She was thankful that she couldn't see his face. His boots, she had noticed, as he got up, were still soaking wet. Where the upper joined the sole on the right one, a small piece of regurgitated green bean had become lodged in the yellow stitching.

'One,' Andy barked savagely. 'Legs together.' The Commander's son disappeared. 'Two…legs together.' 'Seven,' he said, more gently, as she got up to the opening. 'Legs together.' She turned and, not knowing or caring whether Chris was looking, kissed Andy on the mouth. Then she stood in the doorway, leaned back and let go.

She tried to count when the air hit her, shouting out the numbers like she'd been taught to, but her voice died in her throat. She couldn't shout because she couldn't breathe. The general sensation of buffeting, cold and asphyxiation felt less like moving in air, more as if she had jumped into Niagara Falls. The ground, which seemed for some reason to be in front of her rather than below, was flickering like old movie footage on a cheap home projector. She had the brief but certain feeling that she was going to die.

There was an explosion around her midriff and she was wrenched violently upwards as the main chute opened. When she'd recovered, she found that the couple of minutes spent floating silently down under the canopy, an experience commonly described as inducing feelings of tranquillity or elation, was an anticlimax. She landed rebelliously on both feet, to see if she could. As soon as she was down, she wanted to go back up again straight away, like a child will come down a slide and sprint back round to the ladder before the exhilaration of the last descent has worn off.

Whatever you said to yourself, she told Andy that evening, once they were back in the Broad Face, when you jumped out of that plane, there was something deep within you that believed it was your last act.

'The strange thing is,' he said, 'that the terror can strike you at any moment. You can get a group instructor who's made three hundred jumps, and he'll be on some low-level training exercise, and suddenly he'll get that late-onset fear, and he'll never make a jump again. You never know,' he said, 'when that moment will come.'

Laura had told Daniel she'd leave for Haverfordwest on Saturday lunchtime, stay overnight at her Aunt Helen's house, make the jump and come home Sunday night. But when Linnell came back to the flat at four on Saturday afternoon, after he'd finished the day shift, he was surprised to find the outside door still unlocked.

When he walked in, he saw her on her knees in the living room. At first he thought Laura was packing, then he noticed that she had every item of her small wardrobe strewn across the floor. She was turning out the pockets of all her clothes. She gave no sign that she'd noticed him arrive. He went into the bedroom and changed into a loose shirt and canvas trousers. He stood in the doorway and watched her. She was crouched down with her back to him. There was something troubling in her movements. She looked like an addict scrabbling round for a mislaid prescription.

He walked up behind her, kneeled down and put his hand on her shoulder. She didn't give a start; she must have known he was there.

'Can I help?' he asked her.

'I lost my damn passport,' she said.

He walked back into the bedroom and began to search half-heartedly through a pile of books and CDs. Was it possible, he wondered, that somebody – Brendan perhaps – had told her that Wales had introduced a visa requirement for Americans? Then, to his surprise, he found it almost immediately. The small blue booklet had got stuck to the underside of a CD case, with what looked like spilled coffee. He peeled the passport gently away from the plastic cover and held it up to see if it had been damaged. As he did so, a small card fell out and landed on the floor. He picked it up: it was a receipt from a cab company in Brighton Beach, Brooklyn. He turned it over. There, in the space where the date and the amount should have been, somebody had scrawled, in biro, the words 'In Yor Bed'.

He put the card back in the passport and handed it to her. Her eyes went straight to his, then she looked away again. 'Thanks,' she said.

'Do you need your passport for a parachute jump?' he asked her.

'Yes,' she said, her voice expressionless.

'You know...you never talk about that. About the parachute jumping.'

'You never ask.'

'OK,' said Daniel. 'I'll ask. Why?'

'Why what?'

'What makes you do it?'

If he hadn't asked her the last time, it was because Daniel had always assumed that, since his own worst terrors were in his mind, stupidity and courage were two sides of the same coin and he risked implying that she wasn't brave, but an idiot. On the rare occasions when she did volunteer some thought about other people's parachute jumps, he'd noticed how her attraction to the sport seemed to have been forged almost entirely from her imagination. She had a tendency to linger over terms such as aviation, descent, or cloud cover, rather in the way that her mother might have done with Biarritz, Cary Grant, or chenille.

She slipped the passport into her back pocket. One time, she told him, she'd come down over strange basalt formations at a place called Rifle, near where Jessica Lee grew up in Colorado. 'I got down, and I could hear these howling noises,' she said. 'There's nothing there, for miles around. Then I saw this one guy from our group who'd landed with one leg either side of an electric cattle fence.'

They sat in the middle of the pile of clothes in the living room. She was leaning with her back against his shoulder, sitting at right angles to him, so she wasn't looking into his eyes, and she told him about Andy, and the Broad Face, and how she couldn't manage to count because of the wind, about the instructors' encouraging mottos, and even about the kiss.

He noticed how she had formed some perverse attachment to the specialist language of catastrophe; things like the Roman Candle effect – a malfunction in which the chute fails to open completely.

'What happens then?' he asked her.

'Well then,' she said, 'you're into one of those rare scenarios that Andy was talking about. What happens then is, it doesn't feel quite like jumping off a table. It feels more like jumping out of an airplane two miles up in the sky.'

'Can you count now, when you jump?'

'Yes. Except now I say Christopher One, Christopher Two.'

'Because of the second RAF guy?'

'Who?'

'Because of the other instructor.'

'Oh,' she said. 'No. Because of the saint. The patron saint of travellers.'

'I think he got struck off.'

'He did. That's why I like him. And he's always worked for me.'

'You're addicted,' he told her. 'It's like a drug.'

'It's not like that,' she said. 'It's not a compulsion. It's more like…it's more like you have this little country house somewhere abroad and you've locked it up and travelled home, but you have this feeling that you've left the bathroom light on. You haven't, probably, but you have this itch to get back and turn it off.' She paused. 'You want to know something? Those low-level training jumps are far, far worse than going from altitude. At two thousand feet, you can still see the motor scooters and the hospital parking lot. On the real jumps, all you can see is the sun and the sky.'

Daniel remembered that Guy Montgomery had told him how he felt calmer in large theatres, which often had a less intimidating atmosphere – an atmosphere which his own career had brought him little chance to savour. In a small playhouse, Montgomery claimed, you could see every face in the first few rows. In a large arena, you walked on stage to a reassuringly vague dazzle, and individual faces were blotted out by the distance across the orchestra pit and the power of the spotlights.

Apart from his unfortunate decision to light up while playing a late-fourteenth-century nobleman, Montgomery's worst experience had been at a tiny theatre in Southport, where he was appearing as Satan in a modern verse adaptation of the mediaeval mystery plays. He was wearing snakeskin tights, a black velvet cape and a devil's mask with horns, made out of papier mâché and elastic. Act Three, after the interval, opened with him sitting on the steps at the front of the stage, with Eve, who he'd successfully tempted, standing motionless behind him, frozen in time, with her teeth sunk into a wax apple. Montgomery had to deliver a menacing soliloquy, during which he would fix his gaze on the most defenceless-looking spectator in the second row, and try to induce a ripple of contagious panic.

'That day I was staring malevolently into the eyes of this young trainee nurse,' he'd told Linnell. 'She'd come straight from the hospital, and she was still in her uniform. I was giving them all this stuff about how I was Prince in this world, but Invincible Master of the dark realm of hell,' he said, 'when I started to feel my mask slipping down off my face. I could feel it going as I was speaking, and I tried to prop it up with my trident, but it didn't help. All the time I was staring into the eyes of this nurse. When it really started going, I saw her put her hand up to her mouth.

'Losing your devil's mask,' he remembered Montgomery saying, 'isn't like your hat coming off. You can hold your hat on. You can toss your hat casually on to the sofa. Anyway, suddenly it slipped off altogether, and I heard this noise behind me like someone trying to start a car with a very flat battery. I found out later it was Eve trying to stifle a snigger, with her nostrils pressed hard against the apple. I heard the nurse let out this little yelp. It had fallen down forward off my face, and I had it dangling around my neck, like a welder's mask when he's stopped welding. It just dangled there on its elastic; I could imagine them all thinking oh well, maybe he'll slip it on again later, if he ever starts feeling devilish again. I dried, totally. I couldn't move; I just stood there, staring into the eyes of this young nurse, looking at her horrified expression and thinking: this girl has come straight from Intensive Care, and she knows disaster when she sees it.'

'You still there?' Laura asked him.

She had been talking about death, Daniel realised, and an idiotic half-smile had appeared on his face.

'What happened to Andy?' he said.

'God knows,' she replied. 'I don't think a whole lot about Andy.'

This wasn't quite true.

She had split up with him after a couple of months, when she went back to the States for the summer. But it was there, in his one-bedroom Witney flat, with its heavy metal posters, its litter of motorcycle gear, and its radiators draped with half-dried T-shirts and boxer shorts, that she had noticed something about herself. She had noticed, as she told her friend Ruth Lloyd at the time, 'that you can bring a man to a point where any movement – you reach out for a light switch on a bedside table, you turn your head slightly so that, in the place where their chest is held against you there is a half-inch movement of their skin on your skin…'

She had stopped at this point, and Ruth was staring at her. She was saying 'their' so as not to say Andy.

'You get to a point where any of these movements,' she continued, 'will make them … '

'Detonate,' said her friend. 'Explode. Like a bomb.'

'Yes, Ruth,' Laura said. 'Like a bomb.' She lapsed into an exaggerated French accent, for reasons her friend didn't understand. 'A beumb. The exploding kind. But it wasn't a bomb I was thinking of.'

Looking back on this conversation, she realised it was the first and last time in her life that she had initiated the sort of risqué banter she sometimes heard from her girlfriends.

'I was thinking of one of those movement sensors in the corner of a room, and they're linked to a burglar alarm, and they go off if a mouse blinks.'

'Oh dear,' said Ruth. 'You must have been bored.'

If she had been bored, Laura thought, then she hadn't stayed bored – or at least looked bored – for long. That capacity for detachment and control was not something she had sustained. It was a paradox of her intimate life that, the more she lived it, the more powerless it left her. She experienced a dwindling tolerance, rather in the way that some people could walk away from their first line of cocaine feeling bemused and indifferent, while the tenth would have them gibbering uncontrollably about wireless telegraphy and flowering succulents. These days, in some way that she resented, her body took her over.

As they sat motionless, shoulder to back in the disorder, like hostages there, with the light outside fading, Daniel told her that he couldn't help but worry about her making parachute jumps.

'Why?'

'Because it's careless.'

'Careless?'

'It's careless about the person who – the man who – likes you. Who loves you. For instance me,' he said, realising to his horror that this was a line he had heard in a song.

She got to her feet, picked up her bag and set off to catch the evening train. When she reached the door, she turned round.

'I'm careful,' she said. 'Up there, I'm very careful. We all are. It's down here I'm careless.'

'Careless?'

'Yes,' she told him, 'I miss things. I don't see things I should see. I'm careless. I don't notice. Like I never notice you,' she said, 'carefully pouring yourself quadruple vodkas.'

CHAPTER 6

He hated him before he met him. He hated him for his name – Alexander Whittington – seven cumbersome syllables which, Daniel thought as he sat on the light railway that carried him out to the newspaper's Docklands offices, might have served as a shorthand for everything he detested about England. The Christian name was pompously unabbreviated, as of course it was required to be in his world. When it came to his surname, however, it was hard to believe that the editor, relaxing among his peers, would answer to anything but Whitters. He hated him before he met him, and when he met him he hated him more.

Steven Peerless was waiting for him by the security desks at the bottom of the newspaper building. It was Peerless who'd persuaded him to come to Whittington's drinks party and, remembering that, Linnell started to resent him as well.

'Come on,' Peerless said, seeing his expression. 'Give it ten minutes. If you can't stand it, we'll go to the pub.'

Peerless hadn't been entirely honest with Linnell even if, as was often the case in his profession, the deception was one of omission rather than a simple statement of untruth. Daniel knew that Whittington had asked if Peerless could bring him along to the early evening function. What Steven hadn't mentioned was that the editor was casting an eye over candidates for the job of obits deputy. Like most of his colleagues, he saw recruiting by advertisement as pointless. 'The Death Squad,' he told Peerless, 'like the Mafia, is not an equal opportunities employer.' If he liked the look of any of his potential assistants, Whittington might take them off to eat, or, as the obituaries editor liked to say, 'to dine'.

Daniel followed Peerless into the newspaper boardroom. It was on the nineteenth floor of the modern office block; a huge space, dominated by the ancient, twenty-foot oak table which had been recently transported from the paper's old offices, an art deco building in Fleet Street. In these surroundings, it looked incongruous and stupid. As Daniel looked round the room he realised, with a pang of rage, that he felt daunted. He could feel the material of the cheap suit that he'd bought for a friend's wedding eight years earlier, scratching his kneecaps.

His mind went back to the time he was taken, as a seven-year-old, to the Post Office Tower in Liverpool. His father had wanted to visit the top-floor restaurant as a treat, because it revolved and because the Queen had had her dinner there. They'd arrived at the tower in their beach clothes from New Brighton; Daniel was wearing his blue shorts with the anchor motif, and he was, he remembered, clutching his cheap shrimping-net. He could remember every detail, from the moment the lift doors opened, revealing a dining room filled with several dozen businessmen who appeared to be dressed for church, to the waiter's sadistically laboured explanation of the menu, which was in French, to their order – three plain omelettes and chips – and the whispered embarrassment when the bill arrived, and his father was ushered into a side room to call Barclays Bank in Old Trafford, to beg them to honour the cheque. And the room – he had complained, as his father led the way, without speaking, to Lime Street Station – hadn't even been revolving. The experience had stayed with him and had left him, Daniel now realised, easily cowed by the sight of rich men at altitude.

It was perhaps the memory of this episode which had so distracted him that night in The Owl, when Peerless couldn't settle his bill.

'Whittington,' smiled the obituaries editor, holding out his hand. He was six foot three, heavily-built and bald. Daniel didn't know what to say back. It seemed absurd to respond with his own surname, his Christian name would be too familiar, and both together sounded pompous. As a result, he murmured something deliberately inaudible and inclined his head slightly, like the Queen. A few minutes later, as he listened to the editor deliver a long and, he thought, rather drunken, celebration of hereditary peers – 'the last, and most brilliant, exponents of English eccentricity' – he recognised that Whittington, as he was universally called, had some quality that intrigued him. He looked about forty, though he could have been almost any age and had, in manner and bearing, the seedy benevolence of the British film actor Alastair Sim. It was hard to believe that this man had written obituaries that, for the English upper classes especially, had brought a new dimension to the fear of death.

Whittington was wearing an anonymous suit in Prince of Wales check, and yet Linnell found it hard to imagine him in anything but tweeds. The editor was the son of a Cornish vicar, Peerless had told him. Before becoming a journalist, Whittington had worked for several years as a teacher in some private rural establishment. Having come to the job late, he'd adopted what he saw as the essential accessories for a journalist: they included a trench coat, a leather document case and a trilby. When he went to functions where he was issued with a pass, Whittington would stick his into his hat-band, in the time-honoured (but extinct) habit of Fleet Street reporters.

But even in this outfit, the former teacher seemed incapable of anything more devious than the drilling of irregular verbs in some minor public school. In the five minutes or so he spent within earshot of Whittington, before the editor was pursued relentlessly round the function room by three other hopeful candidates who, Linnell noticed enviously, appeared entirely relaxed in these formidable surroundings, he hardly looked at Daniel and asked him nothing. His regal nod had blown it. He rejoined Peerless. They slouched by the bar – a linen-covered table near the door – and started to drink.

He lit a cigarette and began to tell Steven about the Post Office Tower, an experience he hadn't thought about for twenty years, and had never revealed to anyone, even Laura, before. 'And the room,' he said, 'wasn't even revolving.'

'Carry on like this,' said Peerless, 'and it will be.'

Daniel was staring at the small selection of spirits, wondering how he could best accelerate the painfully gradual process of intoxication, when somebody took him by the arm and started walking him down the room. It was the kind of over-familiar gesture that made him want to spit and which nobody who knew Daniel had ever done twice. But the grip was like a vice and the hand was the obituary editor's.

'You think,' said Whittington, as he steered Linnell towards a quiet corner of the room, 'that I'm an upper-class cunt.'

Daniel looked at him, genuinely shocked by a noun he had not pronounced himself since his schooldays. Whittington's amiable beam, he noticed, had not altered.

'And up to a point,' the older man went on, 'you may be right. But I think,' he added, 'that we could get on.'

Four hours later, he was sitting alone with Whittington in a run-down Chinese restaurant by a roundabout in Limehouse. As a venue for meeting the editor, who had a reputation as a gourmand, it would have been unlikely at any time. Now it was after midnight, and there was a black Labrador roaming the kitchen area, a sight which, for some reason, put Daniel instantly at ease.

'I am a heterosexual,' said Whittington, suddenly, with volume and determination.

His declaration coincided with the abrupt end of a piece of Chinese instrumental music and had, Linnell noticed, turned the heads of their fellow diners, a group of five muscular East End builders. Jesus, thought Daniel. He tried to think how best to limit the damage of this dangerous turn in the conversation. 'Good,' he said loudly.

The background talk, and the music – now, curiously, flamenco – resumed.

'Which makes it, to my mind, all the more appalling,' Whittington went on, 'that for three years at school, I was routinely buggered. Buggered,' he repeated – Linnell, still anxious about the builders, could feel himself flinching, as if from a gunshot, every time he heard the word – 'by boys, and buggered by men.' Daniel stared down at his sweet and sour prawns. 'Buggered,' Whittington repeated. 'I expect you can guess,' he added, 'what they called me.'

'Dick?' said Daniel.

'No, actually,' said Whittington. 'Turnagain. Turnagain Whittington.'

'Oh, fuck,' said Daniel.

'Fuck is right, Linnell,' said Whittington. 'Fuck is right. When can you start?'

'I'll come in Monday,' said Daniel.

CHAPTER 7

To sit on a moving train and stare out of the window, Daniel had read somewhere, is to have all the sins of your life come down on your shoulders. Something happened to him on trains and – though it would begin with a subdued contemplation of his past – things didn't usually stop there. Depending on his mood and the length of the journey, he would often move on to be gripped by a powerful desire to reorder his life.

It might not be too late, he would tell himself, gazing out at some farm outbuilding or power lines, to atone for his mistakes by gaining some new and fulfilling expertise. Given tremendous application, self-sacrifice and other qualities long extinguished from his real existence, he might, even now, become a surgeon. As he went on to ponder the practical obstacles – seven years of intense study on top of the school science background he didn't have, the crippling expenses and his age, almost thirty – he would start broadening the range of possible outlets for his talents. From then on it could be anything: Mandarin Chinese, veterinary science, or aikido. He would burn with the same brief passion for each as it came into his mind and yet when he got off at his destination, it was all forgotten.

One of the things he'd noticed when he boarded the light railway which ran from the City of London to the newspaper offices was that no such thoughts occurred to him. It wasn't because he was on his way to his first day in a new career: deputy obituaries editor, well-paid though the position might be, was hardly a title that would stifle his other employment fantasies. It wasn't the job – it was the train.

A flimsy contraption made of toughened plastic and fibreglass, its carriages felt more suited to a monorail in a theme park than to the ancient, solid railway tracks it ran on. Its cars had been painted – not even painted, he noted bitterly, but pre-cast – in the colours of the British flag. The last time he had seen an engine in such patriotic livery had been in a television documentary on the Sudan, broken down and shimmering in the heat of a remote, parched landscape. This railway broke down as well – just outside Limehouse, for about ten minutes – as he was making his way to Whittington's office. He gazed down at the track it had usurped, a converted section of what used to be a main overground line east out of the City. Those rusted steel rails were built for the kind of trains people called rolling stock, with robust, properly upholstered carriages – the kind that made you dream in them. Trains that were made to be pulled by the sort of locomotives which – whether from his memories of black and white film versions of *Anna Karenina*, or some more primitive source – had always been connected in his mind with sudden death.

The light railway felt like a monorail, too, because it ran above the neighbouring houses, level with the sixth floor of the few tower blocks that hadn't been flattened to make way for Executive Apartments. 'Mummy,' he heard a young girl say, as they went past one tenement, with sheets and underwear flapping on washing lines that obstructed its thin, demeaning balconies. 'Why are those people in prison?'

Daniel had been apprehensive of telling Laura about his new job.

'You know, my dad hated newspapers,' was the first thing she told him. 'When I was a girl, he'd pick up one of those massive articles in the *New York Times* magazine and he'd say, "Three words are enough to describe any experience."'

'Too fucking right,' said Daniel.

'Anyway, I think it's OK,' she said.

'Really?'

'Really. You're not that great a barman you know. Don't flatter yourself. I think it's OK,' she went on, 'so long as...'

'Yes?'

'I don't want you to turn into one of those people. One of those people with money.'

'Which people with money?'

'One of those assholes.'

*

It was ten o'clock by the time he walked into the reception area at the bottom of the tower. He collected a pass and took the lift to the nineteenth floor. Rosa, Whittington's personal assistant, met him as he came out of the doors.

Rosa Dalmau was Catalan, though she looked more Middle-Eastern. Her body shape and her general air of asexuality made him think of the lean, villainous high priests who appear in old Hollywood films about an Egyptian mummy's curse. Daniel followed her across the open-plan office. She was wearing flat shoes; even without heels she must have been six foot. Little was known about her in the office, though her older sister Angeles, a doctor who belonged to a medical group dedicated to helping casualties of famine, was occasionally interviewed by the foreign desk. Rosa herself never talked about her family.

The fact that this otherwise reserved young woman had forged a harmonious rapport with Whittington had led the office gossips (in a newspaper, Daniel soon learned, that meant almost everyone) to suggest that they were lovers. It was an accusation that had never had a hint of confirmation.

On the wall behind his desk, Daniel noticed, Whittington had fixed a large noticeboard. It was backed with green felt and protected by two oak-framed glass doors. Walking over to it, Linnell saw that, in the centre of the display, there were two pictures. One was a dog-eared sepia photograph of a handsome black agricultural worker in a hayfield, with his arms round his wife and three children. The print had a jagged hole in its top corner, and was stained with spots of something that looked like cocoa. The other was a portrait of Long John Silver, crudely painted in primary colours, on a page cut from a Victorian children's edition of *Treasure Island*. Below it was the quotation: 'Them as die will be the lucky ones.'

By ten fifteen Whittington still hadn't arrived and Rosa directed Daniel to the café on the floor above. As he crossed the open-plan office, the first thing that shocked him was the waste. He had imagined, from the leader columns exposing the indolent excesses of miners, bus drivers or hospital porters, that the paper would be run with ruthless efficiency. His first instinct was to go around retrieving the dozens of expensive padded envelopes he could see discarded in the large circular bins all around the floor. At the desks of the various departments – each consisted of ten or twelve computer terminals set out around one large oval table – journalists and secretaries were beginning to arrive. They sat down to scrutinise messages on their screen, or buried themselves in intense-sounding telephone conversations. Most of them, he would gradually discover, had – like the manual labourers they derided – simply perfected the invaluable art of looking busy.

He bought a black coffee from the machine and sat down at a table next to the window. Looking down, he realised he was more than two hundred feet in the air. The windows ran right down to the floor, so that his right foot and his right shoulder were touching the glass. Staring at his shoe, he could also see, a couple of inches to the right of it, the derelict sites by the river below. If he fixed his gaze there for a while and ignored the sounds coming from the café, there was no way of telling the building was there at all. To judge from this perspective, he might have been sitting there on that chair with only a few square feet of carpet supporting him. For all he knew, Daniel thought, torturing himself, his chair could be perched on the top of a two-hundred-foot aluminium pole, so that any movement to the right or left would cause him to overbalance and fall to his death. He started to feel nauseous, and walked back upstairs leaving the coffee untouched.

As he approached the desk for a second time, he saw Whittington, who grunted a welcome and waved towards a vacant chair opposite him. The editor then went back to reading through copies of the morning newspapers. There was a second pile on the desk, in which each paper had a printed label with his name on, stuck to its top right-hand corner. His selection also contained publications from Spain, Italy and France.

Daniel glanced across at his two new colleagues. They were, undeniably, a curious pair. A stranger catching sight of them in less formal surroundings – eating in a restaurant, or talking on a bench in the park – would have asked themselves what possible circumstances could have brought them together. Whittington was an odd mixture of fastidiousness and inelegance. His hands and feet were of a size that had some of the less serious-minded women in the advertising department tittering behind the water cooler. For some reason he always carried cash – large amounts of it – and paid for everything from a roll of twenty-pound notes he kept in his back pocket. And yet, at the same time, he had an indefinable style. He kept two pairs of reading glasses around his neck, supported by strings that, when you looked closely, were composed of tiny aluminium beads. There was something graceful and reassuring about the way he would spot a headline he wanted to investigate, then unfold the tortoiseshell arms of his spectacles. It made Daniel wish his own eyes had gone too.

The reading glasses were rarely lowered when Whittington was going through the tabloid newspapers. Editors pretended to scorn the popular press; privately, they envied its speed on stories, its fierce libel lawyers, and its massive readership. Every morning for two hours, Whittington scoured these papers for news of the living, looking for suitable subjects for his professional attention.

The fatal hint could take various forms. It could be an actual illness. It could be a report that a star had been partying too vigorously. It could simply be somebody who had – to use one of Whittington's favourite expressions – 'that feeling about them'. The editor circled an article about Dean Sutherland, an elderly crime writer who had suffered a fall at home during a dinner party. He pushed the page across the desk to Daniel. Linnell knew about Sutherland, who had written a spectacular best-seller in the fifties, but had managed nothing as good since.

The pattern of his career could be plotted as a steadily declining graph. Sutherland had been tormented for the last forty-five years by the maddening knowledge that every book – every line – he wrote would get a slightly poorer reception than the one before it. The article said that the writer, who had discharged himself from hospital, had just published his latest work, a collection of short stories called *Class X*. 'Worth a look in the morgue?' Whittington suggested.

The morgue was the bank of filing cabinets that stood behind them. Each was crammed with beige envelopes marked with the name of an obituary subject and stored in alphabetical order. All of these subjects were still alive. The contents of the envelopes ranged from virtually unusable 'cuttings jobs', hastily compiled from archives by a bored library assistant, to thoroughly researched, intimate life histories written by business associates, former partners, lovers and others too well-briefed for the subject's good. At the end of each obituary there were contact details for prominent friends, enemies and the article's author.

For most of the morgue's seven thousand occupants, the shock of discovering they were held here, and were in the frame for Whittington's daily round of lethal tombola, would have been as nothing compared to their unease at the contents of the files, had they been able to examine them. But the morgue – a painstaking and old-fashioned form of data storage – was maintained precisely to ensure secrecy: the subjects of computer files having, theoretically, the legal right to inspect personal information held on them.

Daniel found Sutherland's file, which contained a page of factual details about his life and a detailed, well-written assessment of his character on four yellowing sheets of paper. They had been manually typed. His waning literary reputation, it reported, had made him cantankerous and driven him into superstition, so that he always wrote in the same kind of notebook, with the same pen, in his lucky shed, in his favourite oxblood shoes. Daniel handed the file to Whittington.

'I spent days – weeks, probably, if you add it all up,' he said, 'in the front pew at St Fimbarrus' in Fowey, listening to my father describing the perils of superstition.' Whittington's voice took on the stern intonation of the preacher. 'In addition to the central symbolic truth of the crucifixion,' he declaimed, 'the very grotesqueness of the punishment and the utter helplessness of its victim may teach each us another truth, and it is this. One never knows what form one's courage will take.' The editor paused. He was clearly reciting the words precisely, from memory. 'The same,' he went on, still in a sonorous, ecclesiastical tone, 'may be said of cowardice. Cowardice comes in many guises. Perhaps the most poisonous of which is superstition, which is the abdication of responsibility due to oneself and to one's creator. Superstition is nothing less than a strain of spiritual fascism.

'Even as a boy,' Whittington added, 'I thought those words ill-judged, bearing in mind his congregation. They loved fascism. They couldn't get enough of it.'

He handed the papers back to his deputy. The Sutherland file looked usable, Whittington told Daniel, but it was five years out of date. 'Any contact number in there for the journalist?' asked the editor. Daniel shook his head. 'Ring directory enquiries,' the editor said. 'Get a number for him.'

It was a sad reflection on the state of the world, Linnell thought, that Whittington could know the obituary's author was bound to be a 'he', and he told him so. The older man didn't react. For all his deep love of the aristocracy, he had done more than any other editor, Daniel would discover later, to subvert the predominance of white, male, public-school-educated journalists on the paper.

'I just think,' Linnell repeated, 'it's a really depressing assumption.'

'I suppose he's like you and me,' said Whittington, without malice. 'He makes the best of the world as the world is.' Daniel was dialling directory enquiries. 'Who is she anyway?' Whittington asked.

'Brian Muirhead,' said Daniel.

'That was our second really sad assumption,' the editor told him. 'You can hang up now. He's not listed.' Daniel looked up, confused. 'He's what you might call ex-directory,' said Whittington. 'Even obituarists don't live for ever.'

Daniel got Sutherland's number from the writer's agent, and rang him at home. He realised, as the phone was picked up at the other end, that he hadn't properly worked out how to ask this irritable pensioner what he had been doing for the last decade. He began with a series of compliments about Sutherland's work. Across the table, he saw Whittington raise his left thumb. Rosa remained impassive, although Daniel thought he saw her eyebrows raise slightly.

'And the new book,' Daniel went on. 'The new book is magnificent.'

'The new book,' Sutherland repeated. 'Yes. Thank you.'

'An interesting title,' said Daniel.

'Yes,' said Sutherland. 'It is. Very interesting.' The writer paused, then spoke again. 'What is it?'

Daniel waited, thinking that Sutherland was joking, but he wasn't. 'It's...' he began, and then realised that he couldn't remember either. At that point there was a raucous whoop and a loud, sustained burst of laughter from the other side of the office.

'Are you entertaining?' asked Sutherland. 'Whom am I addressing?'

Daniel hung up.

The noise had come from the sports department, whose desk occupied a nearby, but far more prestigious, space, further away from the toilets and closer to the panoramic view from the windows. The usual atmosphere on their desk resembled an office party nearing its peak. The sports editor was Sean Linahan – a figure whose corpulent self-belief reminded Linnell of the French actor Gérard Depardieu. Linahan was a compulsive gambler from Newcastle, with an unfussy attitude to writing. His garrulous wit meant he was often on television, talking about football or giving horse-racing tips, and this second career had somehow exempted him from the norms of office behaviour. Quick-witted and fearless, Linahan enjoyed mocking his less voluble colleagues in other departments, yet always left obits, his nearest neighbours, alone.

Obituaries was dismissed by other departments as a sleepy retreat; some kind of fault line between this world and the next. And yet the potential it offered for unpleasantly abrupt developments was far greater than in some of the more fashionable sections such as foreign news, whose reporters, especially the younger ones, had a tendency to posturing and self-indulgence. 'They can say what they like,' Whittington told him. 'But even in a war zone, you have time.'

However stressful the day promised to be, Whittington always went for lunch at twelve thirty, and was rarely back much before three, sometimes much later, leaving Rosa to watch the news coming in on the PA wire and finish the pages alone. He took Daniel to a dingy, overpriced brasserie five minutes walk from the office, down by the water.

'What do you think of Linahan?' he asked as they sat down.

'I think he's terrifying,' said Daniel.

'You won't have any bother from him,' said Whittington. 'You know, there was a time when he whistled the funeral march every time he walked past us. What I did in the end was to get Rosa to ask him his date of birth. He's very superstitious, like most gamblers. The thought that we might have him in the morgue petrified him. He shut up after that.'

A couple of years earlier, Whittington added, Linahan had been forced by the editor-in-chief to commission a report on rugby union from a prize-winning lyric poet who had an amateur interest in the sport. The editor had read one of the writer's articles in a literary magazine, in the course of which, Whittington recalled, the poet had complained that British sports-writing was 'cliché ridden, obsessed with national stereotypes, and written by people whose minds are deader than their metaphors'.

'So anyway,' Whittington said, 'they made Linahan send this poet to cover an international in Cardiff. He faxed in his copy. I watched Linahan read it. He scrawled this one alteration, then tossed it to his deputy, who gave him this ferret-like nod. When they'd gone home, I looked at it. It said, "Insert anywhere – Leaden-footed Welsh defence." In his own way,' he added, 'he's magnificent.'

Whittington liked to socialise with the sports desk and occasionally attended their drunken late breakfasts, held on Mondays at Bar G, a converted canal boat moored close to the offices. On the face of it, Daniel observed, this was one of journalism's more unlikely liaisons.

The obituaries editor looked almost hurt. 'You are from Lancashire,' he said. 'So I imagine you know Blackpool.'

'Yes,' said Daniel.

'Which means you are familiar with one of our greatest national institutions, the Grand Hotel, just down the coast at Lytham St Anne's.'

Daniel nodded.

'Well, I am like the Grand,' said Whittington. 'Within striking distance of the vulgarity, but not part of it.'

They'd been in the restaurant for about half an hour when they were joined by the paper's crime correspondent, Simon Roylance. Looking at an undated picture of Roylance, with his thick dark hair and heavy-lidded, vivid blue eyes, you might have taken him to be a leading man from the old Hollywood school of combat and seduction. This first impression was never sustained, mainly because of Roylance's habit, when an idea occurred to him, of jerking his head backwards and staring madly at a far corner of the ceiling, as if he had just spotted a banknote taped to it. He was on excellent terms with Whittington, who knew him to be a dependable indicator of which individuals were most likely to make an unscheduled departure from their life of crime.

Although he was in his late thirties, Roylance still spoke with the sort of exclusive accent his younger colleagues had learned to camouflage. His unreformed vowel sounds had proved surprisingly helpful in dealing with hardened gangsters, who considered him no more capable of exerting credible influence in their own world than a visitor from Neptune. And yet there was something they respected in the way Roylance covered their chosen field, with great enthusiasm and no trace of moral condemnation. He had begun his career as a cricket correspondent and he approached crime in exactly the same spirit: observing it, in the pure sense. Though the job required him to spend long evenings in the company of the police, or their informants – in the course of which he was given privileged knowledge of the most barbarous and revolting kind – he never once expressed a personal view of the perpetrators. There was a distance about him; a deliberate failure to engage.

Whittington interrogated Roylance about a recent series of gangland beatings, with a view to anticipating the consequences, should the recriminations escalate. The names they mentioned meant nothing to Daniel, and yet, listening to these matter-of-fact exchanges, he found himself caught up in the narrative much as you might become engrossed in a detective story, to the point that he forgot how alien a world he was in. The realisation came back to him abruptly, with one of Roylance's typically theatrical movements. It happened as the waitress brought over a tiny plate containing a single sliced kiwi fruit surrounded by a few delicately shaved whorls of sorbet. 'Ah!' said Roylance, clapping his hands and rubbing them together with exaggerated glee, 'pudding!'

It was as if he was being served something massive and possibly illicit. It wasn't this that annoyed Daniel though; it was the way he said pudding. He caressed the word with an irritating jokiness that evoked every aspect of the English upper classes' nursery fixation – nanny, the dorm, and – well – pudding. There was an unusual emphasis on the first syllable of the word, and a curious pronunciation of the 'u' so that, had you been writing it down phonetically, it would have been more like pooding. Except that it was a sound that defied transcription, in the same way, he reflected, resentfully, that London journalists were never quite convincing when they quoted Yorkshire people as saying 'booger'. And it wasn't pudding anyway – it was a kiwi fruit. A kiwi fruit, he thought, however you cut it up, is not pudding. Pudding, Linnell said to himself, as the conversation around him continued and he gathered his wits for a silent voyage into fury, was pudding.

Daniel drifted off into a bitter reverie, in which he pondered the way that, when he had begun to mix with Roylance's class, he had been obliged to learn new names for familiar objects, rather as a migrant from some far-flung village in Burkina Faso might have to abandon tribal terms for the mainstream vocabulary of the capital. What Roylance was eating was transparently a sweet, or a dessert – both nouns he had learned not to use, roughly at about the same time that serviette had had to mutate imperceptibly into napkin, and lounge gave way to living room. In vocabulary, as in life, Linnell thought, rich wrapped poor like paper wraps stone. What was worse was that – despite his simmering rage over Roylance's pudding – he had to admit that he had come to hate the old words too. The bungled grandeur of serviette, for instance. There was an awful pathos about the way that the humble and the uninitiated had done their best to sound genteel in order to please their betters, only to be derided for it. Why, he asked himself, was there no posh term for launderette? Because, he reflected, they had some alternative – a washing machine, a spin-drier, a geezer, a chap.

It was like the sense of uncertainty that gripped every sensitive English dinner table when someone asked to go to the...to the what? Toilet? Too crude. Loo? A middle-class compromise. Lavatory? The week before, he had arranged to meet Laura in the coffee bar at an art gallery in the East End. He arrived early and – noticing the crowd of artists and wealthy collectors, and presuming himself to be in the heart of Napkinland – asked a young art student the way to the 'loo'. 'Toilet,' she said, by way of correction, in a voice which, for all its carefully honed glottal stops, proclaimed the comfortable suburban apprenticeship she was trying to shake off. He remembered a radio play he had once heard where a berserk aristocrat was asked if he knew the way to the lavatory. 'The lavatory?' came the reply. 'Call it the bog, man, and be damned.'

And how English, he thought – he had become an infant at the table, staring vacantly into space as Whittington and Roylance discussed grown-up affairs – that this coyness should relate to eating and defecation. When he was a child, it had been breakfast, dinner and tea if you're good. Breakfast was still breakfast. Dinner, though, was now lunch, and tea was now dinner but could also be supper, a word that native speakers of Napkin sometimes invested with a slight irony whose meaning he felt he had not yet grasped. The subtleties of supper might be worth mastering. But no booger in this town, he thought, with a futile surge of venom, is ever going to get me to call a kiwi fruit a pudding. He looked up and noticed that the crime correspondent was staring at him, waiting for an answer.

'Pardon?' said Daniel.

'I said are you settling in OK?' asked Roylance.

Linnell nodded. It was only later, as he was staring at his shoes in the lift, that he remembered, with a twinge of embarrassment, that, in this company, that last Pardon should have been a What.

CHAPTER 8

In the evening Whittington took him down to the Printer's Devil, a cavernous pub in the shadow of the paper's offices. Hastily constructed by a brewery when it learned of the newspaper industry's impending relocation to Docklands, the Devil was a prefabricated warehouse, shoddily camouflaged with antiqued plasterboard and imitation beams. By way of acknowledging its target clientele, one corner of the vast building was occupied by an old printing press. Unlike the rest of the furnishings, which had been modernised to look old, the machinery gleamed with a brilliance it could never have sustained in use.

Behind the press, on a stud wall with a plain brick façade, there were varnished wooden signs, with gothic lettering burned into them in the style of the mass-produced name-plates that hang outside suburban residences with names like 'Dunroamin' and 'Belle Vue'. In a doomed attempt to foster a literary atmosphere, the signs had been inscribed with well-known proverbs. They were out of sight of the bar, and most had been defaced by the regulars, who had taken to scoring the flimsy wood with steak knives, and snapping off their opening or concluding phrase. The tradition had begun accidentally on the pub's opening night, when a drunk had broken a sign in such a way that the fragment left hanging on the wall bore the comforting message: 'Hell Hath No Fury'. Gradually, its neighbours were also abbreviated, so that the surreal display now included mottos such as 'Marry in Haste', 'The Devil Finds Work', 'The Camel's Back' (this last had been supplemented by a crudely-gouged exclamation mark) and 'Dogs Lie'.

Other truncated slogans had been scrawled on the brickwork in felt marker. One recent addition, in an uneven hand, read 'I Didn't Get Where I Am Today'.

'The true definition of a Cockney,' Whittington said, as he reached for the bottle of Alsace, fully submerged in a stainless steel container next to their table, 'is that they were born within the sound of Bow Bells and that, however hard they try, they can never master the correct use of an ice bucket.'

The editor's disenchantment with the Printer's Devil was warmly reciprocated. A couple of weeks earlier the whole of Whittington's department had briefly been barred from the pub, in a gesture which, considering the obituarists' generous contributions to its profits, the Devil could hardly have undertaken lightly. The rupture in relations occurred immediately after the obituaries desk's Christmas karaoke party, at which Whittington, dressed as an undertaker, gave his now traditional yearly rendition of 'I Will Survive'. It was a performance which offended another, recently bereaved, party in the main bar.

But the real trouble, according to Whittington, had come later when Tony Ellis, the paper's tiny librarian, who had been fired that morning – and had gatecrashed the private function accidentally, by not leaving the pub, where he had been since noon – took the stage. 'He gave a memorable and distinctive reading of the song "Born to be Wild", Whittington said, 'which ended with him stamping on his own spectacles and kicking in the karaoke man's speakers. Then he ran away through the fire door.'

Even outside the Printer's Devil, the obituaries department was beginning to be noticed. For decades before Whittington arrived, obits had been the backwater of British journalism, a place editors retreated to in their twilight years, often as the result of some costly error of judgement.

Whittington had, almost incredibly, made obituaries fashionable without deserting the paper's favoured subject-matter of generals, dowagers and viscounts – although such figures might now share the page with an LA drag queen or a chanteuse. Within weeks, and without anybody noticing the transition, he had turned the pages into the most vibrant and compelling section of the newspaper. The managing editors, whose own interest was generally restricted to features that might attract perfumiers, record companies and other major advertisers, never read obits, but they did scrutinise reader surveys. These showed that – apart from the old, who had a morbid reflex that made them turn to the obituaries pages first in any case – all ages were now reading the section. Whittington's style was especially popular among the young who, with the greatest amount of disposable income, were the most sought-after readers.

He approached the job with a unique combination of talents: he was deeply fascinated by the aristocracy and spent his holidays visiting stately homes; at the same time his instincts were eccentric and renegade. 'To say he was on the road to madness,' he had written of one Conservative MP, 'would be to invite ridicule. He was not on the road to madness: he had arrived there, bought a house, and was renting out rooms.'

It was this sharp tone in his writing that had come close to getting him dismissed. He occasionally added a wholly fictitious detail to an obituary: a reclusive film star, for instance, might be described as having a secret passion for orienteering, making balsa-wood aircraft, or collecting clinical thermometers. On a couple of occasions, he had printed the obituary of somebody who was still alive. Such accidents, which had happened to most obituarists at some time, but seemed to plague Whittington, had become far more frequent following the introduction of new technology. In the old days, a press agency's correction of a premature death notice arrived in the form of a printed sheet of paper, which would be carried across by messenger from the news room to the obituaries desk. Now, such an amendment would be just one line among dozens of news releases on a tiny screen, and was easily overlooked.

'At such difficult moments I often think of the ninth Earl of Denbigh,' said Whittington, taking delivery of a lobster bisque. 'Heir to a vast, dilapidated estate which would have required the ruthless guile of a young Bonaparte to hold it together. Instead, he spent sixteen years working on his never completed monograph, *The Sheepdog in Dickens*.'

'I can't understand,' Daniel said, 'how you're so caught up with these people...who are so used to being on top.'

'That's the thing,' said Whittington. 'They aren't on top. Not any more. I mean take this poor devil the Duke of Radley...' He pulled a yellowing newspaper cutting out of a file he carried around with a view to preparing a collection of his obituaries. 'Bankruptcy court...his son a heroin addict...It ends with him blowing his brains out with a borrowed gun in Holland Park.' He started to read. 'Convicted on eight charges of cheque fraud and two of theft, Radley was working as a washer-up in a Reading hotel where he was dismissed for stealing teaspoons shortly before he perished by his own hand. He will be remembered for his bold and innovative interpretation of the Radley family motto: Death before Dishonour. Do you know,' he added, 'that, at the time of his death, he was living in a numbered house in Leatherhead?'

Forty years earlier, Whittington said, Dylan Thomas had died without any of his obituaries even mentioning the fact that he enjoyed a beer. 'It all used to be concealed in the code,' he said. 'Things like "He never married", which could mean anything from a lifetime spent cruising the public lavatories of the free world to...well..."He never married."'

Whittington's achievement had been to take the code, understand it, and turn it against itself. One of his numerous run-ins with the paper's senior editors had come after he wrote an obituary of a school headmaster in West Yorkshire. 'He never married,' it read, 'because hypocrisy, as he was fond of saying, was not a word in his Lexicon, and because he was a proselytising homosexual who liked to spend his evenings sashaying around Hebden Bridge in a skirt.'

'And so it is,' Whittington said, 'that we tend to call the deceased a "tireless raconteur" rather than a windbag and prefer to say, of an Oxbridge don, that "his door was always open, at any hour of the day or night" than to call him...'

'An alcoholic?' Daniel ventured.

'An alcoholic,' Whittington replied, 'with implications of gross sexual impropriety with students. He tended,' Whittington went on, sounding like a quiz-master, 'to become over-attached to certain ideas and theories...'

'Fascist,' Daniel replied.

'You're getting the hang of this,' said his editor. 'These phrases have been immortalised,' he added, 'and exist in a little-known volume which you can find in the British Library.'

Daniel read through the small handful of cuttings in the file. '"In his later years,"' he read, '"the Earl of Carnforth increasingly dispensed with aspects of social etiquette he regarded as useless. Among guests at Carnforth Castle, he enjoyed a reputation as an uncompromisingly direct ladies' man." Rapist?' Daniel asked.

'Not quite,' said Whittington. 'When he used to have overnight visitors, especially young women, the Earl would knock at their bedroom door in the early hours and ask if they would like "to meet Sir Percy". As the Book of Hebrews says, he added, "Sin doth so easily beset us."'

CHAPTER 9

Every time he walked out of the building, in those first few days, Daniel found himself overtaken by a sense of leaving a world of unreality. He was reminded, heading out into the dark night air, of the occasional memory he had of his father leading him out of the pictures as a child. Leaving the paper, like the cinema, in daylight, meant that the disorienting effect of resurfacing from another, alternative universe, was intensified.

Back at The Owl, his former colleagues rarely asked about his new job – perhaps because, through Steven Peerless, they already knew more about obituaries than they needed to, perhaps because Daniel never brought up the subject. But then, at Laura's birthday party, a couple of weeks after he'd started at the paper, when he was sat round a table with Peerless and all the regular staff, the conversation turned to his work.

'Don't you ever worry,' asked Rachel, who was sat opposite him, 'about spooking the people you're filing away in those drawers?'

Daniel hesitated. It was the same thought he'd once voiced to Peerless, but hadn't been troubled by since. Keen to steer the subject towards the broader area of superstition, he told her about Dean Sutherland and his writing rituals. 'God knows why he carries on with them,' he said, 'when it's so obvious they don't work.'

'It's because he's in one of those areas of life,' Laura interrupted.

'What?' Rachel asked.

'One of those areas where hard work alone isn't enough...to get you out of trouble. Like gambling,' she added. 'Or bullfighting.'

'Or typing,' said Peerless. He'd just accepted a job, he announced, as deputy editor on the foreign desk.

'What's that like?' Laura asked him.

'It's OK,' he said. 'Less typing. More money. Everything has its drawbacks. Long hours. Wearing a tie.'

'Ed Franks,' Daniel interrupted.

Peerless sighed and shook his head.

Franks was the paper's chief war correspondent. The editor's best man at his recent second wedding, he had abandoned the foreign reporter's traditional role as dispassionate observer and made his name by parading his own emotions at scenes of catastrophe. He began his career as a television reporter and once famously wept on camera by the gate of a refugee camp. This appalled his producers, who fired him, but endeared him to the public, many of whom found his capacity for hand-wringing empathy even more attractive in print.

'The other day,' Peerless said, 'he told me that he's got twelve different ways of asking distraught widows the question "How do you feel?" Of course the answer is always pretty much the same: "Bloody great Ed. Yourself?"'

Franks' reports were littered with references to his humble beginnings in a terraced house on a challenging West London estate called White City, where he claimed still to live, though it was common knowledge on the paper that the reporter had left the area years earlier, in favour of a large detached house in the more affluent suburb of Acton.

'He filed this tearful report from a refugee camp in Peru last week,' said Peerless. 'And when he rang up to make sure it had the headline he wanted, he kept complaining about his hotel being full of "Manuels" and "the tinted tendency". So like I say, every job has its drawbacks.' At least, he added, his new position meant he didn't have to go on the Obituarists' Outing in a fortnight's time.

'Outing?' Daniel repeated.

'Christ. Haven't they told you about it?'

'No.'

'It happens every year,' Peerless began, 'and they...look, just make sure you take two – no, three – days off afterwards. Put in for it now, before the rest of them get round to it.'

'We could go away somewhere,' said Laura. 'Somewhere we don't know. Where,' she asked Daniel, 'do you think would be good?'

'Lourdes,' said Peerless.

At around two in the morning, Brendan closed the bar. Laura climbed the iron ladder up to the trapdoor, very unsteadily, carrying a glass of Spanish brandy. Her legs disappeared as she pulled herself through the ceiling hatch into the flat. Daniel had a black coffee at the bar with Doyle. 'You know something?' the barman said. 'I've never once seen her do that sober.'

Daniel followed her up.

'I know,' she said, as he struggled out on to the living room floor. 'We'll go to your mate's place.'

'Pardon?'

'Fowey.'

'OK,' he said, pleased. It was rare, he thought, that they went anywhere together. Resentfully, he remembered the frantic search of the apartment that had delayed her last departure, and which had remained unexplained. 'It's in Cornwall,' he said. 'Make sure you've got your visa with you.'

She disappeared and returned holding her passport, which she handed to him. He opened it and, still loose inside it, found the New York taxi receipt inscribed 'In Yor Bed'.

'I guess you saw that,' she said, 'didn't you?'

He nodded. 'What is it?'

'It came from this fortune teller on the boardwalk outside the freak show at Coney Island.'

'Is Coney Island still there?'

'Just. And anyway this gypsy told me all this stuff.'

'Like what?'

'Like she told me I had a brother called Paul. Stuff like that. And then,' she added, 'I asked her when I would die. And as soon as I did that, she wouldn't say anything. So then I asked – well, where then? Where will it happen? And she still wouldn't answer.'

She swallowed the rest of the Spanish brandy.

'So I was getting up to leave and – I mean you can imagine, that unnerved me totally.

'I can imagine it so well,' said Daniel, 'that I wouldn't have asked her.'

'I said, "I can't go; I can't go now." Then I remember I said, "Don't speak it – write it." She just stared back at me. And that's what she wrote down.'

'So now,' he said, 'you carry that cab receipt around with you when you go, and er...' He'd never found a reassuring way of saying parachute. Nobody had. She said nothing. 'Could you jump without it?' he asked her.

'Yes,' she replied, almost too quickly. 'No. Well...I mean...I'd rather not.'

If Daniel's daily journey between the café and the newspaper didn't shock him more in those early days, it was because obituaries, by contrast with the formality of other sections of the paper, had a distinctive character that had not been imposed from above. Whittington's popularity with readers was the cause of bitter resentment among some of his fellow editors, not least because it allowed him a degree of licence in his public dealings with the senior figures who tyrannised them. Once, at the daily editorial conference, the paper's editor had launched into a protracted lament at the state of the nation.

'Everywhere one goes these days,' he complained, 'there are pools of vomit, men gibbering to themselves, old people thoughtlessly cast aside and young women selling their bodies without the slightest hint of remorse in their eyes.'

'And that,' Whittington interrupted, 'is before you've left the building.'

And yet, curiously enough, even the tower block was not entirely insulated from the desperate privations of the real world. When a chauffeured car or taxi drew up outside the newspaper's main entrance, its passenger had to climb three steps, then cross a marble floor the size of three tennis courts – still open to the elements at its sides, but kept immaculately polished – before they walked in through the automatic glass doors. The first point of contact for a guest arriving by road was not the imposing line of uniformed security men who waited inside the main lobby to check identity cards and issue day passes, but Carlton, a homeless man in his fifties. Carlton spent the whole day waiting outside, on the marble steps. When a car arrived, he would rush forward to open the rear passenger door. He slept in a hostel at Limehouse, but arrived every day at 6.00 a.m. in a threadbare suit which he pressed roughly every night using an iron and a tea towel, though every attempt at restoration only served to underline its second-hand provenance. When the weather was cold, he would show up well-wrapped in an ancient greatcoat, gloves and overshoes.

Carlton, who had brought his family over from Montego Bay in the seventies, had worked as a mechanic in Tower Hill until he left home one morning as usual, and never came back. He had taken to the streets without explanation or warning – not, as is usually the case, the streets of another city, or even a more central part of town but, to the anguish of his wife and children, the public areas of his own neighbourhood.

Before he found his niche as the paper's self-appointed usher, Carlton had sold magazines for the homeless. He'd moved his pitch to the front of the building when it was still a construction site. On the first day the management arrived, they walked past Carlton, whose chronic insignificance in their eyes endowed him with a kind of invisibility. By the time they did notice him, he'd already bought the suit, and he'd been opening car doors for weeks – nobody was quite sure on whose authority – so he stayed. It was a private source of satisfaction to some senior figures on the paper that the first face strangers saw on arriving was West Indian. It created the illusion of an enlightened approach to equal opportunity employment, an area in which the company's real record was undistinguished.

Most visitors and some employees would give Carlton a pound for carrying their luggage, or just for opening their car door. Executive editors, especially those with working-class origins who were returning from a long lunch in a sentimental frame of mind, might give him far more. He carried an ornate-looking walking stick. His shoes were cheap, but always immaculate. It was a legacy from his first months on the street. At that time, Carlton's clothes had been so ragged that he'd noticed how the eyes of wealthy passers-by would instinctively drop to his footwear. Shoes were the truest indicator, in their eyes, of the depth and duration of a man's distress; more so than his shivering, emaciated frame, the tear-stains etched into the dirt on his cheeks, or (given the number of motionless bodies sleeping in city-centre shop doorways) death itself.

He almost never spoke. When he accepted money from visitors, Carlton gave a slight nod, all the time staring at a point just above their left shoulder, as if he had seen a ghost behind them but was too polite to say so.

There were rumours that Carlton had amassed a tremendous fortune through frugal living and hoarding tips but, since any attempt at conversation was unreciprocated, these stories could never be confirmed. On his way home, he would occasionally stop off in the Printer's Devil, where he would stand silently at the bar and drink a single light rum with sweet ginger wine before returning to the hostel at about nine in the evening. Every other detail of his life was a mystery. On one occasion two drunken restaurant critics brought him a glass of 1988 Château Pétrus from a nearby restaurant. They had been engaged in a furious argument about whether food and wine of great quality requires a practised palate to appreciate it. One of them had bet five hundred pounds – far less than the price of the bottle – that Carlton's senses would be transported by the taste of the exclusive vintage, which he carried up to the West Indian on a silver tray.

Carlton took the glass, drained it, then spat the red wine on to the marble floor. He did this not from impoliteness, but out of real unease, as if he suspected he might have been served something containing blood, or cleaning fluid. He put the glass back on the tray, knelt down, and mopped up the spilt wine using his own white cotton handkerchief. To the great surprise of the onlooking gourmets, it was linen and perfectly laundered. He stood up again. Then, to their further astonishment, he spoke. 'Forgive me,' he said. 'I never liked them brackish drinks.'

CHAPTER 10

If the obituaries department was not the most glamorous on the paper, there was one respect in which its staff were envied. Obituarists, along with the thirty or so regular contributors to the pages, were allowed to go on Whittington's annual outing – a day trip, usually to a military cemetery, war memorial, or some other location that might put them in the right mood for writing more obituaries. The source of funding for the generous catering provisions on these outings was a mystery that other departments on the paper had often pondered, but never explained.

How, Linnell asked, not really expecting a reply, did Whittington manage it?

'It's quite straightforward,' said the editor. 'I simply commission every regular writer to produce their own obituary – or, if they've travelled with us before, which they nearly all have, to update their existing file – and pay them the maximum fee, which they then contribute, in cash, straight into what I believe is known as "the kitty."'

The scheme was undetectable unless anybody betrayed it, a course of action which – since the idea provided funds of around three hundred pounds per head even after deductions for travelling expenses – was in nobody's interest.

There was a cash bonus, Whittington added, for the obituarist who guessed the number of travellers still conscious at the end of the day, which was formally marked by the closing of the bar in the Grosvenor House Hotel in Mayfair.

'Out of last year's field of thirty-one starters,' he explained, 'only eleven made it to last orders. Of course a couple always drop out before the off and we occasionally have one or two fallers.'

Casualties in recent years had included Suzanne Stiles, a young rock critic, who had fallen off the platform on to the track at Victoria – 'the return visit to the London terminal,' said Whittington, 'is our equivalent of the second time over Bechers Brook' – and had only been rescued by the quick thinking of her older companions. Cyril Edwards, an expert in Japanese fine art, had come to grief at the same station three years earlier. 'He sprinted on to an escalator,' the editor recalled, 'shouting: "I bet you bastards didn't think I could spot the down one." It was the down one,' Whittington continued, 'but it wasn't in operation. He fell very badly; he got up and struggled on, but he's still got the groove marks in his forehead.'

This year they were going to Dunkirk, ostensibly for the purpose of visiting nearby war cemeteries. The group had been told to assemble at eight o'clock that Saturday morning in the main buffet at Victoria. Daniel had spoken to the contributors on the phone, but met few of them face to face, and he eyed their group carefully as he entered the self-service café, wondering who was who. He spotted Charles Crosthwaite, their royal obituarist, who was often on television, and two young women writers of about his own age: Stiles, and another less reckless-looking writer on installation art. Harder to place, however, were the twenty or so military historians, most well past retirement age, who were retained because of their contacts with the Second – and even, in a couple of cases, the First – World War.

Members of this group, though their recollection of distant events could be extraordinary, were sometimes less accomplished when it came to remembering the more recent past. Sitting in groups of three or four in the modernised buffet, with its plastic seats and fluorescent lights, they looked ludicrously out of place. If you took a Polaroid of this scene, Daniel thought, these figures would come out in black and white.

He spotted Whittington, who was sitting with one of the writers Daniel had once met briefly in the office, Edward Devereux, an army historian who was in his eighties. 'Go easy,' Whittington had said when they were first introduced, 'his memory plays up.' Seeing Linnell walking towards him across the buffet, Devereux tried to stand, but couldn't, because his plastic chair was riveted to the floor; he struggled out from the table and shook Daniel's hand. 'How hard it is,' Whittington was saying, as Daniel joined them, 'to picture those 340,000 men struggling away from the beaches of Dunkirk.'

'This is the way,' said Devereux, taking his seat again, 'with all mass suffering. I often think about the incomprehensible scale of the slaughter at Stalingrad. The greater the outrage, the harder it is to comprehend. Take the ninety Jewish infants, all orphans, shot in cold blood in Belaya Tserkov on 20 August 1941, on orders from the chaplains of the 295th Infantry Division of the German Army. I can see from your expressions how, more than fifty years on, this information affects you. And now,' he continued, 'I invite you to imagine the agonies of the 1.1 million Red Army soldiers killed at Stalingrad, or even the 33,771 Jews slaughtered by Sonderkommando 4a in the ravine of Babi Yar. Not easy,' he said, 'is it? It's the 33,770 that cause the trouble.'

God Almighty, Daniel thought, I hope my memory plays up like that when I'm eighty.

Crosthwaite, the royal correspondent, joined them.

'Charles!' said Devereux. 'This is Alexander Whittington, whom you know' – Whittington nodded – 'and this is Daniel Linnell. Daniel and I,' he added, 'fought in Algiers together in the war.'

Daniel opened his mouth to speak but, as he did so, noticed Whittington give a barely perceptible shake of the head.

At Dover, the ferry (to propose the tunnel, Whittington said, was to court mutiny) was delayed for two hours because of heavy seas. The party was ushered into the ship's VIP lounge, which had its own private bar. The bill, Whittington would later reveal, had reached four figures before the vessel had cleared British coastal waters. The ferry was hardly out of dock when he was summoned upstairs to the control room.

'Is there a mistake?' Whittington asked.

The purser shook his head, and hurried the editor up an internal staircase to the bridge. It was packed with veteran obituarists, two of whom were former marines who had been invited up by the captain. Word got around, and the visiting party had swelled to fifteen by the time it reached the control room, where several of them had taken to prodding eagerly at the radar controls and video display units, while the senior members of crew, greatly outnumbered, tried to concentrate on navigating, occasionally swatting at them like flies.

'Three at a time,' barked the ship's captain. 'Tell them three at a time. Like they have to in the sweetshop.'

Behind the captain, Whittington could see Jane Denselow, his architecture correspondent. Denselow, a formidable widow in her early seventies, had somehow inveigled herself into this privileged party, and was yanking hard on a large yellow lever. 'I wonder,' she roared, 'what this one does?'

'Keep an eye on Patrick Fitzgerald,' Whittington told Daniel, pointing out a tall, gaunt figure among the group they herded back down the steps.

'Keep an eye on him? What do you mean keep an eye on him?'

'If I may quote from his account of his own life,' said Whittington. 'Sober and upright for most of his years, the latter stages of his naval career were tarnished by his fondness for setting off flares in situations of no immediate nautical emergency.'

When they disembarked in France, they were met by a coach that took them to Chez Bertrand, a restaurant which, Whittington explained, had three things to recommend it. 'One, the chef, who has earned the Bertrand its international reputation; two, the fact that they have never encountered us, en masse, before; and three, there isn't a revolving door.'

Daniel had taken this list of criteria as a joke until he saw the obituarists, some on sticks and one with a walker, making their way towards the entrance.

'Do you think,' he heard one of the more mature contingent saying, 'they'll have thingy?'

'Thingy?' replied his colleague.

'You know – er, thing...drink it cold...drink it at room temperature...mix it with soda. It's on the tip of my tongue.' A pause.

'Wine?' asked his friend.

'Wine, yes,' came the reply. 'That's it.'

They sat down for lunch at one long table; Daniel found himself between Charles Crosthwaite and Jane Denselow. It was a shame, he told Crosthwaite, that they didn't have more time to wander around the town on their own.

'I love the French,' Crosthwaite declared suddenly.

'Why?' Daniel asked.

'Because...I've never had to think why before. Because they have a better time than we do. It's the same in Spain actually, and Australia, and Wales.'

'And Kenya,' added Denselow.

Could a foreigner, Daniel wondered, ever begin to comprehend the wealth of personal history conveyed – to a British listener – in those three, commanding syllables? Twenty years in the colonial service had left her with a brusque, assertive manner capable of instilling great fear, especially in men.

'And Norway,' a voice croaked, with bizarre urgency, to her left.

'And Norway,' said Crosthwaite. 'Thank you Devereux.'

'Perhaps,' Daniel suggested, 'you just don't like England.'

Crosthwaite, who had written a whole book about the Queen Mother's shoes, gave him a mortified look. 'As I was saying,' he continued, 'I love the French. But on these outings, we do try to minimise contact with the locals.'

'Remember Anthony Adams,' snorted Denselow.

'Adams went off on his own,' said Crosthwaite, 'when we went to Paris in 1992, because he wanted to see Napoleon's tomb. He'd been swotting for months with this blasted phrase book. He was almost eighty by then – he's no longer with us I'm afraid – so he never got past the first chapter: Accident and Emergency. He kept mixing it all up; it was beyond him at his age. All the way over there he was banging on about *Où sont les toilettes?* and *Avez-vous l'heure?*

'That means "What time is it?"' Denselow interrupted.

'And,' Crosthwaite went on, '*Au voleur*!'

'That,' his colleague added, 'means "Stop Thief".'

'So we got to the Gare du Nord,' said Denselow, 'and we were walking across the concourse, and we got in the cars. Anthony wandered off, and we lost him for a while. He'd just got right under that enormous clock they used to have suspended from the roof, when this young girl bumped into him and spilt coffee on his coat. While he was sorting himself out, these young chaps…

'We believe now,' interrupted Crosthwaite, in a conspiratorial tone, 'that these men may have been her accomplices …'

'These young chaps,' she continued, 'snatched Anthony's briefcase, and legged it.' She motioned a waiter to open a new bottle of Sauvignon and had swallowed her first glass, Daniel noticed, before the echo of the cork had fully subsided. 'They snatched his briefcase,' she continued, 'and he stood there in the middle of the concourse shouting what he thought meant "Stop Thief" – "*Avez-vous l'heure! Avez-vous l'heure!*" He was screaming it over and over again – "*Avez-vous l'heure! Avez-vous l'heure!*" – and waving his arms around like a madman, and all these French people were coming up to him and pointing up at the clock. He looked up, but since he was directly underneath it, he could only see the square metal bottom of the casing; he thought they were gesturing "up yours", and he started giving them that vulgar French crooked arm thing.'

'The station police ran across to him,' she said, 'and he was still at it: "*Avez vous l'heure, avez-vous l'heure*"... One of the officers grabbed him, and the other turned up the sleeve of his uniform and started pointing hard at his watch. Of course Anthony didn't know what the hell he was up to; he thought the chap had gone insane. Then he rolled up his own sleeve to show them that he had a watch as well.'

'Except that he hadn't,' said Crosthwaite. 'The French blighters had snatched that too.'

By four o'clock they were still on the hors d'oeuvres. The boat back to England left at six. Across the table Daniel could see Patrick Fitzgerald demolishing large tumblers of red wine. He was drinking at the same brisk, steady rhythm he would maintain for the next ten hours, but even a couple of minutes spent at his shoulder was enough to inspire incredulous sidelong glances from a group of French farmers who were stood behind the elderly writer, queuing for a table. Somewhere, deeply embedded behind their appalled gaze, Daniel thought he could detect a sort of grudging admiration, an implicit acknowledgement that Fitzgerald's reckless presence had endowed the afternoon with a certain unforgettable, tragic magnificence. But the only expression you could make out on the man's own features – the only recognition of the terrible self-inflicted onslaught on his body – was a contemptuous half-smile. For an hour or so, Linnell restricted himself to bottled water; Fitzgerald gave him an unwelcome glimpse of one of his possible futures. At the same time, the old obituarist revived memories of some scene Daniel had watched flickering on celluloid years earlier. It was a black and white image that he remembered as a formative moment from his childhood, and yet couldn't place.

'I'm not sure,' Jane Denselow said, 'that we're going to make it to the cemetery.'

They didn't make it to the cemetery and, in the end, they almost missed the return sailing. Daniel wouldn't have been sorry if they had, especially when he noticed several of the party in conversation with a group of Chelsea supporters who had been over to make bulk purchases of export lager. One – who was being addressed in what looked like an aggressive manner by Edward Aston, the RAF historian – had the word 'nutter' cut out like type, and dyed royal blue, against his tightly-cropped hair. Aston had tottered very slowly towards the group, supporting himself on his walking stick, holding a French beer glass that was inscribed with the word 'Meteor'. He had made the most of the outing, aware that, like several of his colleagues, he would be returning, when they reached land, to an old people's home.

Worried, Daniel edged closer to the pair. 'Shite,' Aston was saying. 'Absolute fucking shite. Never, never say that. Never say the good old days. These are the good times. Now, when you're alive, and you're warm, and you're breathing.'

By quarter to eleven the survivors were in the bar at the Grosvenor House. 'Eight left – not bad,' said Whittington towards midnight. Loud whoops and cackles greeted every new bottle of Veuve Clicquot champagne, which was now being openly ordered from the bar staff as 'thingy'. Whittington pulled out a wad of fifty-pound notes from his inside pocket. 'With that delay,' he said, 'I thought we were going to end up over-budget. But there's still nine hundred quid left.'

At midnight, the barman rang a single stroke on a brass bell: a sign that the hotel had stopped serving to non-residents. Daniel saw Patrick Fitzgerald standing with the small of his back pressed against the bar for support. As the bell's unforgiving resonance was dying away, Linnelll remembered the film image Fitzgerald's bravado had put him in mind of. It wasn't, as he'd expected it to be, a melodrama involving Ray Milland, or Bogart, or Spencer Tracy. The memory came from another, more dramatic, arena. It was the sight of Muhammad Ali on the ropes in the first six rounds of his fight in Kinshasa in 1974, disdainfully offering no resistance to the furious onslaught from George Foreman, observing the punishment that was being inflicted on his body like a disinterested bystander, almost glorying in it. And he emerged from the evening – though God knows what price he would pay in the long term for this perverse triumph – radiating, from his battered and swollen features, a kind of victory.

The bell precipitated a fracas at the bar, with Fitzgerald and Jane Denselow at its epicentre. The hotel manager, discreetly positioned in a nearby alcove, was observing the party with an anxious look. Fitzgerald, having been refused further service, placed a hand on the counter to steady himself as he tried to distil his resistance into one irrefutable argument.

'I...' he said. 'I...am...*a very important man*.'

This declaration – though true, or at least arguably so – drawing nothing but mirth from the staff, Denselow intervened. 'I feel,' she said to the head barman, 'that we have disappointed you in some way.'

'On the contrary, madam,' he replied, 'you have come right up to my expectations.'

Whittington walked over. 'What they mean,' he said to Fitzgerald, 'is that they're closed.'

'Bollocks,' Denselow replied.

Without speaking, the editor walked back to Daniel's table and sat down. 'To continue our racing analogy,' he said, 'I think Fitzgerald is in a condition that might best be described as "thrown rider".' He pulled out his roll of notes and went up to the hotel manager. Whittington pressed all the money into his hand, and appeared to whisper something to him. The manager walked over to the bar, and the angry clamour subsided. He handed the cash to the head barman. 'An order for Mr Fitzgerald and his friends,' he said, his dour expression unaltered. 'Please give them a case of thingy,' he added, 'and a room.'

Unnoticed against the wild applause, Whittington walked to the door. Linnell shared his cab to Victoria.

'It's a real shame,' Daniel slurred, 'that we didn't make it to the cemetery. It must have been a terrible break with tradition.'

Whittington smiled. 'To be quite honest with you,' he said, 'we've never made it to the cemetery.'

CHAPTER 11

When he opened his eyes on the Sunday morning, the first thing he saw was Laura's black holdall, packed and ready, near the door. For a moment he thought she was leaving him. He could barely remember how he got home; the trip to Fowey could have been a bargain he'd struck in another incarnation. He got up and began to pack his own things. He could hear Laura downstairs in The Owl, talking to Rachel. As he lay in bed, the hangover hadn't been quite so bad as he'd feared on first waking. Once he was up, even the simplest task took twice as long as normal. Objects such as zips and keys seemed to conspire against him. The process of packing reminded him of a documentary film he'd once seen of a man trying to make an omelette on a Russian space station.

Daniel tossed his cheap camera and a few clothes into his own bag. He stared at himself in the full-length mirror, haunted by the fear that, in his distracted state, he might have forgotten to put on some indispensable item, such as trousers. It was then that he imagined, mistakenly, that the nights in Cornwall might be far colder than London. He reached for the cardboard box full of clothes that he'd stored on top of the wardrobe when he first arrived. Inside, he found a few worn-out socks and faded pullovers; he pulled all the garments roughly out on to the floor. He glanced back into the box, to be sure it was empty, and it was then that he saw it. A thick winter scarf, composed of rainbow-coloured bands, it had become snagged against one of the large brass staples at the bottom of the container. He sat down, overcome.

Daniel freed the scarf with great care, handling it almost as if it had been alive, or at least capable of pain. It was hand-knitted, from the type of coarse wool that, for anyone who could afford to choose, had long gone out of use. He pressed his face into it, hard. He could feel its fibres scratch against his lips and his fingers. It had no smell any more, other than the damp air of storage, and yet it evoked her presence more powerfully than any perfume, photograph, or voice recording, and it froze him into remorse.

He'd met Jude at university in Liverpool and he could still remember the moment she'd given the scarf to him, one afternoon just before Christmas as she was boarding a coach to take her to her parents in Aberdeen. Jude was the one thing that had made college bearable. Daniel met her when he moved in to share a small terraced house she shared with her sister.

Jude had been adopted when she was three, in the days before a host family's suitability was rigorously scrutinised. She knew nothing about her birth parents except that her mother was Malaysian and her father was English. Her benefactors, as they saw themselves, had rescued her on an uncharacteristically generous impulse, one that swiftly waned, and which they came to look back on much as a drunk might recall the night he had presented his life's savings to a beggar, on a whim.

Their resentment of Jude descended on them just as their fit of charity had: rapidly, and fully formed. The difference was that their resentment never went away. They resented her. They resented the expense of keeping her. They resented her easy smile and her delicacy of manner. They resented her racial origin – tolerance of which had formed the centrepiece, in their minds, of their original act of kindness. They took away her name, Luu Thi Nam, and made her answer to Judith. That she was adopted was obvious to anyone: both her parents had sand-coloured hair and were heavily-built. She had once shown Daniel a photograph of her walking along a road, dawdling behind her father. Even the family dog, a boxer, was ahead of her. It had struck him, looking at their expressions, that, had the image been in sepia and not Kodachrome, it might have come from an exhibition on the slave trade.

There were family holidays that she never went on. If she did go, she had the smallest room, like she did at home. In their company, she'd always had the smallest of everything: the smallest share of meat, of battered cod, of life. 'In any case, of course,' she told Daniel, 'I *was* the smallest.'

When she'd fallen in love with him, she told him, it was like coming home to a feeling of space.

'With you,' she once told him, 'I'm in this massive room, with a big open fire.'

'Lit?' he'd asked her.

'Lit,' she replied.

Bright, though never encouraged at school, she'd left home at seventeen and, when he met her, she was studying law. She'd been there a year when her flatmate moved out and she agreed to take in her elder sister. She took pity on Stephanie – a natural blonde who had noticed at an early age the arresting potential of barmaid chic – because her sister begged her and because she too was on the run from her father who, Stephanie implied, had attempted to abuse her, though this was a claim she never repeated once she'd got her own rent book. Things changed when Stephanie moved in and found a secretarial job at a local bank. She went back to treating Jude in the old way. When she was ten and Jude was five, Stephanie had put her sister on the front of a shopping cart in the supermarket and pushed her as hard as she could into a large pyramid display of tinned peas. The older girl heard, but never saw, the collision. By that time she was already running home, where she entered the house with the cry 'Judith's been bad again'.

Still holding the scarf, Daniel remained motionless, with the distracted look of a man listening to a tragedy on a pair of invisible earphones. He thought he heard someone call his name, and he was going to get up and leave, but something made him relive the drama, as he always did, right through to its awful last act.

After the Christmas holidays he'd arrived in Liverpool on an evening train. He stopped off at the pub and reached Jude's towards eleven. Stephanie let him in. Her sister's coach had been delayed, she explained, and she'd be back around half midnight. With great ceremony, she went to the fridge and pulled out a magnum of Spanish champagne, which she said was one of her Christmas presents, and opened it. At 3.00 a.m., when Jude had still not arrived, Daniel disappeared to her room and fell asleep or, to be more accurate, unconscious, still fully dressed. Precisely at what time he'd been woken up by the touch of an unfamiliar naked body, he couldn't be sure. What he did remember was coming to again, for a second time, at around eleven, to find Jude, in her coat, hat and gloves, staring round the door at him as he lay there naked on the bed, next to the dishevelled figure of the sister who, albeit in a supporting role, had made her life a misery for twelve years. She didn't speak; she just turned on her heel and left. She didn't slam the front door; she was in shock, and she left it open. He leapt up to follow her, but he landed heavily on the cheap wine glass he'd left by the bed, which shattered and cut deep into his right heel. The blood had come pulsing out immediately, on to the thin grey carpet. It occurred to him later that if he'd been sober, he'd have followed her out into the street even though he was trailing blood, screaming, or naked. But he was still drunk, and therefore modest, and by the time he'd pulled on his jeans, first backwards, in his haste, soaking the front of the left knee with blood, and wrapped a handkerchief around his right foot, then put a shoe on his left, and hobbled to the door, she was gone.

He struggled back in and put his shirt on, and stared at Stephanie. 'You knew,' he said, 'she was on the overnight bus.'

She raised one eyebrow, a trick she had practised. He picked up his jacket and the knitted scarf, and limped out.

It was the last time he'd set eyes on Jude. He went round there the next day and every day for the next few days, and there was no answer. The phone was dead. The conclusion of the affair, which he remembered as one of the most appalling moments of his life, was that he got a card a week later from one of her friends telling him that Jude had left university and gone to work in London, serving on a counter in a department store. He'd poisoned Liverpool for her.

He picked out a sweater at random and stuffed the other things back into the box, with the scarf at the bottom. He bound the lid down as best he could with a small, narrow roll of sellotape, and lifted it back on to the wardrobe. He couldn't bring himself to throw the scarf away, but he had to get it out of sight. He could hear – unmistakably this time – Laura shouting his name from below, and a minicab driver sounding his horn.

'Coming,' he called, and left, locking the door behind him.

CHAPTER 12

Daniel and Laura spent a week at the Fowey Hotel, an old-fashioned establishment with deep pink interior walls and white-painted, wooden window frames. There was an ancient lift with brass fittings; even for the elderly, taking it to the second floor was slower than walking. Screwed to one of its oak walls was its name-plate: 'The Express'.

They had a room with a four-poster bed, which they first laughed at, then came round to. There were breathtaking views across the river estuary. An uncovered red and white motor launch, with twelve seats, ploughed back and forth all day, making the five-minute crossing to the small village of Polruan on the opposite bank.

They got up late every day, and wandered down though the terraced gardens and out to the village. In Fowey itself there was almost nothing, except for a handful of pubs, some new dogs for Laura to photograph, a second-hand bookshop, and a small Chinese restaurant. They both liked the genteel desperation of these small British resorts. Daniel took dozens of pictures of Laura sitting on the harbour wall, or reading in The Lifebuoy, the local café.

They boarded the small launch themselves one morning and had coffee in Polruan's riverside pub, then came back to the hotel for lunch. The restaurant had the same magnificent view over the water. There were a couple of London wine merchants in the bar with their wives. The men sounded a little drunk, and they were talking, slightly too audibly, about their yachts, and the café cellars of Richmond. They started to gush about a painting that hung over the urinals in the hotel's downstairs gents': a masted schooner called the SS *Great Britain*. One of their sons, a precocious-sounding eleven-year-old, was glued to the window, standing a little too close to Laura's shoulder, writing down the names of passing ships in a notebook. She stared out of the lounge windows, past the boy, back down at the small vessel.

'Did you notice,' she asked, 'what that boatman on the ferry had tattooed on the fingers of his left hand?'

'It said Hate,' Daniel told her.

'What about the right?'

'I didn't see that.'

'I didn't either,' she said. 'He had a glove on it.'

Alan, the hotel's elderly porter, came up to reception and, not realising that he could be overheard, spoke to the receptionist. 'By Christ,' he said, in his strong Cornish accent, 'I had some drink in me last night.' The hotel manager hissed him to silence.

'Boy Chroyst,' said Jeremy, the loudest of the two dealers, and the boy's father, a few minutes later, when the porter had gone, 'Oyve aaad zum drink in me today.'

Daniel's eyes met Laura's. He knew her well enough by now to sense the onset of the mood that had routed the drunken executives in The Owl. She glared at the vintners. From time to time one of them would glance over at her, troubled by an intermittent unease, much as a man might look at a suspect package in his Underground compartment.

'It's incredible,' she said, turning back to the river, where a tug was moored mid-stream, and a couple of fishing boats were heading inland from the mouth of the estuary. 'I've seen that same scene all over the world: little fishing boats, and those guys shifting lumber…you could be anywhere.'

What was really amazing, Daniel said, was to see any traditional industry left in a country whose infrastructure had been so beaten down in the last twenty years.

'Piss,' one of the wine merchants said suddenly. His statement was prompted not by Daniel's industrial elegy, but the house white wine, and it was delivered within earshot of – if not addressed directly to – the young waitress. She hovered uncertainly for a moment, then left the room, making the first few steps backwards.

A few minutes later, a container ship came into view. It was a flat-decked, rusting beige monster, its prow inscribed, preposterously, with the word 'Superiority'. The young boy called the name out. 'Yes,' said Jeremy, with a mischievous increase in volume and a glance to their table. 'For some curious reason, I imagine that ship to be American.'

Laura turned to the young boy with the notebook, who was still at her shoulder. 'May I ask you something?' she said. 'Where is the port of origin?'

'What?' The boy looked startled.

'The port of origin. On a ship. Where do they mark the port of origin?'

'On the stern,' said the boy.

She turned back to face the water. As the back of the boat went past, she got up, walked over to the boy's father and, gently but firmly, twisted his shoulders so that his eyes were facing the narrow stretch of river. 'I know you're drunk,' she said. 'Because you said so. But can you still read?'

He said nothing. His wife, who looked livid, got up. She went to the window. '"Superiority",' she read. '"London."'

'How did you know?' the wine merchant asked Laura, in a conciliatory tone.

'How did I know? Let me ask you a question,' she said. 'Is there any other country in the entire world you can think of that would possibly have the downright fucking brazen insanity to give its name the prefix of Great? Well?'

'Well...' he said.

His wife steered the child next door, into the drawing room. From behind the reception desk across the corridor, three pairs of eyes looked on in silence.

'Let me help you then,' Laura went on. 'Not even the most mad, arrogant, syphilis-crazed dictator of what you would call a Third World Banana Republic would do that. And,' she went on, 'if a country really was winning – if it called itself that and it really was – in the terms you respect – Great, it would be ludicrous. It would be fucking pathetic. Great America. How does that sound to you, Jeremy? "Superiority",' she said again. '"London."'

There was an uncomfortable silence, broken by the faint, but distinct, sound of somebody clapping in the next room. The wine merchant glanced through the door, thinking that the applause had come from the old delivery man, who could pay for it later with his job, but the only hands moving belonged to his wife. Laura sat down. The party left in silence. When Daniel and Laura went up to their room that night, on the bed they found a bottle of house white wine and a red rose, delivered anonymously.

It was the sort of incident that would occur in London every few months. But there was something about Fowey – it might have been its air of affluent tranquillity, or the conservative views expressed by many of the locals – that encouraged her capacity to foment unease in public. Only the next day there was a lively exchange in The Lifebuoy with a table of elderly residents who had gathered to advocate the reintroduction of the death penalty – immediately, and for a new, almost limitless, range of offences.

'I'm not saying you're wrong,' he said, as they were leaving the café. 'You're right. But can't you just ease up a bit? We're on holiday.'

When they came back to the hotel, Alan, the porter, was standing by reception. Laura began talking to him about the Polruan ferry.

'You know the guy who runs that boat,' she said.

'Keith,' he replied.

'You know he has Hate tattooed on his left hand.'

'Yes,' said Alan.

'Have you seen,' she asked, 'what he has on his right hand?'

'Yes,' said Alan.

'Does it say Love?' she asked him.

'No,' he said.

'It says nothing,' Daniel ventured, offering him a way out, 'doesn't it?'

'No sir,' he said. 'It says something.' A silence. 'It says Hate as well.'

In the week they spent there, he found his initial exhilaration at being with Laura was tempered by a new emotion: anxiety about whether or not she would stay with him. In the past, as Robin Robinson had reminded him, she hadn't stayed. With anyone. Perhaps the beginning of a great affair was like an early one-nil lead in a football match against superior opposition: a brief moment of euphoria that soon gave way to unease about a catastrophic reverse. Late one night, when they were sitting on the balcony outside the hotel restaurant, they saw a couple climbing the steep steps that led up through the gardens below. The man was in his fifties, the woman ten years or so younger. Both were expensively dressed. They were holding hands. Halfway up, believing herself unobserved, the woman stopped.

'Hold me darling,' she said. 'Hold' rhymed with 'foaled'. She kissed him.

'How long do you think they've been together?' Laura asked Daniel.

'I don't know,' he said. 'A week?'

'Why,' she said, 'because of that kiss?'

'No,' he said. 'Because they've got that look – as if they believe that absolutely anything is possible.'

'It is,' she said.

Daniel and Laura walked inside, back to the bar. 'We don't do that, do we?' Laura asked.

'What?'

'*Hoaled* me, daahling.'

'No,' he said. 'Do you want to?'

She clung to his arm like a proud new fiancée. 'It's a bit tacky,' she said, 'don't you think?'

The barmaid, who was heavily pregnant, was getting the drinks when the only other customer, a retired military man, began lecturing the expectant mother on the etiquette of breastfeeding.

'I'm not against it,' he said. 'But when you get these young women doing it here, and in the breakfast room – I think it's disgusting.'

'Steady,' Daniel whispered to Laura.

The barmaid gave the man a meaningless nod of assent. She handed Laura her drinks.

'You want one?' Laura asked her.

'I'll have a Britvic,' the girl said.

'Yeah,' said Laura. 'You have a Britvic. And you know what?' As a concession to Daniel, she leaned across the counter and whispered, 'You feed your kid where you damn well please.'

The girl smiled. 'Did you?' she asked Laura, not lowering her own voice.

'Did I what?'

'Did you breastfeed?'

'I...'

It was the first time he'd seen Laura lost for words – she looked shaken, almost. 'I...no,' she went on. She smiled. 'I've never had call to.' She picked up the drinks.

'You mean you've never had kids,' said the barmaid.

'I mean I've never had kids,' Laura said, sounding slightly irritated.

'Would you?'

'I'm sorry?'

'If you did have a baby,' the young woman asked, 'would you breastfeed?'

'Yeah...well...' She looked at the elderly local. 'I would if I was here. And I definitely would if I was in the breakfast room.'

On their last night in Fowey he lay in bed with one side of the curtains open to the sea, while Laura sat in an armchair in the far corner of the room, watching a British film from the forties. Daniel picked up one of the books she'd bought from the second-hand shop. It was a collection of poems called *Lament of the Border Guard*, and Laura had left it open and face down, to keep her place.

He began reading the poem, called 'What Made Him Do It?' about a man who had flung himself off a building.

'"Maybe the spring was too wet,"' he read, '"that summer too hot, and at the end of it no one came to pick his tree. He died a windfall."' He put the book back, and fell asleep.

She woke him up as she got into bed. 'It's a shame you missed that picture,' she said.

'Why?'

'Now just let me be sure I get the plot right,' she replied. 'He's an Oxford organ scholar who gets his draft papers at the start of the Second World War. He has scenic walks with a virgin from Dover, then – this is the final scene, before he leaves for the Front – the verger lets him play the Bach toccata at Canterbury Cathedral. That's British movies all over. Always the lowest fucking common denominator. You know what? You could hold me now.'

He woke at three. She was asleep on his shoulder. He eased her back on to a pillow, and moved a strand of hair that had fallen over her eyes, tangled with sweat. He reached out for a bottle of water on his side of the bed, congratulating himself on not having woken her, but when he turned back, her eyes were open.

'Laura?'

'Yes,' she said.

'Will you marry me?'

He'd thought about proposing in a general sort of way, but his question, when it came, was entirely impulsive.

Just as he asked it, a passing tanker sounded its foghorn on the river below. He thought he could detect a very faint smell of diesel enter the room.

'No,' she said.

He picked up the bottle and drank from it, then handed it to her. 'Was it the tanker?' he said.

'It wasn't the tanker,' she told him. 'I like the tanker.'

'What then?'

'It's what it does to people.'

'Who to?'

'Everyone,' she said. 'You've seen them, right? I've seen them too. I've seen Kate. I've seen my mom.'

'You know,' he said, 'when you…when we…sleep together.' He felt himself squirm at the phrase. He stared out across the bay, wondering if he could have found a better one. He glanced over to see if she was laughing at him. She wasn't.

'Go on,' she said.

'You…mentally, you…'

She was sitting with her knees pulled up against her body, with the sheet trapped under her chin. 'I drift off,' she said. 'I drift out.'

'You drift out.'

'Yes,' she said. 'I like it.'

'But,' he said, 'how will I know when I've got you?'

She laughed. 'You're doing OK, kid.'

When he got back to work the following week, he went for lunch at the Printer's Devil with Whittington and Rosa. Ed Franks, the chief foreign reporter, was at a nearby table. He'd come in that morning on a flight from Texas, and he was sitting with the paper's deputy editor. The foreign writer looked travel-weary, and drunk.

'Hello Franks,' Whittington shouted. 'How's life in Acton?'

The reporter responded with a bitter glare.

'I said,' Whittington continued, 'how's life in…'

'White City,' Franks shouted. '*White City*. Not…' By this point the bar, filled with his colleagues, had fallen silent. 'Not fucking Acton,' he said.

Returning to the office, Daniel noticed how swiftly the first excitement of his contact with the newspaper world had dissipated. The moment at social gatherings, for instance, when he was asked what he did for a living – never something he had looked forward to – now inspired positive dread in him.

Linnell, who had never written a line which was not connected with a death notice, found himself seized by a mounting envy of the star interviewers on the newspaper, journalists who, according to office rumour, were paid unimaginable salaries and were flown first class all over the world, to lavish hotels where they ran up bills that might have strained the pockets of the wealthy stars they were sent to interview. But it wasn't this that he coveted most. He was still, genuinely, without great financial ambition.

What he envied was the people: the chance of meeting writers, film producers and artists – though the truth was that most of the cinema figures who fascinated Daniel, like Alfred Hitchcock and Preston Sturges, were already safely installed in Whittington's World, and, of those that weren't, few would have interested the commissioning editors on the paper's colour supplement. Daniel knew that, but still couldn't help wondering what it would be like to meet them face to face; to be associated, just for a moment, with the world of great performers who were rich, glamorous, talented and – that most desirable of all qualities – still alive.

He found himself giving sideways glances at the leading profile writers when they walked towards him across the open-plan office, which, since the obituaries desk was next to the toilets, even they occasionally did. By contrast with the mood of the articles these interviewers produced – which was distinguished by a degree of spite and brutality that would have shamed even his own department – he was surprised to notice that the writers, who were mostly women, were retiring, even timid, in person, and rarely made eye contact. They were like he was, people who were only brave when their subject had – in his case in the fullest sense of the word – departed. And that, he said to himself, was not very brave at all.

The best known of the paper's interviewers, Sheila Stevens, was an exception. She was in her mid-fifties and had a lucrative parallel career as a television chat show host. Stevens hardly ever came into the office but, when she did, enjoyed taking the opportunity to exercise her bibulous wit. Even Paul Harkes, the paper's formidable news editor, told Daniel that, when he was out with a large party that included Stevens, he had more than once found himself suffering in silence rather than risk ridicule by leaving the table to go to the gents'. Fortunately, Harkes told him, his agonies were a thing of the past, since the kind of places you were most likely to encounter Stevens these days were the Polo Lounge in the Beverly Hills Hotel and La Coupole in Paris.

All of which meant that, on the Tuesday night when Daniel was sitting with Laura upstairs at the Araucaria, a long-established and unpretentious Greek restaurant in Crouch End, he thought at first that he had imagined the familiar voice that was broadcasting at some volume from the only other occupied table. He'd got back to The Owl at about eight, and changed into a pair of jeans and a collarless white shirt, whose round neck protruded slightly over the top of his black crew-necked pullover, creating an effect that looked vaguely familiar. In the sepulchral light of the Araucaria, he said to himself, style hardly mattered.

They'd been in the restaurant for less than a minute when he heard Stevens. She was with a young journalist from the Glasgow paper where she had begun her career – a geographical coincidence that had allowed the man this rare audience although, as she boomed every few minutes, their meeting must be 'purely social', and everything she said off the record. Daniel struggled to take in the situation. Stevens never gave interviews, though she was often asked, and her protective attitude to disclosures about her own life resembled that of a hardened pickpocket towards her own wallet. The young man, who might easily have been her grandson, was giving flirtatiously admiring looks to Stevens, a woman whose many qualities were not widely felt to include voluptuousness. 'When I first met her,' Harkes had told him, 'I thought she was a guy.'

The pair looked as if they had begun their conversation over lunch, and both were in the state that Whittington would have called 'convivial.' 'Yeah,' she said, 'and he's as convivial as a newt.'

It wasn't a matter of eavesdropping; you couldn't help but hear. As the evening wore on, Stevens' tone lurched from the boastful to the confiding. 'Sure,' she told her junior escort, 'I've made stuff up. I mean – it really doesn't matter that much when you know what you're doing. When I was starting out, I once fabricated a whole interview with a young rape victim.' Daniel, who had counselled several women who had experienced the real crime, found his mood switching from curiosity to fury. He looked at the young Scotsman, who had greeted the remark with a vacant beam worthy of Stan Laurel. 'And you know,' she added, 'I interviewed real rape victims later, and it was uncanny how right I was.'

Daniel stood up and turned towards the journalists. Another table behind him was now occupied, he noticed, and the two young couples sitting there turned to look at him. A moment later, even Stevens, noticing him on his feet, and staring, fell silent. Daniel felt Laura's hand catch his, something she never did. 'Hey,' she said, under her breath, 'don't play out of your league.' She was right of course, but sitting down now would look even more foolish than going on.

He walked down towards Stevens' table. 'Would you mind,' he said, 'keeping your sexist fucking voice down.' Daniel fell silent, a little surprised at himself – he hadn't intended there to be adjectives. Stevens tilted her head back slightly and looked at him, without recognition. 'Dimitri,' she called. The owner who, Daniel later discovered, had been serving her here for almost thirty years, appeared at the top of the stairs, looking anxious, accompanied by a waiter. 'Oh, shit,' he heard Laura mutter.

Stevens paused for a second – just long enough, Laura told him afterwards, to ensure that every eye in the place was on him. 'Dimitri,' she repeated, pointing at Linnell's round white collar, protruding from his black crew-necked sweater. 'It appears that we have a clergyman in the restaurant. How did he get in without a tie?' The waiter and the owner burst out laughing; one of the women at the table behind him tried, and failed, to suppress a snigger, and the sight of her set off the rest of her table as well. Daniel stood in the middle of the room, trying to think of a devastating response, and not finding one. Before he turned to slink back to his table, he felt himself suffering that least journalistic of symptoms, a blush.

As he and Laura were walking down the narrow staircase, he heard the restaurant's downstairs room, which was fuller, and its kitchen, which was in customers' view, ringing to the latest bon mot from its most famous patron: '...clergyman in the house...get in without a tie'.

Laura was unusually quiet as they walked the few hundred yards back to her flat. 'Daniel,' she said, as they were standing on the fire escape and she was searching for her keys, 'Never do that to me again.'

He was about to make some smart reply along the lines of...was it really credible that God – who he sometimes imagined in front of a huge map of the kind that feature in the control rooms at army HQ in British wartime films – was it really possible that God would ever again manage to push the magnetic rectangles representing Laura, Dimitri, himself and

Sheila Stevens on to the same square at the same time again? He stopped himself. This sort of thing didn't happen to Laura – not on the receiving end.

A couple of days later he went in to the paper early, and looked up Stevens' obituary on file. The file name was marked with a star; a sign that this was not the version to be published. In the case of colleagues he strongly disliked, Whittington kept one, mildly barbed, obituary on the main computer. The real one would be stored on the disks he kept in an old hollowed-out copy of a Victorian book called *Lives of the Saints*. 'As a profile writer she was admired by all classes,' he read, in the concealed version, 'though Stevens, in her manners and instincts, as in her gender, was the polar reverse of a gentleman.'

Daniel loaded the file in to edit. 'Admired by all classes,' he wrote, 'though a stranger setting eyes on Sheila Stevens for the first time would have found her, in her manners, instincts and in every other way apart, perhaps, from gender, the polar reverse of a gentleman.' He replaced the file and went out for a coffee.

It was rare, in the ordinary course of things, that obituary writers would have any contact with their subjects. Occasionally, however, if there was real urgency and no other way of researching an individual, a writer would be sent out by Whittington to interview them, usually in the guise of an admiring young freelance eager to boost the subject's fading career by writing a feature in their honour – an article that, to their knowledge at least, would never appear. It was ethically dubious – shocking, even, Daniel thought at first – but preferable to the alternative introduction of 'Hello – I am your obituarist.'

One such case was Hugo Savage, a Soho artist who – Whittington had learned from Professor Cooper, a heart consultant at St Mary's Paddington and one of a number of medical professionals he cultivated – had recently refused to have the triple heart bypass operation that had been recommended for him. 'And he's coming up for seventy,' the editor told Daniel. 'It's amazing you know; sometimes they chug along quite happily, then one of these anniversaries comes along, and the candles and the sparkling wine just finish them off.'

Savage – thin and rakish in the newspaper photographs Daniel had seen of him, taken thirty years earlier – had been a promising abstract painter in the fifties, but moved out to Italy around 1960, and disappeared from public view. His trouble, as he once said of himself, was that he lost all interest in art if there was any prospect of 'enjoying a woman or a decent Bordeaux', and in recent years he had rarely unfolded his easel. Food, however, was his real vice. Savage, according to the cardiologist, was still a regular at his local café Reno's, where they offered an English breakfast known as The Seven Deadly Sins. 'The Professor can't remember what Savage said they all are,' Whittington said, 'except that one of them is black pudding.'

Savage, persistently lobbied by Rosa, who told him she was the arts editor, eventually agreed to meet Daniel at a restaurant in Fulham on a Saturday night. In the afternoon, Daniel stopped off at the dry cleaner's near the office to pick up his suit, then went to the chemist to collect the photographs from Fowey. He was about to go back up to Crouch End to change, when it occurred to him that he would need a small tape recorder – real interviewers, he knew, always had one. By the time he'd chosen one, bought the tapes, left the shop, returned to buy the right batteries, and spent half an hour in a café finding out how the machine worked, he realised he had no time to get back to The Owl and get ready, and he decided to go straight to meet Savage as he was.

When he arrived at the venue – an expensive Thai restaurant on the Fulham Road – Savage was already there, sitting at the table Daniel had booked in the painter's name. He had already embarked on his first course, a massive soup dish called Floating Market. He glanced at the artist, who these days looked as if he had been blown up with a bicycle pump full of Beaujolais, and for a moment thought he might have got the wrong table.

'I thought I'd open my innings with this,' Savage said to Daniel, indicating a bottle of potent Czech lager. Next to it was a plate that looked like a marine autopsy.

Daniel was feeling more and more guilty about the deception he was practising, especially as Whittington had told him he felt sure that Savage was 'at that stage in the great journey of life when – how should I put it – his tray table has been returned to its upright position'.

Hugo Savage was, unusually for a man with Bohemian instincts, not a great drinker, but he did appreciate good vintages, and he'd ordered a bottle of Pauillac, which Linnell, looking at the wine list, thought at first must have its decimal point in the wrong place.

Daniel pushed his collection of shopping bags under the table, bumping against Savage's feet. He felt less and less at ease. He was in a pair of dark green jeans, Dr Martens boots, and an old pullover. Savage's clothes were such that, were he to have been seated in a doorway instead of this prestigious restaurant, he might have collected a few pounds in loose change by the time Daniel arrived. But the relaxed style of his own outfit had not stopped him staring briefly in surprise at Linnell's.

Daniel noticed his look, but made no comment. He knew nothing about how a profile writer might set about an interview, but sensed that this was not the time to produce his baffling tape machine. He tried to chat generally to Savage but, what with the food on the table, and the painter's famous reticence when speaking for publication, all he got back was a succession of monosyllables, grunts, and further questions. Occasionally Savage would ignore him altogether.

Had he known from the start, Daniel asked him, that his career would be in the fine arts?

'Well, I suppose I'll have to say something,' Savage growled, 'yes or no, so...I'll say yes.'

What details Linnell had about his subject came from a Mayfair art dealer friend of Whittington's who had stayed in occasional touch with the painter. Savage, the dealer had said, was currently reported to be living alone, in a small flat in Chiswick. He had been married six times, and most of these liaisons had been with models far younger than he was, in Tuscany, where he had lived since he left England. He'd returned to live in London only two years ago because he had run out of money and perhaps also because his health was failing. This long absence from Britain made things especially difficult, as it meant that none of Whittington's usual network of informants had any information that wasn't vague or out of date.

Daniel's main task was to discover the whereabouts of his subject's third wife. Caroline Savage, Whittington told him, was rumoured to have stayed in contact with the artist, but apparently regarded her three years of marriage to him as one of her less astute decisions, and was believed to be frank and loquacious on the subject of her former husband's shortcomings. Unfortunately Caroline seemed to have disappeared, and Whittington was afraid she might be dead.

Attacking the Pauillac, which had the taste of burnt rubber that Daniel associated with expensive red wine, and didn't particularly like, he asked if Savage had any news of his immediate family.

'Nope,' said the painter, defiantly.

He tried bringing up the name of Caroline, who Savage was believed to have thrown out of a first-floor window in his Tuscan villa.

'All I can remember,' the artist said, with a look which indicated that further mention of his third wife would not be prudent, 'is her toes. Her toes,' he went on, 'were like monkey-nuts.'

At one point, after an uncomfortably protracted lull in the conversation, he asked the artist – who had served nine months in a Florence prison for possession of cocaine, and was widely believed to have killed a man – whether he had been on holiday recently. Savage stared back, hard, at Daniel. The artist looked like a man peering at a Magic Eye picture he believed might be a page of meaningless blobs assembled as a practical joke.

'No,' replied Savage, still giving him the same wary look. Silence. 'You?' said the artist, with a sarcasm Daniel didn't catch.

'I went to Cornwall,' he replied. 'I've just got back. I've got some photographs.' He bent under the table and pulled open his holdall, breaking the bag's clasp in his haste. He found the yellow paper wallet of pictures, took it out and handed it to Savage. 'That's my girlfriend,' he said, his head back down, fumbling with the bag's fastener, 'at Fowey harbour.'

Perhaps some small disclosure of his own private life, he thought, might encourage the artist to reciprocate. He sat upright again. Savage was staring at him once more, but this time he had a new, and menacing, look.

'Are you taking the piss?' he said.

'Cornwall,' said Daniel, 'for a week.'

Savage snorted.

'That,' he replied, 'is a mongrel.'

He tossed the pictures – thirty-six shots of the dogs of Fowey – back to Daniel. The painter stared away from the table, as if appealing to some invisible referee.

'Bugger,' said Daniel.

'You know,' said Savage, filling both their glasses – the first gesture of personal recognition Linnell had experienced from him – 'you're not very good at this, are you, Adrian?'

'No,' said Daniel.

Savage began to talk about the early sixties. He had moved to Chianti, he said, after Anna, his first wife had come into some money and they had bought a small vineyard. He was still brusque, but seemed to have relaxed slightly since the dog incident, probably because he had decided his interviewer was so hopeless as to pose no real danger. Daniel, deciding that Savage was at least as mad as the people he had counselled in Maple Street, began talking to him as if he were a Resolve customer, showing concern and using silence to prompt him. They began, in a small, fitful sort of a way, to communicate.

Savage drove out to Florence, he said, with a friend who was a retired poet, in a decommissioned army lorry they'd bought at an auction in Didcot. 'It had eight axles and it weighed six tons,' he said. He'd loaded it up with all his poet's tackle: writing desks and musical instruments and incense and prophylactics and God knows what. 'All I've ever needed,' he added, 'was a bottle of Scotch, an easel and my shotgun. Anyway, it was January, and we started climbing up into the Alps as night was falling. There was snow everywhere and black ice on the road, and the only thing we had with us were two litre bottles of Drambuie. I thought we were going to die there. All these nouveau-riche bastards in saloon cars stuck behind us as we crawled up through the snow at eight miles an hour, in first.'

Daniel nodded, wondering how he could twist the conversation away from the gear ratios of Heavy Goods Vehicles and back to his guest's first experience of marriage. 'Anna,' he said clumsily, 'your first wife, Anna...'

'The contempt one feels,' Savage roared, 'for those puny vehicles one could print into the tarmac with one flick of the wheel.'

By a quarter to midnight Daniel was no wiser about Savage's personal life. On the table in front of him was a bill for almost five hundred pounds, and they were the last two people in the restaurant. He asked if Savage would like another coffee. The artist nodded but, when the drinks arrived, pushed his away untouched.

'What – in your opinion,' he said, '...what would you say was my current state of health?'

'I...you look fine to me,' said Daniel.

'Fine,' Savage snorted. 'Try again.'

The game, Daniel thought, was almost over in any case. 'You're fucked, aren't you?' he said.

'Correct,' said Savage. 'Correct.'

He took Daniel's hand and pressed it to his wrist. 'What do you feel?' he said.

'It's fast,' Linnell replied.

'How fast?'

'It's very fast.'

'And?'

'And?'

'Is it regular?'

Daniel, tormented more than ever by his deceit, shook his head. He felt like bursting into tears, and he was on the verge of confessing everything. Precisely the state, he thought afterwards, that he had been supposed to induce in his interviewee.

'Some men's hearts are, in a certain sense, like a grenade,' said Savage. 'Mine is one of them. My heart is like a grenade,' he added. 'And the pin is out.'

Daniel paid with his credit card, and they stood together on the pavement outside while they waited for a taxi for the artist; Linnell told him he would try to get the last tube. Savage looked at him.

'You know,' he suddenly said, 'I'd hate to be a journalist.'

'Why?' asked Daniel.

'Because I think it would mean meeting people I genuinely admired and they'd treat me like a wanker,' said Savage. 'Thank you for dinner.'

He climbed into the cab, but then motioned the driver to wait, and wound down the window. He leaned forward and, half-crouching in the back seat, held out his hand. Daniel shook it, but gathered from Savage's peculiar grip when he did so that the painter was not expecting a handshake; either that, or he belonged to some particularly demonstrative Masonic order. Then he understood: Savage was pushing a piece of paper into his hand. God, he thought, was he that pitiful? Was it supposed to be his taxi fare?

'Thank you,' he said, and stuffed it into the front pocket of his jeans, without looking. Once Savage's cab was safely out of sight, Daniel ran to Fulham Broadway station where he just caught the last tube. Laura would have taken a taxi all the way, he thought, as he sat down in the empty carriage and the doors closed. He'd have to get a cab anyway, once he got to Victoria. He got to his feet, put his hand in his pocket and pulled out Savage's crumpled note. It wasn't money, he discovered, but even more bizarrely, an old prescription. Daniel turned it over and noticed two lines which had been hastily scrawled over the existing print, in biro. The first read 'Caroline Savage, née Terry 00.33.1.45.58.52.16.' The second, which had been underlined twice, took longer to decipher, but once he had made it out there was no mistake. 'Adrian,' it said, 'I know what you are.'

CHAPTER 13

It started as a joke. They were sitting in the upstairs bar of the Cheshire Cheese in Fleet Street, a pub Daniel disliked for its suffocating oak decor, and for its clientele – a mixture of tourists, City bankers, and veteran journalists who had remained pathetically attached to this, their old meeting place before the trade, and the world, moved on.

Whittington turned up at the pub around eight, straight from lunch. It was only the second time since they'd met that Daniel had seen him drunk to the point of being out of control. Shortly after he arrived, the editor produced a copy of *Who's Who 1976* from his canvas holdall. This didn't surprise Linnell unduly: old editions of the reference book, of little interest to most readers, are popular with obituarists eager to unearth inconsistencies in the lives of the famous.

'Interests,' said Whittington, turning to the entry for one recently imprisoned life peer. 'Contract bridge and hare coursing. No reference here,' he added, 'to masturbating in the lifts at Covent Garden tube station at noon.'

The book stayed on the table and, as the evening wore on, Whittington, who had been reinforcing pint glasses of the tepid ale with double shots of malt whisky, periodically opened it at random and prodded his finger at a name, exclaiming: 'Dead...Dead!' The room was crowded and noisy, but people were beginning to look.

'Dead, yes,' Daniel said, in response to one such outburst. There was a pause. He was drunk himself by now, and he realised that he had spoken purely in order to shut the editor up, and without any thought of what he would say next.Whittington gazed at him expectantly. Looking back at him, a kind of panic gripped Linnell. 'Dead...' he heard himself saying, 'but where?'

'Highgate Cemetery,' said Whittington, who was, amongst other things, a walking directory of the graveyards of the world. 'He went there in 1991. Some people – some friends of his – took him there. They took him there, Linnell,' he added, with the exaggerated clarity of a man speaking to a lunatic, 'because he was dead.'

'Yes,' said Daniel. He seized on the first thought that came to him: a premature visitation of the infant school piety that sometimes accompanied his hangovers. 'Dead. But...in heaven?'

Whittington gave him a look of vicious scorn. 'Don't be a moron Linnell,' he said. 'None of these lads is there. These are the great and the good of the United Kingdom.' He held the massive volume inches from Daniel's nose. 'The earls, the judges, the cabinet ministers and the newspaper editors. Take this book fifty years from now,' he went on, 'and you could rebind it and sell it as *Who's Who In Hell*.'

The phrase stayed with Daniel and, in idle moments, he would think of how such a book would be assembled. At first he imagined it as a historical work confined to the dead, with such obvious candidates as the Marquis de Sade, Gilles de Retz and Caligula. When he started talking to people about it though, the names they suggested were always contemporary.

'I'd be in there,' said Laura.

'Rubbish,' said Daniel. Then, more seriously, 'Don't joke about these things.'

'I'd be in there,' she repeated. 'I'd be in there with Herod, and David Etherington.'

Daniel had talked to her about Etherington, whose obituary he'd just completed. A dissolute Old Harrovian now operating as a slum landlord, he had recently accepted a huge advance from a major publisher for his memoirs, a scandalous volume entitled *Lights Out*. There were eight descriptions of sodomy in its first thirty pages, including one involving a pupil who had grown up to be a father of three and was a serving archbishop. The book, which had been passed on to Whittington in manuscript form by a friend at the publisher's, had eventually been deemed unprintable. He had, characteristically, refused to return the advance which, he pledged, would be 'spent, as any publisher's funds should be: instantly, and on pleasure.'

Though seventy-five, Etherington was a well-known face in the crack houses of South London, and he had served two years in Brixton, in the fifties, for his part in the theft of a Vermeer painting which had never been recovered.

Etherington. His was the first name and then, on the quieter days in the office, when the deaths were the elderly, the addicted and the reckless, whose obituaries had long been prepared, Daniel started to make lists. Gradually, and for his own amusement at first, he completed the first detailed entries.

Who's Who In Hell, he decided, had to be essentially an entertainment, and he resolved, where possible, to exclude child murderers and architects of genocide unless, like Nero and Caligula, they had already benefited from that remarkable transition whereby the most savage of crimes becomes bleached by history. It was curious, Daniel reflected, how the names of historical criminals – like Jack the Ripper or Dick Turpin – eventually acquire a glamorous resonance which makes them strangely untouchable and no more deserving of horrified blame than characters in fiction.

'I can't have the modern equivalents,' he said to Laura, 'of these guys who…who are totally, you know…how should I say…'

'Guys who have Hate,' she told him, 'on both their hands.'

Working at home, or in the office on a Saturday morning, when the desk was deserted, he sketched out entries for Lucrezia Borgia, Stalin and Paganini, the last of whom was widely reputed, as one of his contemporaries put it, to have been 'dealing with the naughty one'. In the flat, Daniel used the old Remington for most writing, out of sentimentality. Once he started the book, though, he bought a cheap laptop computer so that he could transfer work from home to the office.

He did include some contemporary villains, such as the Longworths, a criminal family of long standing with their base in North London, on the grounds that their founding members were colourful figures, and were all either dead or jailed for life. Details of the murders and savage assaults they committed had faded in the public memory. The name of Longworth was beginning to benefit from what Daniel thought of as the Jack the Ripper effect. To some, they were already heroes.

He composed entries for the original Longworth brothers, Edward and Terence (like kings, saints and many of their colleagues in the world of organised crime, they preferred to be addressed with the full form of their Christian name). Between them, the two had orchestrated three decades of brutality from adjacent terraced houses in Camden. For years, they had laundered their money – as they were still laundering it – through a scaffolding business. This was conducted, unbelievably, under their own name. Many builders found that hiring them minimised unreliability in other subcontractors.

Underneath the Longworths' own houses, whose exteriors had been painted white in the continental style and were decorated with cheerful window-boxes, a passage connected the two cellars. There in the basement, the brothers had committed acts of torture which Daniel, freed from the normal restrictions of libel or other intimidation, described in some detail.

Aware of the need to fulfil the expectations aroused by the book's title, he didn't stint on providing details of the corpses, shattered marriages and casual violence for which the family had been responsible. 'The Longworths,' he wrote, 'were unusual not merely for the viciousness and the persistence of their homicidal instincts, but for their assiduous recruitment of almost every member of their extended circle. Thus when Charles was sentenced to thirty-five years in 1988, he was swiftly followed into prison by his wife, ex-wife, two lovers, his uncle, architect, and cleaner.'

The Longworth dynasty, like Cromwell's, might have continued indefinitely had it not been for the incompetence of its chosen successor, Terence's son, Gerald. Daniel had originally planned a brief sketch of the weak-minded heir as light relief but, once he'd completed it, Gerald Longworth's entry turned out to be the longest of any of the family. His mother Eileen – rich and remorseful by the time Gerald was born, in the early seventies, sent the boy to Cringle Hill, a minor public school in North Yorkshire.

'His London accent,' he wrote, 'had him cruelly mocked at boarding school, with the result that he pleaded for, and was given, elocution classes. When he left after four unhappy years, he was spurned by his family on his return to London, where he attempted, with limited success, to reacquire his native Cockney. The result was a bizarre, dramatically unstable accent that commanded little authority in daily life, but made him the subject of some interest to professors of linguistics. Cringle Hill failed to instil in Gerald the arrogant self-regard, physical resilience and talent for duplicity that he might have acquired at Wormwood Scrubs or Eton,' Linnell wrote. On Whittington's advice, he had found interesting material in the school magazine, which was held in the British Library. 'But one attribute that Cringle Hill did successfully develop was Gerald's resonant tenor voice. His gift for light opera,' he went on, 'proved to be of little use to him when he returned to Praed Street, aged sixteen, following the imprisonment of his father and uncle, charged with administering the family empire, which by now was dominated by drug dealing and prostitution. His natural inclination was to sloth, punctuated by occasional benevolence. Longworth took pity on one young prostitute and sent her to Malaga with five thousand pounds, instructing her to start a new career, which she did – as a blackmailer, by post, with Gerald Longworth as her lucrative victim.'

According to his cuttings file, Gerald was now living alone in a one-bedroom flat in Islington, and was in and out of prison on charges relating to petty theft and handling stolen goods. His brief but catastrophic reign in Praed Street, Linnell judged, nevertheless merited an entry.

'He was capable of great malice, and would fly into a rage, especially at accusations that he was insufficiently robust, and too lazy, for a life of crime,' he wrote. 'Like many of his compatriots in other areas of life,' Daniel added, thinking of the nepotism in the office around him, 'he was plagued by self-loathing which sprang from the knowledge that he had taken the natural path for the truly mediocre: adopting his father's profession, and doing it less well.'

The book was coming together faster than he'd hoped, and compiling it was proving to be strangely addictive. Whittington declined Daniel's proposal that they write *Who's Who In Hell* together, but he was a vital source of suggestions, especially subjects from the ranks of the Anglican Church and the Conservative Party. The editor arranged for him to meet his own literary agent, Robert Balfour, a dour-looking Glaswegian in his early forties, who was widely feared in his profession – at the Printer's Devil.

They arrived early and met Steven Peerless reading through copy at the bar, with a melancholic yet irritated expression.

'Bad news?' Daniel asked.

'More stuff from Ed Franks,' Peerless said. 'He's at a railway station in Germany.'

He handed the print-out to Daniel. The article, which related to a high-speed train crash in which 170 people had died, was entitled 'Amputation Fears for Baby Greta'.

'At least you can change that headline,' Daniel said.

'I can't,' Peerless said. 'He's the editor's best mate. He can write his own fucking headlines.' He took back the sheet of paper. 'You know what the worst thing is?' he told Daniel. 'It's not just Franks now. He's spawned a whole school of foreign reporting. They stick together. They phone in copy together. They borrow each other's handkerchiefs.'

'Even so,' said Whittington, 'you can't say he's got the safest job on the paper.'

'It's like a lot of things in life,' said Peerless. 'It depends how you go about it.'

'Still, we'd better get him on file. Will you do his obit?'

'Sure,' said Peerless.

Diffident and inscrutable-looking when he first arrived at the Devil, Robert Balfour's manner changed dramatically when he had read Linnell's single-sheet outline of the project. Suddenly galvanised, he looked up at Daniel with a sort of awed astonishment. Even half an hour later, when Whittington announced he had another meeting, and called a cab for Balfour, the agent's expression had not quite faded. 'I'll call you,' he told Daniel, as he was leaving.

It was the kind of look, Linnell told Whittington when they were alone at their table once more, that he'd only previously seen in films.

'That's right,' said his colleague. 'On the face of a villain opening a suitcase filled with untraceable virgin banknotes. Don't go to him by the way,' said Whittington, after Balfour had gone. 'Make him come to you.'

'He won't come to Crouch End,' Daniel said. 'Will he?'

'He will,' said Whittington. 'I will too, if you like.'

'Yes,' said Daniel. 'Right. Thanks.' He mentally scanned the area for a place where he could take the editor. Not The Owl: the prospect of sharing a table with Brendan and Whittington made him feel faint.

'What's your other meeting tonight?' he asked Whittington.

'Simon Roylance.'

'Oh God.'

He decided to wait, for Whittington's sake, until the crime correspondent arrived. By the time he did, it had occurred to Linnell that Roylance could be a useful source for his own research. After twenty minutes' discussion with the reporter, Daniel had covered several bar-mats with the names of historical criminals. 'I'm going to go easy on the living,' he said.

'Who've you already got in there?' Roylance asked.

So far, Daniel told him, his only active felon was Gerald Longworth.

'Oh dear,' said the crime reporter. 'I wish you'd never told me that.'

'Why?' asked Daniel. 'He's an idiot isn't he?'

Roylance made no comment. 'It's just that...I'm having a drink with him,' he said, 'tomorrow, at The Archers in Whitechapel.'

Whittington leaned forward. 'You're not planning to, er...bring the subject of this conversation up?'

Roylance shook his head, looking offended. 'No, no,' he said. 'Of course I'm not.'

'Well, then?' asked Daniel.

'It's just that...' Roylance hesitated. 'If you've told me, then I imagine you've told other people.'

'One or two,' said Daniel.

'And the thing is that, if he asks you, you have to tell him.'

'Why?' asked Whittington.

Roylance looked uncomfortable, and squinted up to the far corner of the ceiling. 'Because he doesn't ask you twice.'

Daniel got home around midnight, and told Laura that Whittington was coming north.

'Don't pander to him,' she said. 'Where do you like? What about Chillies?'

It was the local Indian.

'*Chillies?*' he said. 'Are you mad?'

'Good God,' said Whittington. He was sitting with Daniel and Laura in an alcove whose walls were made of frosted glass etched with images of nude copulating gods. The ceiling at Chillies was concealed by a dense mass of plastic creepers and other artificial vegetation. 'It's never occurred to me before,' Whittington told them, 'but now I come to think of it there's practically no restaurant I know that wouldn't be improved by foliage.'

'Magnificent,' he exclaimed to the waiter, gesturing at the décor. 'Will it rain?'

The editor was a keen admirer of Indian cooking, as he was of most countries' cuisine, but things started badly when he sent back two bottles of red wine. By the time he was tasting the third, described on the label as a Saint Emilion, the atmosphere had become strained to the point that even

Whittington knew he had no option but to accept this last vintage, whatever its condition.

The waiter was standing behind him as he tasted it.

'That's fine,' the editor said, giving a furtive, horrified grimace to Laura. 'That's fine. That's very nice indeed.'

'If you say so, sir, it is my duty to believe you,' said the waiter. Whittington turned round to see what could have inspired such a remark. Their host pointed at the wall in front of them. 'The mirror, sir.'

At which point Alexander Whittington, the scourge of weakness, hypocrisy and fornication as practised by the nation's establishment, blushed deeply.

Balfour arrived ten minutes late. 'The great thing with this book,' he said, 'is to make sure you go for the most dramatic, the most lurid characters possible.'

'Can there be any other profession,' Laura said, 'which could worry that the most evil souls in the history of creation might not be bad enough?'

'Pol Pot,' said Whittington, 'King Herod. Margaret Thatcher. Judas.'

'I'm not sure about Pol Pot,' said Daniel. Balfour laughed.

'No,' he went on. 'I'm not. Because this book has to be an entertainment. I don't want to play God.'

'You have to have Pol Pot,' said Balfour. 'He killed a million people.'

'But even one death sells,' said Laura. She looked at Whittington. 'As we know.'

'In the end,' the editor said, 'I don't think it matters that much. The great thing in any endeavour of this kind is to include some people who definitely don't deserve to be there, and to omit a few people who do. I imagine it is a principle the deity will apply; that would be half the pleasure of mingling, whatever one's destination. Readers,' he went on, 'love to work themselves up over errors of omission. They're never happier than when they're furious.'

Balfour got a call on his mobile, and walked to the other side of the restaurant.

'What do you think of him?' Whittington asked Laura.

'I think he's a fucking weasel,' she said.

'Careful,' said Daniel. 'He may be a fucking weasel, but he's not fucking deaf.'

'So what would you call him?' Laura asked the editor.

'He is a weasel,' Whittington replied. 'But sometimes you need a weasel.'

'What's the first name you'd put in this book?' Laura asked the editor, as Balfour rejoined them.

'I can think of one man I would nominate,' said Whittington. 'Though he died many years ago, and his name would mean nothing to you.'

'A literary agent?' Laura asked.

'A doctor of medicine,' Whittington told her. 'It's a curious thing,' he added. 'We live in an age which prides itself on the notion that any concept may be embraced, yet judgement and damnation represent our last great taboo. I recently listened to an hour-long radio debate on the difference, if any, between the human brain and the artificial intelligence of the most advanced computers which never once mentioned the concept of a soul.'

'Where will you end up?' Laura asked him.

Whittington smiled. 'I hope to be in the livelier domain.'

CHAPTER 14

Robert Balfour's enthusiasm and urgency proved infectious. After Daniel had signed the contract the agent negotiated, and banked the publisher's advance, he became increasingly frustrated that he couldn't devote himself to the project more solidly. He worked on the book for an hour or two in the evening, at the office, and at the weekends. He was sitting at his desk at ten o'clock one evening when his direct line rang.

'I need to talk to you,' Laura said, when he picked it up.

'I'll see you in an hour.'

'I'm downstairs.'

He met her in reception. They walked across to the North Pole, one of the few old pubs the developers had left standing.

'What time are you leaving for work tomorrow?' she asked him, as they stood at the bar.

'I don't know…eight thirty?'

'Jesus,' she said. 'When am I supposed to see you?' She raised her voice slightly. They'd become the centre of attention in the pub. They didn't see many Americans at the North Pole. He bought two beers and they sat down.

'Let's go somewhere,' he said. The idea had never occurred to him, but the more he thought of it, the better it sounded.

'Do you think we can?'

'Sure,' he said. 'I'll ask them for twice as long as we want. I believe that's how it works. Where do you think?' he asked her. 'Fowey?'

'Yes,' she told him. 'Fowey. Great. I mean, if we stay there for long enough, you never know, we might get that guy on the ferry to show us his other hand.'

The jukebox was playing Chuck Berry's version of 'Promised Land'. He knew the song so well it made him feel physically sick.

'Hey,' she said. 'Aren't we forgetting something?'

'What?'

'We're people with money now.' Daniel laughed.

'I can take you to Vesuvio's bar in San Francisco,' she said. 'We can drive up Highway 101 and watch the sun go down over Monterey. We can wake up in a cabin, under the redwoods at Big Sur.'

Daniel stared at her. He'd never thought of going to America before. 'I don't want to wake up in a cabin,' he said. 'I don't want to go to Big Sur.' And then – his voice seemed to come straight from his subconscious – 'I want to go to Kansas.'

'*What?*'

'I want to go to Kansas,' he said. 'I want to see Joshua.'

'What's Joshua?'

'Joshua you told me about,' he said. 'Joshua who lives in Sally's bar.'

'Jasper,' she said. 'The catfish. Hang on – I'll have to think about this – no.'

'When did you last go back?'

'Two years ago. For Kate's wedding.'

'Where did you stay?'

'With my parents.'

'Why?'

'Because if I hadn't – since you ask – it would have left my mother in pieces. And that wasn't the plan.'

'No. And how did that go, when you stayed with your parents?'

'It...' she lapsed into Brendan's broad Yorkshire. 'It were bloody awful mate.' She paused. 'You don't know my dad.'

'I want to know your dad.'

'Believe me,' she said, 'you don't.'

'Let's get a cab,' he said. 'Let's go and eat.'

'I brought the car.'

'Why?'

'Because I needed to talk to you.'

'It takes ages in the car.'

'It takes ages,' she said. 'But it feels faster.'

She drove them up through East London, towards the Agra.

'What's he like, your dad?'

'He's mean,' she said. 'He's mean with money. He's mean to my brother. And he's mean...'

She drew up too sharply at a set of traffic lights, and avoided the car stopping with a jolt by easing off the brake at the last minute. 'To me.'

'Why?'

'Why?' The lights changed, and she accelerated away. 'How do I know? Because he got fucked up in Korea. Because he caught me naked with his gardener.'

'Did he?' Daniel asked.

'Did he which?'

'Both'

'Yes.'

'Blimey,' said Daniel.

She laughed. 'He loses it. When he does, it's really, really scary.'

'How often?'

'About every year or so.'

'When?'

'Well,' she said, 'it usually happens about when I arrive. My friend Kate calls him the PG.'

'Parental Guidance?'

'The Psychotic Gentleman.'

'Does he like Kate?'

'He hates her.'

'Why?'

'Because Kate doesn't do things right.'

'Don't you want to see Kate?'

'I would love to see Kate.'

They pulled up outside the Agra and took a table under one of the pictures of Muhammad Ali.

'OK,' she said. 'Why are we discussing this? Oh yeah, I remember. I want you to see the Monterey harbour lights at nightfall. And you want to meet my dad.'

'I want to go to Kansas,' he said, 'because it's part of you. Because it's special.'

'You're damn right it's special,' she said. 'It's so special I haven't set foot in it for two years.'

'Let's go then,' he said.

'What are you,' she laughed, 'twisted?' And then, as if she'd suddenly thought of a point that would end all argument, 'You'd have to sleep on the sofa.'

She was speaking in the second conditional, he noticed, and when she took out a cigarette, she didn't offer him one. He took heart from these things. They were negotiating.

'That's OK,' he said.

'That is *not* fucking OK.' She leaned towards him and took him gently by the forearms. 'Look at me,' she said. 'I don't understand. What would you get out of this? A cheap drama? A free holiday?'

'I'll stay at the hotel,' he said.

She laughed out loud. 'Oh, shit.'

'Isn't there a hotel?'

'Oh, there's a hotel,' she said. 'There's a hotel all right.'

Laura struck a match, and lit the cigarette. 'So,' she continued, 'you stay at the hotel. Actually when I think of you there, I'm getting to like this idea. And while you're staying at the hotel...what is it you get out of this?'

'I hadn't thought. If I'm honest,' he said. 'I think it might be...'

'Yes?' She was laughing gently and shaking her head in disbelief. 'Come on – try me. I can't wait.' She blew smoke into his face, playfully.

He drew in his breath and held it for a few seconds. As he breathed out, he closed his eyes. 'A family.'

'Fuck you,' she said, in a tone of tenderness and defeat. She handed him the lighted cigarette. He drew heavily on it. There was smoke in his eyes and he felt he might be about to weep. She got up and came round and sat on the bench seat next to him, and put her head on his shoulder too firmly and too fast, like a dog would.

'OK,' she told him. 'But just remember – this was you, not me.'

'Shall we say "love" now?' he asked her.

'Don't push it,' she said.

The next morning he arrived late, to find Whittington already editing copy at his screen.

'He was rarely found in the advanced and hazardous positions occupied by the photographers whose pictures accompanied his reports,' he read, out loud, to Linnell, 'and critics privately doubted whether the reporter truly possessed the degree of bravery he implicitly attributed to himself in his despatches. Readers might have been forgiven for thinking that this prudent journalist from Acton had entered into a lifetime wager to use the first person pronoun as frequently as possible: the more terrible the disaster, the more regularly the word occurred.'

'I see,' said Daniel. 'Peerless has delivered.'

'Nobody who had ever heard Ed Franks speak about himself,' Whittington continued, 'could have doubted his capacity for deep and lasting affection, and yet the difficulty he had in extending the emotion to others, particularly to non-UK citizens, made foreign reporting a curious choice of career.'

Whittington lowered his reading glasses. 'He can still do it,' he told Daniel. 'He's been a serious loss, young Steven.'

'*Lives of the Saints?*' Daniel suggested.

'I think filing it there would be wise,' Whittington said, 'pending a change of editor.' He began to work through the gossip columns in his pile of tabloids. 'If I grasp the subtleties of these reports correctly,' he said, 'we live in decadent times.'

'Would you mind,' Daniel asked the editor, 'if I went to America?'

'For ever?' asked the editor, with a weary inflection, and without looking up.

'No,' said Daniel. 'For a month.'

'No,' said Whittington. 'So long as I can get Julian Cave to cover for you.'

Rosa called the freelance. 'Julian can do a month,' she said, 'but only if you can leave this Monday.

'I can,' said Linnell, in a slightly deeper voice than usual. He had no idea of whether he could or not, but he was feeling overtaken by events and he had to sound resolute.

'Can Cave come in tomorrow?' Whittington asked her. She nodded. 'Take the rest of the week off,' he said to Daniel.

'OK,' said Linnell. 'Yes. Right.' He looked at the calendar. It was Wednesday already.

'Monday?' said Laura, when he got back. 'Shit.' And then, 'Do you – do we – really want to stay a month?'

He nodded.

Laura went down to the bar to talk to Jessica. When she came back up a few minutes later she was holding her diary. She'd fixed up a parachute jump in Wales, she told him, which was just a couple of days after they'd got back; anything else she could rearrange.

She rang her friend Kate, then called her mother to say she was thinking of coming. Mrs Jardine was out, but phoned back a few minutes later to leave a message. There was a note of rapture in her voice – a surprise, Daniel said, considering what Laura had said about her relationship with her parents.

'My mom's OK,' said Laura. 'It's just that her life's been a bit like Belarus.'

'What?' asked Daniel.

'It's been a history of eclipse and surrender.'

She booked the flights the next morning. He'd hoped to devote his few free days to completing his obituary on Gerald Longworth, but he ended up spending one day queuing to replace his passport, which had expired, and another in the bookshops of the Charing Cross Road, collecting research material, mostly true crime paperbacks with garishly illustrated covers, to take with him. The night before they were leaving, Laura was working downstairs in the restaurant. Her two small bags were packed. She'd left fifty pounds propped up on the mantelpiece.

'What's that?' he asked her.

'Burglar money,' she said. 'If they're honest, that's what they take.'

Daniel found an old suitcase in the boxroom and filled it with clothes. He crammed the paperbacks into a holdall that he planned to take as cabin baggage.

He sat down, turned on the laptop and began work on a last paragraph for Longworth.

'Taking his career as a whole,' he wrote, 'the pinnacle of his achievements in public life was probably his celebrated performance in his boarding school's end-of-term production of the musical *Mary Poppins*, in which Longworth played Bert the chimney sweep, a part originally taken by Dick Van Dyke. Since the American's Cockney was the most famously botched attempt at a regional accent in the history of talking pictures, the role of Bert was an unusually appropriate one for Longworth, whose own amorphous, constantly shifting speech had caused him, even in adulthood, to be mistaken by strangers as Scandinavian, or Welsh.

'A reliable police informant,' the entry continued, 'swore on oath that

Gerald Longworth had never killed a man. But he had stood aside and seen them die – dozens of them – and if his instincts were less fatal than those of his more famous predecessors, they were more gratuitously sadistic. Gerald Longworth was unusual, in the normal run of men, in that he was consistently at pains to seem worse than he was. To his family, his relatively modest criminal record showed not a lack of malice, but of application. He was not so much a good man,' Daniel wrote, 'as a bad man who never quite put the hours in.'

He saved the file, and made two copies on disks which he put in an envelope and stored in the desk drawer. It was only as he did this that he realised how attached he had become to the project, and how determined he was that it should work. He closed the drawer with a new feeling of satisfaction. He went down to the bar and sat with Brendan while Laura cashed up.

'OK,' she said, when she came over and ordered a coffee. 'Shall we?'

At eight the following morning, they were at Heathrow, standing in line for the British Airways flight to New York. As they inched forward, Daniel had difficulty in lifting the small holdall, which held his research books and his laptop computer. If each life can, indeed, be weighed in scales of judgement, he thought, it was unlikely that any single passenger had ever assembled a bag packed quite so densely with sin.

The queue was moving slowly, to the obvious frustration of the man immediately behind them, an obese, grey-haired figure of about sixty. He wore steel-rimmed spectacles with lavender-tinted lenses, and he was sweating heavily. He kept checking his watch, even though the flight wouldn't board for another two hours. He had a suede coat and a black leather suitcase with gold combination locks. The case looked brand new – a retirement gift, Daniel guessed, given that his manner suggested he wasn't accustomed to travelling economy, or waiting. 'Jeffreys,' he read on the man's luggage tag, made out of leather and perspex. 'Everdene, Hoylake.'

They got to the front and the woman on the check-in desk – Andrea, he read off her lapel badge – checked their hold bags through. She was American, and she had a fixed professional smile of a kind he imagined he would come to know far better by the time their month abroad was up. If Andrea was a car, he thought spitefully to himself, you'd have thought she'd left her indicator on. Then, to his alarm, she explained that she needed to weigh the cabin luggage. She checked Laura's bag, which held a bottle of red wine from the café, a small towel and a paperback. Daniel stooped to pick up his holdall. Guy Montgomery, he remembered, had once showed him how actors pick up polystyrene props in a way that implies tremendous weight; he'd never mentioned the opposite technique, which would have disguised the fact that he could barely lift the small bag on to the rubber conveyor.

'That's way over sir,' the woman said, looking at the digital counter, still smiling. 'Way over.'

'I have to take these things,' he said.

'I'm sorry sir,' she told him. 'Do you think your wife might carry some of your belongings for you?'

'Sure she can,' Laura said. 'Give her a call. She's a very accommodating woman. You'll have to ask her though. She fucking hates me.'

He decided to remove the laptop. To reach it he had to unpack most of his books, which he placed on the check-in desk. He saw Andrea glancing at the covers. Facing towards her were several eye-catching paperbacks, variously decorated with portraits of Hitler, Dr Crippen and Jack the Ripper. These characters, crudely drawn against vivid backgrounds of hellfire, bleeding torsos or mass graves, had been invested with more maniacal and forbidding qualities than even they ever managed in life. He noticed her eye fall on a large volume in a black dust jacket whose title, written in letters formed by coiled serpents, was *The Complete History of Sin*. He pulled out the laptop, handed it to Laura, and put the books back.

The computer alone, it turned out, brought her bag over the limit.

'And you sir,' Andrea said, her smile now tinged with a small gleam of malicious satisfaction, 'are still at double the cabin allowance.'

'Charge him the excess,' said Laura, wearily.

'I can't do that ma'am,' Andrea said. 'The flight is full.' Behind them, the man with the new leather case tutted loudly.

'The flight is full,' she repeated, turning to Daniel, still smiling. 'It's a matter of the gross cargo. That means,' she added, as if talking to a spaniel, 'the weight of the whole aircraft. That's why we have the cabin luggage restriction.' She waved towards the line of impatient passengers, and raised her voice. 'It's so we can be fair to everybody.'

'Oh come on man,' said a voice behind them. It was the passenger with the black suitcase again. Daniel looked at him. 'Well do *something*,' the man said. 'For God's sake.' He jabbed his index finger down at his watch.

There was a woman with him. She smirked. Daniel felt fire rise in his blood. He took a step to the right, so that his knee caps were level with the rubber conveyor, and he was visible, from the shins upwards, to Andrea. He noticed her stiffen slightly, as if she feared some physical attack.

'How much,' he asked her, 'would you say that I weigh?'

'I don't know,' she said. 'I don't...I can't...no...'

'You can,' he said politely. 'Go on.'

'I don't know,' she said. She looked him up and down, and, once she'd done that, she was committed. 'A hundred forty?' she guessed.

'Correct,' he said.

He turned so that he was sideways on to her, and extended an open palm towards his irritated fellow passenger. 'And how much,' he added, 'would you say for Mr Jeffreys here?'

There was a silence, and a surge of collective embarrassment. 'What I'm saying,' he went on, in a tone of apparently puzzled reasonableness which, he realised, he'd learned from his travelling companion, 'is that if you're really concerned about gross cargo, you should weigh us, and our luggage, together. Because the thing is,' he continued, a little surprised at himself, but aware that the situation had taken on a dynamic of its own, 'that if you weigh me, and my books, and my clothes, and my computer...' He paused for a moment. 'Then all of us, all taken together...we will all weigh less than Mr Jeffreys.'

Mrs Jeffreys looked to her husband for some reaction, but he was looking not so much offended as perplexed; almost as if he thought that Linnell might have hit on something. Daniel turned back to face the check-in woman, who was staring up at him with a new expression. Her smile had gone and she looked like somebody who had been rolling her eyes, but somehow got them stuck at the highest point of the arc. Then she looked down again without speaking and pressed a button. The printer spat out two boarding cards and luggage receipt tags, which she handed to him. 'Take them,' she said. 'Board Gate Eleven.'

There were no baggage problems on the New York to Kansas connection. Laura, who was used to long haul flights, slept most of the way from London; Daniel took out his laptop and started to work through his paperbacks. Even before they'd sighted the American coast, he had finished with more than half of them, because his entries were short and the material he was looking for was specific.

Just as they were preparing to check in for the flight to Kansas, he tipped almost all of the books into a waste bin.

'Why are you putting them in the trash?' a young girl asked him.

'I'm putting them in the trash,' he told her, 'because they're trash.'

CHAPTER 15

The plane was making its descent into Kansas, and he saw Laura staring fixedly out of the window, oblivious to her immediate surroundings, contemplating another, more dramatic, sort of landing.

'Is it now?' he asked her.

She looked down again to gauge the height, and then nodded. 'Twelve thousand feet. No wind; light cloud. That'll do it.' She gave an exaggerated shiver.

'What is it?' he asked. 'Are you getting that late-onset fear of free fall?'

'No,' she said. 'It's worse than that. I was just thinking we're getting nearer and nearer to my dad.'

'Why do you really think he's so mean?'

'I knew his parents, OK?'

'Or your grandparents, as they're more commonly known.'

'Were known,' she said. 'They're dead now. My dad's dad was this little guy – very quiet, very particular. He wanted things done just so.'

'What things?'

They were jolted in their seats as the plane descended. 'Aviation,' she said. 'Grammar. Gardening. Everything. Do it right. Like it was done when he was growing up in Bunker Hill in 1900. And his wife was this furious monster with a will of iron. She was really awesome. My mom said she used to throw stuff at him.'

'Stuff?'

'Crockery, you know. Knives. Bottles. I believe she used what was close at hand. I don't think she collected that stuff specially, you know. She improvised. And my dad's like both of them. He wants everything just so, when of course it never ever is, even now he's totally fucking loaded with money. And at the same time he's got his mother's temper.'

'What happened to him in Korea?' Daniel asked.

'He doesn't talk about that a whole lot,' said Laura. 'My mom once told me he escaped an ambush by digging down into the undergrowth, and hiding there for hours before he could get back to camp.'

'I guess he's probably not alone there,' said Daniel.

'No,' Laura said. 'But she told me he was holding the wounded body of his best friend. When they finally came out, he was dead. He carried him back to be buried. His name was Paul Preston.'

'You remember that,' Daniel said, surprised.

'I remember his name,' Laura said, 'because my brother was named after him. Paul Preston Jardine. And his widow is Paul's godmother. And she's dying.'

At Kansas City they boarded a twenty-eight-seat light aircraft to Salina, where her brother Paul was coming to meet them. Salina is thirty miles east of Bedford, up Interstate 70, the hypnotically drab highway that crosses the state from east to west. On its 2,000-mile route from Baltimore to Cove Fort, Utah, the I-70 slips almost unnoticed through Denver, Indianapolis and Saint Louis, but it thunders straight through the tiny heart of Bedford and past its central hotel, the Red Carpet Inn. Daniel had booked himself in here for the whole month, after Laura told him that her father, Stewart, who had inherited the rigid propriety of his Scottish grandparents, had indeed insisted that, if his English guest slept at the house, it would be alone, in the spare bedroom.

As the plane began its approach, Daniel stared down at Salina's water tower, railway line, and neat wooden rooftops.

'Does Paul still go up the grain silo?' he asked her, as they neared the airfield.

'I don't know,' she said. 'But what matters is, he could. He's thirty-two, but he still could. Any day.'

'When were you last in touch with Paul?' Daniel asked her.

She took a few moments to reply. 'Last week,' she said.

'What took you so long to remember?'

'I was just thinking,' she said, 'that I could have answered "never".'

Paul had moved out to his own place a couple of years back. He lived alone in a makeshift camp that consisted of a caravan and a couple of run-down trailers, off a dirt track half a mile up the road from the family house. He made the locals uneasy. His one truly dangerous tendency was his interest in large fireworks, in that area of the Chinese art where display rockets begin to overlap with munitions – a passion which, fortunately enough, he shared with most young men in the area. When he left school, he worked as a porter in the hospital. For the past year or so, Laura told Daniel, he had been making an uncertain living as a mechanic.

'He also does some work as a cab driver. But that's kind of sporadic.'

'Sporadic?'

'He has a problem with his car,' she said. 'Not everybody goes the distance. Paul's not like other people. He has this weird thing of...well you'll see, he's incredibly nervous. If there's something he's supposed to do that he can't, he never confronts it. He just doesn't do it. Even when he's bound to get found out later.'

'So why does he behave like that?'

'Because it's the easiest way out at the time. Because that's how he deals with the world.' She stopped and put her hand on his. 'Let me ask you something,' she said. 'Don't ever lose your temper with Paul.'

'Why do you say that?' he asked her.

'Because people shouldn't,' she said, 'but people do.'

He was there waiting for them at the airport, a balding, dark-haired figure in a flying jacket. He greeted them without making eye contact, then accompanied them to the airport's small car park – following half a step behind, Daniel noticed, rather than leading his younger sister. His car, a black Ford Taurus his dad had given him, looked ordinary enough. He loaded their cases into a moulded plastic luggage container on the roof.

Daniel sat next to Paul in the front; Laura stretched across the back seat in what was roughly the foetal position, with her fingers in her ears: some exercise popular with seasoned fliers, Daniel supposed, to relieve trapped pressure. 'Why don't you put stuff in the trunk?' he asked Paul, trying to practise his American. Laura's brother smiled and turned on the stereo. It was 'If Everybody Looked the Same' by the Groove Armada and he'd chosen it because it was British and because it would make Daniel feel at home.

In the second after Paul pushed the button, Daniel thought for a moment that a bomb had gone off in his head. The volume was at such a level that the demands it placed on the human frame had less to do with in-car stereo, more with the rigours of lift-off in the early days of manned space flight. Curiously, once the initial shock was over, it wasn't the strain on his eardrums that made the experience so unbearable, but the awareness that his internal organs, helpless against the massive, thudding assault from the four-four beat, had begun a kind of independent motion that neither willpower, nor tightening of the stomach muscles, could do anything to arrest. Though the car's motor was still switched off, and the wheels were not turning, it never occurred to Daniel that he could have opened the door and got out. It never occurred to him, because he couldn't think. Nobody could have. It was too loud. He looked at Paul, who pulled the ring from a Coke can, drank from it, and offered it to him. Daniel shook his head. Paul turned the volume down to a deafening but more bearable level, and laughed.

'That was smart,' he shouted to Daniel.

'What?'

'That was smart,' Paul repeated, 'that you said no to the Coke. The first few times, most guys throw up.'

'How loud was that, Paul?' shouted Laura.

He glanced at a meter under the dashboard. 'One forty-one,' he said.

'What does it go to now?'

'One five two. Want to...'

'No, Paul,' she said. They pulled out on to the small service road which led down to Interstate 70.

'Oh yeah,' Paul said to Daniel. 'The trunk. There's no room in the trunk. The amp's in the trunk.'

He drove them not to the Jardines' house, but to the Red Carpet Inn, where they arrived just before five thirty. 'I told the folks we'd be in for dinner at nine,' she said. 'So we can hang out.'

They walked into what would have been an ordinary two-storey motel, except that the Red Carpet, as its name suggested, had pretensions. The floor was covered in scarlet carpeting barely thicker than felt. It had been put down everywhere, even in the bedrooms, but with no underlay, so that the first-time visitor, without knowing why, was instantly struck by the feeling of having entered somewhere down at heel and cheap. And yet the carpet, if it failed in its attempt to radiate regal splendour, did give the hotel its one truly distinct characteristic.

Laura and Daniel walked across reception, and put their bags down. Behind the desk, Lucy, the blonde receptionist – in her early twenties, but already clinically obese – closed her copy of *Glamour* and smiled at them. It was a kind, genuine expression; not at all the smile, Linnell found himself thinking, of an American, or a receptionist.

'Eighty dollars a night, OK?' she said to Daniel. He nodded. 'Er…do we tell him?' she asked Laura.

'Yeah,' said Laura. 'Go on. He's all right. He's with me.'

'OK,' said Lucy. She came out from behind the reception area. She was wearing grey jogging trousers and plastic sandals. She walked round and stood next to him.

'OK – you're from England, right?' she said. 'So you're polite, right? OK – shake hands.'

Bemused, he held out his hand and, as she touched him, a static shock raced up his right arm; it was so powerful that his first thought was that she must have been carrying some gadget from a joke shop.

But by the time he'd been walking around the Red Carpet for a couple of hours, Daniel, like most of the regulars, could be seen slapping his hand against a metal banister, or door handle, every couple of minutes or so, to discharge the static that was generated by that thin acrylic carpet and the soles of his shoes. The slap had to be a quick, deliberate movement: if you hesitated, the shock was prolonged, more unpleasant, and pretty much as bad as if you hadn't bothered in the first place. There was a popular discharge point outside the entrance to the hotel bar: a bronze plaque celebrating the visit here, in 1963, of Richard Nixon. It didn't mention that he only stopped here because his bodyguard's car had a flat tyre; neither did it commemorate the fact that the future President didn't even come in, but simply climbed from the back of one limousine to another in the car park. Seeing the regulars touch the Nixon plaque on their way into the bar, in the early evening, you might have taken them for members of a religious sect in thrall to some ancient ritual.

'The charge is worse some days than others,' Lucy told Daniel. 'It's bad today, because it's overcast.' She noticed him looking relieved. 'It's bad today,' she repeated. 'But it's never good.'

At eight that evening Daniel and Laura walked the half-mile from the hotel to the Jardines' house on Grant. As they turned into the drive, they saw

Paul's black Taurus parked at the end of the path by the front door. The car was empty and the driver's door had been left open. Next to it was Angela Jardine's Ford Focus. A pair of feet in black training shoes were sticking out from under the back of her mother's car. She aimed a firm kick at the soles.

'Where is he?' she said.

Paul's head appeared from under the car. 'Dad's up at the Elks Club,' he said. He pulled himself out. There was dust in his hair, and gravel sticking to his shirt. 'I thought I saw an oil leak,' he said, brushing grit from his shoulders.

The three of them walked round to the large garden at the back of the house. On the lawn, which needed cutting, somebody had dumped a small mountain of topsoil. Next to it was a pallet stacked with paving stones. Daniel noticed what looked like the charred foundations of a small outhouse. The neat, geometric shapes of the overgrown flower-beds suggested they had once been immaculately kept.

The Jardines' two-storey house was built out of clapboard in the traditional style, which gave the building, viewed from the outside, a sort of tidy innocence. Inside, the walls were covered – smothered, you might almost say – in furnishing fabrics and these, like the similar materials covering the sofas and the headboards on the beds, radiated claustrophobia and airlessness. The furnishings had been chosen by Laura's mother Angela, who once told her daughter that she only ever felt comfortable in a house if she felt sure it was thoroughly insulated from the ground it was built on. To emerge from Angela Jardine's bathroom and its colour-co-ordinated suite, with matching carpet, towels and shower curtain, was to know the relief a fly feels as it struggles free from a pot of apricot yoghurt.

Laura and Daniel waited in the living room. Paul went to look for his mother, but came back saying she was still in the shower. His sister sat on the sofa, with her feet on the coffee table. Daniel got up and walked around the room. He kept his hands clasped behind his back, as if he was a principal in some ceremony where posture mattered.

Between the living room and the kitchen there was a serving hatch – this, like the somnolent ticking of the carriage clock, and the framed family pictures in a glass cabinet, reminded him of his childhood in England. Next to the photographs in the display case, there was a faded beige cushion, embroidered, in a child's clumsy hand, with the words: 'To Daddy: A Daughter Is Just A Little Girl Who Grows Up To Be Your Friend.'

'Laura did that,' Paul said with pride.

'When?' Daniel asked.

'Last week,' she replied.

'That's my dad,' said Paul, still looking into the display cabinet. He pointed at a black and white photograph of a young man of about twenty, sitting on a motorcycle, staring straight into the lens. Next to him, standing, was a smaller, dark-haired youth with a cigarette in his mouth and a black puppy in his arms.

'I guess the dog's not around any more,' said Daniel.

'Neither's the owner,' said Laura. 'That's Paul Preston.'

They heard a car draw up on the gravel drive. Stewart Jardine walked in through the back porch into the kitchen, looking flustered. He was wearing a black suit; Daniel could see him, through the hatch, as he took off his jacket and tie. He rolled both sleeves up and undid his top shirt button, a habit he'd retained from the military. He came in and shook hands with Daniel. There was a thick silver ring, the younger man noticed, on the middle finger of Jardine's right hand. Stewart nodded to Paul and smiled at Laura, but did not embrace her.

Jardine excused himself and went upstairs to change. As he turned his back, Laura motioned to Daniel and led him towards the main door, with the thought of having a smoke on the front porch. Linnell halted abruptly, however, as he crossed the main lobby. If Mr Jardine had left matters of décor to his wife, it was Stewart, not Angela, who had given the house its most immediately striking feature. When he came home to Bedford from Korea, where he was decorated, the pupils at St David's High School presented him with a life-sized model of himself in uniform, standing to attention. It was made from a blown-up photograph fixed on a rigid card mount, in imitation of the full-scale images of movie stars which used to be placed in the town's cinema foyer.

Mr Jardine brought his likeness home and stood it in the lobby, where it had remained ever since: partly as a joke, partly out of his subconscious desire that the figure would stand as a reminder of the need for unblinking vigilance in an uncertain world. Its solemn eyes, glazed with duty, had greeted every visitor to the house for the last forty years. 'Just remember,' Jardine called out from the top of the stairs, when he saw Daniel standing motionless, staring at the dummy. 'You're outnumbered.'

On the face of the real man, the innocent features of the young cardboard soldier had become tempered and lined with age. Time and experience had done these things. Paradoxically, of the two Mr Jardines it was the dummy (who had stood, his broad, guileless face unshielded, as Laura and her school friend Kate had entertained young men in the hall when the family were away – and, once or twice, when they weren't) whose eyes had witnessed the fuller repertoire of carnal indulgence. These days, Kate taught English at St David's High School, and the fresh-faced lieutenant was only noticed by newcomers to the house. 'He's like a blemish on the paint,' Laura used to say to her friends, the first time they came round. 'After a week or two, you just stop seeing him.'

Daniel walked out on to the front porch with Laura and lit a cigarette.

'I know what you're thinking,' she told him, 'but just let me warn you that it's a thought I've found myself having the first time I met anyone who brought real trouble into my life.'

'Which is?' Daniel asked.

'*Actually* he's not that bad.'

They sat down on the porch, side by side on a wooden swing with a canopy. It looked like something out of a fifties musical.

'You know what I noticed when he shook hands?' Daniel said.

'That he's an elk?'

'He's a what?'

'A mason.'

'No.'

'Well he is.'

'I noticed his ring. He doesn't look like the kind of man that wears a ring.'

'He isn't,' she said. 'It was his buddy Paul's. His wife left it to him.'

They had dinner that evening in the sitting room, which was brightly lit by an overhead electric light. Mr Jardine said grace, at the end of which Daniel, keen to conform, said 'Amen' over-firmly, with an American 'a'. Nobody else spoke. He caught Jardine looking at him, wondering if he'd done it because he was a sarcastic atheist, or a religious fanatic.

Mrs Jardine wore her straight grey hair tied back; her blue linen skirt was so scrupulously pressed that she reminded Daniel of a ward sister. And yet he could sense in Angela some of the strength and vitality that were so brazenly prominent in her daughter. Over dinner though, Laura's mother said little, Paul nothing. Stewart Jardine brought out a tepid bottle of

Beaujolais, which he opened ceremoniously with an ornate silver corkscrew. Daniel and Laura drank the thin wine with reluctant moderation.

Stewart talked to Daniel about the seven years he'd spent in Britain and told him how, one summer, he'd taken the family around the country in a camper van. The places he mentioned, Daniel noticed, were all close to the nation's more prestigious stately homes.

'Do you remember that vacation, Laura?' her mother asked. As she waited for a reply, Angela Jardine got up and picked a piece of gravel from where it had lodged in Paul's hair, just above his ear. Laura glared at her.

'No,' she said.

'How old were you?'

'She was eleven,' Stewart Jardine interrupted, reproach in his voice. 'How could she remember?' he added. 'That was a very long time ago. That was when we were all young and innocent.'

Father and daughter exchanged a look of cold rage. Mr Jardine had devoted his life to repelling certain tendencies in the modern world – drugs, popular music, casual sexual intercourse – that she had drawn into his home, just as some young women attract poltergeists.

'What's that pile of stuff in the back yard?' Laura asked her mother.

'Planting medium,' she said. 'And new stone walls. We wanted to re-lay the back garden. But,' she added, turning to Daniel, 'I don't like planting things out. And we haven't got a...we haven't got...' She stopped herself.

'A gardener,' said her husband. As he spoke, his eyes were raised to the angle of the wall and the ceiling.

'I could help you with that,' Laura said to her mother. 'I could help you with the garden.'

The corners of Stewart Jardine's mouth tightened.

'I have great admiration for the British,' he said, looking straight at Daniel.

'Why?' Laura interrupted.

'Because,' he replied, not taking his eyes off his guest to look at her, 'the best of them have retained their sense of dignity and honour.'

Daniel glanced at the bottle of Beaujolais, which was empty. Laura disappeared into the kitchen.

While she was gone, Angela started asking her husband about his meeting at the Elks Club, where they had been planning the annual veterans' dinner.

'When is it?' she asked him.

'Two weeks today.'

'How many guests?'

'Seventy,' he replied.

'No Jerry Cole,' she said, in a voice of condolence.

There was a muffled pop from the kitchen.

'No Donald Jolliffe,' he told her.

'I don't think I knew him,' she said.

'Well he passed away just after Jerry did,' he said, 'of motor neurone disease.' He invested the last words with a note of scorn, as though they described some new fad, like breakdancing: a younger man's useless invention.

Laura returned with the bottle of Bordeaux she had brought from The Owl. She'd opened it using her pocket knife.

'Every year we're one or two less,' Jardine said. 'We're having a collection this time,' he added, 'for Rita Preston.' He turned to Daniel. 'Her husband was killed in action,' he said. 'She never really recovered. Now she's living alone in Sarasota.'

'She has no medical insurance,' Angela told Daniel.

'And multiple sclerosis,' said Laura. She picked up the bottle and filled a glass for herself and Daniel. Paul never drank at the house.

'When a person dies,' Stewart Jardine said to Daniel, 'why don't the newspapers just get their best friend to write about them?'

Daniel thought of an obit of the Earl of Stapeley that he'd read on the plane. Whittington had prepared it alone, in his absence. The article was accompanied by a recent photograph of Stapeley, a former consul, being dragged off by security guards, seconds after he'd danced on stage uninvited, to assist a Brazilian stripper with the finale of her act at a nightclub in Faro.

'I don't know,' he said. 'I never thought of that.'

'A good friend would probably write it for nothing,' said Jardine. He paused. 'How much,' he went on, 'is your room at the Red Carpet?'

'Fifty dollars,' said Laura, before Daniel could speak.

'Good grief,' said her father.

The dinner ended, as every dinner did, with Mrs Jardine turning to her husband and saying 'Wash or dry?', a ritual which he unfailingly completed with the single word 'wash'.

Around eleven, Laura borrowed her mother's car and drove him back to the hotel. Daniel sensed that, in many ways, he conformed to the kind of character her father admired: he was British, from the old world. He had a job and a university education. But none of that could hide the fact that Jardine fundamentally didn't approve of him.

'I know I'm doing something wrong,' he told Laura afterwards, 'but I don't know what it is.'

'You have that one fatal quality,' she said, 'that he's come to despise in all his potential son-in-laws. It's called something in common with Laura.'

CHAPTER 16

Daniel had expected to loathe the United States for its materialism and phoney politeness. Instead he found himself immersed in a welcoming, unpretentious community that consisted mainly of wheat farmers of German descent. Bedford was a typical small Midwestern town, almost to the point of parody, with its combined post office and general store on Main Street, and the gaily-painted houses, each with its own driveway, outside mailbox, and well-kept lawn. As a connoisseur of the street map, he noticed immediately that in its town plan, as in most things, Bedford had been faithful to the American model. Built on a neat grid system, its streets, running east to west, had been numbered, and were crossed by a dozen or so vertical roads with names like Franklin, Jefferson and Pine.

Daniel hired a beaten-up Buick convertible from Zindler's Garage on Walnut and Fifth and, bowing to local practice, gave up walking out of doors. He found himself acclimatising to the puzzling quirks of local driving, like the state law that allowed a right turn on a red light, so long as the road was clear.

Right across from the Red Carpet, on the other side of the I-70 – connected by a footbridge which, though it must have been at least forty years old, had been thoughtfully constructed with ramps, not steps – was the school where Laura's friend Kate taught, and, just visible behind its buildings, the whitewashed walls of St David's Church.

The day after they arrived, he went over with Laura to visit Kate at work. He felt anxious and slightly sick as they walked across the footbridge. He tried to persuade himself it was jet lag, but it wasn't. It was something to do with the fact that he hadn't set foot in a school for over ten years, and he wasn't used to being around children; that, and the knowledge that it was Kate who had led Laura on some of her less modest excursions.

From what Laura had told him, he expected Kate to be thin, dark and sorcerous. But her looks were more of the kind that might have appealed to Charles II: her face was full and moon-shaped. She spent most of her money on clothes, and she'd amassed a huge reserve wardrobe. 'Teachers are like royalty,' she told Laura. 'We can't be seen in the same dress twice.' Kate had shoulder-length strawberry blonde hair that she lightened with the help of her other extravagance, herbal shampoo, imported from France. She was married to Bob, a biology teacher in Salina, and she had betrayed him passionately and with great stamina practically from the day they met. There was a rumour that she had slept with the immigration officer who stamped her visa form when she and Bob arrived in Paris on their honeymoon. This story, though widely circulated in Bedford, was generally disbelieved, though it was one that Laura, who knew Kate better than anyone, confirmed.

They sat in for the end of Kate's lesson, where the senior class was reading *Macbeth* out loud. She was the kind of teacher that parents dreamed their child might meet: expansive, generous and fun. Daniel was sitting with Laura behind the teacher's desk, aware that the eyes of most of the class never left him once. Some of the children rarely saw people from Kansas City, never mind Europe.

Afterwards, the three of them went to eat in the school canteen. The dining hall, like the school, Kate explained, was open from six in the morning till ten at night. When the children weren't there, the buildings were used for adult education classes. He told her how he was working on a book, but he hadn't been able to bring all the research material he needed.

'If you go down to the library and talk to Miss Hammond,' Kate said – she and Laura exchanged glances – 'she can order stuff in for you on an inter-library loan.' At this point, he must have looked doubtful. 'You'd be surprised,' she said. 'They can get you pretty much anything you need.'

When her senior class had read Shakespeare, Daniel told Kate, their Midwest accent brought the words a new quality, an endearing innocence. 'Yeah,' she said. 'There is that. And then there's the fact that they don't have a clue what's going on.' Perhaps, he said, they were just too young to have any real understanding of certain things, like mortal fear, vengeance, or blood lust. 'That's right,' said Laura, pointing at Kate. 'That's where she comes in.'

Daniel found himself falling into step with the gentle rhythm of the small town. After lunch, he'd drop into the office of the *Bedford News*, the neighbourhood newspaper, which came off the presses daily, at two thirty. Once a thriving concern, the *News*, which was produced by its seventy-year -old editor and proprietor, Mr Reynolds, and a staff of three, had shrunk to six pages. These days, the front page was generally dominated by wheat prices and school fêtes. In more prosperous times, the reception area at the *News* had contained a couple of leather armchairs, a coffee table and a portrait of Mr Reynolds' grandfather, the founder. Now, it served as the town stationery shop.

In the late afternoon, Daniel and Laura took to calling in at the Prospect Café on Main Street. The Prospect was narrow and cramped, with six stools at the counter and three small tables, but it was Bedford's only real bar. And in the early evening, as Laura had promised, Sally Da Tores, the owner, tuned the television set to a cable station that provided non-stop coverage of proceedings at Westminster, for which Sally had developed a perverse appetite. Their host, who was divorced and, judging from her dark, weather-beaten features, must have been near fifty, was especially enthralled by the House of Lords. She was thrilled, she said, to meet a real Englishman.

'It's great – it's just great,' she told Daniel. 'You know,' she confided, 'there are people in this town who have never even heard of an early day motion?'

What was it, Daniel asked her, that she liked about the upper chamber – the clothes? The majesty? The seriousness of the debate?

Sally, who was originally from San Francisco, a town she'd most appreciated in the sixties, thought for minute. 'I like the way,' she replied, 'that they all look like they're on acid.'

She noticed Daniel looking at the large aquarium, at the other end of the bar. 'That's Jasper,' she told him, pointing at a catfish who looked uncomfortably large for his tank. 'He's fifteen.'

'Great,' said Laura. 'Next year he'll be able to order wine with a meal, right?'

'Not in the state of Kansas,' said Sally.

'Actually he already knows about Jasper,' said Laura.

'Really?'

'Yeah. It's Jasper's fault we're here.'

Most evenings, they had a tense, floodlit dinner with Laura's family. Daniel dreaded the silences, which were of a length that would normally only occur if the people round the table were staring at a chess board, or a hand of cards. But there were no cards. And all they had to stare at was each other.

One night, after a particularly excruciating gap in the conversation, Stewart Jardine shifted in his seat and said, 'I'll give you an Oliver for Twenty.' Bored, embarrassed, and desperate to inject some life into the gathering, he'd forgotten that Oliver had been a childhood secret between Laura and Paul, and hence one that he was not supposed to know about, though of course he did know and he had known for years. No sooner had he spoken than a shudder ran round the table. It was an almost tangible current of discomfort, which passed from Jardine to Laura, on his left, through Daniel, who was opposite him, and came to rest in Angela, who was sitting on her husband's right. She turned towards him and silenced him once more, with a look of scorn. 'Dry,' she said. Jardine got up without speaking and retreated angrily to his tea towel.

That night, like most nights, Daniel left the house at around ten thirty, took the Buick back up to the Red Carpet alone, and stopped in the bar for a drink. He would sit on a barstool for a while, then go up to his room, and fall asleep watching a vintage movie channel. He'd be woken around 10.00 a.m. by Laura, who let herself into room fifteen, where the late mornings passed with an intensity that – it occasionally occurred to Daniel over dinner – her father, had he known of it, would never have spoken to him again.

By the time he showed up at the Red Carpet for his nightcap, Lucy would have moved over from the reception desk to the bar. The owners had her stay there until midnight at least, even though there were rarely more than a couple of customers. She'd sit on her stool with her magazine and an orange juice, or a miniature bottle of a noxious pre-mixed cocktail called Hot Damn!, listening to the hotel's two CDs, both dispiriting collections of country-and-western songs. He'd sit there with her for the last hour or so, and she'd tell him about the stars she'd read about in *Glamour*. The first night he was there, she asked him if he had met any of them, 'you being a writer and all'.

'Look,' said Daniel, 'I...I really don't have anything to do with the, er...' He stopped. Lucy was looking at him so expectantly, he couldn't think of anything to say but the truth. '...the living.'

She gave an exaggerated shiver, and told him how most of Bedford believed there was a ghost who walked the verges of the I-70 and flagged down passing motorists.

'Have you seen him?' Daniel asked.

She attempted a smile, then her eyes went down, and she fell silent.

Lucy loved animals; if she got drunk, which was rare, she would start to talk about how she was planning to get out of hotel work and move to Salina and enrol for what she called 'ved-air-ee-neer-ee-an' classes. It was cruel to say it, but listening to her pronounce that word – to borrow an image from one of her favourite creatures – was like watching a showjumping horse drag its trailing back hoof over the puissance fence and almost, but not quite, dislodge a brick. When she got that last, sixth syllable out, she looked at him and smiled.

By the end of his first week in the United States, Daniel had already forgotten why he had been so sure that he'd hate it there. He'd expected America to be uniformly modern, and he'd been astonished to discover that Bedford seemed, in almost every detail of daily life, more old-fashioned than Britain. You could see it everywhere; from the packaging of soap and canned fruit, much of which had survived apparently unchanged since the fifties, to the rusted nodding donkeys – primitive oil pumps that stood motionless in the surrounding fields.

This old-world atmosphere was at its most intense in public buildings, with their immaculately-swept corridors, solid oak doors and cast-iron radiators controlled by round Bakelite dials with a finely serrated circumference. Every detail contributed to an atmosphere of scrupulous order that brought back memories of his childhood in the north of England.

He'd noticed this air of burnished propriety in Kate's school, but it was even more pronounced in the library. A single-storey redbrick building, it had one large room with parquet flooring and eight long desks in beech veneer, set out in two rows of four. Each desk had space for six readers, and each space was numbered with a small engraved oval brass plaque, a little smaller than the tag on a dog's collar, set into the surface of the wood. At the front of the room, on your left as you came in, was the desk occupied by Miss Hammond. The main desks were directly in front of, and facing, her. To her right, against the side wall, there were three individual wooden chairs with no writing tables, facing across the room. Fixed on the wall above them were three wooden signs, with stencilled red letters on a white-painted background; they read 'No Talking', 'No Smoking' and 'No Eating'. On the last of these signs the 'No' had been underlined twice, in red marker pen, presumably to deter any debate over grey areas like chewing gum, or mints. Quite why the three extra seats were there, Daniel couldn't begin to understand. The wooden chairs, like the other forty-eight readers' seats, were generally deserted.

School parties came to the library in the morning; in the early afternoon a few of the poorer residents – that was another constituency of the Midwest, the rural poor, for which Daniel's vision of the United States had left him unprepared – would come in to read one of the three reference copies of the *Bedford News*. Otherwise, the library was barely used. In England, Daniel thought, it would have been demolished twenty years ago and turned into a video store. Here, nobody minded. The library had to be there, and decently maintained, in case anybody needed it, the same as the firehouse or the gas station.

Daniel came in and sat down at seat eleven, facing Miss Hammond. He got out his laptop, meaning to reread his *Who's Who* entry for Gerald Longworth. The machine had barely begun to crackle into life before she was standing over him. 'Typing,' she explained, with a stern yet weary intonation, like a constable reciting the caution, 'isn't allowed. Typing,' she added, 'disturbs other readers.' He looked around the empty room. She walked back to her desk.

Janice Hammond had been at St David's Junior High with Laura and Kate. It was only while she was taking her librarian's course, in Topeka, that she turned to evangelism. If Christian dedication was on the retreat in the outside world, things were very different in Bedford County Library: since Hammond had taken over, six years earlier, the Bible Studies section had quietly annexed an extra fifth of the library's shelf space, entirely obliterating several other sections, such as the occult and erotica. In her profession, as in her faith, compromise was not a notion Janice Hammond privately entertained or publicly tolerated.

Daniel sat by his extinguished screen for a few moments. He was about to turn the machine on again to see what form his ejection would take, but hesitated. Both the library and Miss Hammond, he reasoned, were going to be important to him over the coming month. If he couldn't force himself to work for a couple of hours in the library every afternoon, he decided, nothing would ever get done. So he left the small machine where it was and walked out to the office of the *Bedford News*. There, in the stationery shop, he bought two large notebooks and a couple of biros. It was only as he was returning with them that he realised he'd chosen the disposable ballpoints because they would be silent on the paper, unlike a felt-tip or a fountain pen. He came back and wrote out one or two additions to the Gerald Longworth entry from memory, so he could type them in when he got back to the Red Carpet. When he got back to the hotel, he found that he'd not saved Longworth to the hard disk. Both his backup copies were in London. A good start. He began to polish his Jack the Ripper instead. The following day, after much negotiation, Hammond agreed to let him have the laptop on, so he could read his notes from its screen, on condition that he didn't type, and he switched the machine on outside, before he came in. 'Bleeps,' she said – Daniel glanced round the deserted room and stifled an impulse to join in with her, – 'disturb other readers.'

Miss Hammond herself – as he was tempted to point out, but didn't – had a small computer which bleeped, and rattled when she typed, but was only used to search the Interstate database of reference books. They were alone, as usual, when he handed her his list of requests. '*The Divine Marquis: A Life of the Marquis de Sade*,' she read, out loud. '*Evil Genius: The Life and Death of Joseph Goebbels*...*The History of the Hell-Fire Club*...' She looked up at him, about to make a remark, but professional etiquette got the better of her. '*Lord Rochester's Monkey*,' she continued. '*The Life of Nero*...' She wrote the titles on a filing card, then entered them into the computer. 'We have them,' she said, 'all except the Marquis de Sade.' It rhymed with Gatorade. 'They're all in Kansas City. Seventy-two hours,' she added. 'They'll be here.'

He drove back from the library to the Jardines' house on Grant. He found Laura in her mother's garden, wearing gumboots and one of Paul's old check shirts, a shovel in her hand. She was digging over the ground that would house Angela's neat, geometric lines of the more orderly kind of perennial.

'Beer?' he asked her.

'OK.' She put down her shovel and walked towards the car.

'Don't you want to get changed?' he asked her.

'For the Prospect?' she said. 'This isn't Salford you know.'

They sat at one of the small tables by the aquarium. The drone of Westminster debate was punctuated, every few seconds, by Jasper spitting out a mouthful of gravel. Daniel looked at the fish.

'Can you imagine?' he said. 'Day after day, just grubbing around in dirt.'

'You'd be surprised,' Laura said. 'It's not that bad, once you get used to it.'

He laughed. 'I never knew you were so keen on gardening.'

'I wasn't,' she said.

'You know something?' said Laura. 'My mom won't touch soil. She won't *say* soil. She once told me she doesn't really like lawns. I said, "Why?" She said, "I think it's because you can't vacuum them." '

'Bloody hell,' said Daniel. 'What do you mean,' he went on, 'she won't say soil?'

'She just won't. I asked her why once, and she said, "Oh – I just hate it." I said why mom? She said, "Soil – it's like sully, besmirch and stain."'

'When I was seven or eight,' Laura added, 'I remember some workmen came to fix the plumbing, and they lifted the floorboards in the kitchen. And mom – I mean she should never have looked down there, but she was like someone with vertigo on a cliff-edge. She just couldn't help herself. And she looked down and saw the foundations, with all that rough concrete and wood, and the brick debris, and the earth. I went over to look too, but she pulled me away. For years afterwards I used to have nightmares about what there might have been down there. But I think she'd just realised how close she really was to the earth.'

They drove back to the house for dinner. Paul was sitting on the front porch.

'My mom makes him come over a couple of times a week,' Laura said.

'Why?' Daniel asked her.

'Because she worries.'

'What about?'

'Everything.'

As they got out of the car, Paul gave them an over-vigorous wave, like a castaway hailing a passing vessel. They sat at the dinner table and Laura's father said grace, this time concluding with a nervous glance in Daniel's direction.

'It's nice that Laura's helping with the garden,' Angela said to Stewart who didn't reply. Mrs Jardine turned to Daniel.

'You know she never did a great deal in the garden before, did you Laura?'

'No,' said Laura.

And then – prompting a reaction in his fellow diners which, though silent, could hardly have been greater if he had spontaneously levitated – Paul spoke.

'When she was eleven,' he said to Daniel, 'she blew up our shed.'

'What?' said Daniel.

'I found this old chemistry book of my dad's,' Laura said. 'It had this experiment where you mixed ammonia and iodine and let it dry on a piece of blotting paper. And once it was dry it would explode. We found this big bottle of ammonia and we went down to the store and bought a load of iodine, and then we poured it all over this stack of old newspapers in the shed. And we left them to dry, with the door open to let the sun in. And then Kate threw a baseball at it. We blew it to pieces, actually.'

'Why?' Daniel asked.

'I remember I got interested,' she said, 'when I read this one line in the textbook. It said, "Even a fly walking over it will set it off." '

After dinner, Daniel sat out on the back porch with Laura. 'Why did Paul say that?' he asked her.

'I don't know.'

'When was the last time he spoke at the table?'

'God knows,' she said. 'He never says anything. Except, you know, yes or no. When he absolutely has to.'

'So why did he say that?'

'I think he likes you.'

This last remark left Daniel feeling flattered and bewildered. 'Does he have any friends?'

'No,' she said. 'Like I told you, Paul's not like other people.'

'What was he like,' he asked her, 'when he was a boy?'

'Pretty much the same,' she said. 'He's always had this thing of taking expressions – like any saying, or proverb – at face value. When we first arrived in England, I remember sitting on the tube with him, looking at some of the station names, like Shepherd's Bush, and Elephant and Castle.

But Paul still mentioned the strangeness of them two years later, whenever we took the Underground. I told him – it's weird how you don't think of the literal meaning of place names in your own country, every time you hear them. He looked at me as if I was crazy. Then he said, "Are you kidding? What about Buffalo? What about Providence?" '

The next morning Daniel called in on Paul at his makeshift camp. Laura's brother spent most of his time in one large trailer. It housed his collections: a display of brightly-coloured labels from wholesale apple boxes, a few toy cars and dozens of tobacco tins. One corner was filled with broken things he had found and adopted: a cheap porcelain donkey in a sombrero pulling a cracked cart, a smashed electric razor, a crushed kaleidoscope. You never knew quite what was going to catch his eye. He was attracted suddenly and completely by things in the way that a child will go through a period of obsession with a particular animal.

In the months leading up to the birth of his first child, Stewart had prayed for a son. His prayers did not go on, as they might have done, to request that this male child should attend Harvard, distinguish himself as a quarterback and emerge as a roguishly popular figure in his fraternity house before settling down and raising a family. It wasn't that he'd taken these things for granted; he'd assumed that they would be within his sphere of influence.

But Paul, far from fulfilling any of these hopes, had grown into a parody of his projected ambitions. Stewart Jardine could remember turning on a public service radio station one Sunday afternoon, and becoming gripped by a drama about a Bronze Age hunter who had covered the walls of his cave with drawings of a monster that encapsulated his greatest fears, only to find that God brought the beast to life to shame, torment and humiliate him. Laura and Angela, he remembered, found the play hysterical. But he wasn't laughing. He was thinking of Paul.

Even at the height of adolescence, his son showed little interest in human companionship, let alone sex. Paul liked to sit up alone with his music till two or three in the morning. He seemed to look upon the prospect of romantic attachment much as an elderly, traditionally-minded bachelor might respond to an invitation to try his hand at pastrymaking.

He was not, Jardine had to admit, a faggot or a heroin addict, but then at least a homo or a user would have been predictable on occasions. The trouble with Paul was that you never had the slightest idea what he was going to do next. True, he had never done anything dangerous or alarming, even if his idea of a good evening involved sitting around in someone's back yard and letting off a dozen cases of cherry bombs – one of the few sorts of local event Paul might show up at, if anybody told him it was happening. He'd sit apart from the other guys. He wouldn't talk to them, or drink. But in his fondness for dynamite, at least, he was normal.

CHAPTER 17

When Daniel returned to the library to collect his order, Janice Hammond handed his books over with a look of concern and suspicion. It confirmed beyond doubt that she'd been glancing at the contents. He opened *The History of the Hell-Fire Club*. A sensational account by an American author, it described how members of the covert society, which flourished in late-eighteenth-century England, gathered to indulge in a variety of activities including Satanic masses, the rape and sacrifice of virgins and, naturally enough, chronic alcohol abuse. They met in a warren of secret caves, specially constructed in a hill on the estate of Sir Francis Dashwood, at West Wycombe in Buckinghamshire. Daniel, more interested in colour than historical accuracy, prepared an entry for Thomas Potter, one of the society's best known, and least virtuous, members.

'The misdeeds of individual members of the Hell-Fire Club have often been exaggerated,' Daniel wrote, 'though in Potter's case, little embellishment was required. The son of the Archbishop of Canterbury, he squandered the family fortune of half a million pounds on women and drink, and was reputed to have beaten his wife to death. An MP, his leisure interests included the writing and conducting of black masses, and necrophilia.'

He stared out of the window. Outside, he noticed, it was pouring with rain. He somehow found himself briefly pondering the many irksome niceties of etiquette that would be avoided by restricting your romantic attentions to the dead. Then, unsettled by this appalling and surreal line of reflection, he wondered if it was only familiarity of use that made a man named Tom Potter sound so much less evil than the Marquis de Sade. Then he thought about the families in Eastern Circle, the road where he'd grown up in Salford. To the best of his knowledge, nobody in Eastern Circle had ever been a habitual drunk, or stolen anything, or had an affair, let alone conjured up devils. They worked long hours in the cake factory or on the railway. They were tired when they got home, and they had tiny, but perfectly tended lawns. Were they morally better than the decadent upper classes? Or were their moral fault lines disguised by circumstance, in the way that poverty can mask a tendency to meanness with money? Were the Puritans right to believe that the flesh belonged to the devil, and that leisure meant wickedness?

It was coming up to three o'clock, and Daniel felt stifled. He'd have gone for a walk round the building if it hadn't been for the weather. Instead, he got up and, under the watchful eye of Miss Hammond, walked across to the reference shelves. He'd done it in the hope of distraction, but couldn't help noticing an elderly translation of Dante's *Inferno*. He carried it back to desk eleven, and he was reading a passage about Ugolino of Sicily (a possible contender, Daniel thought, if only on the strength of having eaten his own children) when he was distracted by the arrival of another reader.

He had seen the man a couple of times before, sitting on a stool at the Prospect. He was in his late thirties with dark, curly hair, turning white around the temples. He wore high-waisted black cotton trousers with thin grey stripes, which looked like a casual variation on a British lawyer's outfit. He had a crumpled grey linen jacket, a white open-necked shirt and an indigo waistcoat. He had a shabby elegance that caught the eye. But it wasn't his clothes that held Daniel's attention. The stranger picked up a copy of the town newspaper and sat down – not at a numbered seat, as you might have expected, but on one of the individual wooden chairs, five yards or so from Miss Hammond.

The man fumbled in his waistcoat pocket and pulled out a tin of the kind once used for throat lozenges. Daniel's eye rose apprehensively to the 'No Eating' sign. He watched furtively as the man opened the lid and pulled out a small amount of tobacco. He found a packet of papers and began, slowly and painstakingly, to roll a cigarette. By the time he'd placed it between his lips, and taken out a book of matches, Daniel was staring openly. The newcomer was sitting directly below the No Smoking sign.

This must be someone fulfilling a gambling forfeit, he reasoned, and to the man's great good fortune Hammond appeared not to have seen the cigarette. But then he struck a match, and lit it.

Daniel looked on, mesmerised, as the cloud of smoke drifted over towards the librarian. He lowered his eyes and tried to focus his thoughts on the less menacing combustion of the *Inferno*. He listened, but still nothing happened. For a moment he wondered if the man was a ghost, and whether only he could see him, but when he looked up again he saw that the smoke was real enough, and that it had reached Miss Hammond, and enveloped her. It was even making her cough. Daniel looked on with silent rage. Why had he been singled out for such rigid enforcement of the regulations? He was tempted to retaliate by typing, but he didn't. The visitor finished his cigarette, which he ashed in the lid of his tobacco tin, then walked out without speaking.

At five, Daniel left for the Prospect. He sat on a barstool near the door. When he glanced to his left he noticed that the man with the waistcoat was there, just a few feet away at the end of the counter. He was smoking, and he was still holding the newspaper, which was prominently stamped, in red capitals, with the words 'Bedford Library – Not To Be Removed'. Behind him, a supplier was piling up crates of orange juice against the wall. The stranger seemed engrossed in the paper, apparently distracted neither by the delivery, nor by the large yellow root beer sign immediately above his head, that lit up for five seconds every half-minute or so.

Daniel had been planning to ask for a coffee, but when he looked across at the stranger's glass, with its deep gold colour and the delicate strings of carbon dioxide bubbles clinging to its sides, he changed his mind and ordered a Rolling Rock.

Sally served him, and handed a beer to the visiting wholesaler, then wandered down to the end of the bar and stared into the aquarium. Daniel could hear her talking out loud, and quite unselfconsciously, to Jasper.

'How many hours a year,' asked the delivery man, who appeared to know her well, 'do you spend talking to that dumb fish?'

'You know,' she replied, 'he's just as smart as you are. He knows every damned inch of that tank. He knows what time the pump comes on, and he moves over to his feeding ring five minutes before it's time for his flakes.'

The man gave a good-natured snort, offered Sally a dollar for the drink, which she refused, and left.

It was too early for the Westminster cable show, and Sally had tuned the radio to the local country station, which was playing an old bluegrass song. There was something about the tune, and the ferocious Southern accent of the vocalist, who was speaking rather than singing, and who sounded unhinged, that was immediately arresting. Daniel noticed that the three of them – Sally, himself and the reckless smoker – were all listening to it. It was a strident religious anthem, ridiculing the various excuses idle parishioners made to avoid church. One woman, the singer explained, stayed away through fear that the crying of her newborn baby might disturb other worshippers. 'And yet what would you do,' the voice said, 'if the Lord thought fit to reward you by taking away your excuse...'

'Jesus Christ,' said Daniel to Sally. 'What is that?'

She shrugged.

'It's the Louvin Brothers,' said the stranger, looking up from his paper. 'Charles and Ira Louvin,' he added.

'Well,' said Daniel, 'I think they're being a bit harsh there.'

'I couldn't agree more,' said the man. He had a strong local accent, but this last expression, and the way he said it, sounded deeply un-American.

'John used to be a DJ,' said Sally, with a note of pride. Something in the way she spoke also suggested that she assumed Daniel knew who the stranger was. 'Over in Kansas City.'

Daniel's fellow customer got up and shook his hand. He sat down on the next barstool. 'John Oakes,' he said.

'Where are they from?' asked Daniel. 'The Louvin Brothers.'

'Rainesville Alabama,' said Oakes.

'What do you call that music?'

'In those books you read down at the library,' said Oakes, 'they'd probably call it a blend of the High Lonesome Appalachian style with Nashville country. I'd call it mad preaching.'

Sally gave Daniel a second beer he hadn't ordered, and offered one to Oakes, who shook his head. He told Daniel that he'd graduated from high school before Laura left the States, but that he knew her slightly, socially. 'I met her a couple of times ten years ago, when she was on vacation from college over there,' he said. 'I was crazy about her,' he went on. 'We all were.'

To Daniel's surprise, Oakes not only knew, but owned, records by many of the lesser-known artists he'd discovered through Doyle at The Owl – Cheb Khaled, The Alabama Three, Kevin Coyne.

'Why did you leave the radio station?' he asked him.

Oakes paused. 'I wanted to be some use,' he said, at last.

'Where do you work now?'

'Over there.' Oakes gestured across the I-70, towards St David's School.

'With the children,' Daniel asked, 'or the adults?'

'Both,' he replied.

Just as he said this, the root beer sign above Oakes's head lit up again, making him look like a cartoon character who has just had a good idea. Daniel winced at the brightness. Sally turned it off.

As a child, Daniel told Oakes, he used to be fascinated by an advertisement they used to have in the centre of Manchester, near the BBC offices in Piccadilly. Every fifteen seconds the red neon sign would light up, flashing the name of Horlicks.

'It would flash what?' asked Oakes.

'Horlicks. It's a drink.'

'It's malted milk,' Sally said. 'One of those sweet bedtime drinks.'

'My dad,' Daniel went on, 'told me you shouldn't look at it too long, because if you did the sign would turn your head, and you'd wind up thinking about nothing but Horlicks all the time.'

'And did it?' said Oakes.

'I don't know,' said Linnell. 'I never looked at it long enough.'

'Right,' said the stranger, 'so it just affects you now and again. Like now.'

'Can anybody,' Daniel countered, 'smoke in the library?'

Oakes laughed. 'You have to understand,' he said, 'that I can't smoke at work.'

'Yes...' said Daniel, impatiently.

'So Janice allows me...she lets me do that on three conditions. It has to be raining,' he said. 'It has to be at closing time, because she's always empty by then anyway, unless the British are in town. And the third thing is that I have to sit right under the No Smoking sign.'

'Why?'

'So that if anyone did come in, they'd know that she hadn't missed what's going on.'

'Bloody hell,' said Daniel.

Oakes looked at his watch. 'I have to leave,' he said.

'I'm glad we met,' Daniel said, thinking he might have offended him.

'We would have...' Oakes replied. 'We would have met anyhow.' He walked outside and climbed on to a small orange moped. He set off – not, as he should have done, down to the interstate and up to the next exit, but driving at speed, without a helmet, up and over the pedestrian footbridge.

Daniel was about to ask Sally Da Tores to tell him more about this curious figure when Laura and Kate came through the door. The teacher sat closest to him, on the stool the man had just left. He told them about Oakes, and the smoke in the library.

'Yeah,' Kate said, 'well he can do pretty well whatever he likes in there.'

'He said he used to be mad about you,' Daniel told Laura. 'I'm glad he said "was".'

Kate laughed. 'Oh – it's "was",' she said. 'It's "was" OK. You needn't worry,' she added, noticing Daniel looking puzzled. 'He's out of the running.'

'Running?' He turned to Laura. 'Is there still running?' He was joking, but underneath there lurked a germ of torment.

'No, dear,' she said, imitating her mother's voice. 'But if there was, he wouldn't be in it.'

'What do you mean?' he asked. 'Is he dying? Is he gay?'

'Not exactly,' said Laura.

'You could say,' Kate said, 'that he's otherwise engaged.'

'Shall we make him guess?' asked Laura.

'Oh for God's sake...' said Daniel.

'You're getting warm,' said Kate.

'OK, OK...' Laura said. 'He's a priest.'

CHAPTER 18

Daniel was in the library for two or three hours each weekday. One afternoon he was working through a pile of books on the British devil-worshipper Aleister Crowley. He was only a few feet away from the librarian's desk, and for a moment he was gripped by an irrational fear that the squalid cruelty described in its pages would communicate itself, by some kind of ESP, to Hammond. In the case of Crowley, the librarian's obvious reservations about his area of research were ones he could understand, if not share with the same fervour. He opened the book at a chapter which dealt with the headquarters Crowley established in Sicily. In the course of his magical career, he discovered, Aleister Crowley, who was from Leamington Spa, fearlessly crushed the skulls of at least two kittens and fed his acolytes on 'Cakes of Light' made from human faeces.

'Circumstances indicate,' he wrote in his notebook, 'that the intellectual capabilities of a mate weighed more heavily with most men than they ever did with Crowley, who committed sodomy with a range of partners including a goat and two graduates of Trinity College Cambridge.

'Surprisingly for a man who perceived the world through a haze of cannabis, opium, heroin, angelica and cactus-based hallucinogens, Aleister Crowley's favourite recreations included ice-skating and mountaineering.' Aleister Crowley's two major expeditions, to K2 and Kangchenjunga, where four of his fellowclimbers died, were disappointing performances, especially for a man who claimed, as Crowley did, that he was "under the protection of the mountain Gods". Moments after the tragic accident at

Kangchenjunga, Crowley walked calmly down the mountain, apparently heedless of the cries of his stricken companions.'

Edward Alexander Crowley, Daniel discovered, had become seized by a loathing of organised religion at an early age. His parents were zealous members of the Plymouth Brethren, who refused him, amongst other things, any access to toys. It would be hard to quantify, he thought, the degree of human misery that might have been averted if Mr and Mrs Crowley could have eased off a little and bought young Edward a popgun and a set of skittles.

'Whatever the truth of his claims to have raised devils and (more usefully perhaps) to have lit candles without the usual accessories,' Linnell's entry for Crowley went on, 'one aspect of his life was undeniable: he was the focus of a strangely contagious tide of distress, misery and sudden death. Life with Aleister Crowley, a fascist in his faith as in his politics, could be demanding, especially for faithful devotees such as his assistant Victor Neuberg. Neuberg, a hunchbacked poet, was compelled to sleep naked in a gorse hedge at Boleskine, Crowley's house on the banks of Loch Ness, for ten nights in a row, with only the promise of a breakfast Cake of Light to sustain him till dawn. But Neuberg returned again and again to Crowley's various households, undeterred by accommodation and catering facilities which many guests might have deemed unsatisfactory.'

He picked up a book about another Crowley disciple, Raoul Loveday. As Daniel opened the volume, written by Loveday's widow, a leaflet fell out. Cheaply printed on lime-coloured paper, it was inscribed, in large print, with the motto 'Rejoice: He died for you.' Underneath, there was a large Celtic cross and a contact number for an organisation called Soldiers of Christ. Their area code, he noticed to his surprise, was in Bedford, although the book had been sent over from Topeka library. He folded the single sheet and slipped it back in the book. Raoul Loveday, he discovered, died in his twenties – possibly from blood poisoning, as Crowley made him slash his arm with a razor every time he used the word 'I' – possibly from an overdose, as Loveday's wife argued, of 'drugs and cat's blood' prepared for him by the Knight Guardian of the Sacred Flame. Crowley himself died in the fifties, broke, in a boarding house near Hastings, on the English south coast.

'Unable to afford the bulk quantities of opiates which had sustained him in his prime,' Daniel wrote, 'Crowley struggled to maintain his reputation for conspicuous excess by demanding ten to twelve spoonfuls of sugar in every cup of tea, which may be one of the reasons why his landlady, interviewed shortly after his demise, told a newspaper that she had been praying for his death for two years.'

He worked his way through the incremental lewdness of Aleister Crowley's sexual adventures, with Miss Hammond's knee-length tartan skirt and thick, flesh-toned stockings directly within his line of vision. He spent a great deal of time lost in thought, staring straight ahead of him, his eyes cast down to avoid catching the librarian's eye. The position of his desk was such that he would occasionally spend long periods gazing, with a platonic vacancy, at her ankles. But now – just as he was pondering an account of one of Crowley's more uninhibited orgies, and wondering how to condense it into a few lines of light entertainment acceptable to a general reader – the librarian slipped off her left shoe and raised her bare stockinged foot, so as to run the toes up the back of her right calf. It was the first time Daniel had ever seen her do anything like this, so that the effect of the movement on her sole reader was to shock him abruptly back into normal consciousness. She could hardly have shaken him more, he thought, if she had stood up and slowly stripped naked.

What secret passions, he found himself wondering, smouldered in Miss Hammond? Passions, perhaps, that could only be classified in those sections of the Dewey decimal system that she had outlawed from the library.

At which point he caught himself, and realised that this was precisely the sort of reflection he most despised in others; a variation on the low-life reflex that prompted middle-aged stockbrokers, sitting on rush-hour trains on the Central Line, to drool openly over girls younger than their daughters, forced by the men's own selfishness to stand in groups between the two rows of seated suits, strap-hanging. It was what happened, he decided, when you read too much Aleister Crowley.

He was struck by the thought that Crowley – whether he was a pathetic charlatan or, as he professed, a genuine fiend – should be left out of *Who's Who In Hell* altogether. It would be the one thing, he thought, that the small bald man, who signed his letters Six Six Six, would have least appreciated. To submerge yourself in the details of his life was to experience the repellent fascination of sifting through the passenger cabin of an airliner that has crash-landed and festered for two weeks in the heat of a Central American jungle.

*

The crowded rush-hour tube, the wrecked Colombian airplane, and various other unhygienic images were still at the back of Daniel's mind as he walked out of the library at five and headed towards the Prospect. Entering the café, he saw a familiar figure on the end stool of the bar. The man had his back to him and was reading the paper.

'Father,' Daniel called out, in his best American.

Oakes looked round. 'Hey Sal,' he said. 'Another beer.'

Daniel sat down next to him.

'Pardon me,' Oakes said. 'I just don't usually mention my job at first. People run away.'

'Really?' said Daniel.

The priest nodded. 'You would have.'

Daniel shrugged. 'Yeah, OK,' he said. 'I would have.'

Oakes handed him the newspaper. He pointed to an article about an incident in Topeka, where a gang had cut off a young man's ear. There was a large picture of the bandaged victim, who had had his ear sewn back on. Daniel cast an eye over it quickly.

'Anything strike you as strange about that?' Oakes asked.

'In what way?'

'I just think it's surprising,' said Oakes. 'I read this story...it has a thousand words about this guy who hacked off the ear, and all this detail of his part in a gang rape in Denver eight years ago, and his crack dependency; half a page about the man who hacked this ear off...which must have taken all of two seconds...'

'Yes?' interrupted Sally.

'And they haven't even put the name of the person who sewed it back on.'

Sally tossed a carving knife into the dishwasher behind the bar, kicked it shut with her foot, and pressed the start button. 'That ain't news,' she said.

'All I'm saying,' Oakes said, 'is that in the newspapers, God and evil are the new taboos.'

'You're preaching, Reverend,' said Daniel.

'I do do that,' said Oakes. 'If you notice it again, stop me. But only if you notice.'

'Let me ask you something,' Daniel said. 'Why did you say we would have met anyway?'

'Because Janice Hammond,' Oakes said, 'is not at all happy about all those books you're ordering. She asked me to talk to you. She told me she prays for your soul. She keeps asking me if I'll pray for you too.'

'And do you?'

Oakes didn't reply. He picked up a half-smoked cigarette from the ashtray and re-lit it. 'What are you up to in there anyway?' he asked.

'Where?'

'In the library.'

Daniel told him.

'While we're on the subject,' he said, 'do you have any ideas about people I might have missed?'

'I believe that my role here,' said the Reverend of St David's, 'is to tell you that if I was you I wouldn't write that book. And to remind you of a rather powerful phrase which you will know as a line from a song by REM: "Judge Not Lest Ye Yourself Be Judged." '

The thought disturbed Daniel, despite himself. He didn't know what to make of Oakes who, Laura had told him, had been out with Kate in his secular days. 'I guess from what you've said,' Daniel had told her, 'that he's not the only man in Bedford who can say that.'

'No,' she said. 'But you know what? She told me he was the best lover she ever had.'

He only ever saw the priest in the bar in the afternoon, and Oakes never had more than one drink in a visit. But he drank beer straight from the bottle, not in a glass, which, Daniel told him, he found slightly shocking in a man of God.

'You know, since you are doing this,' Oakes said, 'you might do worse than to think about Robert Johnson.' He looked at Daniel for some sign of recognition, and didn't find any. 'You know,' he went on, 'who Robert Johnson was, I suppose...'

'He wrote "Love in Vain".'

Oakes nodded. 'But other themes recur in his work. Like he also wrote "Hellhound on My Trail". And he also wrote "Me and the Devil Blues". And he died when he was twenty-seven.'

'How?'

'Stabbed. Or poisoned. Or ritually sacrificed. Like many things in life,' he added, 'it depends on who you choose to believe. There's a book on him by this guy called somebody Finn who played blues harp for Muddy Waters. He says Johnson...' He paused, and pressed his lips together tightly. 'He says Robert Johnson sold his soul to the devil in exchange for his gift.'

'What do you think about that?'

'I think it's most likely nonsense,' said the priest. 'I don't go for that stuff.'

'Isn't that stuff your living?' Daniel asked him.

'Well... ' said Oakes. 'I'm just telling you I'm not convinced that those things happen. If they do, I don't believe they'd happen fast. I think they would be slow. It wouldn't be a sudden vow; it'd be a creeping...it'd be...insidious. It would be a kind of gradual consent.'

'Like with Hitler,' said Daniel.

'You know in my sermons,' Oakes said, 'I sometimes use this line from a songwriter called The Jazz Butcher. You know him?'

Daniel shook his head.

'Well you should do: he's British I believe. It goes: "One day I met the devil, he was sitting in a bar; he bought me sixteen rum and cokes and then he went too far." I guess that's what I mean. Gradual consent.' He paused. 'But there's no doubt that some of those old blues musicians, of Robert Johnson's generation, that they still believed in voodoo.'

'And?' Daniel asked.

'Look,' said Oakes. 'You see me here. And when I'm here, and when I'm walking around town, I don't usually come out with my breviary. Not every priest does. I still like to have a beer in the afternoon. But I am a priest. I comfort the living. I bury the dead. I believe in the existence of evil, and I believe in salvation through Jesus Christ. And I don't believe in voodoo.' He looked up at Daniel. 'Even if I think I agree with them that there are certain things you would be well advised not to mess with. It's like what I told you; it's like the Spanish say: *Menus Mal*. Be on the safe side. There's a line in that book on Robert Johnson I've never forgotten. It says: "Magic looks exactly like reality – only the effect is different." '

Daniel looked at Oakes, not understanding exactly what he meant. 'Anyone else?' he asked. Oakes smiled, and shook his head.

Daniel's schooling had given him a thorough grounding in hell-fire Puritanism but, like most of his generation, he had lately developed a revulsion at orthodox Christianity. It was this last reaction that the priest had somehow managed to circumvent. He told Oakes how, the first time he set eyes on him in the library, he felt a sudden fear that he was no more real than the ghostly hitchhiker on the I-70.

'You know, when the good old boys off the farms come in to church at Easter,' Oakes said, 'I use this story about a hitchhiker, who's in such a

:sperate hurry to get to the destination on the cardboard sign he holds up
at he's forgotten what it is. He just holds the board up anyhow, without
'er looking at it. Guys stop, and they look at it, and they say, "Oh, yeah,
imb in – that's in Illinois, or that's in Montana, or North Dakota." Then
: goes off with them. They all pick him up, but he can never find the
ace.

'And finally this old guy stops for him in a beat-up Dodge Shadow and
: says, "Young man"' – Oakes's voice took on the exaggerated Southern
iety of the Louvin Brothers – ' "there ain't no place of that name on any
ate map."

'The young man stops, and he says, "Yeah – but people always pull
ver, like you did. And they pick me up, like you did." And the old guy
ys, "Yes, that's right son: put your thumb out often enough and you'll get
iere." And he turns over the board and it says "Perdition".'

'Just how exactly did you become a priest?' Daniel asked him.

'There was one guy on the radio station,' Oakes said. 'I'd known him
or years; he used to be a screenwriter – a very successful one – and then
e came across these Methodists and he got born again...he got to be very
tense. He did the religious show on a Sunday morning. I was talking to
im...he was called Bill Phythian and he used to have this live programme
alled *My Favorite Things* very late on a Wednesday night. These minor
elebrities would go on the show and...he'd have this tacky routine where
e'd ask them to list their belongings. Usually it would be like, The Lone
anger's stunt man's understudy, people like that. And this week the guy
idn't show up. I was in the station getting my show ready and Bill burst
i, in a panic, and asked me to go on his programme. Then at the end of
ie show he asked me – this was always his last question – what three
iings would you ask for, if you could be sure nobody would ever find out.
ike we used to say round the station, if you'd ever seen his listener figures
nd you had something to say that you wanted nobody else to hear, then
ou'd know Bill's late-night Wednesday show was as good a place as any
o say it...'

'So he asked me what I'd want and I said, "Well, Bill, I'd like the
omplete bootlegged recordings of the Bob Dylan 1966 World Tour..."'

'I've got those,' Daniel interrupted, in a way that sounded, he realised
oo late, both boastful and tremendously stupid.

'Second,' Oakes said, 'I said I'd ask for a unique and captivating
voman. OK,' the priest added, 'before you say anything – you've got that

too. I know that. And then I said, "Oh, yeah, well – if this is *really* private Bill – I'd ask for eternal redemption.'

'As a joke?' Daniel asked.

'As a joke,' Oakes replied. 'And that was that. Then about a month later I passed this terrible wreck on the Interstate. The guy died in my arms. And the last thing he said was, "Please Lord, don't let me die this way."

'This was not a man of God,' he added. 'The last time I'd seen him, he was in the jailhouse. I gave a police statement. It was only when I was driving home that I realised I was still covered in his blood. And I started to think...if I was in that position – I mean if I was lying there, alone, on the highway, confronting my own death, I would be, literally, goddam terrified. And the truth is that is exactly what I'd ask for. Not last, but first. We all would. You know why? Because it might not be three wishes. It might be one. It's like I say about Robert Johnson, *Menus Mal*. That phrase also means less evil.'

Daniel looked at him, astonished.

He was trying to think of a reply when he saw Laura coming through the door. It was Sally who spoke next.

'What do you think of the rest of us?' she asked Oakes. 'What do you think of us poor damned sinners?'

'I think you're like Jasper,' he told her. 'You know how the light works. You know every inch of your tank. You know what time the flakes appear. You know where the food comes from.'

'It comes from the big pink hand, right?' Laura said.

Oakes laughed.

'Do you miss anything?' Daniel asked him.

'I could use more money,' Oakes said. 'I was born in Melbourne Australia. My mom's still out there, down on Marine Parade in St Kilda. I get over to see her once a year, and I have to borrow the air fare from my sister, or I have to go to the bishop, and beg. And I miss...well. I miss. I miss what you'd miss.'

He packed up his smoking materials and headed for the door, then stopped. 'I really shouldn't be telling you this,' the priest said. 'But you could make a very good case for Saint Ignatius of Loyola.'

'Saint who?' asked Daniel.

'He founded the Jesuit movement,' said Oakes. 'And he sort of pioneered the Inquisition. If I remember rightly he killed a coupla guys.'

It was hard to believe, Daniel said, that Oakes had dedicated himself to the same discipline that so preoccupied Janice Hammond.

'Oh well, you know...the thing is, I'm still kind of interested in life too, you know. I mean Janice...Janice's kinda...her life is ordered. She saw the light and now...what can I tell you? With Janice, now, it's Horlicks all the time.'

CHAPTER 19

No life, of course, is quite so serene as it appears. At family weddings or at Stewart's work reunions, Angela Jardine would occasionally drink too much Napa Valley champagne, take to the dance floor without her husband, and jitterbug with a feverish determination that discomforted her friends and horrified Jardine, who knew that such moments, though rare, hinted at some other life she could have had.

As for Stewart Jardine, Daniel knew, because Laura had told him, that at night, if he was disturbed by an unfamiliar noise – it usually happened when Angela's breathing changed, through some shift in movement – he would begin to dig frantically, like a dog, into the mattress. He would carry on digging, even after the bedside light was on and his eyes were open, until his wife had woken him fully and soothed him to sleep again. It was a legacy of that day in the Chorwon Valley, south of Pyongyang, where he'd saved himself by burrowing down into the undergrowth. More than once Daniel had looked at Stewart across the dinner table and wondered whether a man who had seen his best friend die in his arms and carried his decomposing body for miles over difficult terrain, could really be quite so appalled by the thought of cannabis, ecstasy or pre-marital sex.

There was only one night of the year on which Mr Jardine might publicly relax his self-discipline. The local veterans' dinner, at the Elks Club, was the sole occasion when Stewart – anticipating sustained reminiscence with his more gregarious companions – would not drive himself home. This year, as every year, Angela pressed her husband's suit and drove him the half-mile to the function.

She waited up, thinking he might ring to ask her to collect him, but then heard him return at half midnight, when Hubert Porter, who'd driven Stewart home, rolled his pickup gently into Mr Jardine's Lincoln Continental, denting the stationary car's rear fender. The collision woke Laura, who went to her window and watched her father climb slowly down from the cab of his friend's vehicle and, without inspecting the damage, walk unsteadily to his front door.

Angela heard him struggling to get his key in the lock. She didn't go to help, for the sake of his pride. Porter's car drove off. The door opened. Stewart came in, holding a brown paper parcel.

He sat down at the kitchen table without speaking, opened the package and tipped out its contents. There was a card signed by the veterans' association, and a large pile of dollar bills, the members' collection for Rita Preston. Stewart counted the money out loud – five hundred and eighteen dollars – then went to the dresser. He took out a padded envelope that he'd already addressed to the widow in Sarasota. He opened the envelope, put in the money and the greetings card and then, slowly and deliberately, sealed it. He took a ten-dollar bill and a registered letter form out of his own jacket pocket, then placed them next to the package on a small table in the hall, ready to be mailed the next morning. He went to the small drinks cabinet in the living room, poured himself a glass of Scotch whisky from a dusty bottle, and went out to sit on the back porch.

Angela made a pot of coffee and put it on a tray with two cups. When she got outside on the porch, she was surprised to see that his whisky glass was already empty. He sat with his eyes closed, and his fists clenched.

'Stewart?' she said. He opened his eyes. She put the coffee cup on the arm of his chair.

'Do you know Jeff Reynolds?' he asked her.

'Young Mr Reynolds,' she said. 'The man with the jeweller's shop.'

'For a quarter of an hour tonight,' he said, 'I listened to Jeff Reynolds talking about his son's next semester at Yale. James Harding told me about his boy's fraternity initiation. Pat Lomas's kid is getting married next month.'

She sat down next to him.

'The only chance Paul will ever have of mixing with those young men,' he went on, 'is after some function, when they fall down dead drunk, and they need a guy to push their gurney down to the trauma room.' He sat back, knocking the cup on to the decking of the porch, where it broke cleanly into two pieces.

He leaned over to pick them up, and came face to face with Laura, who'd come down, in bare feet and a robe, for a bottle of water from the fridge. She was kneeling, and she already had the broken cup in her hand. Neither spoke. Laura went back into the kitchen, threw the broken cup in the bin, and went back upstairs.

'I was just coming back with Hubert Porter,' he told his wife. 'He said, "Isn't it wonderful that Laura's back home?" I said, "Oh – why?" He said because when they come home, that's when you remember the child in them. Their first church service. The day they learned to ride a bike.'

'And what did you say, dear?'

'I didn't say anything,' he told her, 'because all I could think of was that time I walked in on her with the black boy in the vestibule. I came down the stairs...'

Angela had her eyes shut and she stayed like that, frozen. He never talked like this.

'And I saw him lying there, face down on the floor. I can remember thinking, oh – he's had an accident. I won't touch him: the way he looks, it could be electrocution. Then I saw her under him. She looked up and she just stared at me. She didn't move, except she put her hand on the back of the boy's head, to stop him looking round and seeing me. She stared up at me with this cold look in her eyes. I said "I came down for a glass of water" and I went back up the stairs. It was like she was the adult,' he said, 'and I was the child.'

Angela helped him upstairs. Then she called Paul, to ask him to come round the next day to pick up the damaged car.

The following morning was the first Mrs Jardine could remember when her husband hadn't got up at seven. He was still asleep at ten, when Paul came to collect the car and took Rita Preston's package down to the post office.

Just after he'd left, Laura got up and woke Daniel at the Red Carpet.

'How is it there?' he said.

'Oh, it's fine,' she told him. 'The war hero got smashed last night and wrecked the car. Paul's taken it off to fix it.'

'So where's your dad now?' Daniel asked.

'He's still in bed with a hangover. We're almost getting on.'

Daniel set off for the library; Laura returned alone to her parents' house. She followed the Lincoln up the drive, with the dent beaten out of the fender and Paul at the wheel. He'd brought the metal fixings for a new garden bench his father was assembling at the end of the garden.

'Thanks, son,' Jardine said, as Paul handed him the brackets. Laura stared at her father; in twenty years she'd never heard him address her brother in this way.

Angela Jardine had planned to talk further to her husband about what he'd told her the night before but, although they were alone for most of the afternoon, the moment never came.

Collecting his latest set of books from Miss Hammond, Daniel noticed that he was almost as embarrassed at the prospect of receiving his order as the librarian was in dispensing it. This new delivery consisted mostly of works by General J.F.C. Fuller, Satanist and tank theoretician, who was Aleister Crowley's first important disciple. Crowley himself had never shrunk from situations of conflict – whether he was fearlessly executing a domestic cat, sinking his specially filed canines into the forearm of an unaccompanied young woman, or crucifying a frog in Detroit – yet he showed no appetite for orthodox military action. Fuller was another matter. After he wearied of celebrating the sleazy magus in the years leading up to the First World War, he embarked on a spectacularly successful army career.

'Working alongside such memorably named officers as Captain F.E. "Boots" Hotblack and Captain 'Slosher' Gifford le Q. Martel,' Daniel wrote, 'Fuller, more than any other single military tactician, was responsible for developing the tank as a means of expanding the swiftness and scale of battlefield slaughter. He ridiculed its victims, especially those suffering from shell-shock, as malingerers "peddling the so-called realities of war". '

On the desk space opposite him, he noticed there was a Gideon Bible; placed there, he was sure, by Hammond. She'd looked upon him with pity at first. Now, after almost a month of his depraved orders, she had come to view him with real dread, a little like a bank clerk who has spent weeks humouring a child who threatens her with an imitation gun, only to discover the weapon is real. He guessed that – fearing for her own salvation – she must have stopped reading his material. If she hadn't, she might have been slightly reassured by the writings of Fuller. His first job as a junior officer in the Ministry of Defence, he read, had been to draw up plans to forcibly march every sheep in Sussex, Kent and Surrey to Salisbury in the event of a German invasion.

By the time he was engaged in this vital mission, Fuller would have qualified for Daniel's almanac on the grounds of his support for Aleister Crowley alone. The son of the rector of Itchenor, near Chichester, he developed a pronounced hatred of the Church, a sentiment that colours 'The Star in the West', his lengthy eulogy to Crowley.

'He cursed the name of Christ,' Fuller wrote admiringly, 'and strode on to seek the gates of hell.' In one biography, Linnell came across a letter from Crowley to Fuller, written in 1908, in which the Beast complains that 'You must be careful – you left a devil behind you last Sunday that came within an ace of killing me. It had a sharp pointed beak (curved), no eyes, no arms or wings, no legs, but a single, tapering tail, balanced on a rounded piece of its own excrement. For some minutes I really thought it was all over for me.'

Fuller went on to be a keen and prominent member of the British Union of Fascists and would have been Defence Minister for the British Nazi Oswald Mosley, had he come to power. 'He once pronounced, with great pride,' Daniel wrote, 'that "all foreigners are niggers to the English".'

He sat with Laura at a table in the Prospect early that evening.

'How's your dad's car?' he asked her.

'You know how Paul's so clumsy, and his balance is so terrible?' she said. 'And yet he's got these tremendous abilities. He can take that car to bits, and put it back together again, without ever looking at the manual.

'When we were playing Oliver,' she said, 'we used to call him enterprising, courageous, masterful. And yet I've always had this feeling that Paul's trouble with this country – no, let's be fair...with this planet – is that it doesn't have room for that one very unusual job, that would suddenly engage all of his interests at once.'

For three weeks after he'd arrived in Bedford, Daniel successfully resisted Angela Jardine's occasional attempts to get him to join her and Jardine for dinner alone. But then Laura arranged to see Kate for dinner in town one night, and her mother knew about it. Daniel could see no option but to forgo the evening programme he would have preferred, sitting in his hotel room, drinking tea and watching Bette Davis films on the cable stations. At least Angela had said that Paul would be eating with them. He agreed to drive over.

Laura was meeting Kate a few blocks away, at Dorothy's. There were no restaurants in Bedford, only diners, and Dorothy's, with its bright lights, gingham tablecloths and twenty-two-ounce steaks, was the most expensive. It was right in the centre of town, on Third and Main, but there were people who had lived in Bedford for twenty years and only been there once, as a treat. Many of those seated at its tables spoke in hushed tones, like penitents in a cathedral.

'You know you could always come with us if you like,' said Laura, when he told her about his plan for the evening. Daniel shook his head. They were in the Prospect; he watched her as she walked down the bar and used the payphone to call Kate, tucking her thumb into the waistband of her jeans. A vague memory of a song came into his mind. He felt himself overcome with a feeling of great warmth for her. When she came back, he put the car keys on the table in front of her and, when she reached out to pick them up to leave for the diner, he took her hand. 'I like it here,' he told her, 'you know that?'

When Kate and Laura sat down, other conversations in Dorothy's were even more muted than usual, as their fellow diners strained to catch the exchanges between these two young women: women who took lovers; women who had been abroad.

For those at nearby tables, the conversation was initially unrewarding.

'I showed the senior class *Sabotage* today,' Kate told Laura. 'You know why I like Hitchcock's films? Because he's obsessed with hands. I love those black and white close-ups of hands. I love hands.'

'Why?' asked Laura. 'I mean there's really only two kinds, right? The ones with the long thin fingers. And the ones with small fat...'

Kate lifted up her own plump hands, with their short, bloated-looking fingers. 'Well, I like those thin hands you were talking about,' she said. 'Even if some of them do belong to brutes. You never know who's going to get them.'

Laura laughed.

'How's he doing at the Red Carpet?' Kate asked.

'The other day he was round at mom's house and I saw him touch a radiator, to earth himself.'

'OK,' said Kate. 'It sounds like he's settling in. I remember one Christmas when I was a kid, Rick Wiseman staggering towards me across the bar, holding up a sprig of mistletoe. I didn't know then what I know

now, otherwise I'd have recognised the walk of a man who was so loaded he'd forgotten to touch Nixon. When he kissed me, I got this static belt. I thought my lips were going to fry like sliced squid.'

'You'd have thought,' said Laura, 'that that might have put you off. You seem to have gotten over it pretty well.'

'Are you crazy?' said Kate. 'It was my kind of kiss. I fell in love.'

Laura snorted into her margarita.

'Anyway,' said Kate, 'you can talk. I've seen you do it, don't forget. I've seen you let these guys pick you up and cherish you, like one of those street kids in Brazil that finds a radioactive crystal on a garbage dump. They take you home,' she said, 'and they think that you're special. And you are,' she added. 'And they just sit there. Glowing. And a week later, they're gone.'

Laura laughed again, but then stopped herself.

'The thing you forget,' Kate said, watching her, 'is that I know you at least as well as you know yourself. And I know when you're getting ready to hang that Closed sign up on your door.'

Laura looked back at her friend. That was Kate's attraction; she was an unusual combination of gentle and direct. Laura hadn't exactly grown apart from her since she'd been living in England and yet, meeting her this time, she found herself resenting something in Kate's character. It was hard to describe exactly, but it had to do with her friend's ability to look very honest whatever the circumstances.

'Remember that Thanksgiving party in Salina?' Laura asked. Kate had got drunk and taken so much cocaine that she'd ended the evening wired to a heart monitor in the emergency room. 'How old were we?'

'Twenty,' said Kate.

'You still do a lot of that?' asked Laura, who had had a brief flirtation with amphetamines at around this time.

'Coke? Oh...you know. Christmas and Fridays. Schoolteachers can't do coke.'

'The criminality,' said Laura.

'The price,' said Kate.

It was fortunate, Laura added, with a tone of sceptical congratulation, that Kate, unlike several of their contemporaries, had never acquired a taste for the hypodermic. Her friend pulled up the sleeve of her cotton top, revealing her unblemished arm.

'Happy now?' she said. 'My mom had that polio shot in her arm, and she hated the idea that thousands of strangers could see her scar, so when it was my turn she made them give it to me in my ass.'

'If only she'd known,' said Laura.

Kate pulled a face.

'In England,' Laura said, 'I once heard this parody of Humphrey Bogart. This guy's walking home after a night of passion and he asks his friend: "What shall I tell my wife – 'Darling, I've been beaten up again?' Let's face it, she's credulous as hell." '

'You know what?' said Kate. 'It's not that bad. Because deep down, they always know. They always know you're cheating, but they blind themselves to it by familiarity, like you say you don't notice that fucking soldier standing to attention in your lobby.'

'Except in Bob's case...' said Laura, 'it's not a soldier he doesn't notice. It's a platoon.'

'What's your problem anyhow? You joined the church?'

'Yes,' Laura said 'Well this one's different. I like this one.'

'Well,' said Kate, 'I think you might be right. I like him. But you know what? You never shake off that thing. That thing comes back.'

'Like coke?'

'Like athlete's foot.'

'No,' said Laura, shaking her head. 'No.'

'Yeah,' said Kate, rapping her knuckle against the metal table. 'Well, like they say at the Red Carpet, knock on wood.'

Towards the end of an evening of glowering disapproval from Stewart Jardine and unbroken silence from Paul, Daniel escaped from the dinner table on the pretext of helping Angela wash up. From his position by the sink, with a tea towel in his hand, he could see Jardine through the serving hatch, sitting at the dinner table with his son. The phone rang. Jardine took the call. Daniel watched him, hoping it was Laura asking if he'd go down to join her at Dorothy's. But he knew in an instant, from Stewart's effusive manner, that the caller couldn't be his daughter. Then his tone changed. He replaced the receiver and sat down next to Paul, looking agitated.

'Who was it?' called Angela, who had her back to the hatch.

'Rita Preston,' Jardine said. 'She was calling about the collection money.'

'Oh, that's nice,' Angela said. 'Was she pleased?'

'Not really,' Jardine replied. 'It never reached her.' He turned to his son.

'That money,' he asked Paul. 'Did you mail it?'

Daniel remained where he was, looking through the hatch, holding a damp tea towel to his chest. Paul didn't respond; he stared down at his shoes.

'You didn't send it,' Jardine continued, 'did you?'

Still looking at the floor, Paul shook his head.

Jardine raised his hand. He'd intended the blow to be firm but controlled, yet once his arm was in the air, twenty years of pent-up anger rose in him and he struck Paul with his full force, using the flat palm of his right hand. The heavy ring on his middle finger cut a half-inch gash across the top of his son's ear. Paul still said nothing and kept his eyes down. Blood ran down the side of his face and dripped off his jaw on to the collar of his white short-sleeved shirt. Jardine drew his arm back again, this time making a fist. Daniel went to step into the sitting room but Angela blocked his path, standing in the kitchen doorway facing him, her hands pressed so hard against the door frame that her shoulders visibly trembled.

Mr Jardine lowered his arm, then said quietly, 'Can't you do one damn thing right?'

Angela took Paul upstairs and staunched the wound. When he came back down with her, his expression betrayed no emotion.

'Go home Paul,' his mother told him.

''Bye, Daniel,' he said.

Daniel walked out alone to the end of the garden and lit a cigarette, sitting on the new bench which Stewart Jardine had assembled using Paul's metalwork, then placed among Angela's neat rows of gardenias and dwarf pines. When Daniel heard Laura's car pull into the drive, he walked down and got in before she could get out and approach the house.

'How did it go?' she asked. She noticed his expression and, glancing up, saw her mother, looking distraught, on the front porch. 'Oh,' she said.

She pulled away and took the I-70 in the direction of the Red Carpet. He told her what had happened, anticipating a furious reaction which never came. Anger was her father's emotion, that she met, and provoked, with infuriating calm. Anger for Laura was a kind of defeat.

'What the fuck did Paul do with the money?' Daniel asked. 'Did he steal it?'

'No,' she said.

'How do you know?'

'Because he never stole anything.'

'What then?'

'Don't ask me,' she said. 'Ask him.'

She turned the Buick around; as they pulled into the dirt road that led down to Paul's camp, they could hear music, though his group of sheds was in darkness. They drew up next to his car. He was sitting in the passenger seat, with the engine off and, to judge by the ambient noise and vibration, the powerful stereo turned up its full force. Laura opened the driver's door and climbed in, briefly releasing a howl of decibels.

Daniel walked over to Paul's main trailer and sat down inside. He turned on the desk lamp. Outside, he heard the noise subside. He looked at the objects around him. There was a small grey plastic horse and an empty tin of shotgun lubricant. One wall was decorated with a yellow poster advertising a brand of ice cream. On the cluttered window ledge, he saw a novelty bottle in the shape of a St Bernard. The whole dog, not just the transparent barrel around its neck, was filled with brandy. The seal was unbroken. It looked cheap and very old. Sediment had formed in its paws; the alcohol had clouded slightly.

The door opened. Laura came in, followed by her brother.

'Hi Daniel,' he said, as if nothing had happened. He was still in the white shirt. It was heavily bloodstained. Paul went over to a tea-chest in the corner and pulled out Mr Jardine's padded envelope, with the registered package form lightly taped to it.

'I'll mail it tomorrow, OK Paul?' she said.

'OK Laura.'

As they were leaving, Daniel pointed out the St Bernard. 'Where did you get it?' he asked.

'Yard sale,' said Paul.

'Did you never think of drinking it?'

'I never felt that low,' said Paul.

'Let's hope it always stays in its bottle,' Daniel said.

'Yeah,' said Paul, as if he wasn't really listening.

Daniel and Laura went back to the Red Carpet, where they sat together at a table in the bar.

'OK,' he asked her. 'What happened?'

'He went to the post office counter in Kaufman's store with ten dollars they'd given him to mail the package,' she said. 'But when he was walking through the store, he saw this trade poster they had in there, advertising some chocolate bar.'

'Ice cream,' said Daniel.

'Ice cream. He said they asked him for fifteen dollars for the poster – they get sent these things for nothing for fuck's sake – and he'd only got five dollars of his own. So he bought it with his dad's postage money. Then Paul said that, as he was leaving with the picture, he heard Kaufman turn to his wife and say, "More money than sense." He said they both burst out laughing. He came home, he hid the parcel, and he said he's not been in there since.'

'Why?' said Daniel. 'Why did he hide the parcel?'

'Like I told you,' she said. 'The easiest route at the time. That's how he deals with the world.'

'Will you stay?' he asked her.

'No,' she said. 'Because if I stay tonight, I'll stay every night.'

'And?'

'And that will drive my mom insane. And I believe we agreed that was never the plan. My father…' she stopped, and swallowed. 'When he came in wasted the other night I heard him say the only way Paul will ever rub shoulders with smart NYU graduates is if he's working as a porter pushing a medical trolley.'

There were tears running down her face. He put his arm round her and she pressed her face against his chest.

'And the son of a bitch might be right,' she said. 'But Paul's none the worse for that.'

They took the I-70 down to Salina. It was midnight and there was a country station playing on the radio. Laura drove. He sat next to her and smoked cigarettes. He loved the brand names, like Kent and, in their blood-red pack, the daunting Lucky Filters. Where he grew up, he thought, you didn't have Kent and Lucky Filters. You didn't even have brand names. You had a make. They only had a week before they went back to London. For all the difficulties he'd had here, he didn't want to go.

'You know what?' he said. 'I think he could have killed Paul tonight.'

'I told you about his temper,' she said.

On the radio, a woman whose voice had a sensual, abrasive quality, was singing a lament addressed to a young suicide. 'See what you lost when you left this world,' it went. 'This sweet old world. The sound of a midnight train. Wearing someone's ring. Someone calling your name...'

He wasn't sure what did it – the night air and the distant lights of the airfield, her laryngeal delivery, or the curious power of these simple images – but whatever it was, as he listened, a shiver ran down his spine.

He looked at Laura and noticed a faint trace of eye-liner that had smudged over the lower lid of her right eye. He'd never noticed her wearing it before. Probably she always did. It was extraordinary, he thought, the obviousness of the things that you could be blind to. They were leaving the lights of Salina behind them, and he thought that he'd never been so much in love. He drew breath to tell her so. Just as he was about to speak they drew up at a set of lights behind an elderly silver pickup with Arizona state plates. Riding in the uncovered back of the truck were five or six Latino kids. Two of them, a young couple, were having a furious row. He was close enough to see that the girl, who couldn't have been more than fourteen, had two teardrops tattooed on her left cheek. The young man was screaming at her, his gestures so violent that he might have been having a fit. He was out of control, hovering on the borderline between brutal language and physical attack. Daniel stared at the hysterical figure, struck by the realisation that, if the boy started to beat her up, he'd have to get out and that, when he did, he'd get shot. Another of the youths, who was sitting with a leg dangling over the offside rear brake light, saw Daniel staring and spat on to the windscreen of the Buick. The lights changed and the truck made an illegal left turn at speed. Laura shifted gently into gear and steered the big car straight on up the road.

It was curious, he said, that a girl should choose the image of a teardrop for a tattoo.

'Two teardrops,' Laura said, 'means that she's killed two guys. It's a gang symbol.'

He put his left hand on the back of her seat and looked up at the night sky. Distracted, he neglected to mention the thing that, a minute earlier, he had been burning to say.

As they came back in to Bedford, the roadside posts flashed past like white-clad sentries standing between them and the dark. In the wheat fields beyond, he began to see alarming shapes. He asked Laura why Lucy had reacted so strangely when he'd mentioned the ghost of the I-70.

'Has she seen it?'

'In a manner of speaking,' she replied.

The receptionist's induction into the mysteries of passion, Laura explained, had taken place one Friday night when Lucy was sixteen, on a dirt track just off the Interstate. She'd been helping out at the Red Carpet bar, where Joe Carr, a local combine driver, had been drinking Red Beer – a mixture of lager and grenadine, which was popular across the state – and scaring her with stories about the ghostly figure that hitched rides from drivers. Carr told her how the phantom was usually sighted on the short stretch of the Interstate she used on the way back home.

Around midnight, Lucy got into her car and turned on to the I-70 to drive the couple of miles west to her mother's. She'd just made the right turn on to the main road when she looked into the driver's mirror and saw a pair of eyes staring back at her. Carr had left the bar half an hour before she did and he'd hidden in the back seat. He had risen up silently once the wheels started to turn. After the initial shock of seeing his reflection, Lucy told Laura, she remembered experiencing a moment of tremendous relief, when she realised that Carr was really there and not a ghost. This respite was short-lived. Since he was not a spectre, but a fellow human being with a warm, beating heart of flesh and blood, he held a knife to her throat and made her turn off on to the track, where he forced her out of the car and raped her in a wheat field.

'She told me,' Laura said, 'that on his breath, she could smell that sweet fruit syrup she'd stirred into the cheap beer she'd served him. And she said that afterwards, he made her drive him four miles back down the road to his trailer.'

'When was that?' he asked.

'Nine, maybe ten years ago.'

'Didn't she go to the police?'

'He'd threatened her, you know, and she was five years too young to be working in a bar anyhow.'

In the end, Laura explained, Lucy had done nothing. The following year she got her own place, a small trailer close to the Red Carpet. In the back yard, she set up a number of wire-fenced pens, where she looked after rabbits and birds that had been injured and found on the road. It was only five years after the attack, when Joe Carr died on the Interstate, drunk, in a wreck on his way back from a party in Topeka, that she told anybody what he'd done to her. Word got around. And that was how Lucy had gained that most unenviable of local reputations, as a woman with a heart of gold and a victim's face.

Laura drove him back to the Red Carpet. 'That girl made me think of my mom,' she said, just as he was about to get out.

'What?'

'That girl on the truck. She made me think of what you told me happened between mom, and her husband and Paul just now,' she said.

'Why?'

'Because I was thinking it's amazing what some people will settle for.'

'Your mother can't say soil,' he said. 'And you can't quite say Dad.'

'You noticed that, huh.'

Daniel held her, then walked into the hotel alone.

It was 1.30 a.m., but Lucy was still behind the bar. He was on his stool by the time he noticed the other customer at his side, Lucy's boyfriend, Tom Karlin. A tall, thin-faced man with wiry fair hair, Tom was in his early forties, fifteen years older than the barmaid. His surname, he told Daniel, came from the French. 'My mom,' he said, 'told me it means Lion-Heart.' Looking at Tom's narrow brow and his tight, small mouth, Daniel thought, it made you wonder if the Victorian phrenologists, who believed they could discern a criminal nature from the shape and features of the skull, might not have been so crazy after all. God knows what Lucy saw in him.

Looking at her, as she talked to the Lionheart across the bar, Daniel thought of one of those plump, soft-eyed wildebeests that appear in wildlife documentaries; one of the young, weaker animals on the edge of the herd which, the viewer realises, will prove too sluggish to prevent a set of predatory claws from sinking into its flanks.

If the atmosphere around the Jardine dinner table made those late-night drinks with Lucy seem like an ecstatic celebration of release, Daniel had learned not to speak freely when there were other customers at the Red Carpet bar. It was the same, come to that, everywhere in Bedford. It is a cliché sometimes misapplied to small town life, but here everybody really did know everyone else. With Karlin, he found himself weighing each word like a politician, assuming that every remark could be re-broadcast. Bedford's citizens were linked, he'd discovered, by invisible and unimagined connections. Tom Karlin, for instance, was a regular visitor to the Jardine household. Tom's main job was as a janitor at the local air-base, but he occasionally worked for Mr Jardine as a carpenter, mechanic and gardener. He sometimes called on Paul, too, who he bullied to his face and insulted as a defective behind his back. Up at the US air-base, which was a reliable source of drinking companions and illicit explosives, Tom had a rent-free dormitory room, but he stored his few possessions at Lucy's place. He spent all his money on his car, a second-hand Chevrolet Blazer he had resprayed in crimson.

Among the town gossips, rumour about Karlin's minor treacheries was rife, but Laura's father didn't know any gossips, and Tom was well practised in radiating qualities that resembled honour and affection. Angela Jardine mistrusted Karlin, but never said so. Voicing such thoughts would have felt like a betrayal of her husband. She had married late, at twenty-nine and, unlike many of her contemporaries who had unlearned their wedding vows within days of the honeymoon, she could remember more or less every word she had pronounced at the service; not because she had made any effort to memorise the lines, but because they represented an honest expression of her relationship with her husband. For Angela, Stewart Jardine embodied not just her dreams, but her ideal.

CHAPTER 20

The longer he spent in Bedford, the more Daniel became fascinated by Laura's unusual brother. Paul had left school at sixteen, gone straight to work at the hospital, and since then had never shown the slightest interest in reading anything he wasn't obliged to. When they first met, he asked Daniel what work he did in London. He explained, as carefully as he could, the way the desk worked. Two hours later, Paul went up to Laura and asked her what an obituary was. And yet Paul Jardine, Daniel noticed, had a dry sense of humour when relaxed; so dry that most people from Bedford took it for madness. And there was something restful about Paul's self-absorption. There was no need to speak if you didn't want to, and he soon learned that Paul meant no harm by his habit of walking over to the stove and making himself coffee, or a steak sandwich, without offering one to you. He never had guests – he had no friends – and the thought simply never occurred to him.

One Wednesday afternoon, with just four days left of his stay, Laura was up at the house on Grant with her mother, who was still distressed after the disastrous dinner. Daniel was at Paul's camp, sitting in his trailer, listening to an End Time Evangelist on a local AM station. The man's missionary rage had him reluctantly captivated, so that he didn't notice Paul disappear outside. A couple of minutes later there was an explosion that Daniel, his mind already on Armageddon, took to be a missile landing in a nearby field. He rushed out to find Paul packing up the detonator coil he'd used to set off a firecracker the size of a mortar. He hadn't done it,

Daniel realised, as a surprise, or as a joke. It was like the coffee: if you felt like a bomb, you fixed your own.

'You like fireworks?' Paul asked him.

'When I was a child,' Daniel said, 'I liked the fireworks, but...you know what? The thing I liked best was going round the next morning, collecting all the burnt-out shells.'

'Yeah?' said Paul. Then he added, in a matter of fact way, without malice, 'Well that's like you're living now, isn't it?'

By the end of the afternoon, Daniel was mixing concrete. Laura's brother wanted it to pour into the Taurus' front-door cavities, because he'd read in one of his magazines that other car owners who enjoyed high decibel levels had found concrete could minimise vibration. They were listening to a dance track called Acid Conga on Paul's main sound system in the caravan: a tiny black Naim amplifier, no bigger than a detergent pack, plugged in to two speakers eight inches square, on each of which a previous owner had painted the symbol of the Red Cross. The equipment's size was deceptive: its power was not far short of the deafening potential of his car stereo.

The concrete had to be applied in sections, so that each layer hardened before the next went in. This gave Daniel a break of an hour or so and, while Paul worked with the trowel, he opened a biography of the seventeenth-century degenerate and poet John Wilmot, Lord Rochester. A friend of Charles I, he maintained levels of drunkenness and lechery that were astonishing even by the standards of the royal family. Daniel already knew most of the stories about Rochester: how he fled when a friend was being bludgeoned to death at Epsom in 1676, how he had the playwright Dryden beaten within an inch of his life, and how he was reputed to have deliberately infected his wife with syphilis, in order to punish a man he believed to be her lover. 'And yet,' he wrote in his notebook, 'he was capable of poetry of great beauty: writing which, had it not depended so heavily on obscenity of thought and language, would today have him celebrated in schools as one of the nation's most gifted writers.'

Rochester, he discovered, was ravaged and impotent at thirty, and dead at thirty-four. 'He was well known for smashing sundials and timepieces,' he wrote, 'and appeared determined to establish so swift a succession of sins that anyone trying to list them would require not so much a calendar as a stopwatch.'

The sun was going down, and he could hear Paul filling in the door cavity with his trowel, which made a gentle, reassuring sound, like waves on a shale beach.

The eulogy at Rochester's funeral, he discovered, was delivered by Robert Parsons, the family chaplain. 'His impieties,' Parsons told the mourners, 'were above the reach and thought of other men. He took as much pains to draw others in, and to pervert the right ways of virtue, as the apostles and primitive saints to save their own souls and them that heard them. This was the amazing circumstance of his own sins, that he was so diligent to recommend and propagate them: framing arguments for in, making proselytes to the great enemy of God, and casting down crowns and coronets before his throne.'

He put the book down and went to mix more concrete. As he got up, he found a cassette on the grass by his feet and put it in the tape machine. The air was filled with the voices of black musicians and plantation workers, interspersed with delta blues which had a raw originality he had never heard before.

'What is this?' Daniel asked.

'I don't know,' said Paul. 'I found it dumped in the trash. You want it?'

'Can you copy it?'

'When you leave,' said Paul, 'take it.'

A couple of minutes later, Daniel called over to Laura's brother to ask him how thick the new batch of concrete needed to be. There was no response. He called a second time and again there was no answer. 'Sorry, Daniel,' he said, when he eventually heard. 'I was dreaming.'

'What of?'

'Timeshift,' said Paul, as though he expected he would understand. 'I was doing Timeshift.'

'What?'

'Timeshift,' Paul said again, looking uncomfortable. He put his screwdriver down and hung his head as if he was confessing to a felony. Timeshift, he told Daniel, was a game Laura had invented when they were both in their teens. 'You have to imagine that you've been sleepwalking for the past three years,' Paul said, 'and that in that time you have formed no memories. And that now – right here – you have just come to your senses. You know who you are and stuff, because you remember everything apart from the past three years, but you have to look around you and start wondering about all this new stuff that you don't recognise, and you have to like...work out who people are and where they came from, and what the hell are they doing with you. But you have to keep talking to them lik normal, and you can't blow your cover by asking them questions.

'So...like in my case, I didn't have this car three years ago. So I'm looking at the car and I'm wondering where it came from. Is it mine? Wha state are the plates from? Why is it so loud? And then I see you. And the I'm looking at you and I'm thinking – who is this guy? A mechanic? H doesn't handle a shovel like a mechanic. A thief? Oh no wait, he can't be he's from England. That kind of thing. It gives you a kind of different way, he said, 'of looking at the world. It gives you a different way to count you troubles. Or your blessings.

'Of course,' Paul continued, relaxing slightly, 'it doesn't have to b three years. It could be one. It could be ten. It's just that I always do three.

'How often do you play Timeshift, Paul?' asked Daniel.

'What do you mean?'

'Once, twice a week?'

'No,' he replied, 'it's...it's more than that.'

'Once, twice a day?'

Paul started to look uneasy again, and Daniel wished he hadn't presse him.

'It's...the thing is, with me...' said Paul, 'it's more like...if I'm honest, he said finally, 'it's pretty much all the time.'

Daniel left Paul's camp around nine and ate at a diner on the I-70. H walked into the hotel lobby planning to go straight up to his room, but h could see Lucy waving at him from the bar. He went in and sat down. Sh handed him a small padded envelope. 'This came for you,' she said. H looked at it: there were no stamps or courier stickers; it seemed to hav been delivered by hand. 'Who from?'

She shrugged. 'I found it just now on the front desk.'

He opened the package and found Paul's cassette tape. With it was scrap of paper, on which was scrawled, in a child-like hand, the unsigne message: 'You furgot your music.'

'Beer?' asked Lucy. She'd been waiting for Tom to show up since eight it was ten now, and she was bored. Daniel looked doubtful. 'Hey – com on, you're going back to your watery island on Sunday.'

'OK,' he said. 'Just one.'

Lucy told Daniel about the animal hospital in her back yard, and hov her only patient at present was a traumatised rabbit. From what he could gather the recovery rate of her charges was poor, but at least when they died there was someone to care, and nobody to rejoice, which was not a position enjoyed, as he was well placed to know, by all of God's creatures. Midnight came and went, and there was still no sign of Tom.

He asked Lucy what she made of Oakes. 'I like him,' she said. 'But I think he's kind of weird.'

One day, she said, he'd come out of church in his clerical robes and assaulted a farm labourer who used to hang around the school gates, aiming to molest under-age girls. 'He was right about the guy,' she said. 'But the thing was, he didn't hit him, you know, in the way you're probably thinking, with both fists raised and his sleeves rolled up, like a British gentleman. He head-butted him like a street fighter. He broke the guy's nose.

'He came in here to see me one time,' she said, 'right after Joe Carr...' She stopped herself, realising what she'd said. 'You know about that, right?'

Daniel nodded.

'Right after Joe Carr...right after he did that thing. He came in here and there was just the two of us in here, like this, and he said, "Lucy, just imagine how wonderful anything would be" – he said, what was it?...I think he said a daisy, or a mongrel, or a string bean...how wonderful each of those things would be if they were the only one in the world. And I said, "Yeah, but there's lots of mongrels and daisies. And there's a whole lot of string beans." I mean there's loads of them, millions of them, anybody knows that, right? You want another drink?'

Daniel shook his head.

'And then you know what he said? He said, "Yeah, but there's only one of you, Lucy; there ain't nobody like you anywhere in the world." What do you think he meant?'

'I think he meant you were special. What did you think he meant?'

'I thought...you know what? I thought maybe he wanted to kiss me.'

'Did he?'

'Did he what?'

'Kiss you?'

'No,' she said.

She told him again how she was determined to save up to go back to school and qualify as a – he braced himself for the word – veterinarian. It was an ambition which, even as she rehearsed it, she knew she would never achieve. Two days earlier she'd left her copy of *Glamour* on the bar and he'd turned to a questionnaire she'd left half-completed. Under the headline 'Is He Mr Right?' and illustrated with pictures of well-known Hollywood couples, it asked readers to respond to a series of questions of varying seriousness. She had left several blank; to others, she had responded with pencil ticks so faint that they were almost indistinguishable. What caught the eye, though, was her answer to question nineteen: 'How often would you say you have experienced orgasm with a partner?' to which she had responded with a tick so firm it had almost gone through the paper: 'Never'.

The stereo behind the bar was still playing the second country CD, a compilation which had just restarted on track one, 'Hey, Good-Lookin''.

'Aren't you sick of this?' he asked her.

She didn't reply. 'Hey,' she said, snatching Paul's cassette, 'let's put this on.'

Before he could stop her, and tell her it was mainly talking, she'd put it in the tape machine, and the exotic, broken voices of Clarksville and Natchez filled the bar.

'Wow,' said Lucy. 'Wow.'

It was a few minutes later, halfway through what sounded like an early Leadbelly track, that Tom reappeared, clearly drunk.

He'd been to a bachelor party up at the air-base. He often came back from such events drunk: as a caretaker and occasional gardener, when he was out with the air crews he felt a desire to prove a capacity for heroism.

Karlin sat on a stool, looking sullen. In front of him on the bar he noticed the cassette cover, which had a photograph of a black musician on the front. He turned it over, placing it face down. He ordered, and drank, three large Jack Daniel's in twenty minutes. He asked for another. Then, just as Lucy reached out to give him the new glass, he slammed her hand down on the bar so that half of the drink spilled. He stood up without touching it. 'Clean that up,' he told her. 'I'm going to my place. Come round later if you want.' As he was walking out the door he turned round. 'Come round later if you want,' he shouted, 'but don't forget to wash that black off of ya tongue.'

He was in his car by the time Daniel realised quite what it was that he'd said.

'For Christ's sake, Lucy,' he said. 'You've got to get out of here.'

She nodded, then picked up Karlin's last whisky and swallowed it in one. Daniel paid Tom's tab because otherwise he knew she'd have had to, and bought her another Jack Daniel's. At midnight, as he was leaving, and she was closing up, he noticed that she was very drunk. He offered to drive her home.

'I'm OK,' she said, a little too loud. 'I'm OK,' she said again, more quietly. 'I'm OK,' she repeated, almost whispering this time, like a child might do for a joke. 'And I'm going home.' He looked at her, worried. 'To my place,' she said. 'OK?'

He went up to room fifteen, turned on the television and went into the bathroom to brush his teeth. Even from there, he could make out the peculiar, clipped tones of the English actor Richard Attenbrough doing his familiar botched impression of a Cockney. He walked back over to the set, switched it off, and fell asleep. He slept solidly until eleven the following morning, when Laura slipped in the door. Solidly, that is, except for a moment at around 3.00 a.m., when he woke briefly with a start of terror. He had been dreaming about a missile landing in Paul's field. He thought at the time that the noise had been in his imagination, whereas in fact it had been a real, but distant, explosion.

CHAPTER 21

The blast also disturbed Mr Jardine who, after a short burst of Korean tunnelling, pulled a sports jacket over his pyjamas and rushed out of the front door, certain that the noise had come from Paul's trailer. But he could see, even from where he was, that his son's buildings appeared to be in darkness. He walked back up to the house and got out the car. He put his foot on the brake, shifted it into drive and, without touching the accelerator, let the vehicle roll down the gravel road to Paul's encampment. It was in perfect silence.

It was as he was swinging the car round to come home that he saw flames: on the other side of Main, towards the Interstate. He eased the car down Lincoln and through the back streets, following the smoke, till he got to the scene. An ambulance was leaving as he approached. Two fire trucks had all but extinguished the blaze, in a small prefabricated building at an address he didn't know. He turned around, and headed back.

The exact sequence of events on that Thursday morning took weeks to be agreed by jurors in the Bedford County court, but things had happened more or less as they were related to Daniel by Laura, who had got it from the staff at the Red Carpet.

Lucy had driven home that evening with a couple of Hot Damn! miniatures that she drank before going to bed. She lay awake for a while, then she was startled by what she thought was an intruder breaking in the back porch. She got up and reached for the first blunt instrument she could find, a marine flare that was on the floor with a pile of Tom's other possessions. It was cylindrical, like the packages she had to unwrap every few days at the Red Carpet, containing quart bottles of liquor, though this one was three times larger. She hid behind the living room door. Then she heard a voice. It was Tom, drunker now, and he was still raging about the cassette she'd been playing at the Red Carpet.

She came out from behind the door and sat down in an armchair. He walked over and put his left hand against her forehead. He pressed her head back against the chair and held it there. She was trembling by now and, not for the first time, she wasn't sure if he was going to embrace her or punch her in the face. He went to kiss her, then grabbed her tongue, hard, between his right thumb and index finger. She twisted herself free from him. 'That ain't right baby,' he said, in a mocking parody of the accents of the cotton workers she'd been playing in the bar. 'Aaah said wash it.' He turned and walked into the kitchen, which was in darkness, and began to fumble around for something.

She turned her head to look at the front door behind her. It was locked, and the only key was on a hook in the kitchen, the other side of him.

'Hey Tom,' she said.

'Yeah?'

He came back out of the kitchen, blinking against the electric light in the main room. Still sitting down, she pulled the safety cap off the flare, which she was cradling in her lap, pointed the firing end of the cylinder at him, and pulled firmly on the two beige detonator tapes. The mustard-coloured cylinder had been under her table for several weeks. When she'd been dusting, she'd occasionally glanced at the label, which roughly described the means of operation, so that the device should not be set off accidentally. Had she turned it through forty-five degrees and looked at the large red capitals running up the side of the casing, she would have encountered the words: 'Danger. In Normal Conditions, Visible for Eight Nautical Miles.'

Lucy's house was constructed before she was born by Irvines, a Topeka firm, in the early sixties. Irvines built many such houses in the area, but their popularity had been based on affordability and speed of construction, rather than sturdiness. When Lucy pulled the cords – an action which caused the cylinder to straighten up so that the main force of the charge was delivered not, as she had hoped, into Tom's genitals, but vertically into the ceiling – the first result was a colossal explosion in the rafters that blew the whole corrugated roof clear of the building. The fireball was restrained by the main section of the charred roofing and the whole lot came to earth together, so that the second detonation occurred when this debris landed on Tom's red convertible, which also exploded.

She might have laughed about it the next year, or even the next day, were it not for the fact that, at the moment of detonation, realising that the flare might tip back further and explode into her face, she had braced the canister against her inner thighs and her abdomen, causing second-degree burns to her torso and upper legs which would require multiple grafts. They didn't operate immediately though, because she was too drunk. That didn't stop the police taking a statement. It was one which would play badly for her in court, especially at the point where, when asked to describe the effect she observed once the device was detonated, she replied, '*Ka-boom*.' She also told officers that she had deliberately fired the flare at her ex-boyfriend.

Laura and Daniel saw her in Bedford Hospital on the Saturday afternoon. It was their last full day in the town; they flew out of Salina the following morning. As they approached, Lucy was on her back, watching a portable TV on which two couples were being humiliated on an afternoon talk show. When Daniel saw her in the ward, he felt suddenly responsible for the whole thing, and he had a vision of Lucy's future that consisted not of a vet's nursing course, but of more nights in the bar, of a reconciliation with Tom, and of her eating until she had attained the fighting weight required of a contestant on these programmes. He could picture her there, in the studio, sat opposite Tom, as they screamed at one another and re-enacted the exchanges of that night.

She told them everything that happened, sounding strangely detached. 'We should have stuck with Hank Williams, right?' she said to Daniel.

As they drove away from the hospital, he realised how much he'd grown to love Laura's home town and, through her town, the country he still called America.

'Mom said will we go up to see her tonight,' Laura said.

'What did you say?' asked Daniel.

'I said yes.'

'Oh shit.'

'Remember,' she said. 'This trip was you, not me.'

On the way to the Jardines' that evening, Daniel became increasingly angry and depressed about Lucy's injuries. Stewart Jardine, seeking to make amends for their last meeting, shook his hand over-firmly, so that his ring pressed painfully into the younger man's fingers, and then held his grip far longer than good sense would have required or recommended. Mrs Jardine thanked Daniel for his help with the garden, which Laura had almost finished, though he'd contributed nothing to the work.

The uneasy warmth of their welcome could hardly disguise the intense resentments that had built up over the month. Mr Jardine was hurt that Daniel had seen more of Paul or even Lucy than him, and that he hadn't stayed at the house. Linnell was furious about Jardine's treatment of Paul. Angela was unhappy that Daniel had spent the night of the explosion drinking – as she was reliably informed that he had – with an overweight barmaid.

None of this might have mattered, were it not for the fact that, just as Daniel and Laura turned into the Jardines' drive, Tom, who had been uninjured and was released by the police after making a statement, was coming out. He was at the wheel of a rented pickup, still sweating from laying a stone path in the garden. Even then, the ill-feeling would never have surfaced had he not given a sarcastically carefree wave to Daniel, so that Laura had to use all her strength to cling to the wheel and stop him attempting to kill the janitor right there, among the cosseted lawns of Grant Street.

So it was that – while his hosts were angered but conciliatory – Daniel was seething by the time he walked into the house. Laura put out the last of the bedding plants, then went upstairs for a shower. Daniel sat down in an armchair in the living room and accepted the glass of whisky Mr Jardine offered him. Stewart poured a Scotch for himself and, soon carried away by the strong alcohol, expressed his sympathy for Karlin, lamenting the fact that 'he will hang around with these women'. At which point his wife inquired, with the transparent look of a decent woman delivering a low blow, 'Did you *know* her, Daniel?'

Jardine retreated into the kitchen. Daniel got up without excusing himself, leaving Angela in the living room, and followed him in there. He took his host by the shoulders. Then he repeated, word for word, every exchange that had led up to the destruction, and informed the older man, in an image which, given time, he would have polished, that his handyman was 'a twenty-four-carat arsehole'.

By the time he had got to the part of the story where Tom was in Lucy's kitchen, reprising his command to 'wash it', Laura's father, he noted with a certain satisfaction, was looking mortified. But the source of his horror wasn't Tom Karlin. It was Angela, who had been standing in the kitchen doorway for the last couple of minutes, in Jardine's view but not in Daniel's. Looking at her now, he could see Laura standing behind her, at the foot of the stairs. She'd stepped out of the shower, her hair wet, and hastily pulled on a dark green bathrobe. Drops of water were still running down over her ankles.

'You are embarrassing Laura's mother,' Jardine said to Daniel, 'and you are embarrassing me. Goodnight.'

Laura walked up to her father and stared into his eyes. She slapped him, hard, across the face. Jardine went to take her hand, to stop her repeating the action. He held her wrist lightly for a brief moment, then let go.

'Why don't you just hit me?' she asked him, in a level voice. 'Like you hit your fucking son. Like you hit your son,' she said again, more quietly. 'Like you hit my brother.'

She turned away and disappeared upstairs. On the parquet floor of the kitchen, faint traces of her bare footprints were left by water, heat and steam. Soon, Daniel, thought, these marks of her presence would disappear for good.

As he opened the front door, he turned round to take his jacket off the coat stand and saw Jardine standing next to his cardboard image: both stationary, both wearing the same fixed expression of grim resolution. Daniel walked out and climbed in the Buick. He didn't start the engine, but counted his heartbeat, which was running at about a hundred and eighty; the pulse rate of most parachutists, Laura had told him, as they leave the aircraft. He turned the key in the ignition when he heard the swift, purposeful crunch of her footsteps on the gravel drive. She threw her bag in the back seat and got in.

'All that was your fault,' Jardine shouted to Laura.

'What?'

'That was your fault,' he shouted, 'because...'

'Go on,' she said.

'Because you made Paul the way he is.'

'Let's go,' she said to Daniel.

They drew away from the house.

'What the fuck did that mean?' he asked.

'What that meant,' she said, 'is that it was the most vicious thing he could think of at the time.'

She put her bags on the floor of his room, and put her arms round his neck, and kissed him – hard, and for much longer than he could have predicted.

'When I was fourteen,' she said, 'I was at home with my father watching this movie where a preacher told his congregation that the three most powerful and terrifying words in the world were "I love you." I said, "That's right Dad, isn't it?" He didn't say anything. So I said, "Which three words would you choose then?" '

'What did he say?' Daniel asked.

'He said, "I remember everything." '

Back in the kitchen, Angela Jardine collected up the unused dinner things: first the teaspoons, then the soup spoons, because grouping the cutlery at this stage made them easier to place in the drawer. She picked up the rose bowl her grandmother had left her thirty years ago, but gripped it too tightly, so that it fell to the floor and shattered. Nobody was disturbed by the noise: Laura was at the hotel, pulling her hastily-stuffed holdall out of the back seat of the car; Stewart had gone out for a drive to ease his nerves. Almost without thinking, he went straight to Lincoln and Seventh, where he pulled up and stared at the remains of the house, Tom's car, and the charred, but still recognisable body of a rabbit, imprisoned in its pen of burnt-out chicken-wire.

He wondered how he might have reacted to the day's turbulence when he was twenty, before the trauma of combat had shattered his nerves; before he had a family and kept a handyman, and the insidious demands of good behaviour had eaten him up inside. Tom, he knew – he had always known for Christ's sake – *was* an asshole. His admission would be doubly confirmed: first at Lucy's trial for assault with a deadly weapon, when his spiteful testimony helped get her sent to Bedford penitentiary for nine months, then two days after the hearing, when Jardine, who had fired Karlin on the night of the verdict, caught him on the premises trying to steal a chain-saw.

As Mr Jardine was turning round to come home, it occurred to him to take a left back up Eighth, which led to the Interstate, walk into their room at the Red Carpet and apologise. He was still thinking about it as he approached the junction of Arlington and Eighth, but the light there was red, not green as he had somehow expected. As he was waiting for the light to change, something altered his resolve. The signal was still red as he eased the nose of the car not left, but right, as Kansas state law allows, towards the distant lights of Salina and his home.

CHAPTER 22

They landed in London early on Saturday morning, in heavy rain. By the time they struggled up the fire escape to the flat roof and dropped their bags outside the front door, it was still not quite seven. Searching through their pockets, they found neither of them had the house keys. Their eyes half closed against the steady drizzle, they looked through the bags and still couldn't find them. In the distance, they could hear the wheezing hydraulics of a refuse truck.

'We'll have to wake Rachel,' she said.

'She must have been working till two last night,' Daniel told her. 'What about Brendan?'

'Brendan?' she said. '*Brendan?* At seven a.m.? Are you crazy?'

Daniel tried the sash window, which was locked. He peered through at the internal metal lever that held it closed, wondering if he could shift it by forcing a penknife blade up into the window frame. Rain was dripping down his neck. He didn't have a penknife. He could still detect traces of the fetid cabin air in his clothes. On balance, he reasoned, gazing at the window lock, it would be worth putting a half brick through the frosted glass pane in the door, and getting a glazier in later. Then he glanced through the window again and saw Laura sitting inside, on the couch. He pulled the bags through the open door.

'You found the keys then,' he said.

'No.'

'What?'

'I didn't find them,' she said. 'It was open.'

They looked round the flat but their few possessions were undisturbed. The small music centre was where it always was; the answering machine was untouched, its red light blinking. The Burglar Money was still there, on the mantelpiece. 'It must have been Brendan,' Daniel said. 'He'll have been smoking when he locked up last night, and he's left it open.'

That night they ate in The Owl with Jessica and Doyle. The barman insisted that he'd checked the flat door the night before, and that it had been double locked. They told them about Lucy and Tom Karlin. Jessica talked to Daniel about his research for the book.

'Have you finished it then?' Brendan asked.

'Not far off,' Daniel told him.

It got late. Laura put her head on his shoulder.

'What is it?' he asked her.

'We're home.'

'Home?' he asked her. 'Are you sure?'

'Home,' she said. 'And I like it.'

The following day, the Sunday, she left for Wales with her parachute and her passport. 'I'll be back Tuesday,' she told him. After she'd left, he called his own line at the office and it rang unobtainable. He wondered if Whittington had taken the opportunity, as was traditional in the newspaper business, of firing him while he was on holiday. He called the obituaries editor's own direct line and still got no answer. Not to worry, he thought; he'd be in there tomorrow.

'We had to change your number,' Rosa told him, when he came in the following morning. 'This idiot kept ringing up.' She wrote the new number on a piece of paper and handed it to him.

'What was it,' he asked, 'double glazing?'

'No,' said Whittington. 'Somebody was playing the death march.'

'What?'

'I wouldn't worry,' Rosa told him. 'Normally it's just April Fool's Day that we get that.'

It was a quiet day on the desk. There was an elderly lord covered months earlier by Charles Crosthwaite, and a West African band leader who'd already been filed by Suzanne Stiles, the rock writer. Daniel and Whittington had lunch at the pub, where they ran into Paul Harkes, the news editor.

'Many lords in today?' Harkes asked.

'One,' said Whittington.

'You know,' the news editor said, 'I think it's obscene that they exist at all, in any form.'

'You would prefer,' Whittington said, 'elevation to the peerage to be a reward for some moral improvement of society?'

'No,' said Harkes. 'I think the best way would be complete anarchy; it should be a lottery, so that all those smart benches would be filled with people chosen at random – itinerant drunks, penniless wastrels and the criminally insane, all gibbering and wetting their pants and drooling.'

'So basically,' said Whittington, 'it's a case of "as you were then".'

Daniel got home early and listened to the telephone messages. The first was from Kate in Bedford, who wanted more details about their last unfortunate evening in the town. The second, which sounded as though it had been made from a phone box, was a poor recording of the death march. Listening to it, he was seized by a dreadful suspicion. He walked over to the desk drawer which held the backup copies of his book. When he opened the envelope, he found no disks, but a blank condolence card.

He went down to the bar, where Doyle was polishing glasses, and he told him what had happened.

'Ah,' said the barman.

'Who do you think it is?' asked Daniel.

'Well,' said Brendan, 'let me put it this way. It isn't fucking Paganini.'

Daniel called Steven Peerless.

'I can't come down,' Steven said, 'we've got Jo's mother...'

'It's important,' said Daniel.

'It can't be that...'

'It is,' Linnell said and for the first time in his life, he hung up without saying goodbye, like a man in a film.

Peerless arrived ten minutes later, looking aggravated. His attitude changed once Daniel told him what had happened.

'OK,' he said. 'At least we know two things. We know it's Gerald Longworth. That's one thing. And we know he's not going to kill you.'

'How?'

'Because – mad as he is – if he was going to kill you, he wouldn't leave a message to say he was going to kill you.'

Longworth's history, said Daniel, relaxing slightly, suggested he was not so much a practised assassin as an idiot.

'I don't want to worry you,' said Peerless. 'But that's what makes me uneasy. There's only one thing more dangerous than a practised assassin. And that's an idiot who has practised assassins for friends.'

'OK,' said Daniel. 'What do we...what do I do?'

'He's asking for some kind of sign,' Peerless said. 'For a start you should print out a copy of what you wrote, tear it up, and send it over to him.'

'I don't have his address,' said Daniel.

'I can get that,' Peerless said.

'I haven't got a copy of the file. It's at the office. He's got them both.'

Peerless shrugged. 'That's what you've got to do.'

'OK, OK,' said Daniel, reluctantly. 'I'll send it from the office tomorrow.'

'Right,' said Steven. 'Get it over to me on news. We'll bike it. Don't worry. See you.'

Daniel sat up late at the bar with Brendan and drank too much. He didn't like to admit it to himself, but when he went up to the flat, he was ill at ease. He'd been drinking tequila, which he wasn't used to, and he slept fitfully. He woke at two thirty. He had a headache and he felt sick. He turned on the light and reached out for a book; the only one within arm's length was *My Sister and I*, an autobiography attributed to Nietzsche, who he'd been considering for inclusion in his book. It was a twisted piece of writing supposedly written by the philosopher in his last days at the asylum in Jena, dominated by incest, demonic imagery, and the swish of bull-whip on flesh.

He would have liked something more reassuring to read. Across the room he could see a street plan of Bedford, but even as he thought of it he knew, like some expiring mountaineer, the effort of those extra few feet was beyond him. He opened *My Sister and I* at random.

'"I am paying dearly for the enchanting dreams of my youth,"' he read. '"The currency in which one pays such debts shrinks as one grows older; we pay in gold for what was received in dross. I say nothing of those intervals in this house when the whole world suddenly seems to break loose in delirious screams and wild cackles punctuated by the blowing of a bugle by a Bavarian lunatic who believes he is the angel Gabriel summoning the dead to judgement..."'

Daniel put the book down, and fell asleep with the light on. He woke intermittently, sweating heavily, his pulse racing, dreaming that Laura's parachute hadn't opened, and that constables were at the door to bring him the news, then that he was confronted after her death by her furious parents. In one nightmare, he was alone in the house on Grant. Her raging, wild-eyed father stepped out from behind his cardboard image, which had a sign hanging round its neck, like the ones by French level crossings, warning of obscured trains: 'Caution: One Mr Jardine May Conceal Another.'

When the doorbell did finally ring it was six thirty. Still submerged in his tormented dreams, he pulled on his jeans and staggered to the door, sensing that his premonition of tragedy had been realised. He felt a shudder of nausea as, through the frosted panel in the front door, he made out what looked like the epaulettes on a police uniform.

When he opened it, he was met by a single punch that knocked him unconscious. Two men dressed in the dark green uniform of London paramedics carried him down the fire escape on a stretcher and placed him in an ambulance parked in the alleyway next to the bar – or rather they placed him in what looked like an ambulance. Its interior had none of the usual medical facilities.

When he came to, it was with the sensation that his head hurt and that something was indefinably, but very seriously, wrong. He looked round for the reassuring normality of his surroundings and didn't find it.

'Laura,' he said, as he usually did at this point, and tried to reach out. It was then that he realised that he couldn't move and that he was upside down. There followed a new, more sickening awareness: he was outside. The strange tableau reeling in front of his eyes was not a continuation of his dream, but a real street, below him. It took a few more moments before he had mastered the critical details of his situation: he was upside down, strapped to a chair, and the chair was dangling from a rope, at least fifty feet above a busy city street. Its name – Commercial Road – like the fact that his head had been shaved, was a detail he would not learn until later.

'Hello!' he heard a jovial-sounding voice call out. Daniel craned his neck up, straining against the ropes that secured him, to see what he hoped would be the face of his rescuer.

The face was six feet above him and it was smiling. He had just recognised the features of Gerald Longworth, when he also noticed that the rope his chair was hanging from was tied to a metal scaffolding pole jutting out horizontally from the building. Longworth, who was leaning out of a window and was far closer to the vital steel pole than he was, picked up a pair of what looked like tree shears and started snapping them around the top of the rope.

'Hello!' Longworth shouted again. 'Am I putting the hours in now?'

'Is this it then?' Daniel said. He couldn't hear himself speak – because of the strong wind, he thought at the time, though later he realised it was the blood pounding in his ears.

'This,' Longworth replied, lapsing suddenly into an exaggerated upper-class accent, 'his not hit. If hi may quote a line from your favourite chimney sweep,' he said, breaking grotesquely but tunefully into song: 'Forbearance is the 'allmark of mi creed.'

There was an eerie silence. Longworth and his accomplices had gone.

Now he was alone, Daniel felt a second surge of uncontrollable panic. This was worse, if anything, than when Longworth was still there. How long, he wondered, could a man stay alive, upside down? He had an instinct to struggle free of his bonds, which he managed to resist. He tried to recite the mottos he remembered Laura telling him about. 'Fear is only a big thing if you make it one in your mind.' A siren wailed in the distance. It seemed to be coming nearer.

He shut his eyes, but that made it worse. Overcome by a fear of vomiting, he opened them again and looked down at the opposite pavement, where he saw a child in a pushchair let go of a lollipop, which dropped, or – from Linnell's perspective – flew up, to the pavement. 'Altitude,' he told himself, 'is safety.' He saw the sweet roll a few inches, and watched a passing workman step on it with his boot. He could just hear the faint crunch when the man shattered its pink spherical top. It was the last thing he remembered until he came round again – in the arms of two strangers, wearing oxygen masks, as they lowered him to safety in a fire engine's pneumatic cradle. When he saw their uniforms, he tried to struggle free, so violently that he almost fell to his death.

When he woke up in St Thomas's Hospital, Brendan was at his bedside. 'You're all I need,' Daniel said. The police arrived.

'I have no idea,' the young constable repeated, reading back Daniel's statement in a dead monotone, 'of the identity of the person or persons who may have caused me these injuries; I do not wish to make a further statement or to seek to press charges.'

His senior officer, an inspector, looked in from the corridor outside. 'You didn't notice a name, sir,' he said, 'on that scaffolding at all?'

Daniel felt he was about to sneeze, but feared that to do so would cause him unbearable pain. He shut his eyes. The urge subsided.

'Would you say…' he called to the inspector. The man walked up to his bedside. 'Would you say that's it over now?'

'From our knowledge of your particular unknown assailant,' he replied, 'I would say so sir, yes.'

The two men left and Brendan came back in. 'Bloody hell,' he said. 'That'll teach you to compare a bloke to Mary Poppins.'

'Brendan…' Daniel asked, as he had many times before. 'What's the damage?'

'Broken nose,' he said. 'Shaved head.'

'Anything else?'

Doyle shook his head. 'No. Except…well…you're going to look like a panda tomorrow.'

'What do you mean?'

'When your eyes go black.'

Daniel stared blankly at him.

'With a broken nose,' Brendan explained, sounding a little exasperated, 'your eyes go black.'

'Did you call Laura?'

He nodded. 'She's on the train.'

'OK,' said Daniel. 'Right then. Let's go.'

'They want you to stay here,' the barman said. 'Till tomorrow. For observation.'

'No. I'm coming today. I'm coming with you.'

'You've got no socks.'

'How do you know?'

'How do you?' Brendan replied.

Daniel looked down the length of the turquoise blanket covering him, but decided not to lift it. 'I don't,' he said.

'Well, then.'

A woman charge nurse, alarmed by these exchanges, walked over to the bed.

'I'm going with him,' Daniel told her, more quietly. 'I don't know if I've got socks. I don't care.'

'In that case,' Brendan said, 'there's something else you need to know.'

He passed him the early edition of the evening paper where, on the front page, Daniel saw a large colour photograph of himself lashed to the chair, hanging over the road. 'They got there just before the fire brigade,' Brendan said. 'Your man gave their picture desk a call.'

Brendan drove Daniel back to North London. He was wearing his bloodstained T-shirt and jeans, together with a pair of black velvet slippers and a West Ham United baseball cap; items which Doyle had found in the hospital shop. Even before he got the hat and the slippers, his discomfort at his injuries had started to give way to embarrassment, especially as the article which accompanied the picture, though it didn't mention Longworth, gave a complete account of the mystery attacker's motive.

Back at the flat, he washed as best he could and got changed. The phone kept ringing. He left it on the answering machine; he picked it up once to speak to Whittington, but ignored the messages from television reporters, other journalists and friends. Peerless called in to say that – better late than never – he had sent the shredded copy of the piece to Longworth. Balfour, the literary agent, left a message, his grave commiseration not quite concealing a tone of hysterical excitement. Whatever else he'd suffered, he told Daniel, nothing could buy this sort of publicity.

He was having tea with Brendan in the flat when Laura got back. She walked in without speaking.

'You were on the radio,' she said, at last.

'I know,' he said.

'In Welsh,' she added. 'My Aunt Helen translated. You know,' she said, 'your name blends into the Welsh language; it could mean anything. If you don't speak Welsh, you wouldn't know it was there.'

'I nearly wasn't there.'

She turned away and stopped speaking. She was crying. 'Is that it now?'

'Is what it?'

'Is that the end of your fucking book?'

'He's not going to do this again,' he said. 'It's finished with...'

'How do you know it's finished with?'

'I just think it's worth...'

She lifted a mirror off the wall and held it in front of him. He was bald, his top lip had been split and coagulated blood still filled one of his nostrils. There were weals around the top of his collar-bone where the nylon rope had cut and burned into his skin.

'Trust me Daniel,' she said. 'Nothing is worth this.'

He looked at her. She looked terrible. She moved towards him, but he turned away.

'I feel...I feel stupid,' he told her.

'What?'

'I feel stupid.'

'Why?' she asked.

He paused. For a minute he thought he was going to weep as well. 'Because I feel...because I *am*...marked.'

'But that,' said Brendan, 'will go away.'

'Will it?'

'Yes,' said the barman.

Daniel took another week off, and read through the work he'd done in Kansas. He restricted his attention to entries relating to the dead, which felt like less of a betrayal of Laura, as they were harmless.

'That weasel rang,' Laura told him one evening.

'What did you tell him?'

'I told him to fuck off.'

'In what words?'

'In those words,' she said. 'Do you know any better ones?'

Daniel's mind kept returning to his experiences at the hands of Gerald Longworth. His anxiety didn't centre around what happened to him above the Commercial Road – that, after all, was something that he knew all about. His unease related more to the question of exactly how Longworth had found him and who was the initial source of his intelligence. In the end, he called Simon Roylance. It was nine thirty in the morning, and there was no reply. Daniel was about to hang up when the crime reporter finally lifted the receiver, and spoke with the dazed civility of a man who is trying to pretend he was awake before the phone rang.

'It's Daniel Linnell.'

'Hello,' said Roylance, his voice relaxing as he understood he was not being roused by a senior editor.

'Did you tell anyone about my book?'

'No.'

'Nobody at all?'

'No,' the crime reporter said. 'Well...I did mention it to a friend of mine, but he's a police psychiatrist. I thought he might be useful to you.'

'What's his name?' Daniel asked.

'Robin Robinson. Why, do you know him?'

'No,' Daniel said and put the phone down.

At the insistence of Steven Peerless, he deleted Gerald Longworth from his records, but secretly placed a disk copy in Whittington's *Lives of the Saints*, by the reasoning that, if this volume ever fell into the wrong hands, a swift extrajudicial execution would be a blessing. He kept the other Longworth family members in. If he'd expected sympathy when he returned to the paper, he was disappointed. Harkes, the news editor, met him in the lift on his first day back. 'Now that haircut,' he said, 'is what I call a Right to Reply.'

PART TWO

CHAPTER 23

In time, some of his experiences in the United States were wiped from his memory. One scene he did recall, though, clearly and repeatedly: the moment when Paul Jardine first talked to him about Timeshift. He remembered it perfectly, because that was the point at which he'd begun to wonder whether Laura's brother was not simply eccentric, but deranged.

And yet, ever since he came back from Kansas, Daniel had found himself increasingly taken with Timeshift. He started to do it when he was meeting somebody at a railway station, or in the angst-ridden few minutes as his own train pulled in to London after a few days away. It encouraged a continual reassessment of your life and exposed its small forgotten failings. You were forced to confront aspects of your relationships which you might have become blinded to by familiarity, in the way that the prospect of moving house can bring back the full ghastliness of some absurd ornament prominently positioned on your mantelpiece, initially for a week, to appease the relative who gave it you, and which has ended up staying there, unnoticed, for years. Timeshift made you see people, or places, differently. You might, for instance, constantly rediscover the beauty and talent of a long-standing woman companion in the way that these things might strike a dazed new lover. Do it often enough, Daniel thought, and you could fall in love with her again, every day.

And he did it now, sitting in the feeble early morning sun. He shut his eyes, took himself back three years, and erased every intervening memory. Opening them again, he began to examine his surroundings. He was sitting in a fenced-off infants' playground, on a small roundabout of the kind he used to ride when he was a boy. It was made out of wooden decking, three feet high and six feet in diameter. You sat on the top of the platform: in the centre there was a large metal knob; six thick iron spokes ran out from it, to give the rider something to cling on to, for those inevitable moments when a sadistic older child crept up and spun the contraption so violently that escape was impossible, such was its terrifying centrifugal force.

He was alone on the roundabout, which was rotating slowly, almost imperceptibly. Even so, the slight movement made him feel nauseous. He had pressed both palms down against the decking, which had once been painted in proud racing green, but was now reduced, by neglect, to bare wood. He could feel a thin layer of sweat giving his fingers purchase on its rough, eroded surface. There was an intense dry irritation at the back of his throat. His achievements in his lost three years had not, he concluded from these details, included giving up alcohol.

But what, he asked himself, plunging deeper into the world of Paul's bizarre mental discipline, could have brought him there? A young Asian woman walked towards him. Did he know her? He glanced into her eyes, but she passed by without altering her expression. In the toddlers' area in front of him, he could see a handful of children playing in the sand-pit. On the other side of the playground, a small huddle of adults was seated in a nearby parents' area, drinking tea or talking on mobile phones.

He pushed against the ground with his right foot. The roundabout creaked into a gentle clockwise motion, and on the quarter turn he saw the trashed club house and abandoned, overgrown facilities that confirmed beyond doubt that he was in England. Looking again, he recognised the ruin of what had been the bowling green in Priory Park, Crouch End. Once the ride had turned through a hundred and eighty degrees, so that he had his back to the sandpit and the children, it stopped. Looking across the main park in front of him he could see two eleven-year-olds in Arsenal football shirts. They were sitting on smashed-up benches, smoking grass, in another segregated section named, on a large black and yellow plaque, 'The Philosophers' Garden'. Apart from being fenced off, this contemplative oasis was not visibly different from the rest of the park except that, next to its striking name-plate, there was another notice, in the same colours, which read 'No Dogs'.

Had he slept there? He looked down at his clothes, which were crumpled but clean. He was alone in a children's playground and nobody seemed to be paying any great attention to him. Had he graduated, he wondered, to proper reporting, so that he was writing a piece on some paedophile group, and observing the area undercover? Was he…? Daniel experienced a real, physical shiver. In the ravening imaginings of a hangover, when he would be gripped by wild enthusiasms, terrible certainties, or anxiety – to the point of finding himself daunted by such familiar challenges as an Underground train, a supermarket or an escalator – he was sometimes capable of thinking himself into the amnesiac ritual too convincingly for the good of his own nerves. Was he…Sweet Jesus, thought Daniel; was he himself a child molester?

He looked at his hands. His fingers were stained a familiar deep yellow, with nicotine. And yet, when he felt in his pocket, he found not cigarettes, but two packets of sweets. He pushed off again with his foot against the cracked tarmac and the roundabout swung round to face the infants' playground once more. As it slowed to a halt, he noticed a light plastic football the size of a small melon was rolling towards him. It was decorated with cartoon characters and it came straight up to him. He put his foot on it without standing up, out of instinct. A boy of about three, who'd been chasing after the ball, was running in his direction. The child reached the roundabout, snatched the ball from under his shoe without looking up at him and ran off with it. After three or four yards, though, he paused, and turned, and put a stop to Linnell's mad reverie with the single syllable: 'Dad.'

Daniel didn't really need to play Timeshift to be astonished every day by the condition of parenthood. Every time Jack called him Dad he had an instant reflex to turn and peer behind him, like a Vaudeville rogue who's been complimented on his honesty. The boy came back and sat next to him on the roundabout, slipping his hand in his.

'Dad,' he said again.

'Yes, Jack?'

'Can we play the ice-cream game?'

'Yes, Jack.'

They walked out of the infants' enclosure and across to the park's café. A large room in a wooden pavilion, it had been built in an age when public amenities were cherished, even flaunted. The café was run by a formidable woman of fifty or so. For some reason he never discovered, she was known to regulars, though never to her face, as Beales, and her ferocious rigidity in matters of detail would have made her excellently suited to administrating the customs and excise department of one of the sterner totalitarian republics. Every great café owner, Brendan used to say, had a song. Each time Daniel set eyes on Beales, he was reminded of a country-and-western tune he'd once heard that began 'I love Germany. I don't care what they've done...'

It had become a game between father and son that Daniel would go up to the counter and choose two scoops of ice cream.

'Which flavour?' Beales would say.

'Strawberry and vanilla,' he would reply, impassive through familiarity, like a spy giving a password in a sixties film.

Jack would cover his eyes as his father brought them back to the table. The boy would taste one of the scoops, and then Daniel would touch his nose with the back of the cold teaspoon, at which point Jack, speaking for some reason in the voice of a robot, would guess the flavour. Daniel always ordered the same two flavours to make it easier, which it didn't appear to, and yet, even though he always guessed wrong, Jack never tired of it.

He came back from Beales' counter with the small bowl and put a spoonful of the vanilla into the boy's mouth, and touched his nose with the cold spoon.

'Banana,' said Jack.

Daniel looked around the room. One other table was occupied, by a group of exhausted-looking parents wearing T-shirts from stadium concerts they had attended in their unmarried days. He spooned a small piece of strawberry ice cream.

'Vanilla,' said Jack.

At the table behind him, the back of one man's shirt advertised the dates of a rap band's tour five years earlier. The area had changed. The old greengrocer's was a futon centre. A shop two doors down from The Owl, which for twenty years had sold plumbing supplies, was now in the hands of a woman who specialised in art materials for toddlers: its motif, stencilled on to the window, showed a cowgirl with a revolver in one hand and a paintbrush in the other, and the name over the shop, which meant Daniel never walked past without wanting to petrol-bomb it, was 'Pastel-Pickin' Momma'.

Jack finished his ice cream and they got up to go. For the last couple of minutes, at the table next to them, a woman had been allowing her five-year-old son to hammer an empty glass hard against the Formica table. As Daniel and Jack got to the door, the glass shattered. Beales strode out from behind the serving counter wearing the look of someone who has just spotted the killer at her murdered granddaughter's funeral. The mother looked back at her with the determination of a woman who had never met Beales before. 'You shouldn't have real glasses,' the mother said, 'in this place.'

Daniel hurried Jack out before they could witness Beales' response, with the controlled urgency of a man leaving the site of an imminent demolition.

They walked back to The Owl, and went round the side of the building and up the metal fire escape to the small apartment where they still lived. The flat roof above The Owl's kitchen, which you had to cross to get to their front door, had become a terrace. When they got to the top of the fire escape, they could see Laura on her knees, emptying compost from a plastic sack into a plant pot. As she turned to look at her son, she took her eye off the bag, and the dry, fibrous soil spilled out over the top of the pot and on to the tarmacked roof. Jack walked over and ran his fingers through it, then put his arms round her neck. He bent down and picked up a small handful of the compost and pressed it against her cheek 'Comfy earth,' he said.

After they got back from Kansas, she'd maintained her new passion for gardening, covering the terrace at the back of the flat with cordylines and camellias in terracotta pots, and poppies in large window-boxes.

'It's strange,' Jessica had told Daniel, watching Laura shifting compost, a couple of weeks after they got back from Kansas, 'how a person's interests can suddenly change, don't you think?'

'I guess there are some things in life,' he said, 'that you just can't explain.'

'I can,' said Jessica.

'What?'

'I can explain this one.'

'Go on,' he said.

'She wants a child.'

'*What?*'

'They can all do it you know,' Jessica said. 'Even the ones that look like they can't.'

He'd not taken her seriously at the time; he'd never met a woman who seemed less maternal than Laura. Then a couple of days later at the flat, as she was talking about making another parachute jump, some impulse seized him.

'You know what Jessica said?'

'What?'

'She said you started spending so much time gardening because you really wanted…' He hesitated, struggling to avoid the mawkish diminutive of 'baby'…'a child.'

'That's right,' said Laura. 'I do.'

'*What?*'

'I said "I do". You want to?'

'Yes,' he said, without thinking.

'OK,' she said. 'You know you said how would you know when you've got me? This is how you know when you've got me.'

Before Jack was born, they'd hesitated for a long time over a name.

'Remington,' she suggested.

'What?'

'Made from American parts,' she explained, 'with British labour.'

For months before he was born they called him Remington; his real name had been the suggestion of Laura's Aunt Helen, the only relative she really appeared to get along with.

'Call him anything…' Helen had said one day, as they sat looking daunted, holding a book of names mostly inspired by Greek gods and Caribbean islands.

'Call him Jack for Christ's sake,' she told Laura, irritated by their indecision.

'Why?' Laura asked.

'Because it's short,' Helen said, 'and it doesn't swank.'

On the morning he was born, they'd waited as long as they could before driving in to the hospital. By the time they arrived, the contractions were coming every couple of minutes, so intensely that Laura could barely walk. They paused outside the double doors of the labour ward and looked at each other, both wondering, stupidly, whether they could go straight in.

'Death knocks,' she said. 'Life bursts straight on through.'

At reception, a sister greeted them. 'All the delivery rooms are full,' she said. 'Would you like to go down to the café for a cup of tea?'

'No,' said Daniel. They sat down. He'd never felt so ashamed of his country.

It was nothing like he'd expected. For the first couple of hours there, they were left alone for long periods, in a room with a broken cassette player. The anaesthetist arrived too late to administer the epidural in time. Laura threw up from the gas and air. It must be the first time, he thought, that anybody would have seen her on the edge of losing all control.

'It's OK,' she said to him at one point, at the height of the pain. 'I can do this.'

The boy was born fast, four hours after they arrived, in a howl of agony. It must be strange for a child, Daniel said to the Portuguese trainee midwife afterwards, to be born to a cry of 'Oh shit'.

'Most of them are,' she said. 'They seem to get over it.'

The door was open to the ward and he could see a hysterical husband screaming for a qualified midwife. The Portuguese woman looked at Laura. She opened her mouth to speak, then didn't.

'Go on,' Laura said.

'What I was just thinking was,' the midwife said, 'why do we live here?'

She left. In that moment, Daniel's anger and resentment had been somehow defused. He picked up the tiny creature, wrapped in a white hospital towel.

'I can't speak,' Laura said.

'Is that your three words for childbirth?' he asked her. 'Three words are enough for anything.' She shook her head.

'What then?'

She smiled, and took his hand. 'Harder than gardening.'

After years of complete self-absorption, the abrupt imposition of responsibility seemed to suit him. Laura, who, like Daniel, had found herself ambushed by the practical consequences of motherhood, slipped into it with surprising ease, day by day, in the way that some rich hostages naturally bond with their Marxist kidnappers.

Even so, it was Laura who had showed more signs of revolting against the insularity and self-indulgence which she'd observed in other new parents. In the two and a half years since the birth, she had got noticeably thinner. One autumn afternoon, four weeks after the boy was born, Daniel was walking along a back street in Crouch End when he passed Patricia, a woman he'd met with Laura at antenatal classes. She was standing on the pavement, leaning through the open passenger door of her small hatchback, fiddling with something on the back windscreen. She waved at

Daniel through the glass. He stopped and asked the time which, she told him, was just before three.

'How's Laura?' Patricia asked.

'Well,' he said. 'She's well.'

He didn't mention that Laura had left Jack at The Owl with Rachel so she could go down to Headcorn airfield in Kent where, in approximately eight minutes' time, she would be flinging herself out of a light aircraft fourteen thousand feet over the Kent countryside. As he walked away, he glanced back at the rear window and saw what Patricia was doing: re-glueing the loose corner of a yellow and black diamond-shaped sticker which read 'Baby on Board'.

The flat over The Owl had remained largely untouched by the presence of a child, apart from the boxroom, which had been cleared out and converted into a small bedroom. To Daniel's astonishment, given the limited size of the main flat, the spare room, once cleared of empty crates and suitcases, turned out to have ample space for a bed.

'Why didn't you throw them away before?' he'd asked her, looking at the huge pile of bags and cases they'd thrown into a skip.

'That's my childhood,' she said. 'I grew up living out of those. This feels terrible. It feels like burning down your old house.'

The café itself had hardly changed, in its physical detail at least. Jessica Lee was still around, though less often; she was spending more of the year with her mother in Leadville, which left every aspect of the running of the place to Laura, Brendan and Rachel who had moved with her son Jordan to a first-floor flat next door.

The staff at The Owl, Daniel had to admit, had become his family. Brendan was still behind the bar and age was making him, if anything, more terrifyingly like himself. And yet, despite his best and most stubborn efforts, the clientele was changing. There were more New Age counsellors; more people who came in scanning the room with that deliberate peripheral vision and exaggerated attention to fellow diners, that was the unmistakable symptom of someone who had achieved minor fame. This being the south of England, Brendan once complained bitterly, The Owl had always attracted the odd person with sunglasses tilted back on their head.

'But now they come in with them first thing in the morning,' he said. 'In November. When it's dark. And it's pissing with rain.'

Daniel's professional ambitions no longer extended beyond the obituaries desk; a couple of months after he was rescued from Commercial Road, Daniel had abandoned *Who's Who In Hell*. It wasn't so much the prospect of a second visit from Gerald Longworth – though that, God knows, should have been deterrent enough. The hysterical scaffolder had posted copies of the stolen disk to all his living companions in Linnell's book of the damned, who included three QCs, a High Court judge and a cabinet minister, and, when he could find them, to relatives of the deceased.

The final blow had come one evening when Robert Balfour turned up unannounced at The Owl. Approaching Daniel and Laura, he opened his attaché case, took out a manuscript the size of a large telephone directory, and placed it on the table in front of them.

'Is that the book?' Laura asked.

'No,' he said. He opened the case again and took out a bound document about half the size of the first. He held it up. 'This is the book. That,' he said, indicating the longer work, 'is the libel report.'

'They won't publish it then?' she asked.

'No,' he said. 'Can we be friends now?' Balfour asked her.

'No,' she replied.

To Daniel's regret, Steven Peerless was in the bar much less often, since he'd accepted his editorial job on the foreign desk. But there were other, new regulars at The Owl. Jonathan was tall, thin and dark, with Middle Eastern features. Although he came every day, he always stood out; he would sit on what Daniel still thought of as Peerless's barstool, near the window. He arrived at ten o'clock, straight from the swimming pool, leafed through the papers with his long fingers, and returned in the late afternoon, when he would order a glass of white wine. One reason you noticed him was that, for reasons Daniel never fathomed, he always wore a suit. He kept his back rigid, as if it was supported by an iron bar, and if he turned to speak to you he would move not only his head, but swivel both his shoulders and his torso, right down to the waist, which made him look aloof and disdainful.

Daniel hadn't warmed instantly to Jonathan. It was his clothes, mainly, his apparently supercilious manner, and the fact that he was a pianist specialising in free-form jazz. But then Laura told him that Jonathan's peculiar posture was the result of a gradual knitting together of the bones in his spine. The condition gave rise to excruciating pain, which explained a distant look in Jonathan's eyes, that sometimes gave him the appearance of someone in touch with another consciousness. He was rumoured to seek comfort in cocaine.

Although he had the solitary, distant manner of a cat fancier, Jonathan owned a dog: an elderly Scottish terrier called Leeds. Leeds' twin, Rome, had died before The Owl was opened; the musician had taken charge of both animals when his brother, who was moving abroad, announced he was going to have them put down. Daniel looked across at Jonathan on his stool, with the dog curled up at the foot of the bar, his nose resting on his shoe. They were always together. Take Jonathan out of there, Daniel said to Laura, and the pianist would dissolve in the daylight. Daniel liked him. They both did.

He lived alone, a couple of miles away in North London, and his days were always the same – a swim, which was supposed to ease his condition, but didn't, then his coffee. When he came back in the afternoon, he'd sit at the bar, composing. He worked on a piece of paper half folded inside a newspaper. Unless you observed him closely, you'd have thought he was doing the crossword.

According to Brendan, Jonathan spent his time writing long, confessional pieces of experimental jazz poetry which had turned out to be far less popular in the UK than the Benelux countries.

'Why's that?' Daniel asked.

'I don't know,' Brendan said. 'I think it's the language thing.'

'You mean he writes these things in Flemish?'

'No,' Doyle replied. 'That's just what I mean. He doesn't.'

These days, he added, Jonathan was able to take the dog touring with him, even abroad. 'He told me he shows up with this portable keyboard and a dog bowl,' Brendan said. 'He said he has trouble finding hotels that'll take pop musicians and dogs. It's funny, but for some reason that seems to surprise him.' The barman paused. 'He showed me one once.'

'He showed you one what?' said Daniel.

'One of his...compositions. One of his own things. It was this thirty-minute song cycle where he played piano, backing tapes and guitar. The lyrics were all about the death of his mother and this traumatic first love affair. He said he was going to perform it at this club in Blackburn. I didn't say anything to him. I wish I had now. He had absolutely no idea where Blackburn was. Or what Blackburn is. It lasted over half an hour. I didn't see him for a while after that. When he came in again, he never mentioned it, for weeks. In the end I got out the Balvenie and I asked him what had happened.

'He said he played it, and he looked down from the stage, round this big hall there, and there wasn't a sound – not a hiss or a clap, nothing. And he got up and walked off stage and he said he could hear the sound of the squeak of the neck of his guitar as it slipped in the sweat off his fingers.

'He went out front for a drink, because there wasn't any in the dressing room, and he ordered a large brandy and he sat down. And this bloke came up to him to try and cheer him up, and he said, "You know, we really liked that last one," and Jonathan, said "Oh yes," and he said, "Yes – the last one; the long one. The one about shagging." '

The Owl's clientele remained mixed, when it came to its customers' age and background. Given the option of banishing one single faction, Doyle would have excluded the purveyors and users of New Age remedies, who now clogged the noticeboard with adverts on coarse beige paper, and pointedly requested one of the No Smoking tables that they knew weren't there. Dee, the only one of these self-taught pathologists who had been coming to the café since it opened, was known behind her back by Brendan as The Idiot Woman.

Oblivious to the lack of thanks, routine civility, or any other response that could have been taken as a sign of encouragement from Brendan, whose rudeness she perceived to be a symptom of chronic hypertension, Dee would occasionally leave him free samples of calming oils. One of the mixtures was called 'Dignity and Vision'.

'She put two drops of that on my wrist one evening,' the barman told Laura. 'I came home blind drunk with my trousers down.'

It was Dee who had provided the unopened 'Optimism and Focus' Laura kept in her bathroom. And it was Brendan, returning from an expedition to a market at Fleetwood, near Blackpool, who'd given her the complementary bottle of 'Scram'.

One evening in the bar, shortly before Brendan's birthday, Daniel heard Rachel suggesting to Jessica that they surprise the inscrutable bartender with a kissogram.

Laura, who was on her way to answer the phone in Jessica's office, paused to speak to them. 'That is so tacky,' she said. The ringing stopped. 'And you know what? He'd love it.'

The phone rang again and this time Laura answered it.

'You're *kidding*,' Daniel heard her say. 'No, come on – it's a great idea. Two weeks? You can stay at the flat.'

Daniel, who had no idea who she was talking to, caught her eye and made a face. 'Or there's Mrs Simpson's,' she said. 'She's got this great little guest-house up the road. That's great. That's really great.' She put the phone down. 'Kate's coming over.'

'When?'

'In a fortnight.'

'That's good,' he said, in a flat tone she didn't seem to notice.

'And Bob,' she said.

'And Bob,' he repeated. 'That's wonderful.'

She looked at him and shrugged, then smiled.

Jessica Lee came up from Devon a few days later with a turquoise business card she'd picked up in Totnes. She handed it to Rachel.

'You know you were talking about a surprise for Brendan,' she said.

'"Charlotte Truman,"' Rachel read. '"Rune Reading and Spiritual Cleansing by Appointment". Oh God.'

'Shall I call her?' Jessica said.

'Are you crazy,' said Rachel. 'He'll go ape.'

Laura picked up the card and dialled the number.

'It's a surprise,' she was saying. 'For a friend.'

Daniel found that, without his having realised it, his head had fallen forward into his hands.

'Which service does he require?' he heard Laura repeat, delighted. 'Both.'

'That's it,' she said. 'She's coming up specially on Saturday. Two hundred pounds, including the readings.'

When Charlotte Truman arrived on the night of the party, Laura, Jessica and Rachel were with Brendan at the long table at the far end of the restaurant. Daniel was working on the bar. As soon as she walked in, he knew it was her: a thin, pale woman with long, straight, mouse-coloured hair, she looked about thirty. She was late, but she wasn't hurrying. She was wearing faded green corduroy trousers, a fawn T-shirt and black plastic shoes. She was carrying a battered second-hand doctor's bag. It had been crafted years ago, every stern exterior detail intended to heighten the owner's air of dignified expertise. In Truman's hands, though, some alchemy had occurred, as a result of which the bag served only to underline the existing impression that she was wholly unqualified for anything. When she came up to speak to Daniel, she put the bag on the bar. It was embossed in gold with the initials of the previous owner: MFC.

He directed her to Brendan's table. She sat down, opened her case and produced a cloth bag which she placed on the table. Daniel had meant not to look, but when it came to it, he couldn't help himself.

'No,' he heard Doyle saying. 'No. Go away. *Now*.'

Jessica brought the woman back to the counter, paid her and offered her dinner, which she refused. 'She says she wants to do someone,' she said to Daniel, 'or she feels she can't take the money.'

'No,' said Daniel. He glanced across at the young woman. She was sitting on a barstool, looking at the clock, wondering, no doubt, whether to find a bed and breakfast or spend the night on Paddington Station. She looked on the verge of real distress. 'OK,' he said. 'But tell her...' – the following phrase, it occurred to him for some reason, was one for which no foreign phrase book ever written could have prepared him – 'no cleansing. Just the runes.'

He took the woman into Jessica's office and closed the door. Already she had brightened. 'Listen,' he told her. 'I have to tell you – I don't believe in this. Either.'

'Doesn't matter,' she said and plunged her hand into the cloth bag. Seated, with her tools in her hands, she had the ease of a penguin as it enters the water and the purposeful focus of a nit nurse. She scattered the pile of small wooden tiles across the desk. They were inscribed with odd shapes and symbols.

'What are those?' he asked her.

'Runes,' she said.

'Oh,' said Daniel. 'Yes.'

'Listen,' he said. 'Don't ask me any questions. No questions.' He glanced at the clock. 'And just tell me one thing about me.'

She nodded, lost in the ritual, and asked him to place nine of the pieces in the shape of a cross, which he did. He glanced across to the door, expecting to see a row of eyes peering through the crack. But the door was firmly closed. She stared down at the tiles.

'In what will be the one great passion of your life,' she said, 'which is to say your current relationship...in your current relationship,' she repeated, 'there is a...there is an...acute...extraordinary...tragic... sexual...' She said the words slowly but absolutely without hesitation or self-consciousness like a Morse instructor reading out a signal transmitted clearly, but at ponderous pace, by a novice. There was a longer pause than usual before the last word. No pause, whatever its length, could have allowed him to anticipate it. 'Compatibility.'

He stared at her – this time, properly speechless. 'Who,' he asked her, 'have you been talking to?' He realised the implication of what he'd said, and he felt like an idiot.

'That's it,' she said. 'One thing.' She picked up her medical bag and left.

To his great relief, he got back behind the bar before any of his colleagues could ask him about what had happened. Rachel came over after a few minutes, and he got away with a non-committal response.

As Brendan was leaving, just after one o'clock, he came up to Daniel. 'Hey,' he said. 'What did that stuff on her bag stand for? Middlesbrough Football Club? Miserable Fucking Charlatan?'

Daniel said nothing.

'What did she say?' Doyle asked.

Linnell, to his own astonishment, told him.

'You mucky devil,' said Brendan.

Daniel locked the bar up for the night, turned out the lights and went up to the flat. Laura was sitting on the window seat in the main room. On the radio, a late night phone-in host was inviting callers to name the pop tune most appropriate to themselves or a public figure. He sat down at the table and, still half-suspecting that Laura might have primed the rune reader, out of mischief, he told her about his experience.

'Jesus,' she said. 'Jesus. Are you kidding?' She walked over and kneeled on the floor in front of him. She folded both her arms across his knees and gazed up at him with a look of great seriousness. 'Hey,' she said. 'What else did you ask her?'

Daniel laughed. 'What – you mean does she do racing tips?'

Laura carried on staring at him, hard. He felt a shiver run through him. 'Don't laugh,' she said. 'Don't joke about those things. Don't joke about us. Because I'm not.'

In the background, a new caller to the phone-in was explaining his attachment to a ballad by Andrew Lloyd Webber. Daniel got up and switched it off. When he looked round, Laura was still on her knees. Glancing at her, he thought she seemed on the verge of tears, but when he got close to her he decided that he must have been mistaken. He sat on the floor, next to her.

'What's our song?' he asked her.

'Sticking with the theme of the rune woman,' she said. She clasped her hands in front of her knees, and pulled them up, and towards her. Her eyes went down to the floor. '"The Hunter Gets Captured by the Game" by Smokey Robinson.'

CHAPTER 24

'I need to do at least four days' shopping,' Kate said to Laura, as Daniel drove their visitors back from Heathrow. 'I only have one dress and one pair of jeans.'

Daniel glanced at Kate in the rear-view mirror. She'd wrapped Jack, who was asleep between her and Laura, in a comfort blanket she'd stolen from the plane. Kate wasn't beautiful, exactly, but there was something – her passion for life, her enthusiasm – that made her interesting, almost desirable.

'Why didn't you bring more clothes?' Laura asked.

Daniel refocused on the early morning traffic. This unbroken conversation from the rear was making him feel like a cab driver. Bob was sitting next to him in the front, but the biology teacher was engrossed in some pages he'd cut out of a glossy travel magazine.

'I didn't bring more clothes,' Kate said, 'because I don't have more clothes.'

'*What?*' Laura laughed, with a strong emphasis on the final consonant.

'I threw away all my size tens a couple of months ago,' Kate said, 'to make me slim back into the eights.'

'And now the eights don't fit you.'

'Right,' said Kate. 'Actually I'm not sure that the tens still fit me.'

'What's that you're reading?' Daniel asked Bob. Kate's husband looked up.

'It's all about this environmental project,' he said, 'in the west of

England. It's quite amazing actually...'

As he went on to describe the tourist attraction, Daniel's attention began to wander between Bob and the North Circular. Certain phrases drifted across to him. 'Geodesic dome...sustainable permaculture...sixty-two kinds of fern.'

'I thought it would be good to stay down there,' Bob said, 'for a couple of days.'

Daniel's eyes rose to the driving mirror again. 'Are you going too Kate?'

'Hmmm?' she said.

'Are you going to Cornwall too?'

'They have clothes shops,' Laura told her, 'in Cornwall.'

'Oh,' Kate said, 'yeah...maybe...yeah, I guess so.'

When they arrived at The Owl, a little after ten, Daniel carried Jack, still asleep, up to his room. Kate, whose energy levels appeared to vary in inverse proportion to the amount of sleep she'd had, was making coffee for Laura downstairs in the bar. He took Bob and the luggage to Mrs Simpson's boarding house, quarter of a mile up the road. It was a place Brendan had stayed in when he first came to London, at which time, he said, there had been a sign in the hall that read: 'Mrs Simpson's: Clean Rooms For Clean Boys.' The landlady now had one attic room with a double bed, and it was there that Bob, who hadn't slept on the plane, was allowed to rest, once he had shown Mrs Simpson his wedding certificate. Daniel returned to The Owl with a spare key. Laura was on the phone in the office and Kate was sat on a stool at the bar, talking to Jonathan.

They had dinner with Bob and Kate that night in The Owl. Once the café had closed, and they'd locked the front door, they were joined first by Brendan, then by Jonathan, who'd stayed later than usual. They sat at the long table at the far end of the bar. Leeds fell asleep on Daniel's foot.

Bob noticed Brendan's Bradford Bulls sweatshirt. 'That's soccer, right?'

Brendan gave him a look of the kind a missionary might give a savage who has never heard the name of Jesus. 'Rugby.'

'So,' said Bob, 'that's fifteen men, right?'

'Thirteen,' said Brendan, 'in rugby league. Fifteen is rugby union.'

'Oh,' said Bob. 'What's the difference?'

Several minutes later, Brendan was still schooling Bob in the details of the six-tackle rule.

Daniel glanced across the table at Kate. She was wearing a black mohair top, and she had a lighted cigarette in one hand and a tumbler of

Algerian red in the other. She was talking to Jonathan, who was sat on Daniel's immediate right, and she seemed to be making more eye contact than was absolutely necessary. Linnell searched through the debris on their table – several empty bottles of beer and wine and a couple of full ashtrays – and found Jack's baby monitor. It was impossible to hear anything at this time of night in The Owl, but he picked it up to check that its small flashing lights were registering no noise from his room upstairs. As he was putting it back down, he thought he saw Jonathan pass something to Kate under the table.

On his left, Bob had succeeded in wrestling the conversation away from the world of sport. 'And you know,' he heard him say, 'it has sixty-two types of fern.'

'It's amazing,' Brendan said, 'that you've managed to keep away for so long.'

'I haven't,' said Bob. 'It's only just opened.'

Kate went out to the ladies'. When she came back, the front of her top was covered in fine white powder. He saw Laura try to draw her attention to it, but then Bob noticed.

'Hey,' he said to his wife, pointing to her sweater. 'What's happened to you?'

She looked down. 'I spilled the talcum powder,' she said. 'In the ladies' room.'

They didn't have talcum powder in the ladies' room at The Owl, or anywhere else in North London, but Bob was a gentleman and that was something he had no way of knowing.

Jonathan was the first to leave. 'Are you going to Cornwall?' Daniel heard the pianist ask Kate as he was getting up.

'No,' she said.

Brendan walked down to unlock the front door for Jonathan. He followed the musician and his dog out into the street.

'By the way,' Doyle said, 'are you coming in here again?'

'I hope so,' said Jonathan.

'Well next time, keep your talcum powder in your own bathroom. If you're not careful,' he added, 'that stuff can get everywhere.'

A couple of days later, on the Saturday morning, Bob set off for Cornwall alone. Daniel took Jack to the park, then came back to The Owl to join

Kate and Laura for lunch. As he approached their table from behind, leading the boy by the arm, he could hear Kate say, '...and he has these beautiful, beautiful hands.' She stopped talking as soon as he arrived.

With Kate around, he was starting to feel the kind of powerless fury traditionally experienced by a wife, when her husband's most dissolute bachelor friend comes to stay. He felt threatened by the knowledge that they had a bond that predated him, didn't involve him, and over which he had no control. He'd started to feel oddly protective towards Bob. In Kate, he saw a risk of reawakening a side of Laura which he'd thought safely consigned to history.

That night when he came in late from work, Laura had put Jack to bed and she was downstairs in the bar going through old photographs, alone at a table, the baby monitor in front of her. Kate was sitting on a barstool next to Jonathan. Daniel was irritated, if not surprised, that she should have met him there so blatantly, in a way that made conspirators of them all. She had on her new British clothes: an expensive-looking crimson dress with a grey silk shawl across the shoulders. She was wearing stockings with seams. He began clearing up behind the bar without speaking to Kate who sounded drunk and gave no sign of having noticed him.

On her way up to the flat, Laura said goodnight to Kate, then put her arm across the musician's shoulders. 'You OK?' she said. He nodded. There was something unpleasantly complicit in the gesture; it looked like a thoughtful tribal chief reassuring a virgin about to be sacrificed. Daniel was behind the bar with his back to them, refilling the ice machine.

Kate took the musician's left hand and began to touch the ends of his fingers, which had been left hardened by years of pressing against keys and fretboards.

'Can you actually feel anything with those?' she said.

'Yes,' he told her.

'Put your hand on my hand,' she said. He placed his left hand over her right; his long, delicate fingers enclosed her small, chubby hand completely, barely touching it, as if he was sheltering a delicate fledgeling. 'OK,' she said. 'Now take me home.'

Daniel, who was sure that Kate knew he could hear this last conversation, picked up a couple of bottles of beer, came out from behind the bar and went back to the flat without saying goodnight to her. He crept past the room where his son was sleeping. Laura was in the bathroom. He opened one of the bottles and stood by the window in the living room. She came over and put both arms round his neck. He slipped out of her grip and turned away.

'What are you thinking about?' she said.

'Bob,' he told her. Even the sound of the name was preposterous; a good name for a victim, like a burst bubble.

'What about him?' she said.

'What about him?' He'd raised his voice without realising it, and he heard Jack stir in the next room. 'Well,' he went on, more quietly, 'for instance – does he know?'

'Does he know what?'

'Does he know that she...' He was on the point of resorting to real vulgarity, then didn't. 'What she does.' He sat down. She came and sat next to him, but didn't try to touch him.

'He knows – he has known – about some of them. Why?'

'Because it makes him look stupid,' Daniel said. 'Because the worst thing about betrayal is that it is so fucking impolite.'

'The thing is that she has these flings,' Laura said. 'She doesn't mean anything by them. They never come to anything. She always comes back.'

'Does he mind?'

Laura breathed in deeply, but didn't answer.

'Why did she marry him?'

'I don't know,' she said.

He put his feet up on a chair, and relaxed a little. 'I just think she's unhinged,' he said. 'I mean it could be anyone. It could be Brendan.'

Laura snorted. 'No. Brendan...I mean we all *love* Brendan, don't get me wrong, but Brendan's pretty ugly.' She shifted in her seat, realising the implication of what she'd just said.

'And Jonathan?' Daniel asked.

'Jonathan...' she tried to say it like a joke, but didn't manage. 'Jonathan's just a little bit ugly.'

Over the next couple of days, with Bob still away, Kate appeared occasionally at The Owl, without Jonathan. She arrived every night at six to take a call from her husband. The one time he rang unexpectedly, earlier in the afternoon, she had just walked into the bar by chance, not with Jonathan but with Leeds. Daniel watched her with the phone in one hand, and his leash in the other. The Highland terrier, who he'd rather liked in the past, had become an emblem of treachery, like Desdemona's handkerchief.

She took the call and then went over to talk to Laura.

'Kate,' Laura asked her. 'Why did you marry him?'

Kate looked her friend straight in the eye, then looked away. 'I think it was like when I threw away the size tens,' she said. 'I thought that one bold step would make me better.'

When Bob came back in to Paddington Station, Daniel refused to go and pick him up. Laura drove him back, alone. When they arrived at The Owl, Kate was waiting, showered and dressed in brand-new jeans and white T-shirt but looking, Daniel noticed, distinctly fatigued.

The following morning, Bob and Kate left for a few days in Paris. Their return flight to the States was a budget ticket leaving from Frankfurt, which meant they wouldn't be back. Daniel felt greatly relieved to wave Kate off, but something about her visit had made him profoundly unsettled.

'What is it?' Laura said to him at last. 'What's got into you? Is it Kate?' Then: 'Is it me?'

'Yes,' he said, more out of spite than conviction.

'What have I done?'

'It's you,' he said. 'Because I think you're like her.'

'No,' said Laura. 'I'm not like her.'

'Robin,' he said, 'told me you both slept with a whole rugby team. In Yorkshire.' She said nothing. 'Was that true?'

'Yes,' she said. 'It was true.'

'How can two women spend a night with fifteen men?'

'Thirteen,' she said. 'Rugby league, not rugby union. I'm not a tart.'

'That isn't funny,' he said.

'You know when Kate was fifteen, she told me she'd read a book where it said that sex was just like shaking hands. She's come to believe that.'

'What about you?'

'With me – looking back, I think it was just that I had to keep on trying.'

'Trying?'

' Till I found one I really liked.'

When he got in to work the next day, a Friday, he saw Steven Peerless coming out of the editor's office. To Daniel's surprise he was heading not for the foreign desk, but for obituaries.

'Ed Franks is dead,' Peerless said.

'Christ,' said Daniel, overwhelmed with guilt at the mockery they had poured on his head. 'When?'

'Last night.'

'How?'

'He was on holiday,' Peerless said, 'in this luxury hotel in Morocco. What the owner said is that Franks had forgotten to take his travel adapter, so he'd unscrewed the British plug off his hair dryer and he was trying to get it to work by pushing the wires straight into the socket. The editor,' Steven added, his features betraying no emotion, 'asked me to tell you he'll write the obit himself, as a special feature for the Review section.'

After lunch, Peerless approached obituaries again. He was holding the editor's article. It occupied the whole front page of the Review section. The headline, in large capitals, read: 'Edward Franks – Man of Action.'

'It was a tragic irony,' Daniel read, 'given the years he spent frequenting the world's most perilous trouble spots, that Ed Franks should have met his end in a villa in Marrakech, the victim of faulty North African wiring. The boldest reporter of his generation, both in his physical courage and his capacity to share his own mental suffering…'

'This is a fucking travesty,' Peerless said. 'Run the real obit too,' he pleaded.

'Are you crazy?'

'No,' Peerless smiled. 'Not that crazy.'

Daniel got up late on the Saturday, as usual, and it was half eleven before he got down to The Owl for coffee. They'd just sat down at a table when Peerless and his girlfriend Jo came in and joined them.

'We don't see you round here so much,' said Daniel, looking pleased. 'How are things? You got nothing on today?'

'No,' Peerless said. 'Or tomorrow, actually. I've just been fired.'

'What? They love you there.'

'Not any more,' said Jo.

'Have you seen the paper?' Peerless asked him. Daniel shook his head. Steven took a copy from the café's news rack and held up the editor's Review front with its glowing tribute to Franks.

'Don't you notice anything?' he asked.

Daniel took the section from him and carefully reread the laudatory first few paragraphs. 'No,' he said.

Then he glanced again at the headline, hugely emblazoned across the page.

'Ed Franks – Man of Acton.'

'Christ,' said Daniel.

'I couldn't resist it,' Peerless said. 'Nobody could have. The thing is, it was just one touch of a key.'

'Didn't anyone notice it in time?' said Daniel.

'Only the chief sub-editor.'

'So what did she do?'

'Nothing,' said Peerless. 'She's been fired too.'

'You mad fucker. Was it really worth getting sacked for something that only a hundred people would understand?'

'Ah,' said Peerless. 'But just think of the joy for the hundred.'

'Let's end like we started,' said Daniel. He opened a bottle of champagne. 'What are you going to do?'

'I'm going to Proteras,' said Peerless.

'What's that – one of those government things?' asked Daniel, imagining it to be some kind of political think tank.

'It's a seaside resort,' said Peerless, 'in Cyprus.'

'It means Fig Tree Bay,' said Jo.

'We're going to buy a boat. And we'll have a dog,' Peerless said.

'And a child,' Jo added.

'When?' Daniel asked.

'Six months,' she said.

He put an arm round each of them. 'That is so great,' he said. 'You got out.'

Whittington, who was now in his mid-forties, seemed to glimpse, in the ever-nearing prospect of old age, an opportunity to indulge the reckless and provocative instincts more commonly associated with youth. He'd graduated from inserting mischievous embellishments in the death notices of the famous, to publishing occasional obituaries of people who had never existed at all. He had only been exposed on one occasion: his lengthy tribute to the imaginary North Korean film director, San Kim Chee, included such a glowing appreciation of his seven-hour black and white epic *Will the Precious Yellow Bird Never Return to Nest on Both Banks of Our*

River? that a Soho cinema discovered the truth when they tried to obtain a print for public showing.

The incident infuriated Whittington's superiors, but the popularity to which he had raised his previously marginalised speciality again preserved him. He would occasionally write features for the main section of the newspaper. His best pieces were on popular culture: he wrote one article on a Trinidadian graffiti artist; such people inhabited a world so remote from Whittington's own experience that he would come away with new, and sometimes memorable, perceptions.

One day Daniel asked Linahan, the sports editor, why he didn't send Whittington to do a story for him on some area which automatically involved intense drama: boxing, say, or rugby league.

'I'll tell you why,' said Linahan. 'Because sending him off to do something is like tossing a lighted match into a huge box of fireworks. You might get nothing at all. You might,' he added, warming to his subject, 'get the rather inspiring effect you're hoping for, if you can make it out, in the middle of a great number of other very distracting things going on all around it. Or you might get a situation that requires the urgent attendance of all three emergency services.'

Daniel dismissed this speech as vain rhetoric at the time. A week later, though, Whittington suggested they go up together to Crouch End for a drink. He'd come to The Owl a couple of times in the past – Daniel was one of the few people connected with obits who didn't regard his work as something entirely divorced from his personal life, like some Masonic club – and yet the younger man still felt a little ill at ease as he waited for Whittington. Laura was at the other end of the café dealing with an aggrieved customer. He was relieved to see that the place was busy and that Doyle was fully occupied with his work.

He noticed Jonathan sitting at the far end of the bar, with his dog. The musician was looking more than usually morose. He waved at Daniel when he saw him come in, but then, shortly afterwards, he left.

'He was in this morning,' Brendan told Daniel, after Jonathan had gone. 'You should have seen him. He was so lovesick and feeble he could hardly press down the plunger in his cafetière.' The way he said it, that last word had five syllables.

'What you have to remember,' Brendan added, 'is that musicians are never happier than when they're moping. Misery's very good for songwriters. Look at it this way – it'll give him another of those thirty-minute song cycles. There should be an escort service where songwriters would go in and pay them two thousand quid, and then some time in the next three months they'd send round a woman to seduce them, break their heart, and leave them bereft.'

Whittington joined Daniel and Laura at a table. He took off his hat but not his coat and was clearly unsettled by the volume of the music. He leaned over towards Daniel, far closer than seemed necessary, and asked him if he would come out with him on a story. He handed him a printed card that read 'The New Continental Club: Admit one'. On the reverse, there was a date stamp of the manually adjustable kind used by librarians. 'Apparently it's an anarchist karaoke night,' he said.

'Whose idea was this?' Laura asked him.

'It was Linahan's,' he told her. 'The sports editor. It's this Saturday, near Westbourne Grove. They have it every year,' he added, 'to raise the money to pay for their anarchy.'

'OK,' said Daniel, straight away, on the grounds that the more time he had to think about the idea, the less he'd like it. He knew of the group, who were famous for their deep, and not unjustified loathing of journalists, especially journalists who looked and sounded like Whittington.

'I wouldn't do this if I were you,' said Laura, to the obituaries editor.

'Why not?'

'Because you'll get lynched.'

A passing waitress handed the obituaries editor a complimentary serving of popcorn in a small yellow plastic bucket. 'Shall we dine?' Whittington said.

On the Saturday night, Daniel arrived early at the venue, an orthodox discotheque in a side-street, in the shadow of the Westway. There was a large shaven-headed bouncer on the door, wearing a dinner-jacket, and at first he thought he'd come to the wrong place. Some of the people who were beginning to file past him had the look of travellers, but the young men's hair was swept back into tight pony-tails, the women were conventionally dressed, and no objections were raised to the occasional customer being frisked. It was raining steadily, but the short queue was polite and orderly. A sign outside the door said simply 'Private Party'. The management at the New Continental, he concluded, had no idea what sort of an event they were hosting.

He handed in his ticket and entered the bar, looking for Whittington. It was just before nine, but the editor was still at home, changing into the clothes he had chosen in Knightsbridge that afternoon, and which he imagined would be best suited to mingling inconspicuously at an anarchist function. As a result, Daniel was already inside when Whittington's taxi drew up in front of the club's entrance, splashing some people already in the short queue. He climbed out wearing full denims and a pair of new black training shoes. He was also holding his trilby, which he'd meant to leave at home, but had brought with him out of habit. He handed his ticket to the bouncer and went to go inside. A muscular arm barred his way.

'No jeans,' said the bouncer.

'What?' said Whittington.

'No jeans,' the man repeated.

'They won't notice in there,' said the editor. 'It's dark.' He paused. It was twenty years since he'd been to a public nightclub. 'Isn't it?'

'No jeans,' the bouncer said again. 'And no training shoes.'

Whittington turned back to look for his taxi, hoping it could take him to some late-night shopping mall, but its tail-lights were already disappearing. Rain was dripping down his jacket collar. He went back to speak to the bouncer. As he reached the doorway, the man gently touched his jacket sleeve and peeled away a transparent sticker giving the garment's size and washing instructions. He looked at it disdainfully, and handed it to the editor.

'Where the hell,' Whittington asked, 'do I find a pair of shoes at this time of night?'

The man shrugged. Disconsolate, Whittington stared down the small side-street, which was deserted. His head dropped. His eyes fell on the bouncer's shoes: black, leather and with cheap plastic soles, but at least as large as his own size twelves. He raised his eyes again and drew breath a little hesitantly.

'No,' said the doorman.

'How much,' Whittington persisted, silently praying that this would be the only time in his life he would ever have to utter this sentence, 'How much do you want for your shoes?'

The bouncer laughed. 'Two hundred quid.' His expression changed as Whittington pulled a large wad of twenty-pound notes out of his pocket.

'Each,' said the bouncer. The editor handed him the money. The man glanced around him, beckoned Whittington into an alley blocked by a large wagon and there, looking conspicuously vigilant, they exchanged footwear.

They were only away for a minute, but when they got back to the door, the bouncer's superior, also in a dinner-jacket, was blocking the way.

'Where the fuck have you been?' he barked.

'Just getting this guy to move his motor,' lied his colleague. He began to steer Whittington through the entrance. The boss barred the way.

'No jeans,' he said, with a spite that, it seemed to Whittington, was unnecessary. The editor felt in the back pocket of his jeans, counted out the rest of his money – almost a hundred pounds – and pressed it into the new man's hand. He handed him his press card.

'I'm a journalist,' he hissed. 'I have got to get in.'

The chief bouncer stood aside and Whittington went through into the hall, forgetting to recover his card. Daniel was in the balcony above the stage, watching a young woman perform a song called 'How Does It Feel to be the Mother of Ten Thousand Dead?' He wandered up to the next floor, where the tables were made out of coffins, and there was a bank of television screens showing a peculiar collage of film clips, jump-cutting between news, elderly Westerns, and children's puppet shows.

It was an intriguing piece of work, and Daniel started talking to the young art student who'd assembled it. Downstairs in the main hall, Whittington was queuing at the packed bar, making the staff wait while he scanned the optics for 'a decent malt'. Not finding one, he ordered a large gin. It was only as the barman was pouring it that he remembered he didn't have any money. This turned out not to matter because his order never arrived. The nature of Whittington's mission had been communicated from the doormen to the bar staff, who had passed around his press card. News of his presence, and even his name, spread among the anarchists, packed tightly in the hall, like static.

Realising he had no cash, Whittington tried to back away from the bar, but couldn't. Behind him there was a tight knot of young men who, he presumed, were waiting to be served. Glancing to his right, he noticed there was no queue. He tried to point this out to the group gathered behind him, when they closed in on him and, with the practised firmness of a rugby pack, drove him to the front of the hall and kept him pressed there, so that the top of the chipboard stage was digging painfully into his ribcage. He felt a single, moderate punch connect with his right kidney. A door opened to the gents' which was to the back of the stage – his final destination,

Whittington presumed, for a comprehensive beating. Then the sound system was turned off. The pressure in his chest eased and the next thing he knew he had been picked up and thrown bodily on to the stage.

'We have a special guest performer,' shrieked one of the organisers. 'From the national press.'

A worrying hiss and rumble grew from the back of the hall. A man at the front of the stage spat on his shoes. Whittington tried to find in himself that place of inner quiet that hostages say sustains them during a mock execution. To his alarm, he saw that the biker in charge of the karaoke machine had turned it back on. A microphone was thrust into his hand. 'Sing,' the biker said, 'you bastard.' For all the terror of the experience, he suddenly felt the preposterous fear that they would have chosen a tune that was well known to everybody in the hall but him. That would make him look foolish. That would show his age. But when the opening piano notes struck up, they were all too easily recognisable.

Daniel was still in the film gallery when he noticed a familiar quality to the voice booming from the main stage. He rushed to the balcony just as Whittington, still dressed in his full Levis, reached the chorus: 'Give Me Money (That's What I Want)'.

The atmosphere in the hall below was one of real menace. On the opposite balcony he could see a couple of youths spitting at the stage. Daniel wondered if there was any way out of this that didn't involve the police and the gossip columns. As the performance went on, however, he noticed a change of mood. Whittington, through heat or desperation, had removed his jacket, revealing, to great applause, a bare chest and the pair of what he'd felt to be modish red braces. He performed with increasing gusto, combining a style that was essentially a primitive version of the twist, with a wrist action once popular with Southern Mediterranean ballad singers, who used to emphasise great passion by stretching out their right hand as if attempting to adjust an invisible wing-mirror.

The backing tape ended, then immediately started again. Halfway through the second rendition, the crowd were bellowing a resounding chorus of 'That's What I Want'. In the instrumental break, the editor strutted the front of the stage and dropped to his knees holding out his trilby, an action which precipitated a shower of coins. Whittington's third performance was preceded by a feverish stamped demand for an encore and a number of camera flashes. Daniel found his mobile and rushed downstairs to dial 999.

He struggled across the crowded dance floor. By the time he felt the cold air seeping in from the exit, Whittington, still stripped to the waist and with ironic cheers ringing in his ears, was being chaired in the same direction. Daniel got out into the street just before his senior editor arrived on the shoulders of his hosts, who threw him with a limited degree of force that – considering his initial reception – was almost affectionate. He landed heavily, on the bonnet of a red Mondeo. With sarcastic gentility, one youth picked up his trilby from the gutter, and handed it to him. As Whittington took it, it jingled slightly.

A waiting line of unlicensed minicabs observed the scene in silence. Whittington's tormentors, to Daniel's great relief, turned and went back into the club. He climbed off the dented bonnet. 'Ah,' he said. 'Linnell. Evening. I'll be with you in a moment.' He began walking back towards the club. 'Never mind your jacket,' Daniel hissed. He beckoned the first minicab, which drew up alongside them in front of the entrance. 'It's not the jacket,' said Whittington, whose upper body was still naked except for his braces. 'I'll just give this chap back his shoes.'

'Fuck his shoes,' said Daniel, and pushed the editor through the open door of the cab. Whittington, observed by the driver in his mirror, wound down his window, pulled off the shoes, and lobbed each in a looping arc over the roof of the cab and on to the pavement. His hat was still on his lap.

'Where to?' asked the driver.

'The Savoy,' said Whittington.

The driver turned off the engine, got out, walked round to the back door and opened it. 'Out,' he said. 'Now.'

Daniel pulled two twenty-pound notes from his back pocket and handed them to the man. 'The Savoy Hotel,' he repeated quietly, 'in the Strand.'

When Whittington emerged from the revolving door at the Savoy, and the lobby staff noticed his naked chest, braces, and spittle-soaked jeans, there followed a second unpleasant collision with the British dress code. This was resolved when the night manager, who was just coming on duty, recognised him. 'A suite,' said Whittington, who sent one of the paper's drivers to pick up Rosa. When she arrived an hour later with a change of clothes, the editor was in a hotel robe holding a glass of champagne, and a waiter was laying the table for three. Whittington disappeared into the bathroom again to dress. Rosa was wearing an expensive-looking, full-length scarlet cotton dress. The speed of her arrival, Linnell thought, meant she must have already been wearing it, at home, when the editor phoned.

It occurred to Daniel that, though he had often listened to Whittington talk about books or films, he had almost never spoken about music. He asked Rosa what sort of thing he listened to. 'I have no idea,' she said, looking at Daniel as though he had asked about some sexual peccadillo.

'You know Jane Denselow,' said Rosa, 'the architect.'

'Yes,' said Daniel, and he described the circumstances in which they'd last met, in the bar of the Grosvenor House Hotel.

'That's the one,' said Rosa. 'I used to know her brother John. He's dead now. He was a concert pianist; I got to know him because he had this holiday home at Cadaqués on the coast north of Barcelona. Anyway,' she said, 'Whittington went out to stay with him there once. There was music in that house the whole time, from the moment he woke up till he went to bed. There was this tremendous sound system that played in every room in the house, even the bathrooms.' She poured herself another small glass of champagne. 'John Denselow told me...' she lowered her voice slightly. 'He told me Whittington was there for a week, and in that time John had played everything from Verdi to Stockhausen to Wagner, and that he never passed any comment on any of it. But he said on the last morning, that he – John – put on a record by Feodor Chaliapin; you know who he is?'

Daniel shook his head.

'He's – he was – this intense Russian baritone,' she said. 'And John said he walked into the kitchen, where of course it was playing as well. And he found Whittington sitting there, sobbing silently to himself. I remember,' she added, 'that he said what shocked him was the way that it was a wholly emotional response, not an intellectual one. And he told me that he did the same thing in the evening, and the same thing happened. He said that watching Whittington listening to Chaliapin was like watching a dog howling to the discords from a harmonica. Except that even a dog can learn to stifle its moans.'

'Why...' Daniel began to ask. As he did so, the bathroom door opened again.

'Just briefly,' said Whittington, taking his place at the head of the table in the suite's dining room, 'just for a moment, I thought that I was going to die up there. I felt a serene detachment as I was coming down through the air towards the bonnet of that big red, er...'

'Ford Mondeo,' interrupted Daniel.

'Ah yes,' said Whittington. 'The big red Ford Mondeo. One never knows,' he added, 'what form one's courage will take.'

Rosa lit a cigarette and put her feet up on the sofa. She reached into one of the dishes and took what looked to Daniel like a very large-armoured prawn, which she peeled in one single dexterous movement. Whittington's self-control while airborne over traffic, she said, was especially remarkable because he had more reason to fear death than most.

'What do you mean?' asked the editor, sounding hurt.

'I mean – well...they'll all be down there waiting for you, won't they? All those lords and the archbishops, and the crackhead drummers and the bisexual goalkeepers. It'll be open season.' Rosa roared with laughter and disappeared into the bathroom.

Daniel, who had swallowed half a bottle of Veuve Clicquot before he'd really sat down, to try to erase the memory of the evening's hostilities, told Whittington – slurring slightly, and in what he believed to be a whisper – how he envied Rosa's great ease in these opulent surroundings. 'It's as if she's realised,' Daniel said, 'that wealth and ostentation aren't the things that really count.'

'The best things in life are free,' a powerful soprano voice sang out from the toilet. 'But you can keep them for the birds and bees...'

She came out, picked up her coat and walked over to the door.

'You're staying I suppose?' she said to Whittington. He nodded. As she was leaving she picked up his brown trilby, which was upturned on a table by the door. She tipped out the small change and counted the money. 'Two pounds twenty-three,' she said. 'It's lucky for you that I'm a woman of discretion.'

After she'd gone, Daniel spent some time in the bathroom himself, failing to wash the New Continental's luminous mauve stamp off his hand. When he came out, he looked for some red wine, and couldn't find any.

'I'll get them to send something up,' said Whittington.

'It's OK,' Daniel said. 'I feel like a walk.'

He went down to the bar and collected a bottle of Bordeaux. He stepped outside for a moment, and in the night air realised he was very drunk. He walked unsteadily back into the lobby and spotted a payphone. He called Laura.

'How's Jack?' he asked her.

'He's asleep,' she said. 'Like he often is at two a.m. How did it go tonight? At the club?'

'I can't talk about that now,' he hissed, glancing around for fear of passing columnists. 'Not here. I'm in a phone box. There are people around. I need to keep my head down. I'll tell you later.'

'He got lynched then?' she said.

'Yes.'

'Told you.'

He glanced up and thought he could see a couple of the hotel staff eavesdropping.

'Is he alive?' she asked. 'Where is he now?'

'He's drinking champagne,' Daniel whispered. 'In a room in the Savoy.'

'Oh,' she said. 'That sort of a lynching. The British kind.'

He put the phone down and went over to the lifts to go back up, then realised he'd forgotten the room number. 'I'm looking for...'

'Four hundred and five,' chorused the receptionists.

'It's a funny thing,' said Whittington, when Daniel reappeared. 'Rosa has a very Catholic view of hell. I wouldn't see it that way at all.'

'No goalkeepers,' said Daniel.

'Or, who knows,' said Whittington, 'bearing in mind the capricious character of the Supreme Being – only goalkeepers'. He walked into the bathroom and picked up his stained denims, which he dropped into the waste bin. 'You might be surprised to learn,' he said, 'that I do have a notion of what hell – or rather purgatory – might be like. There are no infernal flames, there are no demons, or implements of torture. There is a huge art deco movie theatre, where you sit between your parents, whether they're dead or not, with God and the Committee in the projection room. The other seats are taken by everyone you've ever known, or betrayed, or deceived. Or – if applicable of course – loved or honoured.

'Then they start the film of your life and it's not edited at all. It lasts for sixty years or whatever, and you see every single incident. So you're sat there, watching it all, thinking, Oh God no, in six months' time I'm going to come back into this flat and drink this chap's entire stock of Mateus Rosé and seduce his blind teenage sister, and you have all those interminable hours to wait for it to happen. Most of the time the screen is in darkness. And at night there's nothing happening except for the occasional – excuse my vulgarity, Linnell – fart, or outbreak of physical intimacy. Neither will enhance your reputation in the eyes of your audience, especially when they have witnessed these acts several thousand times and noticed that, despite their monotonously repetitive nature, they still appear entertaining to you.

'I imagine them to have installed a surrender button next to the seat of the deceased,' Whittington continued, 'which you can press to remove yourself straight to hell. I see that as round and illuminated, with a red triangle pointing downwards, like the ones we have by the lift. You spend seven or eight years wondering whether or not to press it, and when you do push it nothing happens. And you keep on pressing it for the next twenty-eight years, until you finally watch yourself peg out on a trolley in some emergency room, with each last sordid detail revealed in wide screen format. When the lights come up, with every eye in the house on you, you're still pressing the button, praying to be carted off for the proper torture, but nobody moves. An usherette holds up a sign that says "Continuous Programme" and the whole film starts all over again.'

Daniel stared at Whittington. 'Are you sure you haven't been overdoing it a bit recently?'

To the irritation of his more serious-minded colleagues on the news desk, Whittington's account of his experience in Westbourne Grove, which spared no detail of his humiliation, captivated more readers than any single report their own sections had run in the past year. The article generated an unusual amount of correspondence. Most letters were complimentary – most, but not all. The owner of the damaged Mondeo, for instance, enclosed a bill for almost three thousand pounds, which the managing editor grudgingly settled.

The obituaries staff were hardly strangers to hostile feedback. Most departments tried to ignore such correspondence. ('I put mine in the bottom drawer for a couple of weeks,' Linahan, the sports editor, once told Daniel. 'After a while, you just have to throw it away, like cheese.') Whittington, on the other hand, would always have a couple of the more vitriolic outbursts from readers pinned on his noticeboard, next to the portrait of Long John Silver and the photograph of the black farmhand. 'My thirteen-year-old son,' raged the correspondent at the centre of the current display, 'has expressed an interest in becoming a journalist, so I have pinned your obituary of Frances White on his bedroom wall, to remind him of the sort of puerile crap he should most earnestly seek to avoid.'

Fellow journalists, Whittington told Daniel, considered the obituaries' noticeboard to be a public admission of his madness. 'But they're wrong,' he explained. 'Behind those two glass doors is the only real air in the whole building.'

His remark was not wholly flippant: the atmosphere on the newspaper was substantially unlike the culture of the external world whose truths it pretended to reflect. One Friday, when Laura had gone off to Brussels with her camera and her parachute, he brought Jack into the office. On the open-plan editorial floor, the effect of the three-year-old was extraordinary, to the point that Daniel might as well have walked in carrying a mermaid or a fizzing cartoon bomb. Except that, in the presence of the child, the most vicious individuals on the floor would start behaving like humans again.

Jack sat next to Rosa for an hour or two; the boy looked absurd, cross-legged on a revolving office chair listening to animal stories on a cheap Walkman. At one point he got down and walked over to stand with his nose pressed against the window pane of the tower block, gazing down at the city hundreds of feet below. He turned and startled half the floor with his next remark, which was delivered with the accidental volume of a novice in headphones. 'My mummy,' he shouted to Rosa, 'can jump down there.'

Whittington, who generally paid little attention to children, looked over at the infant. 'To those trapped on the editorial floor,' he said, 'the sudden arrival of something from the real, daylight world, the place of living, oxygenated humanity, is appreciated. It is noted. It wreaks havoc. Anything,' he added, 'will do: an Airedale, a badly-played chord on an old ukulele, lit candles, a boy. They cluster round such things, like a cargo cult round a postcard of the Duke of Edinburgh. They gabble. They gape. They stand about.'

His 'they', Daniel said, sounded hypocritically superior.

'Perhaps,' Whittington said. 'And yet we do differ from them in certain ways. For instance, if we see a close friend in trouble, we help.'

Between Whittington and his senior editors there had grown an increasingly bitter distance, and his survival was ensured simply by his proven ability to galvanise the readership figures. One evening, not long after the karaoke episode, he was sitting with Daniel in the Printer's Devil. One of the paper's cartoonists, using a black felt marker and a can of plain white emulsion he'd found in a cupboard next to the gents', was adding a picture to the wall of incomplete quotations. It showed a fat, elderly ram seated in a large editorial office, preening its fleece and leering at a couple of gambolling young ewes. When he'd finished, he scrawled the caption 'A Sheep as a Lamb'.

'We admire our senior executives,' said Whittington, 'in the way that a black dog sticks faithfully by its beggar in the tube, even though he may be maniacal, lice-ridden, or schizophrenic. We blind ourselves to it, but our nose tells us what the world thinks of them. We have observed more closely than others the self-abasement and daily cruelty of which they are capable. And yet still we walk to heel.'

Daniel picked up the evening paper, which contained a report on a fiercely contested local election whose first paragraph contained the phrase 'a roller-coaster ride'.

'A roller-coaster ride,' Daniel remarked. 'God, how the news editors love those words. The more times they get them in a story, the happier they are. Those six syllables,' Linnell added, 'thrill them. Their magic never fades. They quicken their pulse. Like bishops, when they hear "Jesus of Galilee".'

'George Bernard Shaw,' said Whittington, who didn't appear to have been listening, 'once said that he was given his own music column in a newspaper precisely as he might have been given a padded room in an asylum. If I may quote from memory, "The first condition was that what I did should be as attractive to the general reader – musician or non-musician – as any other section of the paper. Most editors did not believe that this could be done. But then most editors do not know how to edit."

'When you observe the senior executives as we do, day by day,' Whittington said, 'rushing about in all directions, with an apparent purposefulness which leads them from one futile collision to another, often with people who are supposed to be their friends and allies, you can't help noticing that what they're really riding is not the roller-coaster, but the dodgems.'

Observations of this sort were not appreciated by middle management. Another source of resentment among Whittington's fellow editors was the way that he seemed to be able to disappear at will, giving little or no notice, for days at a time, calling in Julian Cave, the young freelance. Whittington had convinced the managing editor that these absences were a medical necessity, because of the effects of daily stress on the ample body that (he had also persuaded them) masked a fragile constitution which could only be adequately restored at one establishment. His destination, 'The Zurich', was, as they understood it, a Swiss-run health farm in the West Country, whose restorative regime apparently depended on a raw vegetable diet, transcendental meditation, and circuit training. According to Whittington these principles were applied with an unforgiving rigour, which made it all the more curious that he invariably returned from Devon looking heavier, more sluggish, and sated.

CHAPTER 25

Daniel woke early. From the silence in the street below, he knew that it was a Saturday. Laura was next to him, lying on her side. Her left arm, which was supporting her head, was stretched out, as if pointing the way to the plastic alarm clock on the floor. When he'd first met her, Laura had an elaborate digital radio alarm, which he'd always disliked, for reasons he wasn't sure of. Eventually it had dawned on him: it wasn't simply the unforgiving red glow of the numbers. It was the fact that you might wake up one morning to discover that the display was showing – as it was this morning – 5.52 a.m.: a time that, because of its terrible leading digit, gave the insomniac a reflex shiver. So different from ten to six, which was almost morning. Invigorated by that insight, he had drop-kicked the electric clock off the roof terrace into the bins below, and bought its cheap black replacement. 'Why not give it to the charity shop?' she asked him when he explained what had happened to it. Because, he told her, that would only transfer the problem to somebody else. 'You're all right,' she said. 'You know that?'

He looked down at the girl. There was something – it could have been the way she often seemed frozen in a state of adolescent revolt – that meant that, even now she was a mother, she never seemed quite suited to a word like woman. A white linen sheet was all that covered her, just revealing the point at the top of her right shoulder and the small tattoo of a rose that she'd had done when she was fifteen, on the well-founded assumption that it would drive her father insane. He could see by her outline that her knees were drawn up in front of her, though not far enough for her position to be called foetal. Even so, he thought, there was something strangely familiar about this posture, to the point that he felt it must have a name. It reminded him of the shape, he suddenly realised, that film directors assign to a chalk body outline at the scene of a murder.

A couple of days earlier she'd asked him if there was anything he wanted, and he'd told her that she needed a decent stereo. Up until then, they'd got by with her battered music centre and his portable CD player. He'd said 'she needed' not just because the flat above The Owl was still so much Laura's territory, but because the insularity of words like 'we' and 'family' was something he loathed.

'You know how we never say love,' he told her.

She looked at him.

'The verb,' he repeated, 'to love.'

'Do you want to say it?' she asked him.

'No,' he said.

'You know Helen, my mom's sister,' she said. 'Well, I went down there years ago with Kate, when we were just out of college. And Helen had this magazine article where it said that on average a British woman has ten lovers in her life. And Kate says to Helen, "How many have you had?" I think she was trying to shock her. My aunt – she'd have been about fifty then – just looked at her and said, straight out, "Three."'

'Then she looked back at Kate like she was expecting a response, and Kate said, "Thirty-four." Helen said, "You keep busy then, dear." And I remember Kate laughed and said, "Yes – why didn't you?"

'And my aunt says, "Because I always fell in love."

'And I said, "Well – you don't absolutely *have* to, you know."

'And Helen looked at me and said, "Have you ever?"'

'And,' Daniel said, 'what did you tell her?'

'I said, "No,"' Laura told him. ' "I don't believe I ever have." '

'And what about now?'

'Now,' she said, 'I'm not sure.'

That first night, when he'd said it, it occurred to him, he hadn't meant it. It was a characteristic they shared. He glanced down at her with great tenderness She hated those words too. He liked her for it.

Looking around the room, his eye went up to the wardrobe and the last unwanted possession that remained to him: the cardboard box full of clothes that he'd brought with him from South London, and which had stayed there, untouched, since their trip to Cornwall, three years earlier. He decided to drop it by the bins on his way down to the bar.

He sat up quietly in bed and his foot reached down a few inches from the mattress to the carpet. He'd finally grown used to sleeping on the floor. He stretched up and took down the box, then picked up his crumpled pile of clothes and placed them on top of it, and crept past Jack's half-open bedroom door. Glancing in, he saw the boy asleep in a bed that, like the rest of the room, was strewn with plastic toys in primary colours. He went on through to the living room, where he got dressed.

Laura was looking after Jack that morning; then they'd arranged for Rachel to babysit so they could meet at lunchtime in the West End to go to the electrical shops. And that was not for six and a half hours. He sat at the window, as he had on that first night, and stared out into the street below. From the next room, he heard his young son cough, then stir slightly. He felt a strong but unspecified urge to introduce some more serious order into his life.

He could begin his new, more disciplined life by going in on his day off to do some extra work, while the office was quiet. Before he left, he thought, he could dispose of the box of clothes. Daniel opened the trap-door in the floor, dropped it through the hole and climbed after it, down the iron ladder into the café.

He went behind the bar, turned the sound system to its minimum volume, and altered the setting to radio. He was greeted by the voice of an elderly Lincolnshire farmer being interviewed over breakfast. He was the master of the local hunt, and he sounded as out of place at The Owl as a rogue signal from another galaxy. He set the amplifier to CD and pressed play. Whatever was in there, Daniel thought, it had to be better than this Grantham pig man's eulogy to blood sports.

The room was filled with an orthodox-sounding white American rock band that mightn't have caught his attention at all if it hadn't been for the words. 'I can saw a woman in two,' it began, 'but you won't want to look in the box when I'm through. I can make love disappear; for my next trick I'll need a volunteer.'

He picked up the box, meaning to ditch it in the yard, but found he couldn't resist opening it first. He peeled off the thin tape and turned it upside down to empty out the contents. It was only now, once the box was inverted, that it struck him: this was where he had left it. If the thought hadn't come to him, he might have missed the scarf altogether – just a corner was visible, at the bottom of the pile of misshapen woollens. Now, with Laura and their child sleeping upstairs, he felt he could dispose of this memory, along with his other clothes, with a degree of equanimity. But when he saw the scarf he found that, within a matter of seconds, he had it clenched in both hands, so tightly that strands of the rough wool were pressed up under his fingernails. The physical sensation was so unpleasant that a cold shudder ran down his spine, and yet he stayed there, in that position, for a minute or two, astonished that even now, after everything that had happened to him, this yard of cheap knitting could reduce him so swiftly to desolation.

He went out the back and threw the box and pullovers in the trash. He was about to drop the scarf in there as well, when he decided – out of respect, he told himself – to dispose of it at the charity shop. He thought about making a coffee, then decided against it. If he didn't do it there and then, he never would. He walked out to the street.

A black cab with its yellow For Hire sign illuminated was approaching from his right, coming north out of London. Daniel flagged it down. 'Docklands,' he said, and got in.

'Oh,' muttered the elderly cab driver, who had forgotten that he'd left the intercom switched on, 'for fuck's sake.'

'If you don't want to go,' said Daniel, 'don't go.'

The man said nothing, and pulled away. Daniel, who was occasionally prey to a suicidal fearlessness when conversing with strangers, was about to make another remark, then didn't. He looked at the driver's short-sleeved check shirt and his muscular arms, heavily tattooed with images including a dagger and a rose. His second rose tattoo, he thought, of the morning. God knows what road had brought the man to this fury. He looked at the driver's photograph on the identity badge displayed on the dashboard: his heavily-lined face, looking weary and fraught. Was this the fate awaiting the infant lying asleep in Laura's old suitcase cupboard? Because even driver C8341, he thought to himself, had come into the world as a mewling infant blinking against the light, the unique focus of the hopes and ambitions of his parents, and even he faced the prospect that he might return, as we all might return, naked and humbled to lay his immortal soul before his maker in the splendour of judgement by God and his ministering angels. A car pulled out of a side-street in front of them. 'Cunt,' said C8341.

He asked the driver to stop off at the charity shop in Limehouse. When they got there he opened the cab door, looked down for the scarf, and couldn't see it. A swift panic mounted in him; the kind of sudden dread that might strike a man who has just flown non-stop to Australia and realised he's mislaid his passport. Then he found it, by his feet. He walked up to the locked door of the shop and fed the scarf through the letter-box. Immediately he felt tremendous relief. He'd done it. It was like closing a door.

Daniel was at his desk before seven. The paper was at its best at this time: there was no one to glare at his creased open-necked shirt, and the only people around were the cleaners dealing with the debris from the previous night's rush for the deadline. Nobody from obituaries would be in until the following day.

Daniel had been working on William Barton, a Liverpool showman Whittington had become interested in. A former non-commissioned officer in the merchant navy, he had spent the rest of his life travelling round Britain with an exhibition of curios: shrunken heads, deformed animal embryos and executioners' swords. He handed the obituary over to Daniel when he learned that his deputy had once visited Barton's stall at Belle Vue amusement park in Manchester. The showman was interesting on several counts, not least because he had lost his right ear. 'Hacked off,' read a sign above the exhibits, which for some reason had been printed in large gothic type, 'by a jealous tribal chief in Port Moresby'.

Even as a boy, Daniel had been unimpressed by the display, which included a freeze-dried herring wrapped in a piece of sheepskin and billed as 'the amazing furry fish'. The shrunken heads, which were from Papua New Guinea, and were real, were almost as pathetic. True horror, as Freud wrote, doesn't spring from the unknown or the exotic, but from the familiar become strange: a childhood doll that, a moment ago, seemed to shift its eyes by itself; a sudden chill in a favourite chair; a dead man playing squash.

The obituary was almost finished, but Whittington had asked him to call Barton to check a couple of details: a request that had less to do with genuine need than with his editor's mischievous instincts. He cut and polished the copy he already had. Then, at nine thirty, he dialled the number. To his considerable relief, Barton never asked why he was calling: his ego and the mention of the name of a national paper was enough.

'My first job was in St Helens,' he said, 'with Barton and Thwaites, the coal merchants. That was my uncle's firm. Then the navy, then the show. I was forty-two years on the road.'

Daniel looked down at Whittington's first question, scrawled on the back of a postcard: True circumstances of loss of ear.

'It was blown off,' said Barton cheerfully, 'when we were sent out for artillery training with the army. It was blown off,' he added, 'at Oswestry, by Private Andrew Steele of Darlington when he cocked up his mortar exercise. Not such a good story that, is it, lad?'

Daniel tried to fight whatever it was in that last word that put him instantly in his place, and failed.

'What is interesting,' Barton added, 'is what happened to me two days later, when I was lying alone in this side ward of a hospital in Crewe, with this bloody great bandage round my head. The morphine was wearing off, and they told me they couldn't give me any more. You have to understand – this wasn't just the outside of my ear. The doctor said my eardrum wasn't so much perforated as blown away. He came in and he sat down in the chair next to my bed. He said, "Barton, I've been a surgeon for fifteen years, but when we were cleaning up your ear, the stuff we got out of there, it was like what you see when you take one of those miniature forks and ease the body of an es-car-gowe out of its shell, in a restaurant in Paris."'

Daniel winced. It was those three French syllables that had done it: Barton's Liverpool accent somehow added a new level of awfulness to this already gruesome image; one which, he realised, would stay with him for the rest of his life.

'Well I'd never been to Paris,' said Bailey. 'I still haven't. And I'd never eaten an...'

'It sounds terrible,' he interrupted.

'Anyway,' Barton went on, 'this deep throbbing pain had begun, and it were getting stronger and stronger, like childbirth, and they said well the top and bottom of it is all we can give you is a handful of aspirin.

'And I called for the nurse. I said, "It's coming back nurse, and it's worse than it was first time, and I'm frightened." And the nurse – she didn't say anything – she disappeared behind this screen on the other side of the room, and then I saw her dress appear; she'd hung it over the front of the screen. And then I saw her hand come out and hang her stockings up there, and then all her other tackle. It were like a silent film.'

'Why silent?' Daniel asked.

'It were silent,' Barton said, testily, 'because my right ear had gone, and

I couldn't hear anything in the other for the bloody bandage.'

'And she came out – she was a Scottish lass, and she was tall, she was three inches taller than me and I was five eight, and that was a good height in those days and she couldn't have been more than twenty. She came out, stark naked, and she sat down on the chair by the top of the bed, and she still didn't say anything. She took my hand and she put it – she placed it – on her kneecap.'

Daniel looked across the room where a cleaner was refilling a water dispenser, trying to ground himself in some other form of reality. 'On your ...kneecap,' he said, accidentally pronouncing the word in a way that could have suggested doubt, though he was certain that, on this occasion at least, Barton was telling the truth.

'Not a romantic word that is it lad?' he said. 'Kneecap.'

'No...' said Daniel. '...sorry.'

'I'd just come back from two months in Aden,' Barton said. 'I thought she'd gone mad. And she just sat there, stock still for about a minute, still undressed, staring straight ahead, with my hand still placed on her...'

'Patella,' Daniel volunteered.

'I'll stay with kneecap,' said Barton. 'Kneecap isn't romantic. But that just sounds filthy.

'And then,' he said, 'she got into the bed and she lay on top of me. I had my hands down by my sides and she had this long, thick, dark, wavy hair and it fell down over my face, and it covered my bandage: this long, thick, dark hair. And in the end I said, "Why did you do that?" And she said, "To see what you'd do." I said, "What do you mean what I'd do?" And she said, "To see if you'd move your hand." And I said, "Well, I didn't move my hand." And she said, "No, you didn't move your hand. And that means I can trust you."

'I had my head turned away from her, staring at the wall to my left, and she had her forehead pressed against the right side of my neck. When she lifted her head up, I remember it pulled at my skin very lightly, as if she'd been sweating. I remember all this,' he said, 'because I'd been taught to believe that such things might cause a woman disgust.'

Daniel was struck by the curious delicacy of that last expression.

A pause. 'You still there?' he said.

'Yes,' said Daniel.

'Good. That's between us then, son.'

Daniel had been wholly unprepared for the confessional mood that had settled on Barton. It was more unnerving, in its own way, than the brusque refusal he had been expecting.

'And what then?' he asked.

'What then?' said Barton, with what might have been a snort of contempt or a stifled laugh. 'What then? Look, you're the reporter. You're the one with the college degree. Have you got a college degree?'

Daniel, startled, made his response, waited for an answer and, when it didn't come, realised he was not speaking but nodding. 'Yes,' he said.

'Good,' said Barton. 'Was it hard, the exam?' He put a hard stress on the word's first syllable, as if he was speaking a foreign language.

'Yes,' Daniel said.

'Well then,' said Barton, without a trace of sarcasm, 'well done. And you know the funny thing is,' he went on, 'I can remember every detail of that day, but I can't remember her name. I don't know if I ever even knew it. And you know, I've only ever told one person about that before. I suppose you can guess who that was.'

Daniel looked down at Whittington's second question: date of marriage. 'Your wife?'

'My wife? Bloody hell, man, my wife? I told Andrew Steele. To make him feel better, although I shouldn't think it did.' There was a pause. 'Eleanor,' he said quietly. 'Her name was Eleanor. I never saw her again, and the next year I was married.'

'Summer wedding?' Daniel asked, lamely.

'November the second,' said Barton. 'Because it's her birthday. You may know it,' he added, 'as the Mexican Day of the Dead.'

Daniel opened the computer file and added a few lines, which made no mention of Eleanor. He printed out the finished version, folded it, and placed it in the morgue.

He found himself staring at a bronze plaque on a pillar opposite him, commemorating correspondents who had died while gathering real news on foreign battlefields. He looked down again, at Whittington's two questions. Jesus Christ, he muttered aloud, taking the name, for the first time in fifteen years, not entirely in vain.

Daniel arrived early to meet her at Tottenham Court Road and stood on the corner by the entrance to the Underground, watching the crowds pass in front of a stall selling T-shirts and football scarves. It wasn't what you'd call a restful scene: his view consisted, for the most part, of mean-faced locals weighed down with plastic shopping bags, jostling foreign tourists who were unwittingly obstructing their route back to the suburbs. And yet – perhaps because he'd been up so early, perhaps because he'd eaten nothing – the movement lulled him, and he drifted off into a half dream. When he heard Laura speak to him, and he focused his eyes on her face, she was straight in front of him and so close that he felt as if he was coming round from a general anaesthetic.

They went into one of the large electrical shops at what he'd learned to call the south end of Tottenham Court Road, near the junction with Oxford Street. Daniel stared at the young salesman, who had perfected a look that combined great solicitousness with desperate urgency. It was an expression that might have useful applications in his own life, if he could replicate it.

They narrowed the choice down to two of the small digital systems that would do least to disturb the uncolonised areas in the flat above The Owl. One was twice the price of the other.

'What's the difference?' Laura asked.

'Features,' said the salesman.

'Features?'

'This one,' he explained, 'has more features.' He tilted his head slightly and paused, waiting for the inevitable question, like somebody telling a knock knock joke.

'What kind of features?' she asked, eventually.

'Features,' said the young man, and disappeared.

Daniel bought the cheaper one and asked for it to be delivered. 'With the really good ones,' he told Laura, 'there's just more things to go wrong.'

They walked into a narrow side-street that wound round the back of the tube station, and into a tiny, dimly-lit Spanish bar. She ordered a bottle of water and two glasses of rosado and sat down at a table in front of the huge chrome jukebox. 'I'm surprised you didn't get the other one,' she said, 'considering.'

'Considering?'

'Considering. Considering that it'll never be turned off. Considering that music's like your comfort blanket.' The barman brought the drinks over and placed them within their reach on the bar.

'You know in the States,' she said, 'some people use music to calm them down at the dentist's.'

'That's my trouble,' he said, 'I'm never quite out of that chair.'

She looked at the drinks, still on the tray where the waiter had left them. 'OK,' she said. 'It's time for your pink water.'

They were only a few minutes' walk from Resolve and the Northumberland Arms where they'd met, but it never occurred to either of them to go back. He had never lost that sense – the sense that normally evaporates in a matter of weeks – of feeling that there was a unique quality to the places she went, the things she did, the brands she used, the glass she drank from; that these things were somehow magical and special. It was a feeling that, though she wasn't the kind to say it, was powerfully reciprocated. Places were important to them. Things could intoxicate them. But nowhere would ever be more special than the place they were now.

They went back to The Owl. However many times he came back here, Daniel thought, there was always a feeling of anticipation as he opened the front door.

When they came in, Brendan was talking to Jonathan who was on his seat at the bar. Leeds was asleep at his feet and the musician was looking through enlargements of photographs Laura had taken of the dog. She went over to sort out the pictures with him; Daniel made himself a pot of tea and sat down at a table. Brendan came over and joined him. The barman nodded towards the musician. 'I went to see him in Soho, at that tourist cabaret he plays in, the other week,' he said. 'I didn't tell him I'd been – he'd have gone berserk. He was playing 'El Condor Pasa' and 'Octopus' Garden' to these Japanese coach parties. They'd put electric candles on his piano. It was fucking terrible. It was like watching Francis Drake commanding a pedalo.'

Daniel and Laura went back up to the flat, where the floor was scattered with more colour prints. Glancing down at them, he noticed a photograph of Jonathan in profile; she had taken the picture into the direct light from an open window, in some place he didn't recognise, and the face was so dark as to be almost a silhouette.

'What's up?' he said. 'Are you starting on owners now?'

She said nothing.

'Are you keen?' he asked her.

She looked up. 'Don't be a lightweight.'

He found himself remembering the spectacle of Robin in that bar, wailing like a hired mourner at a Saudi funeral. Don't think these things, he said to himself. You'll draw trouble to you.

And yet he couldn't help looking down at the picture again. That strange rigid posture, and the angular outline of Jonathan's heavily-shadowed face might have haunted him when he went back to work the next week, except that the best thing about the obituaries desk, for him at least, was the way that its intermittent bursts of frenzied activity could mask deep-seated unease almost as well as the bar work. If there was a time when your pulse raced, and you felt slightly sick and dizzy, he confided in Whittington, as they were leaving, one Friday night, it was now – when it was over, and you were still too fired up to go home. 'That,' Whittington told him, as they walked across the ground floor, towards the main exit, 'is why we have to go to this vile public house.'

They looked out. The Printer's Devil was only a few hundred yards away, but the rain was coming down in sheets, and there was an unpleasant chill in the air. Whittington put on his hat, strode out, and began to engage in some discussion with one of the paper's limousine drivers. The editor got in the front seat, and beckoned him over. Daniel put his head down and sprinted out into the deluge, across the large marble floor. When he reached the car, Carlton was already there, at the rear door, holding it open for him. Daniel turned to press a pound into his hand. It was at that moment that Daniel glanced up at the doorman's face. Seeing Carlton, he fell, rather than sat, back in the car, which pulled away. He sat in silence, ashen-faced, for the short journey. When they reached the Devil and sat down at a corner table, he clutched suddenly at the editor's sleeve – like a child, but with far more force – so that it hurt, though Whittington didn't allow his face to reveal it.

'You know what you said about we're different from them,' Daniel said.

'What?' said Whittington.

'About how we're different from them,' he repeated, 'and if one of us gets in trouble, we help.'

Whittington stared at him. 'Are you all right?' he asked.

'No,' said Daniel. 'I'm not fucking all right. I'm in trouble.' There was a moment's silence. 'I am in trouble,' he said again, 'and I need help.' He stared at the wall.

'What is it?' Whittington asked.

'It's Carlton,' Daniel said.

'Carlton,' the editor repeated, slowly.

'Carlton,' said Linnell. 'Our Carlton.'

'Carlton...the doorman,' Whittington replied. Daniel nodded. 'What's up with him? Did he say something to you? He can't have – he never speaks.'

'That's the trouble,' said Linnell. 'I mean – that's what makes it worse. He never speaks and...' He paused. 'And he's wearing my scarf.' His grip relaxed.

'Carlton stole your scarf?'

'He bought it. And now...he's outside the whole time and now...he's going to be wearing it every day. And I need it back.'

'Why,' the editor said, 'did you sell it to him?'

'He bought it...he must have bought it, from the charity shop.' He hesitated and, as he did so, sensed that recovering the scarf would lead him into recounting the most anguished and sordid scene from his past.

Whittington put his briefcase down on the table and put on his trilby. He got up, and walked back out into the driving rain. Daniel sat alone. He felt like a man waiting for the result of a biopsy. It was half an hour before Whittington reappeared – this time in the car again – with Rosa. He was empty-handed.

'Bad news I'm afraid,' he said. 'I offered him twenty pounds for it. He was taking it off, and then he changed his mind.'

'He said,' Rosa added, 'does that mean it's – you know – valuable. Like that old bottle of wine.'

'And then,' Whittington said, 'he put it back on. I told him it was for you. And then he said, "Why does he want it?" I tried persuading him some more, but after that he wouldn't say anything else, only that: "Why?" '

'Shit,' said Daniel. He was about to get up himself, then realised that he was in no condition to attempt any explanation but the truth. He had a vision of confessing, out there on the marble forecourt, surrounded by impatient executives; each more painful sequence of his dishonour interrupted by Carlton opening a door and pocketing a pound.

'Tell me,' said Rosa. 'I'll go. Tell me,' she repeated. 'And I'll tell him.'

He shot anxious glances at the next table, where his colleagues from news and sport were dangerously close to being within earshot.

He told her about Jude and Stephanie; about how he'd stepped on the wine glass, and bound the deep wound with the handkerchief. Rosa got up and left. When she returned, she was carrying an opaque supermarket bag that only half-concealed the scarf, with its thin bands of colour. In the meantime Linahan and his deputy David Dixon, intrigued at the mysterious drama unfolding so close to his own table, had joined the obituarists.

'He says you can have it back,' Rosa said, as she sat down, 'on one condition.' She paused. 'That you send it back to her.'

'What?' said Daniel.

'So I told him you would.'

'Why?'

Rosa shrugged. 'I'll do it,' she replied.

'How?' he asked her.

'What's her surname?'

'Mayer.'

'OK,' she said. She took out a small pad, and wrote it down. 'Jude Mayer won't be hard to find. Any message?'

'No message,' he said.

Relieved, he became reckless and voluble, like a freed hostage. 'I can still remember,' Daniel said, 'that day she walked in and found us. It was the third of January.'

'In the unlikely event that you are ever in charge of a small central American state, and find yourself deposed by a coup d'état,' said Whittington, 'it's the date that your enemies might name the main public square after.'

Daniel attempted a smile, but the obituaries editor didn't return it. He looked taken aback. It wasn't that theirs was a wholly unconfiding sort of relationship; more the realisation that broaching so intimate a subject in the presence of Linahan and Dixon was little short of suicide.

'What's Jude doing now?' Rosa asked, quietly.

'You know what...' he said. 'I got a letter from this friend a couple of years ago. He told me she's become a Buddhist priest.' Linahan struggled to suppress a snort. Whittington looked at his fellow editor with a flash of real anger. It only lasted a second, but Daniel thought for a moment he was going to hit him. He didn't. Hitting people wasn't how Whittington dealt with the world.

'Don't laugh,' Whittington told Linahan, 'you'd be surprised. He's got devastated ex-girlfriends in senior positions in most of the major religions. There's a Sikh, isn't there Linnell, and an Anglican and a Hindu. I believe he also disappointed one of that lot that lay their bodies out on a grating on the top of a huge cooling tower, to have their bones picked clean by vultures. I can't remember,' he added, 'what they're called.'

'You know what?' said Dixon. 'You lot should get out more. You should spend more time with the living. You never know,' he sneered. 'Try it. You might like it.' Rosa glared at him, and told him to shut up. 'Shee is fraaaahm...Baaarthelona,' Dixon said. 'She know nothing.'

He pronounced the name of her home town like a sheep. 'Catalans don't lisp the "c" that heavily by the way,' she told him. 'We say it more like you would, in your normal voice – like a snake.'

'I don't know why you come here,' Dixon told her. 'You don't drink. You don't er...'

'I don't fit in,' she interrupted. 'I don't fit in. I believe in God. I believe that we die and live again. I believe in reincarnation. I believe that we are judged. I have certain instincts. I can tell looking at you for instance,' she said to Linahan, 'that you are a man who, like me, is visited by the ghosts of his ancestors.'

'Holy shit,' said Dixon. He roared with laughter, and looked to Linahan, waiting for him to deliver the coup de grâce, but the editor sat there, pallid and silent, his eyes down.

'I learned a long time ago,' she said, 'that the world is a very dead place if you have no ambition to make it better. But to have that ambition, you need a way of seeing it new every day. It'll be new for you tomorrow,' she said to Dixon. 'Because you won't remember a word of this.'

A couple of minutes later, the sports writers got up and trooped off. ' thought this was a piss-up,' Dixon said, 'not a fucking prayer meeting.'

'You know,' she told Daniel, 'I don't avoid them because I think I'm better than they are. The reason I don't talk to them is that I know I am everything they despise.'

'Yes,' said Daniel, without thinking: he was still distracted by the scarf.

'Have you ever been to see Harkes with an idea?' she asked. He shook his head. Like many of his colleagues, he generally tried to avoid the new editor. 'I have,' she said. The story, she explained, was about a woman in Peru who was six months pregnant when she was taken captive by her political enemies with her boyfriend. They anaesthetised her, and when she regained consciousness her unborn child had been cut out of her and replaced with the head of her executed lover. 'His skull had a single bullet wound to the temple,' she told him. 'It had been sewn into her, apparently with difficulty, by a qualified surgeon. She died after the stitches burst. And before she died, she made a formal statement about what she had seen inside her.

'I can remember, as I was telling Paul Harkes that,' she went on, 'I had a great fear that I was going to burst into tears, or vomit. I told him all that, and when I told him – it was just before lunchtime and I remember he was looking at his watch as he spoke. He said, "The thing is – we've done Peru."'

The story, she explained, had come through her sister, the missionary doctor. Daniel suddenly told her the worst thing about Jude: that for all she had endured at the hands of her own adopted family, she had been the only person who had seemed able to offer him any real consolation over the death of his mother, once he'd returned after the funeral, on the road his father had helped to build.

'You know one night I came home to find my mother in tears,' Rosa said. 'Her mother had died. She was beside herself. I said, "Mama, she was eighty-three. And you are forty." She said, "Yes – but it's a terrible thing to be an orphan, whatever age you are." '

In the taxi on his way home from the pub, Daniel was astonished to discover how, even now the scarf had physically disappeared, its legacy of mental distress had not quite vanished with it.

He'd felt ill at ease ever since Kate's visit, even though she was now safely back in Kansas. Daniel caught himself being short-tempered, especially with Laura. He drank more than usual, which left him feeling paranoid and anxious in the mornings, especially in areas of confinement, such as Underground trains and lifts. His days would generally begin at six, when Jack woke up, so that he'd often had only three or four hours' sleep, occasionally none. On the way to work, he sometimes found himself unable to board tube trains. He would sit for twenty minutes or so on one of the platform benches, until he felt confident he could stand up without passing out, or vomiting.

Daniel's unease didn't go unnoticed by Whittington. He started trying to think of a way to distract his troubled deputy, who he believed might be on the verge of a mental collapse.

That night he called Rosa, late, at home. 'I wonder,' Whittington said, 'if there's some story we could send him on. Something that would take him out of himself for a bit. He looks awful.'

'You're away yourself from next weekend,' Rosa said. 'For a week.'

'Ah...' said Whittington. A guilty note had entered his voice. 'Yes,' he added. 'To the health farm.' There was a silence at the other end of the line. 'To the Zurich,' he said. 'Well, we can get Cave to come in.'

The following Tuesday afternoon, Whittington picked up a press release and passed it, as casually as he could, to Daniel. 'You could go and talk to this one,' he said. 'You could even do a piece on him for the arts desk. It might amuse you.'

Daniel nodded, though as he did so he realised he had no interest in writing about the living. He glanced at the page, a photocopied press release advertising a new musical by Ralph Bennett, who'd been a minor British rock star in the seventies. *Longwood Nights*, according to the publicist, was a rock opera based on the last years of Napoleon Bonaparte. 'My God,' said Linnell, reading aloud. '"This three-hour epic is not so much a musical as forty-nine-year-old Ralph Bennett's artistic rebirth.' What would he say if he knew it had been passed straight on to the obits desk?'

Whittington shrugged.

'Black cab?' said Daniel.

'I'd rather you didn't,' the older man replied. 'He's in Belgium.' He paused. 'Where was the Savage widow?'

'What?'

'Where does she live, the Savage widow? Wife, I mean. Italy?'

Daniel checked Hugo Savage's file, and found her number. 'It's Paris,' he said.

'If you can find her,' Whittington said, 'see her on your way back.'

Rosa fixed a meeting with Bennett in Brussels. The singer, whose press cuttings indicated a capacity for truculence, said he could only manage that coming Saturday, in the evening. Back at the flat that night, Daniel asked Laura if she wanted to go with him; half-heartedly, because he knew that the pressure of having to write a real article wouldn't be eased by sharing a hotel room with both her and a small child. She went over to the desk and handed him the guidebook she'd bought there. 'You know what,' she told him, 'I think I can live till Tuesday without seeing Brussels again.'

He took the tube down to Waterloo on the Saturday morning, and went into the Eurostar office to collect his ticket. There was something peculiar about the atmosphere there. He couldn't work out what it was at first. Then it came to him. It was the staff. When a customer approached, their expressions were transformed from the familiar British look of sullen despondency to ingratiating cheerfulness. When the client left, he noticed, they allowed their fixed smile to fade slowly, and their expression took on a hint of regret, as if they were privately disappointed that, since the passenger had not given the word, they couldn't, after all, come home with them, worm their dog, and re-grout their patio.

He remembered a newspaper article he had read about a Salford teenager who had been threatened with the sack from a Manchester burger bar after he refused to say 'Have a nice day' to the customers. When the manager insisted, he developed a way of investing the phrase with such unmistakable bile that, as the management argued at the industrial tribunal, 'it was the equivalent of being served your dinner with two raised fingers.'

He got on the train. It had a pinched, ungenerous feel to it, like the economy cabin of an airliner. He stared out of the window. As they pulled away from the platform, he began to wonder if it was really too late to find his niche elsewhere – as a prison visitor on death row, a medical auxiliary in Eritrea, or a playwright. He could be a playwright in Belgium, he thought. He started to wonder how he would handle the requirement of doing media interviews in both French and Flemish, once he was famous for his first drama: a classic comedy, he decided, about a philanthropist who was blind to the extent of his own generosity, called *The Imaginary Miser*.

He unzipped his canvas bag and pulled out Laura's guidebook to Brussels. As he opened it, a piece of paper fell out. He glanced at it. It was an old hotel bill. He was about to throw it away, then examined it more closely, out of boredom. It was dated three weeks earlier, and the name at the bottom was Laura's.

He was admiring the stamp from the Flemish hotel – 'The Rembrandt', whose name was majestically reproduced in indigo and small capitals, surrounded by an oval border – when his eye was caught by an entry in modest blue biro, just below it. In the box marked Guests, there was a neatly-written figure two. And, underneath, in the section labelled Extras, the single, handwritten word: *Hond*.

He half rose out of his seat, from that compelling desire to move that often accompanies the sudden onset of shock, nausea or palpitation. The few other people in the carriage, he noticed, had their eye on him as he remained, half-sitting, half-standing. He walked down the aisle to the smoking car and lit a cigarette. He went on down the train. He wondered if there was some other explanation. Perhaps she'd gone there with her aunt. Perhaps *hond* didn't mean what he thought it did.

He came to the restaurant car: a preposterously flattering term for this coach that had been designed to cater for travellers who ate standing up, struggling to control thin plastic trays that buckled under the weight of a burger, or cheese on toast. But the carriage was completely empty, apart from a blond, middle-aged man behind the serving hatch at the far end. The last time he'd seen this amount of open space in a railway carriage was in the buffet car sequences in films like *Some Like It Hot*, and *Palm Beach Story* where a euphoric party of elderly bachelors unleash their dogs, and their rifles, in the bar, to the alarm of their fellow diners. A buffet car you could walk about in was inextricably connected in his mind with financial ease and frivolity. It was no fun here though, he thought, and he remembered Whittington's remark: 'It might amuse you.'

He heard a cough. The Belgian had come out from his serving hatch and was advancing towards him. There was an exaggerated purposefulness about his walk, of the kind often affected by pubescent boys. There was something about the man that he instantly disliked. He looked tremendously clean. He looked like a man who might have run marathons.

The Belgian had one finger raised, and he was wagging it from side to side like a metronome, a gesture that brought a fleeting, unpleasant thought of pianos, and Jonathan. The barman, he noticed, was fumbling in his breast pocket for something. He brought out a round beer-mat, decorated with a No Smoking symbol, and held it up in front of his sole customer with the impassive stare of a veteran referee. Daniel looked at the Belgian, then at his No Smoking sign, then at the carriage windows where, for some reason, he couldn't see another one. The man handed him the beer-mat.

Daniel looked around for an ashtray, and didn't find one. He took the lighted cigarette in his right hand and, on impulse, closed his palm over it with such speed and force that, to his surprise, he extinguished it without burning himself. The barman's expression changed from indignation to horror. Then he turned and walked back behind the counter, assuming that this was a party trick that British travellers rehearse for such moments. Linnell dropped the cigarette in a bin and walked up to the bar. 'Coffee,' he said.

'Anything to eat with that?' the Belgian replied in heavily-accented English – over-attentive, as if to show that the cigarette episode was forgotten.

'No,' said Daniel. 'No. Are you Flemish?' he asked the barman, in English.

The man glanced past him into the empty diner, as if looking for witnesses in case his response precipitated an assault. Seeing nobody, he nodded, hesitantly.

'What is *hond*?' Daniel asked him.

'I'm sorry?' asked the Belgian.

Daniel found a biro, reached for a paper napkin, and wrote the word on it.

'Ah,' said the barman. '*Hond*.'

'Yes,' he said, impatiently. '*Hond*. What is *hond*?'

The man looked for his own pen and couldn't find it. He picked up a thick felt marker, took the napkin, smoothed it flat and, with great care, wrote out the English translation. Daniel looked at the word, written in large black capitals. The ink had begun to seep out into the surrounding paper, so that the letters were starting to merge, but even once it had dried a four-year-old could have read and understood it. The man's pen, he noticed, was stamped in silver with the words 'Indelible Marker'.

'*Hond*,' said the Belgian. 'Dog.'

'Fuck,' said Daniel, out loud.

He took the Underground to Bourse, one of the main squares, then walked the last two hundred yards to the place he'd booked: the Hotel Valmore, a small, depressing establishment with thin brown carpets and the lingering smell of vacuum-bag and air-freshener, its choking pine scent concealing God knows what.

At six thirty he went out to meet Bennett. At first he thought he'd arrived at the wrong address: it was a dour-looking café full of old men playing chess, with stuffed animal heads on the wall. Then he saw him – a wasted-looking figure in his fifties, wearing a leather biker jacket and drainpipe black jeans. His fingers were weighed down with an amount of cumbersome silver jewellery which, given his age, suggested he was either deranged or very famous. He was at a table by the bar with a man of forty or so, who was dressed in a conventional lounge suit.

He was about to introduce himself when he noticed that Bennett's companion, who was speaking French, was in great distress, and seemed on the point of tears. Seeing this, Daniel kept on walking past the table, and sat down on a barstool with his back to them. 'It's just that I sometimes think I'll never meet another woman, at my age,' the man was saying. 'Of course you will,' said Bennett. 'You're still young. You've got – ' the entire room could have joined in at this point – 'your whole life in front of you.'

The man with his life in front of him left, and Daniel walked over and sat down in the vacant chair. They shook hands. The singer had a black coffee on the table in front of him. Daniel ordered a beer and, when the barman asked which he wanted, he pointed at random to a bottle behind the bar. It had a vile, sweet, cloying taste. It was very strong.

'What do you think of it?' asked Bennett.

'Disgusting,' said Daniel. He drank it quickly and ordered another.

To his great relief, he found that he didn't need to talk: Bennett was already describing his musical, and how it was named after the house where Napoleon died in exile, on Saint Helena. 'He was poisoned, you know,' the singer said.

His interviewer nodded, with the counterfeit bonhomie of someone humouring a madman. As he worked his way down the second bottle, though, Daniel began to be drawn in by Bennett's account of the fetid, claustrophobic atmosphere of the Emperor's last residence. By the third, it sounded good. 'Would he have liked rock and roll?' he asked.

'He'd have loved it,' said Bennett.

'He would, wouldn't he?' said Daniel. 'He'd have fucking loved it.'

He looked at the singer, who had embarked on a long, comprehensive account of the symptoms of strychnine poisoning. He stared at his heavily-lined face, his delicate gold-rimmed glasses, and the small silver skull hanging from a ring in his left ear. He slightly resembled the British comic actor Charles Hawtrey. Twenty years of failure and exile had extinguished the crude egotism that, according to the few interviews in his newspaper cuttings file, he was once renowned for. His thoughts returned to his own life.

'Hey, Ralph,' he said, interrupting the older man.

'Yes, Daniel,' said Bennett.

'What's the worst thing that's ever happened to you?'

'When I was doing the coke,' he replied, 'I remember coming round in this hotel room in Antwerp. There was this woman there, lying on the bed wearing nothing but a black slip. I remember thinking she looked very old; she must have been thirty. She was saying something to me. I could see that she was holding something in her right hand, but I couldn't see what it was, because I didn't have my glasses on. She had a cigarette in her mouth all the time she was talking, and she held this blurred object out to me. Then finally she said, "Ralph – are these teeth yours?" '

'Were they?' asked Daniel.

'No,' said the singer, laughing. 'They fucking weren't.'

Bennett took him to a small, dim, oak-panelled restaurant where each table was set apart in its own alcove, with wooden benches for seats: the ideal setting, Daniel thought, for his interviewee to confess every triumph and regret of his life. Bennett noticed his distracted manner. 'Is something wrong?' he asked.

Quite why it was, he wasn't sure, but Daniel told him about Laura, Jonathan and the dog.

'I don't know if this helps at all,' said Bennett, 'but I've seen his one-man show. He's bloody awful.'

'The funny thing is,' said Daniel, 'I can't quite hate her for it. Her last boyfriend, Robin, said to me, "You know fidelity, it's just something she hasn't got in her." He meant like some people can't blow smoke rings, or do algebra, or whistle.'

'Or buy my albums,' said Bennett.

It was one in the morning by the time he got back to his hotel, and he was still with the singer. They sat in reception and Daniel asked the night porter to get them some beers. The night porter declined.

'The gentleman,' Bennett said in French, pointing at Daniel, 'has just lost his wife.'

The man disappeared and came back with six bottles of Duvel. Bennett handed him a note worth five times their value.

'Condolences,' said the porter.

Daniel had been fumbling in his own pockets and pulled out what he thought was money, but turned out to be the crumpled hotel receipt. He staggered behind the reception desk and smoothed it out. Then he placed it in the fax machine, dialled The Owl's number, and pressed send.

CHAPTER 26

He woke at ten the following morning and the memory of the previous day struck him again, like a death. He went down to reception, desperate for distraction. 'Where can I go,' he said to the middle-aged woman behind the counter, 'on a Sunday morning?'

'The flea market,' she said, before he'd quite stopped speaking. Her response had an improbable swiftness that made her sound like a ham actor. She handed him a Metro map and circled a station on the outskirts of town.

He came out of the Underground and noticed a silent procession of people, which he joined. After ten minutes they arrived in a small market-place, filled with dozens of stalls. Some were wooden, with overhead canopies; most consisted of no more than a few second-hand items spread out on a groundsheet. Daniel's eye was caught by one particularly tragic vendor on the edge of the square. Even in an English junk shop, he'd never seen such a woeful display of abandoned possessions. He noticed, laid out on three filthy double blankets, an orange vinyl three-piece suite from the seventies, a broken radiogram and a carpenter's plane, rusted and useless. As he looked at them, all strength went from his legs. He sat down on one of the plastic chairs.

By his right foot he noticed a brown suede nodding dog. On its back, the covering material had worn away to reveal a shiny patch of pink plastic. It provided, in what was otherwise a crude and un-lifelike model, an uncanny recreation of the mange. The dog's head – remarkably, given the state of the surrounding exhibits – did still nod, and was moving gently in the slight breeze; Daniel stared down at it vacantly.

The stallholder, an elderly man with the build of a wrestler, snapped at him in Flemish. Daniel, flustered, but certain that if he got to his feet he would faint, stayed in his colourful seat. He pointed at the nodding dog. 'How much?' he asked, in French. The man handed it to him. 'Ten pounds,' he said, in English. To the trader's amazement, his customer paid without arguing. It was a form of rent, he told himself, for the orange chair. When he got up to go, a few minutes later, he slipped the dog furtively back on to the man's display, then set off for the nearest bar, a glass-fronted café called the Green Doors.

He went in and sat at the counter, on the barstool nearest the door. As he did so, he felt a tap on the shoulder. He looked up: it was the stallholder, carrying the dog, which he placed in front of Daniel, on the zinc. He walked away without speaking.

He glanced round at the Green Doors' clientele. Sitting at tables in its dark interior, he could see a number of market traders. Some had begun setting up at five in the morning; it was eleven now, and they were drinking beer and eating slices of cheese, or sweet biscuits. At another table, closer to the bar, was a group of six students who clearly hadn't been to bed at all. One or two, lulled by the suffocating warmth flooding out of the kitchen, were about to succumb to sleep. On the other barstools, to his right, he could see two or three marginal-looking old men talking to themselves. From time to time one of them would break off from his monologue to beg a drink or a cigarette from the students. To his surprise, nobody tried to approach him. This, he concluded, was probably something to do with the dog, which was on the bar in front of him, nodding vigorously in a draught from the front door.

He ordered a large black coffee. After a while one of the more reckless geriatrics wobbled down the bar and asked him for money. Daniel put his hand in his pocket and handed him all his change. The man, who had newspaper stuffed in his shoes, turned and walked down to the CD jukebox. Suddenly the gentle, soporific atmosphere of the bar was flooded – at deafening volume – with the sound of The Platters singing 'Ebb Tide', a ghastly ballad in six-eight time. The old man waltzed round the room in time to the song, holding a plastic mop he'd found against the wall, singing along at the top of his voice in a strong Flemish accent. His guttural pronunciation of the phrase 'I rush' in particular, was so distinctive that

Daniel realised the moment would never leave his memory. Nobody paid the man any attention. This was clearly not his first performance.

In front of him, behind the bar, the elderly barmaid was making sandwiches out of rillettes, a coarse pork paté that came in a large white plastic tub. When she first opened it, on the sink below the bar, directly in front of him, it had looked almost attractive, until he noticed that the virgin sheen of white that covered the mixture was an inch-thick layer of pig fat. As soon as she'd prised off the flimsy plastic lid, she dipped her fingers in the fat and smeared it around her marriage and engagement rings, to make them easier to slip off.

His thoughts drifted to the story Laura had told him about her and Kate sleeping with a whole rugby team. It should have told him something that her faithlessness was the source of amusement even to her. Infidelity, he remembered her saying once, was her way to get out. He felt Laura had conspired against him – not just with Jonathan, but with Kate.

When the café owner had eased her rings off, she pressed them down into a small piece of soft pink soap on the draining board, for safe keeping. They stuck there; the soap, he noticed, had a thin, ingrained line of grey dirt which ran down its whole length and made it look like a swollen prawn. He was gazing at her hands, wondering whether this would be the lowest moment in his life; whether existence could hold nothing, even the moment of death itself, that would be more depressing, when the strains of 'Ebb Tide' started up again. He paid, picked up his dog and left.

When he got back to the Valmore there were six uniformed policemen in the foyer. 'Ah,' one of them said as he arrived. 'Doctor.' Daniel shook his head and went on upstairs. He shut the chipboard door behind him and sat on the bed, still holding the dog. He stared at the fire regulations, printed in red and black, in English, on the door. 'One: Keep your sang froid.'

He took a shower. When he came out, he changed into a clean T-shirt and fell asleep on top of the bed. He awoke, sensing some presence in the room. He looked up and physically started, as if he had seen a ghost. He could see her sitting by the cheap desk, in front of the mirror. She was writing something and she looked as though she'd been crying. He had a sudden vision of what she must have looked like as a child. She hadn't noticed that he'd woken up. He felt an impulse to go over to her, which he resisted.

'Say it,' he said.

'What?' Laura lifted her head, but she still wasn't looking at him.

'Say it,' he said. 'Don't write it down. Say it.'

There was a long silence. Her head was still down. 'I don't know what happened to me,' she said. 'I went crazy.'

He could hear the heavy tread of police boots on the stairs.

'Somebody died here last night,' she said.

'Really?' he said. 'Not just us then.'

'You know...years ago,' she said – he shut his eyes in exasperated fury – 'my Aunt Laura, the one from the South, she used to tell me how the trouble in the world wasn't really anyone's fault. She'd explain how, if this one guy Mr Dexter was fishing in a catfish pool near Decatur Alabama, and if he accidentally knocked his whole bait tin into the pool, then that would lead to more catfish, which meant less flies – or more birds...I can't remember which, and then that gradually drove up the price of imports, and then she'd follow this line of rational connections that would explain how it was basically Mr Dexter's bait tin that made Hitler invade Poland and started the Second World War.'

'It's called catastrophe theory,' said Daniel.

'It's weird,' said Laura.

He glared at her. This digression might have enraged him even more than it did, except that she seemed to be rambling, through grief.

'She could prove to a stranger how Dexter started the Second World War. And I...I mean no disrespect...but I am smarter than she was. But I don't understand why I did this.' Daniel said nothing. 'I think I've lived with the thought that, for me, it was something that didn't count,' she said.

'What do you mean,' Daniel asked, '"it"?'

'Faithlessness,' she said. 'I thought that was just how I was. That it was something I had. Something like a condition. Like epilepsy.'

'That's right,' said Daniel. 'That's just what it's like. Except that you've got that very rare strain; the contagious kind. Jonathan had it too. I can just see you both there in the Hotel Rembrandt, foaming at the mouth, and your legs thrashing about.' He paused. 'Just don't expect me to hang around to watch your next attack.'

She said nothing.

'Couldn't you even find your own fucking lover?' he said. 'Why don't you just live with Kate, and cut out the middleman? Whatever happened to that speech about finding the one you really liked? Three weeks later you're boarding a train with him and his fucking dog.'

'I was already there,' she said. 'He came over. He was working. He showed up at my hotel. He was so upset. I gave him a drink. I felt sorry for him. And then…' She stopped. 'And then he wouldn't go away.'

'Oh for God's sake,' said Daniel. 'Can't you do better than that?'

'He told me he'd been thinking of killing himself.'

'Oh really,' he said. 'He'd been thinking of it. Hard?'

'He wouldn't go away,' she said, more quietly.

He saw her eye fall on the Brussels guide she'd lent him.

'Where is the Rembrandt?' he asked her.

She said nothing, but put her hands in front of her face.

'Where's Jack?'

'He's with Rachel,' she said. Her voice had stayed level, yet he could see tears running down her face. Still, he didn't move towards her.

'I just had to tell you that I've changed,' she said. 'And he's gone.'

'Who?'

'Jonathan. He's gone. To Toronto.' She stopped. 'And that when I came back after those two days I walked into my apartment – into our apartment – and I vomited. I went down and talked to Jessica.'

'Jessica?' said Daniel, gripped by a new wave of fury.

'I said what will he do if I tell him? What will he do if he finds out that I'm not – that I wasn't – the person he thinks I was? And she said, "He'll leave. I know him. He'll go." And I knew she was right. With the really good ones,' she added, 'there's just more things to go wrong.'

He walked past her, into the small bathroom, out of sight. He picked up the thin tablet of soap, cupped his hands under the cold tap, and pressed his face into the water. The coarse soap went in his eyes, and blinded him.

'I want to ask you something,' she said, through the wall. 'If you'd put a message with that fax last night, what would you have said?'

'That I wish I'd never set eyes on you. That's what I'd have said…' He pressed his face into a towel then, still holding it to his face, stepped back into the bedroom to complete his sentence, but when he opened his eyes, she'd gone.

'…last night,' he continued, to the empty room. 'But I wouldn't have meant it.'

On the desk in front of him he found the piece of paper she'd been writing. 'You're my one,' the message read. 'I swear to God, that life is over.'

She walked out without looking back and went straight back to England. When Daniel got to Brussels' southern station later that afternoon, he felt that some irresistible force was directing his footsteps towards the London train. He could talk to Caroline Savage, he told himself, any time – on the phone if he had to. This was a moment, he sensed, that could alter the whole course of his life. But when he saw the queue of English schoolchildren and day trippers queuing to go north, he snapped. When night fell that day he was not in The Owl but in a hotel room in Paris as he'd first planned, sitting alone and staring at a street map of central Brussels, looking for something he couldn't find.

CHAPTER 27

As Daniel lay in room seven at the Hotel Moreau in the rue Saint-Lazare, dazed by his catastrophic expedition, Whittington was in a taxi, approaching his destination for his own week away.

The Zurich was a private hotel in its own grounds. The main building was a whitewashed villa in the nineteenth-century Swiss style. Its clean, angular lines pleaded for an Alpine backdrop. The hotel would have looked out of place anywhere in England, but it was especially incongruous here, hidden away in the Devon hills. Dusk was closing in as he got his first glimpse of its familiar wooden balconies, from the top of the long drive which descended through a series of paddocks towards the main entrance. Whittington tried to remember his reaction when he first saw the building, many years ago, and couldn't. But for a stranger to set eyes on the Zurich in this gently rolling landscape, it occurred to Whittington, would be no less extraordinary an experience than walking out of Euston Station and seeing the sea.

Whittington rang the bell, which went unanswered. He sat in the empty lounge, in view of the lobby, to wait. The editor's face was well-known at most of London's traditional restaurants, but his appetite was only ever fully satisfied here. Built in the 1890s as the private residence of a Swiss banker, the Zurich had no health and fitness facilities as such, though it did have a large bar, a snooker room, a cocktail lounge, golf course and fishing lake. But for Whittington it wasn't the click of the ivory balls, or the hiss of a deftly cast line that enticed him with such punishing regularity, so much as the sounds that came from the kitchen. The owner, Patrick Anstruther, had remained recklessly loyal to French cooking of the old school, with its thick, cream-based sauces.

The obituaries editor sat in the lounge, waiting, and breathed in deeply. Rising from the massive, ancient stoves in the basement kitchens – only a few yards, he reflected, below his feet – he recognised the rich aroma of that evening's main course, which, in a matter of minutes, God willing, he would be served: a thick cassoulet that had been simmering lovingly for the past thirty-six hours. The surface of the dish, Whittington guessed, would be coated with a generous sheen of melted goose fat. There was an English element to the menu, but it was restricted to breakfast – a defiant selection of streaky bacon, sausages, black pudding and fried bread – and to the puddings. These were heavy suet mixtures so dense that, to quote one of Anstruther's other regulars who had written the owner a letter of thanks from hospital, by contrast with the Zurich's plum pudding with Devon cream and Armagnac butter, eating his barium meal had been 'like swallowing a child's portion of Instant Whip'.

The Zurich's high prices and spectacular location sometimes attracted young business executives. Anstruther tried to deter them by putting up a sign announcing that corporate clients were charged double for all services, but they took this as a public acclamation of status and it only made them like the place more. The business travellers considered the hotelier a freak. In his absence, keeping an eye on the door, they ridiculed him with the circumspect bravado of the cowed. In the evenings such clients would go out to the local pubs, which had juke boxes, live bands, young women, and other attractions unavailable at the Zurich. Patrick Anstruther, though a misogynist, had no objection in principle to women guests. His fanatical commitment to noise abatement, however, had intensified over the years.

Whittington had waited in silence for fifteen minutes or so when the hotelier walked into the lounge, apparently by chance. The editor noticed how his host's belly – no other word would do – was comfortably enveloped in the long lap of his white poplin shirt, decorated with a matrix of faint brown and yellow lines. It was the only design – the only single shirt, some whispered – that he ever wore. Clearly preoccupied, he saw Whittington, then strode over and attempted to deliver the manly embrace that his girth rendered every year more elusive.

The obituarist, meanwhile, felt a substantial joy rise in his soul. But his real devotion was to the Zurich, not to Anstruther. Whittington spoke of

Patrick as a friend, it was true, but he would never have dreamed of meeting him anywhere but here. Like some character enslaved by a rare and humiliating sexual deviation, arriving at his bordello, the gratitude he felt for the proprietor was tinged with resentment, of the kind any of us might feel towards the individual who has identified the dark heart of our most secret shame, and set out to cater for it.

As he embraced him, there was a muffled squeak from the front entrance. Anstruther turned in a flash of fury and hurled himself through reception and out of the front door into the dark. Taken as a whole, the furious intent of the movement was more impressive than its velocity. Even so, it was as fast as Whittington had ever seen Anstruther move. Judging by the original noise, and the urgency of the hotelier's response, he imagined the problem to be vermin.

Then Whittington heard frantic scrambling noises from outside; he walked to the lounge window and peered out. There in the bushes, a couple of feet away, he could just make out a young man in an expensive-looking suit engaged in a discussion with Anstruther, who was holding him by the ear. The man had been crouching in the rhododendrons under the lounge window, speaking into a mobile phone, a device that was prohibited at the Zurich, not just in the house, but anywhere within the grounds. Whittington watched as the executive – an internationally-known designer of computer database systems – remained silent, wearing an Oliver Hardy look, as Anstruther took the telephone in one of his large hands, crushed it like a prawn cracker, and returned it to its owner.

It was, Whittington reflected, a minor incident. Anstruther's temper was short and explosive, but it was rare that he lost it completely. When he did, his usual abruptness would give way to an exaggerated, forelock-tugging servility, and it was this last symptom which – though it generally passed unnoticed by most guests – inspired dread in the staff, who knew that it presaged unpleasantness.

One such mood had descended on him the day Anstruther had met Michael, a former taxi driver who now worked as his barman. Michael had come to collect his girlfriend Helena, Anstruther's chief of staff and head waitress. It was late and the restaurant was crowded. Patrick was at the head of a large table entertaining friends. When Helena served the main course, venison stewed with forcemeat in a heavy sauce of red wine and blood, the owner noticed that one dinner plate was missing. He snorted and shouted at Helena to bring another, which she forgot to do. He served his guests, insisting that they start without him, and then hailed another young waiter, asking, in a meek sort of way, if he would bring the missing plate.

When it still didn't appear, Anstruther emptied a ladleful of the mixture on to the tablecloth in front of him and ate it off the starched white cotton, with his fingers. Helena finally brought him the plate. He thanked her, and scraped the spilled portion of the casserole on to it. As she was walking back to the kitchens, he launched the plate at her like a discus. It smashed against the door frame, a few inches above her head, covering her hair and clothes in flecks of the tepid, coagulating sauce and in shards of broken china. Michael, who was sitting at the bar, waiting to drive Helena home, walked over to Anstruther and, without waiting for him to stand up, delivered a punch to the owner's jaw that might have sent another man through the partition wall. In this case – it might have been because his fist connected with his victim's chins, or simply the result of Anstruther's great bulk – the blow merely rocked him back on his chair. For a moment, his entire weight was balanced on its two back legs, which snapped with a noise like two pistol shots.

Anstruther was helped to his feet by his friends. Without speaking, or attempting to staunch the flow of blood from his lower lip, he walked over to the bar, poured two malt whiskies, and handed one to his attacker. The next day, he offered him the job as barman. Michael, whose previous occupation had taught him to be pragmatic in the face of brutality, accepted. Anstruther never said he was sorry but then, in thirty-five years at the Zurich, he never had.

The owner came back in after his altercation with the software engineer, but made no mention of it. Whittington followed him into reception. Anstruther reached up for the key – twenty-seven, as always – and placed it on the desk in front of the editor. As the metallic resonance died away, there was total silence, broken only by the faint sounds from the kitchen below, where the haricot beans in the cassoulet phutted softly on a gentle heat, as a reminder, as if any was needed, of the mixture's terrifying flatulent potential.

Anstruther noticed a small fragment of circuit-board, which had flown out of the man's phone, sticking to his shirt cuff. He took it off and dropped it into the waste bin with a look of distaste.

'Full board?' he asked.

'Full board,' Whittington replied.

CHAPTER 28

When Daniel woke the next morning he called Caroline Savage and told her he was writing a feature on her husband. He arranged to meet her at La Tartine, a yellowing, old-world bistro on the rue de Rivoli. Its clientele consisted of workmen in overalls and wine enthusiasts enticed by its range of affordable vintages served by the glass. It was not a place frequented by the professional classes. There was nothing there that would interest them and much that would not: the undeferential owner, Monsieur Alain, the large jar stuffed with floating pieces of frightening-looking grey cheese, the thick fog of cigarette smoke, which had brought the high ceiling and walls to a shade of beige that, in the unlikely event anyone ever wanted to recreate it, no Hollywood design team could ever replicate.

He noticed her straight away – she looked all wrong in there. He had expected a raddled Bohemian, like Hugo Savage, and he'd dressed accordingly, in an unironed shirt whose cuffs he hadn't thought to button, and torn jeans. She had turned away from the bar counter, where she'd just bought cigarettes, and was making her way back to the corner table where she'd already settled. She was wearing an elegant knee-length sleeveless black silk dress and grey court shoess. Though he had no way of knowing it, her elegance came from the same school as Carlton's: this was her one good outfit. She was a talented, though not remarkable, painter, and she gave English classes, as he once had. She was in her mid-forties; her shoulder-length fair hair was tied back, and she had a pair of sunglasses propped up on her head.

He went over to her table and introduced himself. There was a bottle of white wine, two-thirds full, in front of her, and two glasses. He poured himself one without asking and re-filled her glass. The last few days had left him careless of social niceties; it was a selfish gesture which, given her past, could not have made her feel more at home. Her table, like the others, had a candle on it, unlit, though the light was failing outside.

'If you want to know what he's like…' she said. 'I remember once, when we were living in Italy, in the village, there was this dreadful case in the paper. It was something that happened in Rome, in a block of flats. This young father had dropped dead of a heart attack and his two-year-old daughter was with him. She'd become hysterical, and she'd shrieked with terror and despair for hours – for days – but nobody paid any attention to her and she died there of thirst; they found her body slumped over him. Anyway I read it, and I wondered how often that sort of thing must have happened.'

'In towns?' said Daniel.

'In towns,' she said. 'Or in the country – at least in Hugo's part of the country. Where he is, there can hardly ever have been a newborn specimen of any animal that hasn't starved to death, waiting for their parents to return, which they never will, because they've been blown to pieces by my former husband. He'd shoot anything. Absolutely anything.

'So anyway, I started talking to him about that newspaper story, and I read him a poem I wrote about it, called "The Unanswered Call". It was about a child dying alone, and a dog waiting for its dead master's return, and a winning lottery ticket that's bought by an impoverished father of six, who drops it in the gutter and never discovers the value of this thing that rots away under a pile of leaves, unredeemed.' She paused. 'It's crap actually,' she said. He looked at her and drew breath, trying to think of some means of disagreeing. 'No – it is,' she said. 'It is crap. It's crap, but it isn't…To a normal person I mean…it isn't complex. I mean the idea isn't that goddam complicated.'

'No,' said Daniel.

'Anyhow I read it to him,' she said, 'and I could tell he just didn't have a clue what I was talking about. It wasn't that he didn't agree, or he didn't sympathise – he just couldn't begin to comprehend what I was saying. And then about a week later, he got up one morning, and he said, "Caroline…you know that poem."

'I said, "Yes Hugo".'

"About the unanswered call."

"Yes."

"I think I know what you meant now. It's like…What you're saying is, it's like that feeling you get when you arrive home, and you realise that you've got a gun in the house that's loaded, but it hasn't been fired."'

She laughed. 'I said, "Yes, Hugo. That's it." He went off looking pleased with himself.' She slipped off her sandals and she tucked her legs up sideways and underneath her on the red leather bench seat. Her toes, he noticed, looked like monkey-nuts.

She told him how she'd left Savage in Italy, in 1986, and tried to return to live in London. 'Then I saw all these people,' she said, 'who had…who had like paid into this system all their lives and were suddenly getting nothing back. It was the most peculiar thing to watch. It was like watching someone going out and writing out a cheque on their own bank account and then having the staff sneer at them as if they'd written a begging letter.'

They finished the bottle. He'd thought she'd be conservative. He'd thought she'd be wealthy. The truth – though nothing in her accent or bearing revealed it – was that she was the daughter of a housepainter from Spalding. He was surprised by her. Outside, night had fallen and he could see it was starting to drizzle. It was four days, he thought to himself, since he'd had a normal conversation with Laura. He told Caroline Savage about the game of Oliver, but he didn't mention who had taught it to him. It was a small detail but it represented, when he looked back on it, a small experiment in betrayal. 'I know a good Oliver for Hugo,' she said. 'Redeemable.'

'You should know,' she continued, sounding slightly drunk, 'that I wasn't with him that long. You could talk to Anna, his first wife…. Christ…she was as big a shit as he was. I woke up one night with her holding a carving knife against my throat. She's still out there, in Tuscany somewhere. I remember reading one time that she'd been rescued one night by the police, wandering around after she'd soaked herself in petrol, in a car park near Siena.' With a mischievous look, she flicked the flint on her disposable plastic lighter, and lit the candle on the table in front of her.

'How long?' asked Daniel.

'How long what?'

'How long were you with him?'

'Two years,' she said. 'OK, maybe three.'

'Till he pushed you out of the French windows.' She nodded. 'I suppose the thing with him,' Daniel added, 'would be to stay away from open doors on the first floor.'

She stretched her right arm up, with the palm of her hand open and facing towards him, revealing a jagged scar that ran along the inside of her upper arm, beginning at her elbow and running across her armpit, at which point it vanished under her dress. 'Who said it was open?' she asked.

The waiter, taking her gesture for a summons, arrived at her side.

'Another bottle?' he asked.

'Yes,' she said, without hesitating. 'I didn't mean to do that,' she told Daniel after the man had gone away. 'But it was either that, or I'd have had to tell him about the French windows as well. And the French windows,' she added, 'were closed. Hugo never opened a door for a lady on the first floor, or any other. If you'll allow me to suggest a phrase of my own for your article, Hugo Savage wasn't a gentleman on any level.'

Daniel, who hadn't slept properly since Belgium, was beginning to feel weary. And yet he was struck by something in her manner which he took as a vague indication – a sober onlooker would have used the adjective blatant – that this woman liked him.

At the tables around them, customers came and went.

'I'd been out with bastards before,' she said. 'To tell the truth…' She leaned forward slightly across the table. 'I've only ever been out with bastards.' She had begun staring at his right hand, he noticed, where he wore a cheap Greek ring made up of three intertwined bands of silver, and she seemed to lose her drift.

'But the difference with him was, he…with the others,' she continued, 'you always felt that their violence, or their fury, or their selfishness hinged, in some odd way, on the decent side they'd deliberately abandoned. And from time to time, you'd see glimpses of that decency and you'd forgive them. That was never a feeling you got with Hugo. You know….'

He noticed that the second bottle, too, was almost empty. He couldn't see how he was going to get out of this conversation uncompromised.

'You know,' she went on, 'he didn't think any more of me – of a woman – than he did of what happened, after he'd pulled the trigger, to one of his clay pigeons. And in the end,' she said, 'he broke me.'

She began to raise her right arm again – an attempt, he presumed, mistakenly, to illustrate this last remark by showing him her scar again. Afraid that this would result in a third bottle of white wine, he grasped her gently by the wrist. Savage, who had actually been reaching up for her dark glasses, in case emotion overcame her, suddenly found that she didn't need them any more. As Daniel's grip relaxed, she lowered her hand so that it was resting gently on his. She held it there, then slipped the tips of her fingers into the unbuttoned cuff of his shirt, and slid them gently up his forearm, which was flat against the table, and into his sleeve. The movement might have seemed over-intimate even in the intoxicating first days of a real affair. He looked at her. Her eyes were not on him, but on the street outside. The next time she breathed out it was audible, and it sounded not so much like passion as great relief.

'Physically...' she said. She drew her hand away. 'Physically...he wouldn't take any more notice of me than if...' She paused. 'It was as if I wasn't there. It was awful, just awful. And I kind of lost interest after that. I left him when I was thirty-three. And now I'm forty-six. And that has been my life.'

The waiter brought the bill, unsummoned. They went outside, and Daniel hailed a cab. 'Take me home,' she said. He held the door open for her, and followed her into the back of the car.

'Hotel Moreau,' he said. 'Eighty-three, rue Saint-Lazare. And first,' he added, 'to...'

'Seven rue Caron,' she interrupted, in a quiet, expressionless voice.

It was a couple of hundred yards up the street. The cab driver, a West African in his sixties, pulled up outside the front door of her apartment block.

'Coffee?' she asked, in a voice which, though hesitant, conveyed an unmistakable commitment to total surrender. She had pronounced the word, she realised to her dismay, with a subtlety worthy of her former husband.

Daniel shook his head, and didn't look at her. 'I...' he began.

She got out, closed the car door firmly but without slamming it, and walked away. The taxi, an ancient Mercedes, didn't move: because of a red light, he presumed, or because of surrounding traffic. But they remained stationary and when he looked up he noticed the driver was looking hard at him in the rear-view mirror.

'Rue Saint-Lazare?' he said, in a tone of voice that suggested that he had never been a man to refuse a coffee. Daniel nodded. 'Now?'

'Now.'

The driver covered the few hundred yards at a tentative pace, as if expecting some further instruction. It was only when he reached Bastille and swung left up the Boulevard Beaumarchais that he finally put his foot on the floor and the heavy automatic picked up speed on the road heading north – in the direction of the Place de la République, the hotel and – it briefly occurred to Daniel – London.

But he didn't return home that night, or the next. The next day, all day, he lay in room seven, on the large double bed, watching black and white films on the cable channels. He loved the Moreau, with its deep red velvet furnishings, the weird stained glass windows in its stairwell, and its elegant high ceilings. The huge bathrooms, last modernised in the early thirties, were like temples, if there are any temples with black and white tiled floors and massive bathtubs and bidets in eau de nil. And it wasn't just beautiful – it was cheap. Most visitors, especially Americans, couldn't bear the hotel's antiquated central heating system. The main boiler shuddered and ground into motion at five every morning and produced a degree of vibration in the pipes which, depending on which room you were in, could have you dreaming that your bed had gone into final rinse and spin. If you did fall asleep again, you were woken half an hour later by the gentler vibration of the first Metro in the tunnel which ran under the foundations.

The hotel used to be a bank, and it was run by Madame Bojéna, a Polish widow. Its most magnificent asset was its lift: a tiny oak cabinet with glass-fronted doors. As a final touch of delicacy, to shield passengers from the rough mesh cage which enclosed the elevator shaft, the windows in its thin wooden doors were draped with lace curtains.

It was a curious thing that the image most constantly present in his mind – from the moment he'd discovered the hotel receipt in her guide-book, to now – was not Laura or Jonathan, or even both together, but Jack. On the second afternoon of his retreat in the Moreau he saw a programme on an American cable service about orphaned refugees.

It was precisely the sort of production which, before he'd had a child himself, he would have dismissed as facile and cynically manipulative – which it was. But he was struck by one interview, with a French doctor who had just left a war zone in Somalia.

The man recalled a conversation he'd had with one young boy who had just watched his whole family cut to pieces with a machete. The attackers let the child live, the doctor explained, so that he could drive a tractor round the village loading up the property of other dead villagers. 'The boy turned to them,' he explained, 'and said that he couldn't. One of them raised a pistol to his temple, but the commando leader stopped him and asked why. "I can't do it," the boy said, "because I'm too young to drive."'

He thought of his son, in his boxroom, and how most days Jack would be lucky to see him once, in the morning, before he left for the paper. Sometimes the child would cling to his arm as he was leaving, and he would have to prise apart the small fingers gripping at his sleeve.

When the programme was over, Daniel dialled the reservations line at The Owl, which was always connected to the answering machine mid-afternoon, and left a message saying he would catch the midday train from Paris the following day, arriving at Waterloo at two twenty that afternoon.

Once it was dark, he decided to go down to the café next door for a drink, but when he tried to stand, he found himself weak at the knees. Give or take a packet of nuts from the minibar in his room, he hadn't eaten since he'd been in that sombre restaurant with Ralph Bennett.

He walked out of the hotel and across the nearby square, which was dominated by the huge church of the Trinité, and went into the nearest cheap restaurant, the Ki-Fok, a small Korean. He ordered two cold spring rolls, wrapped in thin sheets of vermicelli, filled with prawns, and mint, and bean sprouts, and a bottle of Côtes du Rhône. An hour or so later, he set off to walk back to the Moreau. Feeling restored and – looking up at the daunting, floodlit façade of the basilica – slightly penitent, he had a sudden impulse to leave immediately for the airport, but when he looked at the church clock he saw it was ten thirty, and already too late. He walked into the hotel and went up to the main desk to get his key.

When he came out of reception, there was a young Vietnamese woman standing by the lift. She was wearing a black, three-quarter-length jacket, and he noticed her because she looked at him as though she was expecting some sign of recognition. When it didn't come, she turned her eyes away. He pressed the button of the ancient lift, which refused to light, because the wooden car was already creaking on its way down. When it finally groaned to a halt, the doors were opened from the inside by a man in a grey business suit. His tie was worn in the brazen manner of a stage drunk, hitched down three inches from his collar. He was wearing no shoes – just a pair of white socks. In his left hand was a half-empty bottle of champagne. It was the kind of public behaviour you could see any day in Britain, but something that Linnell had rarely, if ever, witnessed in France. The man pushed past Daniel and flung both his arms round the woman. This last movement sprayed champagne across the carpet, but he didn't notice. 'You are more beautiful,' he slurred, 'than in my dreams.' Daniel was in the lift, looking out, by the time the shoeless guest said this. The man had his back to him. The woman's face was clamped against his right shoulder in his unyielding embrace, and she was looking straight at Daniel. If nothing else had happened that night, he would have remembered that moment for ever, simply because of her eyes: fixed on him, staring over that bear-like shoulder, their expression impassive. Her stare met his and she looked away again.

He went to close the lift doors and go up to the fourth floor, when the amorous businessman began to walk backwards and, in a sort of reverse three-legged waltz with the young Vietnamese, got in with him. Two in the lift was uncomfortable at the best of times; three could have worked only for fasting blood relatives.

'Going up?' Daniel asked. It was a feeble attempt – there being no basement – to break the tension.

'Up?' said the businessman, with coarse innuendo. 'Up? Yes. Oh, yes.' Squinting at the brass plate of numbered buttons, he pressed five, then flung himself into a passionate embrace with their fellow passenger.

Daniel went into his room and turned on the bath taps. He took the peach-coloured tops off each of the small plastic bottles of shampoo by the sink, and tossed them into the tub without reading what they were. He found a Jo Corbeau CD, put it on his portable machine, got in the bath, and fell asleep.

He was woken about twenty minutes later by breaking sounds from above. The shouts were barely human; it was the voice of a man who had gone berserk. Daniel got out, found a clean pair of jeans and a T-shirt and lay on the bed watching a Bette Davis film in which a lighthouse keeper's previously solitary life had been seriously complicated by the arrival on his remote island of two identical twins with radically differing moral standards. A few minutes later he heard a soft but urgent knocking at his door. He opened it and the Vietnamese woman burst past him into the room without speaking. Blood was pouring from her mouth. Her jacket was gone and she was wearing a khaki-coloured knee-length dress which had been torn across the shoulder. She motioned to him to lock the door to the corridor; Daniel drew the bolt across. She switched the bedroom lights out and retreated to the bathroom – the furthest place from the door. She sat on the edge of the bath and put her head in her hands. She was shaking.

Blood was trickling slowly between the fingers of her right hand, which she'd placed over her mouth; it dripped down on to a pile of newspapers he'd left strewn about the floor. He walked in after her and switched Jo Corbeau off. 'Put it back on,' she said quietly, in French. 'Please.' Upstairs, the screaming and crashing had started again, though its tone was less frenzied.

He endured a brief moment of peculiarly English torment, when he noticed that the bathroom floor was covered not just with old newsprint, but also with discarded underclothes. She pointed to the sink, asking with a gesture if she could use it. He nodded. She went over and started to rinse her mouth. Daniel watched the blood mix with the water running over the porcelain. He handed her one of the hotel's large white towels.

'If he comes down,' she said, 'don't answer the door, for God's sake. He's a maniac.'

'Who is he?' Daniel asked.

She kept her eyes down. 'He's a customer,' she said.

He motioned her to sit on a wooden chair in the bathroom. He turned on the harsh overhead light; he stood over her and she tilted back her head so that he could look into her mouth. His right hand was supporting the back of her head; his left was under the uninjured side of her face. She kept quite still. It reminded him of the way his parents used to examine him when he was a child. One violent punch had forced one of her teeth through her upper lip. The tooth, her upper left canine, was hanging from a single sinew. He found a small dry white facecloth and a pair of nail scissors. He cut the tooth free and put it on the side of the sink.

'There are some jobs,' she said, 'where it's easier to perform the work than be the recipient. Like dentist.'

'Or,' Daniel added, 'firing squad.'

She shook her head quietly. 'No,' she said. 'Not firing squad.' She shifted from French into heavily accented English. 'US Air Force bomber command.'

He looked at her. She was just about old enough to be the younger sister of the naked, Napalmed girl whose photograph had become a defining image of the Vietnam War.

The rumble overhead had died down altogether, probably because their neighbour had passed out. Daniel found some towels, ran the bath and left her in there. By the time she came out, he realised, it would be safe for her to leave. The thought didn't engender in him quite the relief it should have.

One of the more perverse ironies of deception is the way that it is practised first on the deceiver, so that they may convince themselves that their action – an invitation to dinner, a gift, the use of a bathroom – is entirely disinterested, and driven purely by benevolence. The kind of thing, to put it another way, that anybody would do.

When she came out of his bathroom wearing the white hotel robe, knelt on a chair next to the bed and asked him to look at her left eye, which was half-closed, and he had to place one hand on her forehead and another on her shoulder, to steady her, and he noticed in her hair an unfamiliar scent of aromatic oil – something, he supposed, that Vietnamese women must prefer to perfume – he was still convinced that he was acting out of simple decency. The door to his room wasn't visible from the lift, so she could have had no way of knowing whose room she had flung herself into. She asked if her eye had glass in it; he told her it didn't. She turned to sit sideways on the chair, facing the head of the bed, at right angles to him. There was a mirror directly opposite her. When he looked into it, he could see that she was crying.

And even when she had lain down on her back on the bed, still in the white gown, and he placed a hand on her forehead again, and she had turned and rested her left arm on his right shoulder, a movement that involuntarily loosened the cord on her white dressing gown, which he then undid, he was still convinced that this was something that, even at this late stage, wouldn't happen.

There was a bruise, he noticed, beginning to spread around her right hip-bone. He laid his hand on it. She winced. Although he had known for sure that, at some point, he would prove capable of selflessness, honour and great resolve, he hadn't been clear about when the moment to display those qualities would come. Now that he thought of it, the opportunity had passed. She kissed him without showing the pain from her swollen lip in a way that was delicate, hesitant and, as she had intended, quite unprofessional.

It was a sign of his devotion to Laura that, when he occasionally began dreaming of being seduced by another woman, the experience swiftly turned into a hideous nightmare, in which he woke up believing that he had betrayed her, and was going to have to tell her, and so might lose her. He would sit up gasping for air, to find that the familiar figure of the American was there, next to him. Except that this time she wasn't.

As a result, the night passed in a kind of ecstatic horror. When he woke in the morning, he felt a momentary relief at the thought that his memories of the Vietnamese woman were simply another unwelcome dream. Then he looked across, and saw a bloodstain on the pillow next to him. The gentle rumble of a Metro train shook his bed. The room was empty. She'd gone.

He heard a rustle from the bathroom. She came back, in the robe again, and lay next to him. She touched the ring on his right hand. 'You know – I once pledged a man my whole life,' she said. 'And now one night, one genuine emotion, or the expression of one true thought – is real devotion.'

He couldn't bear the thought of her leaving, and never seeing her again – not through any desire for prolonged intimacy, but because if she went now, this sight of her would be the last he would have in his life. The idea brought the moment of his death tangibly close. He told her so. She showed him her identity card. 'Ly Thi Tien' it said. '28 rue de Kabir, Belleville 75010.'

As his midday train pulled out of the Gare du Nord, Linnell was alone on his bed again, watching a Trevor Howard film from the early-thirties. It was set on an eerie ocean liner and, after an hour or so, it transpired that Howard's character and all his fellow passengers were dead and on their way to judgement. When it was over, he switched the set off. The film reminded him of the correspondence that seemed to exist between certain forms of public transport and guilt, introspection and death. As the picture ended, a Northern Line train was approaching Waterloo carrying a young woman who was struggling to stop an infant from leaping up and down on his seat with excitement.

When the Paris train arrived they were stood, hand in hand, by the arrivals gate, as hundreds of faces streamed past. Then the automatic doors, which had been kept permanently open while the main body of passengers came through, closed – first intermittently, as the concentration of travellers eased, then for good. A woman cleaner was circling Laura and Jack, picking up litter with a steel claw on a stick. Then Laura noticed that the woman had stopped what she was doing and was staring in her direction, pointing to Laura's side. She looked down: Jack was in tears.

'Come on,' she told him. 'We'll get an ice cream.'

They went to the station café, where he ate a cornet, still crying.

'When's Daddy coming back?' he asked her.

She didn't answer. He began repeating the question every few seconds with a maddening, flat intonation.

'I don't know, Jack,' she told him. 'You know – there's something I have to tell you. I can't control everything that happens in the world.'

'I want to go home,' the boy said. He put the cornet down and left it on the table, half eaten. In the back seat of a taxi crossing Waterloo Bridge, she looked up at a billboard advertising a game show where couples spoke to each other while connected to a lie detector. She gazed west down the river and wondered whether – now that instruments could monitor heartbeat and blood pressure with such minute accuracy – there might one day be machines that could recognise other shifts in emotion, such as a woman's sorrow giving way to rage.

Daniel persuaded himself that he had decided to stay in Paris to think – to decide his future – except that, once here, he didn't. He felt not so much distraught as concussed. He went out and wandered around the city's large record stores, pausing occasionally to spend money he didn't have on boxed sets he would never play. He sought out distractions with such zealous determination that he started to experience a feeling of disconnection from the world. Had he been back in Bedford, he thought at one point, he'd have been able to go up and lie for a day, undisturbed, on Paul's grain silo. He returned to the street where he'd once lived in the north-east of the city, off a square called Stalingrad – a name in perfect keeping with his mood – but he called on nobody. He walked down to the North African café where he used to eat and stared through the windows. He could see familiar faces among the customers, and the same staff. They all looked more careworn, overweight, and five years older. He remained on the street outside, invisible and, in his mind at least, untouched by age, like a ghost. He immersed himself so completely in the idea that he imagined that, had he stepped into the place, the people who remembered him would have screamed and fled.

On the Friday lunchtime, by which point he'd been away for a week, he finally arranged to see a friend, Alice, a woman he'd worked with when he was a teacher in France. She was ten years older than Daniel and she'd come over in the seventies from Canada. He met her in a café at Les Halles, a claustrophobic tourist area that reminded him of Covent Garden. Alice was permanently broke, but had always insisted on being in the centre of town: she lived in a flat which, in her home country, would have only been considered useful as a cupboard.

Alice had arrived in Paris as a party girl and had wound up penniless, and often drunk. He talked to her about his meeting with Savage, his life as an obituarist and, mostly, about Laura, who had met Alice briefly in London, in the first weeks of their relationship. It was late afternoon when it struck him that Alice had said nothing about her own boyfriend.

'How's Louis?' he asked her.

'Louis has throat cancer,' she said.

'Do they think…' he began.

'In a month,' Alice told him, 'he'll be dead.'

He stared out into the square, where shoppers and commuters were beginning to head towards the Metro. The waiter brought the bill and he took out his wallet.

'When I knew you,' she said, 'you always had notes just stuffed into your back pocket.'

'If I was lucky. I always tried to travel light.'

She picked up the small leather wallet and felt inside it. 'OK,' she said. 'Where do you keep it then?'

'Where do I keep what?'

'The picture of your son.'

'I haven't got a picture,' he said.

'You should,' she said. 'I'd have liked to see him.'

She emptied a substantial pile of coins and notes out of the wallet and held it in her hand. 'You know what?' she said. 'A picture of a boy doesn't weigh much.'

'I don't carry his picture around,' said Daniel, 'because I like him so much it would break my heart.'

'Go home now,' she said. 'I've seen her with you, remember? She loves you. I've never seen you like that with anyone.'

The moment shocked him back to life. He walked back with Alice, up the dark passageway and the two flights of stairs that led into her block. Upstairs, a family of Albanians who had no papers and were doing miserably paid piece work, had set up an industrial sewing machine which ground away at deafening volume for twelve hours a day. It was no place, Daniel thought, to be sent home to die.

Alice lay down on the bed. He picked up the phone and booked a seat on a train leaving Paris at eleven the following morning. He looked around;

his friend had fallen asleep. He found a sheet of paper and sat down to write a fax to Laura.

He found himself gripped by the emotional paralysis that he associated with writing thank-you notes to grandparents. He sank into the grudging style that suggests the writer is being charged by the word, at so punitive a rate that to write a phrase in full, especially any endearment, might mean instant ruin. 'Back tomorrow,' he wrote, 'five p.m.' and he scrawled his signature. He slid the sheet into Alice's fax machine. When he saw the paper feeding through, he pressed what banknotes he had into the inside pocket of an old jacket she'd hung on a chair and left, closing the door softly. Back on the street, he exhaled very deeply – he couldn't help himself – with the abnormal force of someone who has just left a plague house. It was a stupid last trace of his childhood belief that cancer was contagious. When he breathed in again, it was to replace the funereal air of her flat with the petrol fumes of the boulevard Sébastopol.

CHAPTER 29

Staring through his compartment window at a stack of oildrums in a
transit yard just south of London, he tried to comfort himself with the
thought that the events of that night in Paris were simply an unfortunate
coincidence; that he was a victim of circumstance.

The truth was that he had come away from his interview with Caroline
Savage – a woman almost twenty years his senior – suffering from the kind
of fatal self-satisfaction that can strike an alcoholic who, after three month
of abstinence, makes the best man's speech at a friend's wedding, preside
over every nerve-racking formality of the event and resists all temptation
but the next day wakes up and goes straight to the nearest pub where he
drinks for eight hours.

Aspects of the episode – his uncharacteristic protectiveness, th
woman's Eurasian origins – went back, he realised, much further than
Caroline Savage, to Jude. What he really hated was the thought that, once
he knew Laura had been unfaithful, some contemptible part of him had felt
he had been granted the licence to commit an indiscretion himself. Th
angst of the traveller – always far greater, as other sufferers have observed
when returning home than leaving, and always strangely intensified when
arriving by rail – hit him with its full force at Waterloo.

The taxi ride to North London, which at normal times wa
interminable, passed in an instant. As Daniel climbed the fire escape t
Laura's flat, it struck him that concealment of what he had done had neve
occurred to him. He opened the front door. He was still standing on th

metal platform outside when she ran towards him – the second time that week that a woman had rushed him in a doorway – and put her arms round his neck, and held him.

She was wearing clothes he'd never seen before: a grey collarless man's shirt; blue and white striped trousers and a cream linen waistcoat. 'Where's Jack?' he asked her.

'He's at the zoo,' she said. 'With Rachel.' She stood back, conscious of some distance in him. 'What is it?' she said.

'You know that guy in Decatur Alabama,' he said. 'Well, he just knocked his bait tin in the water.'

'Listen,' she said. 'I'm so sorry. What can I say?'

'No,' he told her. 'I mean...it's happened again. It's not you.' He couldn't look at her. 'It's me.'

She stared at him, appalled. 'I feel sick,' she said.

He looked back at her, astonished. He'd subconsciously thought that, given her apparently cynical attitude to her own romantic history, she wouldn't mind. Instead, she looked destroyed. She walked into the room and stood away from him, her head forward; her dark hair fell forward over her face. He went to touch her but she put both hands against his chest and pushed him away, hard.

'It's a shame you never thought of that move,' he said, 'when you were with that fucker in Belgium.'

'I guess you were just out there with your Get Out of Jail Free card,' she said. 'You just couldn't wait to get banged up.'

She kneeled on the window seat staring out at the street.

'When I was twelve,' she said, 'I remember my mom saying to me, you know one thing you have to remember is that sex is a far more intimate thing for a woman than a man. And I remember I said, "Why, Mom?" and she got embarrassed. And then she said, "Because with men all that plumbing is on the outside." And I thought well, yeah but – men are still *there* aren't they, when that stuff happens? You're both still there, together.'

'Do you still think that?'

'Yes.'

She walked over to the bedroom, and came back with a handkerchief. He'd never seen her with a handkerchief.

'Tell me about it,' she said. 'All of it.'

He told her about Savage and the Tartine, about the Vietnamese woman and the bruise and the broken tooth.

'Yeah,' she said. 'Well, I know how it can get, in the heat of compassion.'

She looked down at her clothes. 'I got these things,' she said, 'because I wanted them to be new. I wanted it – I wanted us – to be new. I feel like one of those guys whose friends get them to turn up at the office party in fancy dress. Except that it isn't fancy dress. And this isn't a party actually, is it, Daniel? It's a fucking memorial service.'

'No,' he said. 'No.' He tried to put his hand on her but she pulled away once more and got to her feet.

'I guess...' she said, and stopped. He had never seen her angry before. She came and sat on his knee and put her arms round his neck and pressed her face against his. He felt a tear roll down her face into his collar. 'What does it matter?' she said. 'It still means...I did this, not you.' She held him tight for a minute and – out of affection rather than suspicion – put her hand in his jacket pocket. She pulled out a small white envelope. 'What is it?' she asked.

'I don't know,' said Daniel, truthfully.

She opened it. Inside was a square sheet of recycled notepaper. It was half-transparent and only its size saved it from being mistaken for cheap toilet paper. It had the single word 'Amour' written on it in capital letters, in pencil. She unfolded a tiny piece of tissue paper which contained – washed and pure white – the tooth that the girl had slipped into his jacket while he was sleeping.

Watching her opening it, he felt horrified. Laura stood at the top of the fire escape. She tore the cheap paper into pieces and scattered them down into the back yard, by the bins. Then she walked down past the garbage and over to a small area of neglected garden. He watched as she scraped a small hole and buried the tooth. He remembered a story he'd been told at school; that when the Irish writer Jonathan Swift died, his executors found, in his desk, wrapped in a piece of paper, a lock of hair belonging to Stella, the woman who had infatuated him and who had died many years earlier. Inscribed on the paper, in the poet's faltering hand, were the words 'Only a Woman's Hair' .

Something about Laura's action – it may have been the way she never looked around to see whether she was observed – made him wonder if she might be losing her senses. When she came back up, he told her for the first time about the nightmares he had about being unfaithful, and how this time he'd woken up to find that it was real. It occurred to him that, though he had always been appalled by infidelity in others, he had never previously remained loyal to any other woman.

She was exhausted, as he was, and she lay down on the bed. He lay next to her and they fell asleep. When he woke up, he felt like he had when he was a child coming home after a general anaesthetic – half-dazed, and presuming that it must be morning and not, as it actually was, late afternoon. They'd been asleep for an hour or so. It would have been longer, but Jessica was down in the bar below them and through the floor they could hear the familiar tones of her Hedy West record. 'If you miss the train I'm on, you will know that I am gone, you can hear the whistle blow a hundred miles...'

'Daniel,' Laura said. She almost never used his name. This is it, he thought, she's off. 'Don't ever bring us to this again,' she said. 'Because I'm not. That life is over.' She put her face against his neck. 'This woman...that woman...her – and that fucking pianist,' she said. 'Think of them as together. Invisible and inseparable. Till death do them part. And when you've done that...' She took his head in her hands, and turned his eyes to face hers, which had filled with tears. 'Marry me.'

In the seconds that followed, Daniel became familiar with a condition he had often imagined, occasionally witnessed, but never experienced: clinical shock. 'I love you,' she said. She disappeared into the bedroom and took off the new clothes. The following morning, she would secretly take them out the back and burn them.

She came back and sat on the edge of the bed in the same shirt and canvas trousers that she'd been wearing when they first met, on that first night in the Northumberland Arms. 'OK,' she told him. 'Let's start again.'

CHAPTER 30

'Oh dear,' she said, as they were in the taxi going down to Camden register office. 'I've just thought of something. Laura Linnell…I'm going to sound like a failed RKO screen test.'

They arrived half an hour early at the building, opposite St Pancras Station. Neither of them had dressed specially for the occasion and as they walked towards the entrance a pale youth tried to sell them some heroin. Daniel shook his head, unable to make himself heard against the traffic. Looking up at the three lanes of vehicles thundering past on the Euston Road, he tried to console himself with the thought of the following morning, when they would be flying out to Montpellier to spend a week in the country with Jessica Lee's friends Michel and Seti.

To his great surprise, Laura had originally proposed arranging their wedding in a local church. This idea had been curtly vetoed by the vicar, an elderly man who had become bitter and irritable even by the standards of the godless. Daniel had suggested that she ask her parents over, and she'd refused.

'Paul?' he ventured.

'No,' she said.

'Why?'

'Because Paul…because that would wreak havoc. I want this to be just family.' She meant Brendan, Rachel, and Jessica, who were travelling down in the Saab, with Jack, and Rachel's son, Jordan.

In the waiting room outside the register office, people were sitting on rows of chairs that were meanly upholstered and had a slight glaze, like seats on public transport. Most were waiting to register a birth or a death; Daniel found himself trying to tell which visitors were which, searching their faces for signs of grief or euphoria. He was overcome by foreboding; the area's combined use brought home a vision of existence as an inescapable conveyor towards the grave.

'It doesn't feel right, this,' was all he said to her.

'Is it me?' she asked.

'No,' he told her. 'It's not you. It's the place. It's too hot. It's too bright. It feels like Christmas in Australia.'

'You know,' she said, 'there's still time to run away. You want to?' He didn't reply. 'Tea?' she said.

They walked out, across the main road and up the slope into St Pancras, towards the buffet. They went through the red, gothic arches into the booking hall. The room, which was in semi-darkness, was lined with dark oak panelling, like a mediaeval banqueting hall. Daniel leaned back against the interior wall, which had six windows, each twenty-foot high and vaulted. She stood facing him. To his right, he could see a number of carved stone figures. Opposite, the five windows of the booking office were enclosed in a section of bow-fronted wood panelling that looked like the stern of a ship.

Standing in the gloom, they could just hear the announcer in the main station reciting a list of place names in a distant, echoing monotone. Through the booking office windows, an electric light glowed with a comforting, dull effulgence. The tiles under their feet were cream and blood red. The cool air of the place drifted into their clothes. Daniel leaned back against the wall opposite the ticket window, his hands in his pockets and his eyes down. She put both arms around his neck.

'This is where we'll say it, OK?' she whispered.

'OK. Right,' he said. 'Say what?'

'I don't know...' she told him, ''til death us do part.'

They stood there for a while in the half-light until they were interrupted by two Spanish women students who came in and started asking them about trains to Durham.

'Next door,' Daniel told one of the woman.

'What?' she said.

'Over there,' he shouted, pointing towards King's Cross. He followed her eyes as she looked up at the clock. They had five minutes.

'OK,' he said to Laura. 'Let's go.'

They walked back over to the town hall, where they found Brendan pacing the waiting room. He was wearing a new tweed suit, which he'd had hand-made in a style that might have appealed to an Edwardian gamekeeper, and there was a fresh carnation in his lapel. Two old women were trying to console him; his clothes, combined with his clear agitation, made them take him for the groom.

'Good God,' Daniel whispered, pointing at his outfit.

'Listen,' said Brendan, 'I never said I wasn't a kit man.'

He ushered them straight into the register office, where Jessica who was hand in hand with Jack, and Rachel with her young son Jordan, were waiting. Jack leapt up into his father's arms. As Laura came into the room, a woman's foot stretched out and half tripped her. She turned sharply and saw Kate, who had flown over alone, uninvited, from Kansas. She handed Daniel a message from Oakes; a card decorated with a picture of wedding bells, attached to a Tamla Motown single called 'It Should Have Been Me'. 'Doing the marriage service, he means,' said Kate, tactfully.

When the short ceremony was over they went for lunch in the bar of an ancient Victorian hotel close to King's Cross. It was a gentle, relaxed couple of hours; by three, the two children were asleep on the alcove seats. A retired couple from Phoenix, cheered by the accents of fellow Americans, were overtaken by generosity and sent over a bottle of champagne.

'Did you get married today?' the woman asked. 'Which church?'

'St Pancras,' said Laura.

She stared out across the taxi rank, towards the station and the platforms. 'You know, they're *so* like cathedrals,' she told Daniel, 'that I can't see why it doesn't work the other way round.'

'What?' he asked her.

'I mean...you never find anyone walking into Westminster Abbey half-expecting the six fifty from Darlington.'

'These are our stations of the cross,' he told her. 'King's and Charing.'

The following morning, as they set off for the airport with Jack, who was clutching his beach ball and Mr Bear, his favourite soft toy, their relief and excitement was tempered by unease. Since Belgium, long-distance travel had become equated in both their minds with trauma and crisis. But their spirits lifted once they'd landed and picked up a hire car, and were crossing the surreal landscape of the Larzac's high plateau, with its curious rock formations. Had it not been for the sunshine and the bleached greens and pale yellows of the undergrowth, they might have been crossing the surface of the moon. They were occasionally jolted back into the real world by an explosion from the army base in the distance.

Daniel pulled up by the front door of Seti and Michel's farmhouse, which was the most distant of a handful of cottages at the end of a dirt track. The garden and drive consisted of a large expanse of meadow turf. Daniel left the car next to Seti's battered red pickup. He'd stopped abruptly, which was just as well, because if he'd gone two yards further, the car would have plunged down a ten-foot drop into the adjacent field.

Michel was away, as he was every weekday, at the housing project in Marseille. They sat around in the garden with Seti until late afternoon, when Daniel went down to the local market with Jack, who seemed not to notice that his hostess couldn't speak his language. On the way back, they stopped in to the Café de la Cavalerie, run by an amiable middle-aged widow called Mademoiselle Lepape.

'Ice-cream game?' Daniel asked Jack. The boy nodded.

'What flavour?' asked Mademoiselle Lepape.

'Two scoops,' said Daniel. 'One strawberry, one vanilla.'

The child shut his eyes and opened his mouth. His father fed him a spoon of the vanilla. 'Chocolate,' said Jack.

Daniel ordered a beer; the setting sun caught the old chrome of the Rock-Ola jukebox that was playing 'Volare'. 'All things considered,' he said to Mademoiselle Lepape, 'life could be worse.' Life could, she smiled.

The father and son would be back every day for the next week, always carrying the beach ball and bear, always with the same order. By the last couple of days, as they approached the counter, the woman's eyes twinkled with complicity. Each visit ended with Jack smiling and dropping a couple of coins into the small pewter plate left on the bar for tips with a bold shout of 'Merci'.

When they got back with the shopping, Monsieur Jean, the next-door neighbour, had arrived and opened a bottle of his farmhouse red wine. Jean was eighty-three and not supposed to drink; he tended to set out with a bottle at around sunset and visit various friends and neighbours. He varied his routine, like a secret agent, in the hope of avoiding his daughter, Madame Sandrine. A director of the chamber of commerce in the nearby town of Millau, she had the thankless task of trying to keep him sober.

Monsieur Jean met Daniel and Jack as they were walking up to the front door.

'Where are you from?' the old man asked.

'England,' said Daniel.

'That's funny,' said Jean. 'I recently met a very beautiful young English woman, from Kansas.'

Daniel put Jack to bed.

'Where's Mr Bear?' the child asked, after he'd put out the light.

He went out to the car, and found the stuffed toy. On his way back in, he picked up the beach ball, which Jack insisted on having near his bed.

'Don't dream about bad ghosts, Dad,' the boy said.

'No, Jack,' he told him.

In the late evening, they were sat around the dinner table with Seti and Léon, one of Jean's friends from the local sheep-farming community. It was hardly a conventional honeymoon dinner; as the evening wore on, the men, Jean and Léon, a Roquefort producer in his seventies, reminisced about the locals' long-standing campaign to stop the army camp annexing their land. For years the farmers had maintained their passive resistance to the military, who frightened their sheep, trespassed on their pasture, and broke their hedges.

Léon recalled how, in the early seventies, they had rigged up their own illegal telephone system, and how they'd sabotaged one army vehicle so that, when the ignition was turned, it shook itself to pieces. 'When that happened,' he said, 'we saw it for what it was: a clown's limousine.'

On the Friday, Daniel offered to drive down to Marseille, to fetch Michel. Linnell's vision of the South of France owed a great deal to the sort of black and white films they showed at The Owl, that began with Charles Boyer at the wheel of a large American convertible with white-walled tyres, rolling along the coast road above Nice or Saint Tropez. He'd expected the whole region to be a more clement version of Bath. He was entirely unprepared for Marseille.

He found his way to the coast road all right, but to his surprise couldn't see much of the sea, which was obscured by warehouses, container depots and rubble. Michel ran La Bricarde, a collection of tower blocks on a hill to the north of the city. Daniel arrived just after lunch. He parked and walked across the pedestrianised square in the middle of the forbidding twenty-storey buildings. He approached the office, which was locked with several large padlocks and graffiti-covered aluminium shutters. There was a note attached to the doorbell with parcel tape, telling him to wait in the café on the ground floor of the nearest tower.

When he turned round, he found that a small crowd of teenagers, all of North African appearance, had gathered, and were staring at him. He could hear music and raised voices coming from a room on the ground floor of the adjacent building. The bar had a door that opened directly on to the courtyard. Its blinds had been pulled down and, as he walked in, it took his eyes a moment to get used to the light. He looked back at the door and saw that the youths had regrouped and were blocking the entrance behind him. The bar at La Bricarde was no bigger than a large hotel bedroom. Looking around, he noticed it had some equipment you would expect to find in any French café – a wooden counter, shelves stocked with Pastis and beer, an ice machine, a jukebox, and a pinball table. Other traditional accessories were absent: among them a till, the framed licence permitting the serving of alcohol, and the sign warning customers of the evils of public drunkenness. A heavy pall of hash smoke hung over the room.

The conversation, which was in French with the heavy accent of the Maghreb, faded like an old pop single as he entered. Daniel took a couple of steps towards the bar, but two youths of about sixteen got up to block his way. He put his small travelling bag down on a Formica table. Wary of Marseille's reputation, he'd closed it before he left the car, and replaced the airline security tape that had been stuck across the zip fastener, so that it couldn't be opened without breaking the seal. 'I've come,' he told them, 'to see Michel Auclair.'

The mood changed instantly. An older man, in his thirties, came out from behind the bar and held out his hand. 'Daniel?' he said. 'I'm Nordine. Michel's been delayed down at the town hall. He'll be here in a couple of hours.' Nordine led him to the bar, and pushed a bottle of Kronenbourg towards him. From habit, Daniel went back to pick up his bag.

The two young men got to their feet and barred his way again. 'Leave it there,' said Nordine. 'If you don't, you'll offend them. Your bag won't be moving,' he added. 'Your bag is a sign of trust.' Daniel stood with them by the bar, listening to the tape machine playing IAM and Jo Corbeau, whose work, his hosts were amazed to discover, he knew. Had he heard Corbeau's new CD? He shook his head.

'You won't find that in England,' Nordine said. 'You won't find that in Paris.'

He warmed to the community, whose conviviality, Parisians had always told him, would be worthless. He realised that the qualities he admired in the Northern French were actually what remained in them of the Mediterranean. With a couple of exceptions, all his new companions were North African immigrants. Most were unemployed, though some did subsidised work around the estate, like litter collection or road maintenance. Nobody would let him pay.

'Do you work?' one of the young men asked.

'I'm an obituary writer,' said Daniel.

It never occurred to him to lie, like he sometimes did. He heard the word go round the bar: *Nécrologue*. God, he told them, that sounds even worse in French. Nordine, the barman, nodded. '*Nécrologue*. Well,' he added, with a grim smile, 'you're in the right place here.'

Michel appeared in the late afternoon. They went back across to his office: two small rooms in a tower which, like its neighbouring blocks, had been thrown up in haste in the seventies, from the cheapest of materials. On the walls behind his desk, where a framed picture or a year-planner might normally be, was a large collection of car number plates. They belonged to vehicles, Michel explained, that had been stolen. The favourite method of despatch was to take a car in the centre of town and drive it to the hill that overlooked La Bricarde's car park. On the top of the hill, there was an unpaved flat area about the size of a football pitch. There, the back seat was doused in paraffin and lit; the vehicle was then driven at speed to the edge of the cliff, at which point the driver dived out at the last moment, allowing the car to plunge over the edge and down into the car park below where, with luck, it would spark new, and more interesting conflagrations.

It was the trouble with the cars, Michel explained, that had delayed him that afternoon. 'Twenty-two times,' he said, 'in the last eighteen months they've done that. Every time I've spoken to the authorities. And they've never listened. But last night was the last.'

Some teenagers, he explained, had stolen the deputy mayor's official limousine, while she was on a visit to explain the recent closure of the local school, which meant that children from the estate now had to be bused three miles towards town. 'I was talking to her...I had my back to the window,' said Michel, 'when she saw her Mercedes being driven away. She got her mobile phone and called the police. They asked her where she was and how long ago it had been taken, and which direction it seemed to be heading in. And then,' Michel roared with laughter, 'they said, "OK, OK. La Bricarde. Five minutes. North. You don't need the highway police. You need air traffic control." So that's twenty-three times.'

He pointed out of the window. At the foot of the hill, a tow truck was removing wreckage from the car park. 'A *shame*,' said Michel. He pointed to the top of the hill, where a group of council labourers were cementing large boulders around the edge of the drop. 'We survive,' he said. 'We survive. We're not the South Bronx. There's no crack to speak of. Because even cheap crack's expensive. What you get here is cheap: prescription drugs and speed. Cheap speed.'

He held the estate together as Jessica had said, by the force of his character and by his physical strength. It was an unspoken assumption shared by the police, the residents and, privately, by Auclair himself, that when he left, the community would crumble into ruin, like some enchanted land in a fairy tale when the Prince leaves the city walls.

They set off at five, with Michel driving. On the way back, he pulled up and parked in Marseille's old port. The atmosphere on the streets struck Daniel powerfully, and straight away: the intoxicating enthusiasm and shared anticipation that you might find in other towns before a big cup game. They sat outside at a bar opposite the quay where the fishermen's wives were packing up their trestle tables.

'What's happening tonight?' Daniel asked. 'A concert? A football match?'

'There's nothing on,' said Michel. 'It's Friday. It's Marseille.'

'What do you think of La Bricarde?' his host asked, as they made their way north.

'I think you do a real job' said Daniel.

'I don't know any British journalists,' Michel said. 'The French ones...' he paused. 'They come down here once a year or so, to write about deprivation. One or two of them have been straight with us. The rest.... I've always felt that the courage of a journalist...' He stopped.

'Go on,' said Daniel.

'At their worst, they're the natural writers of letters behind a guy's back, to his boss. They have the fleet-footed valour of the schoolroom sneak.'

As they approached the house, they heard the sound of raucous laughter. 'Oh dear,' said Michel. 'Jean's here. Have you, er...'

Daniel nodded.

They sat around for an hour or so. Michel disappeared into the kitchen. A few minutes later, the front door opened to reveal Madame Sandrine. She was a woman of about fifty, in a grey business suit, wearing a lot of make-up. She'd only just got back from work and she looked incandescent. 'Out,' she shouted to her father, without saying hello. Monsieur Jean ignored her. Seti introduced Sandrine to her English visitors.

'So,' she said to Daniel, 'you've been to Marseille.' She paused. 'Still got everything?' He smiled. 'Seriously, you have to watch yourself down there. Those people ... They're not to be trusted.'

He told her about his bag, and how they had made him leave it unattended, and how the tag hadn't been broken.

'Is it this one?' she said, pointing to the small canvas holdall.

He nodded.

'Well, I hate to tell you this,' she said, 'but it's broken now.'

'Shit,' said Daniel. He pulled back the zip, and pulled out the wallet with his passport, travel documents and money, all intact. He put his hand in further and found a package, roughly wrapped in a page from an Arabic newspaper. Opening it, he found a small lump of cannabis and a CD – *Jo Corbeau: Chansons*.

'Who gave you that?' she said.

'A friend,' said Daniel.

'You,' she said, turning back to her father, 'are a disgrace.'

Hearing her voice, the old man rallied. 'You know,' he said, 'we always thought that she would never marry. Because' – a look resembling mortification appeared on the face of Monsieur Jean's daughter – '...because she wet the bed until she was thirteen. But then – incredibly – she was the first to find a husband.'

By the time Michel served dinner, Madame Sandrine had given up and left, but Jean – now joined by his friend Léon – was still there. It was amazing, Daniel said, that they had managed to hold the army at bay for so long.

'The military might seem to have everything in their favour,' Léon said, 'but we have three great advantages over them. We have time, we have invention, and we have fearlessness. We are Errol Flynn,' he added, warming to his subject, 'to their lumbering Basil Rathbone. We are a light-footed Brazilian winger to the heavy dependability of their German full-back.'

'We have,' added Jean, who was slumped in his chair with his fly buttons unfastened, 'a certain elegance.'

'A certain elegance,' said Léon. 'Thank you, Jean. 'We are Oscar Wilde to their Marquess of Queensberry. We are the corner grocer to their American superstore. We, er...' He hiccuped, and fell silent.

'They are the powder,' said Seti. 'We are the flame.'

On the evening of Daniel's first day back at work, in the Printer's Devil, Whittington handed him a news cutting about Professor John Sherratt, a leading vivisectionist. There was a photograph of the scientist; a man with a thin mouth and gold-rimmed spectacles. He was staring forlornly at the smouldering remains of his detached bungalow, named, as Whittington told them, 'somewhat optimistically, *Mon Repos*'.

The putty in Sherratt's new windows, reglazed after they were blown out in a lesser explosion five days earlier, could barely have dried, Whittington noted. 'The Professor has never read the spectacular opening of Joseph Conrad's *Under Western Eyes*,' he said. 'If he had, he'd know that, circumstances permitting, one bomb is followed by another.' With that in mind, he added, it was time to get him filed in the morgue. 'Violence,' he said, 'is a terrible thing. But it's hard to feel great sympathy for a man who spends his weekdays plugging Beagles into the mains.'

He spoke to Rosa about which writer would be best placed to prepare Sherratt's obituary. Daniel's attention began to wander. He found himself gazing around the cavernous bar, and the awfulness of the building, which familiarity had gradually obscured, struck him once more. He stared at the Wall of Proverbs and the new slogans that had been scrawled there by his drunken colleagues.

It was heartening, Whittington remarked, when he noticed his deputy peering at the graffiti, to know that even the most formidably bland surroundings could, by means of a little criminal damage, be invested with real atmosphere. Rosa started to talk about an establishment in Barcelona called the Tiger: an old-style dance hall with a gallery, a hardwood floor and a twelve-piece jazz band. Its clientele, she told them, ranged from OAPs through to teenage club-goers.

More remarkable than its varied public, she said, was the Tiger's system of admission. The club was open from 9.00 p.m. until 2.00 a.m., when it expelled all its customers, and closed its doors. It reopened at three thirty, by which time there would be a queue stretching the full length of the narrow street, besieged by hawkers who set out their stalls on the opposite pavement, selling stolen cigarettes or deep-fried doughnuts. 'And even when the queue does begin to move,' she said, 'it takes ages to get in, because they only let people in one at a time. An old man in a porter's uniform opens the front door, motions you in, then closes it behind you. Then you're standing alone, in a dimly-lit lobby, about half the size of an average lift.'

Then, she explained, the main door behind you would be closed, and an oak panel in the wall you were facing slid open, to reveal a hole about the size of a letter-box. The hole was, for most clients, roughly at the height of their nose and, through it, there came a mixture of scents: spilt beer, tobacco, and a half-invigorating, half-repellent note of sweat, pheramones and cheap musk. This last perfume belonged to Nuria Calderon, the owner, who would stand behind the wall and peer at every new arrival through the slot.

The visitor, Rosa explained, would remain in the tiny lobby in silence, for a second or two before Calderon would speak the single word '*Endavant*' – enter – and a door would open in the wall to the customer's left. This procedure went back to the days when Nuria's mother had opened the Tiger during the Spanish Civil War, when such precautions were commonplace in the city. The fact that the practice survived more than six decades was the more bizarre since, to the knowledge of anybody who worked there, nobody had ever been refused admission.

Rosa added that when Nuria had first stood there, fifty years earlier, to examine the procession of faces – each one, whether it belonged to a priest, a midwife, a railway worker or a murderer, greeted with the single word '*Endavant*', intoned without feeling – her eyes had been heavily coated in mascara and, legend had it, carried so powerful an erotic charge that male visitors who had returned her intense stare had been driven mad, or close to the point of ecstasy. There was little danger of that now: alcohol, tobacco and age had given the whites of her eyes a yellowish translucence, like albumen. 'Even now, even tonight,' Rosa said, 'they will be queuing up outside the Tiger – like souls waiting to be born.'

'Like what?' Whittington said.

'Souls,' Rosa repeated, 'waiting to be born.'

'I'm surprised you should say that,' said Whittington. 'I was just thinking that it sounded exactly like death.'

In the closing stages of Rosa's reminiscences they had been joined by the sports editor Sean Linahan, who was with his temporary secretary Louise, a resting actress in her late twenties.

'It's a funny thing,' said Rosa, 'how when you're standing in a queue, or sitting opposite a row of faces in the Metro, you start to wonder about those strangers: their intimate hopes, or joys, or disappointments; through what connection of blood, or shared acquaintance, your existence might be linked with theirs. You could argue that our natural appetite for gossip indicates a desire for total knowledge,' she added. 'But what would be the consequences if we really did know everything? If we knew the secret passions behind the neutral stare of a stranger, or the betrayals and confidences that passed between our friends, without our knowing?'

The table remained in silence. Linahan drew breath to make a sarcastic remark, then checked himself. He had been disappointed, when he arrived, to notice that none of his sportswriters were in the Devil. In their absence he'd hoped that, by joining a larger group, he would be able to engender a spirit of flirtatious banter that might inspire Louise to indicate – by a subtly perceptible gesture, coded allusion, or some other technique available to a resourceful woman with a theatrical background – her desire to be escorted to the Mount Pleasant Hilton where an older, more experienced man might make love to her until she lost all sense of time, place, or propriety. Rosa's weird speech had left the table gripped by morbid introspection – precisely the kind of ambience that he had been keenest to avoid.

Yet Rosa Dalmau's philosophical excursion had its greatest effect not on Linahan but on Whittington. As she completed her last remark, the obituaries editor was fidgeting with his coaster and staring fixedly towards the wall of abbreviated proverbs, as if for guidance. His colleagues didn't notice his reaction and, if they had done, they might have taken it for boredom or preoccupation rather than for what it was – the look of a man who, several weeks earlier, had been taking breakfast in a secluded West Country hotel with a young American woman, in whose intoxicating company he had come as close as he ever would to revealing certain intimate truths of his life.

Jack had cried himself to sleep in the black cab on the way home from Waterloo, and Laura walked up the fire escape with the boy in her arms. She came in to find no messages on the answering machine, and the flat still deserted. She called the obituaries desk and asked to speak to Whittington, but Rosa told her that he'd gone down to Devon. Rosa would have said more but for the fact that – since Daniel had been missing from the office for three days since he left for Belgium – she knew the cause of Laura's unease but had no idea how to address it.

Whittington was at the Hotel Zurich, Rosa explained, near Bigbury, in Devon. She read out the number, which Laura wrote down on her hand. That night, she left Jack next door with Rachel and Jordan. She woke at four thirty in the morning and stared out of the window as the light was coming up over the city. She sat up and looked down at the inked message in her left palm, then gathered together some cash and a chequebook, and called for a cab to Paddington.

She was sitting outside, on the front window ledge, with her back to the café's illuminated mascot, when the car arrived. Even though she had no luggage, the driver, a Greek Cypriot of around fifty, got out and hurried round to open the passenger door for her before she realised what he was doing.

She sat in the rear left seat. The driver's hair was almost gone, though the years had done less to erode an adolescent libido which – as the cheap cologne, the strawberry air freshener, the gold bracelet, the Nat King Cole tape and his priapic chivalry declared – had survived undiminished.

'Are you American?' he asked.

'Yes,' said Laura.

'Are you married?'

'No,' she said, wishing instantly that she'd said something else.

'How old are you?'

'Thirty-two.'

'So why,' he asked, 'you not married?'

'That's my problem,' she told him. 'I was twenty-eight before I got any common sense.'

It was a casual enough remark but one which seemed to have left the driver speechless. He drove on, his expression unaltered, through a set of traffic lights. His bottom jaw, she noticed, had slackened, and his mouth was slightly open.

'That light was red,' she told him.

'Sorry, sorry,' said the driver. At the next set of lights, which was green he pulled up, and put the handbrake on with a jerk. He half twisted round to face her.

'You...you *like* common sex?'

'Sense,' she told him. 'Common sense. I was twenty-eight before I got any common sense.'

The Greek drove on, uneasily silent now. They passed Chillies and she recalled how Whittington had blushed over the wine: it was that single memory, more than anything, that sustained her belief that it might be worth speaking to him.

It was just before nine when she came over the brow of a hill in the taxi she'd taken from Plymouth station and took in her first sight of the Zurich. Laura walked into reception, where she was immediately struck by an overpowering smell of roast lamb, soft fruit and spices; a smell that, even to somebody who had been up for almost five hours, was very wrong for that time of the morning. She rang the brass bell on the reception desk, which Anstruther, who was in the kitchens, heard and disregarded.

She sat down and reached over to a nearby coffee table, where the hotelier had laid out half a dozen leather-bound menus in the place where the magazines should have been. It was impossible for anyone who was raised, as Laura was, on the thin, ascetic dishes of the eighties and nineties, to cast an eye over the Zurich's menu without pondering the consequences of sustained exposure to its daunting regime. If she had lacked the imagination, or the stomach, to picture the result, it was amply illustrated a moment or two later, by the arrival of Anstruther himself, his vast bulk crammed, as usual, into his checked shirt and his ancient tweed suit. He swept past, apparently without having seen her.

Laura struck the bell again, unaware that anyone who rang twice, especially when Anstruther was alone in the hotel, not only surrendered any hope of their host's prompt arrival, but courted the prospect that he might never appear at all.

She rang a third time and started to look at some of the canvases hanging in the entrance hall. They were grotesquely distorted nudes, painted, though she didn't know it at the time, by the artist Hugo Savage, whose progressive self-demolition had been accelerated by his numerous visits to the hotel in the late-sixties, usually in the company of one of his young women models. Anstruther was fond of boasting that his own huge girth had long made him incapable of orthodox sexual intercourse, a claim which few doubted, though some speculated privately on how he could have known. An alien, seeing Patrick Anstruther as he finally appeared in the lobby, striding towards the slight figure of Laura Jardine, might have doubted that the two belonged to the same species. She whispered to him, and he pointed into the restaurant, towards a corner table by a window, where a solitary diner had his head turned away, facing the open fields, apparently lost in contemplation.

CHAPTER 31

Whittington was staring out of the window towards the Zurich's golf course. He had slept badly after a late supper of claret and blue stilton, and he was so well submerged in that half-state between waking and unconsciousness that, when he looked up and saw her sitting across the table from him, he was no more surprised than if her face had appeared to him in a dream.

Patrick Anstruther walked over to their table and handed Laura a black coffee she hadn't ordered.

'My God,' she said to Whittington, as the owner disappeared, 'he's massive.'

'He is massive,' he replied. 'He has to be. If he wasn't, he couldn't do what he does. When a man is massive, as when a woman is beautiful, different things happen to him.'

He shifted uncomfortably in his seat, realising that this remark could be construed as heavy-handed flattery, which he hadn't intended it to be. There was a moment of great awkwardness. She hadn't known quite why she'd come and now she was here she didn't know what she'd say.

Then, perhaps because Whittington's apparent indifference to romantic attachment seemed to place him outside of the world of physicality, like a phantom or a priest, perhaps because of the unreal nature of their surroundings, she told him about what had happened in Belgium. She had no idea of what Whittington might say in return, but that lack of expectation scarcely prepared her for his response.

When she'd finished speaking, he sat for a few moments in silence, then began to relate an episode which, he said, had been described to him by his two elderly great-aunts, concerning a black soldier who had fought alongside the British during the Boer War.

'This happened in their mother's house in Cape Town, when they were eight or nine years old,' he said. 'They sat on the floor of their kitchen; it was mid-morning, and Charlotte, their mother, asked them if they'd help her mix an apricot glaze for an apple tart she'd just taken out of the oven. As soon as she'd spoken those words, a man staggered into the kitchen, with wounds in his arms and legs. He had two bullets in his upper left shoulder, and one in his left thigh, although of course they couldn't tell that then. He stood there, breathless and panic-stricken, as if he feared pursuit. He was losing blood. They went to help him, but before they could treat his injuries the Boers arrived, asking if they'd seen a fugitive.'

'The soldiers,' he went on, 'commandeered the house, and Charlotte had to hide him then, just as he was, in her own wardrobe on the upstairs landing. She pushed him in there, with her ball-gowns and her hat-boxes. Her husband was away fighting with the cavalry, though frankly I don't see how things could have passed off any better if he'd been there.'

Laura stared at him. There was something unnerving about the way Whittington was talking. It wasn't simply that what he was saying bore no relation to anything she'd said to him; it was to do with his attention to the minutiae of this narrative, a level of detail that was clearly not of his own invention, but a faithful account handed down to him and perfected, so unhesitating was his delivery, by God knows how many hours spent dwelling on the scene.

'As she went to bed,' Whittington continued, 'she pushed a bottle of water through the wardrobe door, and in the night the girls crept up to leave him food, which he never touched. The Boers were in the house for three days, and when Charlotte looked in just before dawn on the morning they left, he was still alive. As soon as the enemy soldiers had gone, the girls' mother put on water to boil, so they could sterilise bandages and start treating his wounds. She went up to the attic window, to make sure they'd really moved off. While she was there, the two girls ran up to the cupboard, but the next thing their mother heard was their screams, and when she came down the attic stairs to look at him she could see that he was dead.'

Clutched between the man's left thumb and forefinger, Whittington said, they found a photograph of himself, baling hay with his wife and three daughters. 'He'd taken a hatpin out of a box in the wardrobe and he'd been piercing the back of his left thumb with it, to stop himself crying out from the gunshot wounds. I have often asked myself how that one trivial pain could mask the agony of a flesh wound. But who knows what happens at such moments? When they found him, the pin had pierced the picture, and it had been pressed straight through his left thumb.

'Before they took his body back to his family, they called Dr Laud, the local surgeon, to ask if he would come to remove the bullets and stitch the wounds before they washed and dressed the corpse, and took it back to his village. Dr Laud refused. Then he said he'd come so long as they understood that he would be charging them four times the normal price. Double, he said, because this was a dead man, which meant that he was wasting his time, and four times because this dead man was – I quote the doctor's exact words – an ignorant bloody Kaffir. I am less an admirer of violence,' said Whittington, 'than I am of mercy. But if Dr Laud were in front of us now, and if he were to speak those words again, here, today, I would have no hesitation, for that last phrase alone, in putting a pistol to his temple and blowing his brains out.' He fell silent, and she saw that tears were running down his face.

'When they took his body back to his widow,' he said, 'they learned how he was a father of four, and how he had been born, and breathed, and laughed, and suffered, and collected food for the poor in his parish, and how, when he had built his own house, he had built it flat, with level, open roofs, because he had a lifelong dread of confinement. One of his daughters told Charlotte that, when they kept a turkey to fatten up for Christmas, he could only bring himself to kill it after his wife had tied a muslin bag around its head, and that even then he couldn't wring its neck, but had to shoot it with a musket, which made the meat useless. And that his most reprehensible indulgence was to sing the works of hymn-writers and classical composers in a full, resonant, baritone. And he died,' Whittington added, 'in that cupboard.' He paused. 'I didn't mention his name,' he said. 'And, though you might not think it from the circumstances of his death, he did have a name. It was Edmund Somers. And he was thirty-eight and I keep a picture of him under glass in my office. I keep a picture of him there so I don't forget that Dr Laud, like Edmund Somers, has descendants faithful to his spirit, who walk among us. And to remind me what true misfortune is.'

Anstruther arrived, and placed a heavy earthenware dish, containing what looked like a small boiled fowl, on the table. He glanced at Whittington and frowned slightly, but made no comment, and walked away.

'It's not that he's heartless,' the editor said to Laura, as he blew his nose into the kind of large, blue-spotted handkerchief she had thought existed only in Jack's story-books. 'It's just that he's had more experience than most of seeing a customer in tears. I have to apologise for my emotion,' he added. 'It has to do with the way the man died.'

'And yet so many of us will die alone,' said Laura, 'in the dark. Of our wounds.'

Whittington looked down the driveway, where two men were emptying a van laden down with mature English cheeses and full cream dairy products.

'But that's just it,' he said. 'He didn't die alone. Or in the dark. And he didn't die of his wounds. Every time they'd been up to see him before, they'd crept up during the night. He had no idea the Boers had left, and when the children rushed in and threw the door open, and the light burst in on him, it was too much. He died then, of a seizure. The doctor, before he presented his bill, took the trouble to tell Charlotte, in the presence of her daughters, that had it not been for the heart attack, the man would have survived his injuries. They flung the door open suddenly like that because they were so eager to save him. I mention these things to you now after what you told me, because when I think of them, as I do every day, it occurs to me that there are few things so bad that a reckless impulse can't make them worse.' He could repeat the story so fluently, Whittington said, because it had been written down in minute detail by Constance and Ruth, Charlotte's daughters.

'They kept in touch with you then?' said Laura.

'That's right,' said Whittington. 'They had to really. They brought me up.'

His father, the vicar of St Fimbarrus', had abandoned him when he was one, for reasons which had never been made clear. Whittington himself believed that his mother must have had an affair and that the clergyman succeeded in forgiving his wife, but not her adulterous offspring. 'Though even his forgiveness of her may be in doubt,' he said, 'since she died in a fall on a flight of steps in the village, when I was three. I used to go down to Fowey and watch him preach, twenty years later.'

'Why?' Laura asked, softly.

'I never spoke to him and he never knew who I was,' was all he said. 'Listening to my father's sermons, I felt he shared something with me; that we had the same sort of dislocation from certain aspects of humanity.'

Laura looked at him. 'That means,' she said, 'that he never got laid, right?'

It was true that Whittington might have belonged to a previous age, where sex with a partner was not obligatory and where a solitary life did not necessarily imply repressed homosexuality. It was his voluntary exclusion from the general experience of sexual passion that gave him his unique, ironic perception of the great power that physical desire exerted over others, which must have seemed as strange to him as if the object of their obsession had been not sex but origami, curling or the lute. Whittington, looking away from her eyes for a moment, noticed how elegantly her straight black hair fell over the upturned collar of her jacket, and found himself reflecting – briefly, but for the first time in many years – that his indifference in these matters might have been perverse or mistaken.

When his father's funeral was held at St Fimbarrus', five years earlier, he told her, he was not among the congregation. 'I got a train down there, the morning before the service,' he said, 'and I checked in to the Fowey Hotel. I went down to the church and I sat in the back pew, alone. You may think me foolish, but at moments I believed that we communicated. Then the cleaner made me leave. I walked out, and when I got to the end of South Street there was a bus about to leave for St Austell. I got on it and then I caught the train back to London. I left all my things in room one hundred and three.'

'Things?' she said.

'I left my bag,' he said. 'I left my hat. I know more than most men,' he added, 'about running away.'

She closed her eyes.

'Don't worry about Daniel,' he went on. 'I know him. He ran away. He'll come back.'

They walked out to the conservatory. As they sat in silence, Anstruther appeared and added another indelible memory to the many she would have of that day, by breaking wind, loudly and at length.

Unusual though Anstruther was, Whittington told her, it was the exceptions to his moods that made him interesting. He was indifferent, for instance, to the usual prejudices concerning race or class.

'In the seventies,' he told her, 'Patrick was the only hotelier in the county – and I mean the only one – who would put up punk bands.'

'This place is so weird,' she said. 'Every time I change position, I get a draught of that smell.' It was rich and decaying and it was trapped in the layers of her clothes.

'It's not to everybody's taste,' said Whittington.

'Yeah,' she said, 'but, Christ, will it ever go away?'

'Think of that smell like some primitive token people used to carry around with them to bring them luck,' he said. 'A rabbit's foot, a shrunken head, or a thigh-bone from a saint. Think of it like a lucky charm, that will always be with you and, when you think of it, it will envelop you and bring you protection from danger.'

She left feeling strangely comforted. As she travelled back on the train, alone, she shifted her shoulders against the narrow seat and that sweet smell came up at her again. It was still in her clothes as she got off at Paddington. She would not try to summon it to her memory for many weeks. When she did, it was because she had just made that same movement, of shifting her shoulders in another narrow seat, accelerating rapidly. She was alone in the South of France, and when she did try to bring the scent to mind, it wouldn't come.

CHAPTER 32

'I knew it was going to be you,' Brendan said to Daniel. It was early one Monday morning and they were at the bar in The Owl, where Daniel had stopped off for a coffee on his way to work.

'What?'

'I knew it would be you,' Brendan repeated, 'that she'd stay with.'

Daniel said nothing. It was barely two months since his return from honeymoon. He was trying to think why Brendan, hardly a man given to exchanging emotional confidences, might have broached such an intimate subject.

'Why...' Daniel asked, cautiously, '...why do you mention that?'

Doyle reached under the counter and produced a thick pile of photographs and postcards that he'd been sorting through. He put up the 'Closed' sign, took the stuffed owl out of the front window and placed it on the bar counter between them. The café was shut closed for the next week, for redecorating. The painters were coming in the next morning. In the meantime Brendan was clearing the shelves and cupboards, and taking down posters. Perhaps, Daniel thought, the barman's new inquisitiveness was a symptom of his ecstatic anticipation of impending leisure, a condition which can make even the most staid figures in a school, or a corporation, behave in unpredictable ways. Jessica Lee was with her mother in Colorado. The previous evening, Laura and Jack had left for France, to spend another week in the Larzac with Michel and Seti. Daniel, after his extended absences in Europe, felt he had to stay and work.

Brendan spread the photographs across the bar. At some time, he said, each one had been up on the noticeboard in The Owl. He leafed through the pictures and pushed one across the bar to Daniel. 'This one,' he said, 'only stayed up two hours.'

'What happened then?'

'She noticed it.'

Daniel looked at it. It showed Robin, the psychiatrist, at a table in the restaurant with Laura. He was presenting her with some kind of gift but, far from looking appreciative, she was staring at him with an appalled expression.

'He used to come in with her, you know, now and again,' Brendan said. 'He came in once on his own, after you arrived. I told him you'd both gone to Walsall.'

'Why Walsall?' Daniel asked. 'Why not...I don't know...Tasmania?'

'Because if I'd said Tasmania,' Brendan replied, 'he might have wanted to follow you there.'

Daniel squinted at the picture again, but he couldn't make out what the present was.

'What's he holding?'

'It's a specially commissioned sapphire eternity ring,' said Brendan, 'set in silver, and engraved with two silver bluebirds.'

'An eternity ring? Isn't that supposed to be for married couples who are...'

'Yes,' interrupted Doyle.

'Oh God,' said Daniel. 'Oh bloody hell.'

'Yes,' said Brendan. 'Exactly. I mean...no, don't get me wrong – he got it straight back. But I remember that look she gave him, when he gave her it. I thought – if you could see that look she's giving you pal, you'd see you're not her eternal bluebird. The way she's looking at you is more like the way a miner in a search and rescue team looks at his fucking canary.'

He glanced at the barman and realised why he'd broached this subject. Brendan knew her past. And he knew she'd gone abroad again.

Linnell didn't say anything, but he could feel that the effect of Doyle's attempt at reassurance was precisely the opposite of the one he'd intended. When Laura had talked about taking the boy down to stay with Michel and Seti for the week, Daniel hadn't even considered her absence as an opportunity for a second betrayal. Considering they hadn't known each other for long, there was an unusual degree of trust between the obituarist and the big Frenchman. It had to do, if Daniel was honest, with a sense that Michel could at some point have slept with Laura, and the certain knowledge that he hadn't. That was one thing. And then the events that blighted their summer had left Daniel not with a heightened foreboding, but a new and unshakeable faith in his wife. Could this be simply the latest form of his idiocy? He thought of Bob, and the talcum powder in the ladies'.

Brendan picked up the photograph. 'Bin?' he asked.

Daniel looked at it again and, for all his new-found confidence, nodded.

At ten that morning he set off to eat with the sports desk at Bar G, the converted canal boat on the river near the office. The sports writers' spirits – rarely subdued – had been raised further by an incident that had occurred as Daniel and Sean Linahan were making their way to the boat, just after eleven. The two men had gone ahead of the others, and they were just crossing the main road in front of their building when a police van tore round the corner, pursuit lights flashing and siren wailing, and almost collided with them. Daniel responded instinctively, by crooking his left hand in his right arm, in the French tradition, at the same time raising his right index finger. 'Very sensible,' said Linahan. 'Belt and braces.'

There was a squeal of brakes as the van swung round and came back at them. Four uniformed constables leapt out and pinned the two men to a wall. Daniel tried to move his head forward but a forearm pushed it back and held it there. He could feel the coarseness of the material of the uniform pressed against his forehead and damp moss and brick against his neck.

'What's up?' asked Linahan. 'Your pies getting cold?'

'Shut it,' the smallest one said. 'We are on urgent police business.'

A fifth, older man, a detective inspector, emerged from the vehicle much more slowly – his movement was almost languid – and walked over to the group. As he arrived, one of the smaller constables had just begun a gloating recital of the formal caution. The senior officer, who recognised Linahan from his weekly appearances on a television football quiz, motioned his colleague to silence. He paused for a moment and gave Daniel and Linahan a look of solemn resignation, as if he was looking at two corpses.

'Any tips for the three fifteen at Wincanton?' he asked.

'No,' Linahan lied.

The detective inspector turned and walked back to the vehicle, reluctantly followed by his subordinates, who adopted his leisurely pace rather than overtake him. They climbed back into the van, which took off again with the same urgency.

The Bar G was a narrow, claustrophobic room containing four cramped tables that could each seat eight. To enter it, you had to negotiate an ornate gangplank, then go down a couple of steps into what served as its lobby: a tiny wooden entrance booth not much bigger than a public phone box. Two passages led off it: to the left were the toilets and a payphone; to the right, the entrance to the dining area. Even the smallest adult visitor had to stoop to get through the doorway; once inside, there was room to stand comfortably, but it took your eyes a minute to adjust to the dim lighting. The seats, tables, and panelled walls were all fashioned out of dark, polished oak, and the only natural light came from small portholes, which were at eye-level for seated diners. Customers on the starboard side had a view of the tow-path and, if the evening was drawing in, practised lunchers had learned how to tilt their head backwards, beyond the inquisitive gaze of a passing senior editor. Daniel was a regular guest at the sports department Monday lunches, which began early, at 11.30, to allow them to unwind after the frantic demands of the weekend, and still be seen in the office in the afternoon.

Linnell and the sports editor sat facing each other at a starboard table, where they were soon joined by four of the desk's staff writers. Linahan gave a laconic account of the officers' intervention that appeared, almost unchanged, in the paper's diary the following day. Then Daniel told them about a case he had heard about when he was at Resolve: a Surrey publican called Brian, whose wife had forced him to consult the sex therapist who was treating him for various anxiety-related symptoms, principally memory lapses and impotence. Brian was a former market trader in his fifties, and he had well-embedded views on psychiatry that led to lively exchanges with his therapist, Siobhan Edwardes, a gifted but serious-minded clinical practitioner.

The landlord had a history of hypertension which, his GP had told him, ruled out the use of Viagra. After a number of stubborn confrontations with Edwardes, he began to soften, and eventually discussed his problem with great frankness. Heartened, she proposed a visualisation technique that required the patient to indulge in erotic fantasies while making love with a regular partner. Brian complained that he couldn't fantasise, because 'I never see any other women undressed.'

'She made him write down the names of all his former girlfriends,' Daniel told them. 'There were eleven of them and they were all from his young life in Gillingham. They had names like Eileen and Rita and Maud. Anyway, he came back the next week saying that he'd tried it, but it hadn't worked because his memory was going, and he could never remember them fast enough. So Edwardes told him to try and make an acronym out of the first letter of each of their names. When that didn't work either, she suggested giving each one of them a number and visualising them in a formation, like in a football programme. Anyway, he disappeared again for a few weeks. When he came back he said things were going better. Then he asked if it was all right if he stopped thinking of Eileen. When she asked why, he said, "I don't know where to start. It's not just that she's one-footed; her distribution's sloppy, she's useless in the air and she refuses point blank to track back. Her whole attitude's all wrong."'

This went down well enough with his colleagues, but Daniel thought he could detect a forced quality in their laughter, as if they felt this sort of knockabout anecdote wasn't really like him, and that he'd told it because it combined two aspects of life he knew occupied much of their own thinking. To make it worse, two of Linahan's women sub-editors had arrived towards the end, and they sat looking mystified yet offended.

Then he noticed that Linahan had leaned forward and was peering through his porthole. Daniel seized the opportunity to console himself by draining his Bordeaux – served, at the Bar G, in glasses that held a third of a bottle – in one go. 'Good God,' he heard Linahan say.

When Daniel looked again, everybody at the table was struggling to get what view they could through the tiny windows. Through his own porthole, he could see the cause of their excitement. It was Whittington, and he was running. The obituaries editor, who often boasted that he had never willingly taken exercise in his life, was heading towards them, chased by Carlton, the doorman, who was waving something at him.

'What's he doing?' somebody asked.

'He's on urgent police business,' roared Linahan, to applause.

Whittington and his pursuer disappeared from view and seemed to have gone past. The sports writers resumed their seats. 'Such grace and versatility,' said Linahan. 'It's like watching a swan playing darts.'

A couple of minutes later, the head waiter beckoned to Linnell. Presuming he was wanted on the phone, Daniel ducked into the Bar G's cramped lobby. As he entered the tiny space, he found himself trapped, face to face, with Whittington. Daniel, instinctively trying to limit the intimacy of this unexpected contact, raised both arms: he could have looked like a boxer squaring up, except that, in the confined space, his fists were trapped between his chest and Whittington's. The editor, who always avoided physical contact, gripped Daniel's raised arms around the wrists, and held them so hard that it was painful.

They stood there in silence. Daniel, thinking his colleague had lost his senses, was relieved to hear footsteps approaching down the gangplank. Whittington's pursuer appeared above them, unable to jump down into the hatch, as there was not room. He looked down and saw Whittington holding the younger man's wrists. They were pressed face to face. The obituaries editor was sweating heavily and still panting. Looking at both men with distaste, Carlton held out Whittington's trilby, which he had picked up where it fell, on the marble entrance hall, and had since been trying to return, and pushed it down on to the editor's head. He gave it a final, exaggerated pat, like a slapstick comedian. Then, for the first time in Daniel's presence, the doorman spoke.

'I'm sorry to disturb you,' Carlton said. 'Don't bother to say thank you.'

Whittington didn't. They stayed there, motionless, the editor – now with his hat crushed down at a peculiar angle over his right eye – still gasping for air, still crushing Daniel's wrists. He was too out of breath to speak. Even when his breathing began to come more easily, he remained silent for a minute or so. Daniel started to worry about what would happen when one of the sports writers came out looking for the gents' and witnessed the scene. 'What is it?' he hissed.

Whittington looked at him. His hands went limp. 'Laura's dead,' he said.

Daniel shut his eyes. He thought about asking him to repeat what he had said, but didn't. He found himself pressing his eyeballs up into their sockets until it hurt.

When he opened his eyes again, Whittington, who had no room to turn round, was walking backwards up the gangplank. As Daniel went out to join him on the towpath, he could still hear the sound of raucous laughter from the dining room. They began to walk back to the office. It had started to rain, but Whittington took his hat off and kept it pressed hard against his chest, like a man beseeching a monarch for clemency.

'What?' Daniel said.

'Rosa had a call from the police in France,' Whittington replied. 'They found her in a river.'

As they walked up to the newspaper's reception area, a self-consciousness came over him. He felt he would be stared at.

'Who knows?' he asked.

'Nobody,' said Whittington. 'Only Rosa.'

They walked up to the obituaries desk, and Rosa led him across the editorial floor to the boardroom. They sat down side by side at the enormous oak table. Spaced out around it there were jugs of water with fresh ice cubes floating in them. Was it somebody's job, he started asking himself, stupidly, to make sure that there were always new cubes in them? Rosa, a woman he hardly knew, took his right hand, still bruised by Whittington's fierce clasp. He had a momentary instinct to snatch it away, but didn't. She placed his hand on the table, and put both hands on his, as if swearing him in to some secret society.

Laura had died near Millau, Rosa said, and her body had been found by a farmer, floating in a stream on his land. The French police said they could make no formal pronouncement as to cause of death, but that the body had been wearing parachute equipment which, to use their phrase, appeared to have malfunctioned. She seemed to have come down through the pine trees, landed in the water, and to have died instantly.

'Parachute equipment? What about Jack?' said Daniel, scarcely able to speak.

According to the police, Rosa told him, Laura had been offered the chance to make a jump in Millau, and gone there on impulse. She had left her son with friends, telling him that she would be back in two hours to pick him up.

'He's still at their house,' she said. 'He's safe, but they don't seem to speak any English.' She handed him a piece of paper with a French telephone number, which he recognised as Michel Auclair's.

He stared straight ahead of him down the room, fixing his gaze on the waistcoat buttons in the portrait of the founder. His expression suggested not so much grief as baffled fury. The three-year-old was with people he barely knew, people who spoke a foreign language, and he was expecting his mother to return at any minute.

Rosa handed him a phone. He dialled the number, and Seti answered. Without saying a word, she put the child on.

'Mummy?' said Jack.

'It's Daddy,' Daniel said. 'I'm coming to see you.'

'I forgot Beach Ball,' said Jack. 'Will you bring Beach Ball?' There was a silence. 'Beach Ball?'

'Yes,' said Daniel.

'And Mr Bear?'

'And Mr Bear.'

The boy blew a raspberry, laughed, and dropped the phone. Daniel hung up.

He walked out through the office, still with Rosa, and they took the lift down to reception. He had begun to feel dislocated from his surroundings, like a man walking across a landscape projected behind him on a cinema screen. She left him sitting on a spotless marble bench by the entrance. He watched the security guards issuing one-day ID cards. Through the smoked glass doors he could see Rosa, who was outside in the parking bay. She approached the chauffeur sitting in the deputy editor's Mercedes and said something to him; he saw the man shake his head. Rosa spoke again, and the driver got out without replying, walked round and, motioning Carlton away, opened the nearside rear door.

Rosa came with him, back to The Owl. They went round to the back entrance and up the fire escape. Daniel picked up his passport and driving licence, Jack's large blue beach ball, and Mr Bear, who Rosa found hidden under Jack's bed. Five minutes later they set off again with the driver.

Daniel had the beach ball under one arm and held Mr Bear in the other hand, like Jack did, dangling by one ear. The driver set off for Heathrow; he dropped Rosa at King's Cross, where she got a black cab back to the office. As they drove off again, Daniel could still feel Bar G's vintage Bordeaux in his throat, with its taste like burnt rubber. They passed Camden register office on the left. Despite himself, he turned to look towards the St Pancras booking hall, though he knew you couldn't see into it from the road. It was only when he arrived at the airport that he realised his jacket and credit cards were still in the restaurant and that he had no money.

When they returned to the office at two thirty, Linahan and his colleague brought Linnell's things back with them. David Dixon, Linahan's deputy, walked over to obits, impatient to taunt Whittington over the bizarre scene on the tow-path. He was holding Daniel's jacket disdainfully, at arm's length, as if he thought it might be louse-ridden. 'River Island,' he said, revealing the label. 'Hardly worth saving really.'

Whittington remained ashen-faced, staring straight ahead of him. Julian Cave, the freelance who covered in cases of illness, was laying out the page. Whittington's fists were clenched and he made no acknowledgement of Dixon's arrival, even though the younger man was standing right in front of him.

Dixon, tottering slightly, waved his hand in front of Whittington's face and snapped his fingers, like a stage hypnotist struggling to wake a subject. 'What's the matter?' he asked, when he got no response. 'Nobody snuffed it?'

'There has been a death,' Whittington replied, but without the expected emphasis on the second word of the sentence.

'Oh dear, oh dear,' said Dixon. 'That's a blow – a death on the obituaries desk.'

The older man got up and grabbed him by his tie, and held him so tightly that Dixon thought he would choke. 'You don't understand,' he said, in a level voice that contrasted with the violence of his gesture. 'It's a real one.'

CHAPTER 33

Daniel walked into Departures at Heathrow Terminal One. He was heading for a bank of public telephones when he heard his name being called over the PA system. At the Information Desk, a woman handed him two padded envelopes which had been biked over by Rosa. In the first, there was a pre-paid ticket to Montpellier, a voucher for a hire car and a hotel, and five hundred pounds in traveller's cheques. At the bottom of the package he found a brown plastic pill bottle. Standing at the Information Desk, he laid the objects out in front of him. He opened the second and pulled out a large bundle of twenty pound notes.

He went to the upper level, where he sat down in Chuzzlewit's, a bar that had been laid out in pathetic imitation of a Victorian pub. He stood motionless for a few moments among the tables and noticed that every eye was on him. He caught sight of himself in the antiqued mirror behind the bar. He was dressed for the office, in a collar and tie, holding a teddy bear and an inflated beach ball; the expression on his face, however, was one of desolation.

He looked further down the bar, where the customers – if not actually carrying beach balls – were already in holiday mood, wearing training shoes without socks, shorts, acrylic football shirts or T-shirts and drinking pints of Chuzzlewit's weak lager. Daniel walked over to a large off-licence opposite, where he picked up an item from the first stand he came to: a pyramid-shaped display of half-bottles of a coffee cream liqueur which he disliked. 'Two for one,' said the woman at the checkout as he paid, giving a suspicious glance first at his luggage, then at his huge handful of cash. 'I have to scan them both. Don't forget your other bottle.' Daniel made no response. She shrugged and he walked away.

He retreated to the shelter of Chuzzlewit's ancient plastic beams, and sat down in an alcove with just two tables, set back from the more raucous atmosphere of the main bar. The other table was occupied by a wealthy-looking English woman, accompanied by twin girls of six years old or so. He put the beach ball and bear on the seat next to him, and made a closer examination of his packages. The ticket, he noticed, first with gratitude, then with alarm, was for a flight departing in thirty minutes. He examined the pill bottle. 'Dalmau, Rosa,' it said. 'Valium: 1mg. One tablet at bedtime. Do not exceed stated dose.' He counted the tablets in the palm of his hand; there were ten. The pills were heart-shaped, with a hole in the middle, as though taking them was supposed to be fun.

Making no attempt to conceal his actions, he replaced six tablets, swallowed the rest, and unscrewed the bottle of coffee liqueur. He put it to his lips and drank the half pint of sweet, cloying liquid without pausing. As he did this, one of the young girls opposite turned and began staring at him. Out of the corner of his eye, Daniel saw her mother place her hand on the girl's head and twist it firmly back to its original position with what seemed to be a well-practised movement, like a mechanic screwing back a radiator cap. 'Don't look, Jemima,' she said.

He went to the bar and ordered a black coffee to disperse the drink's viscous legacy of cream and vanilla. 'My name is Kevin' he read on the young barman's over-sized lapel badge. 'I am here to help you.' As he swallowed the coffee, he could feel the cheap whisky at the back of his throat. 'Help me Kevin,' he felt like saying. 'Help me now.' He remembered how Laura drank whisky with espresso. 'With a coffee,' she said, 'you get it twice.'

He boarded the flight, and he was making his way down the aisle when a stewardess stopped him to tell him to deflate his beach ball. 'You can blow it up again sir,' she said, suppressing a snigger, 'as soon as you get off.' He ignored her and walked on. As he did so, he felt the woman deftly remove the boarding pass which was sticking out of his shirt pocket. 'I must apologise,' she said, a little flustered. Daniel stared at her. 'Turn round,' she said. 'You're in Club.'

He sat down in a window seat near the front of the aircraft and fell asleep. As he half recovered consciousness, he noticed two pairs of eyes staring down at him. The faces below the eyes, he noticed, were covered by a dark-coloured cloth. At first he thought he must have collapsed and he was being examined by surgeons. Then he noticed that the eyes were young and bright, and decided they must belong to Islamic virgins. He drifted off and when he looked again the eyes had gone.

He came to properly and sat up, alarmed. The pairs of eyes had reappeared; they belonged to the twin girls from Chuzzlewit's, who were peering over the back of their seats to observe the strange man sleeping behind them. Their lower faces were hidden by the top of their seats, which were covered with a small dark blue square of protective cotton. It was only when he looked out and saw suitcases being loaded on to a French baggage truck that he remembered where he was, and why.

He picked up the hire car, a large green saloon, and pointed its nose north on the main highway that led to Michel's farmhouse. He switched on the headlights, despite the bright sunshine, and put his foot on the floor. As he crossed the plateau of the Larzac, the lunar surroundings added to the feelings of unreality he had about the day's events. He turned down the track that led to the farmhouse. When he got there, he told himself, it would be all right.

Daniel pulled up by the front door and parked, as he had once before, next to Michel's battered red pickup truck. As he turned to walk the few yards to the house, he saw Jack standing in the doorway. The boy clapped his hands and laughed repeatedly – his only instinctive response to great pleasure of any kind. 'Daddy,' he said, giving the word a special, rising intonation that he reserved for this, his favourite expression. 'What *we* gonna do?'

He went to pick the boy up. A pair of wet jeans, hanging on a line next to the front door, flapped in his face. He carried Jack round the back of the house to a small stone outhouse Michel used for storing wood. The door, rarely opened in summer, had wedged itself shut. Daniel had to give it a violent kick to get it open. As he did so, he heard what sounded like a mortar – a stray shell, he supposed, from the hated army firing range – exploding very near them. Jack pointed at a large crow that had landed on a wall a few feet away. 'Blackbird,' he said.

He went in to the cool woodshed and sat down on a pile of chestnut logs. He put the boy on his knee and held him tight. 'You're hurting me, Daddy,' said Jack. Daniel could hear raised voices from the neighbouring houses, and the whirr of cicadas. 'Daddy,' he went on, 'where's Mummy?'

'She's in the hospital,' he told him. 'She's in the hospital because she's poorly.' Poorly. A child-like adjective he hadn't heard since he had been an infant himself, in Eastern Circle. The boy didn't seem to understand it. 'She's in the hospital because she's not well, Jack. She's in the hospital because she's sick. She's in the hospital,' he went on, 'because she's dead.'

Jack made no reaction. He led the boy by the hand back into the sun, and they returned to the front of the house. There he saw that a small group of neighbours had gathered on the drive next to Michel's red pickup and were staring down the drop into the next field. They were looking at the hire car which, as he had forgotten to put the handbrake on, had slid forwards, plunged down, and was now on its roof.

He didn't speak to them, but took Jack straight into the house. He walked into the kitchen where he found Michel lowering his telephone, held by the main phone wire, into a bucket of water. Seti had vomited on it when she took the first call from the police. Daniel sat down and lit a cigarette. A couple of neighbours appeared in the hall, wanting to talk to Michel about the car. The Frenchman took them outside. Daniel sat with Jack in silence again and stared at the large television across the room, which was showing a video Seti had put on to distract the boy: an American cartoon he didn't know, which showed a flock of flying pink horses fluttering around a waterfall.

Jack sat on the sofa in silence. Daniel remembered the beach ball and the teddy bear. He went out, walked past Michel and the small group of onlookers who were gathered in his garden, and clambered down to the overturned car. He could see the toys, which were now lying in the middle of the roof. Daniel tried to open a door, but couldn't. He found a rock and put it through the front windscreen, an action that drew a gasp of horror from one of the onlookers. He pulled the objects out, threw them up ahead of him, then hauled himself back up the wall and took them into the house.

Back in the kitchen, he gave Jack the toys. 'Say hello, Mr Bear,' he told him. The boy stared ahead of him and said nothing. Then Daniel listened as Michel, speaking – thank God, he thought afterwards – in French, told him how Laura had phoned the previous evening, saying she'd tried before she left London to arrange a jump at Millau and hadn't managed it, but that she had been offered the chance to fill in for a cancellation on a free-fall jump for charity. She'd used a borrowed parachute. Seti walked in, glanced at Daniel, then looked away and shook her head. 'I'm going down to talk to the police,' she said. 'Catherine's taking me.' Catherine was the neighbour. Seti picked up her mobile phone and a shoulder bag, and started heading for the door.

'Put something on first,' said Michel. His wife stopped and looked down, and noticed for the first time that, apart from a short red T-shirt, she was naked. She turned and went back into the bedroom.

'I'm worried about Jack,' said Daniel.

'What is it?' asked Michel, looking at Jack sitting quietly on the sofa.

'I'm not sure,' said Linnell, 'but I think he's stopped talking.'

Daniel took the boy out into the garden and kicked the beach ball towards him. Jack turned away and sat down against the rear wheel of Michel's pickup. The driver's door had been left open, to stop heat building up in the cab. The keys were still in the ignition. Daniel lifted Jack into the passenger seat, got in, started the engine and drove back up the track towards the village. He turned in to the small square, and stopped outside the Café de la Cavalerie, Mademoiselle Lepape's small bar. He walked into the café, which was empty, carrying the child. It was late afternoon by now and the owner, who had just reopened after her siesta, was cleaning the coffee machine and had her back to them. Daniel sat Jack at a table by the window. 'Ice-cream game?' he asked. The boy said nothing.

Daniel walked up to the counter, and Mademoiselle Lepape turned round. She gave him a delighted smile of recognition and waved at Jack, who ignored her. 'What colour?' she asked, with a conspiratorial smile. She had already taken a scoop of vanilla and was reaching for the strawberry.

'Any colour,' said Daniel, in a voice without expression. Lepape, her smile fading slightly, drew breath to make a remark then – noticing the fierce look on her customer's face – thought better of it. Had a stranger been queuing behind him, and had they observed the abrupt change that his look produced in the woman's manner, they would have assumed he'd pulled a gun and demanded the takings.

Mademoiselle Lepape placed the small bowl of vanilla and strawberry on the counter. Her nerves on edge, she knocked the small pewter plate, used for returning small change, off the counter. It fell down to the marble floor tiles, and landed by Daniel's feet. He turned, ignoring it, and carried the ice cream over to the table where he had left his son. As he walked, the tiny plate spun louder and faster on the ground; the noise it made was the kind of dull flourish that a bored timpanist might produce to greet an acrobat's somersault. Its echo rang out horribly across the empty café, and it seemed to hang in the air.

Lepape, unsettled by the silence which followed, came out from behind the counter and switched on the bar's ancient jukebox at the mains. The machine was only used in the evening, and she pulled the plug at eleven every night, even if money had just been put in it, for fear of complaints from the neighbours. The next day there were always unplayed selections remaining. The machine clicked into life, and an ancient vinyl single dropped on to its turntable. To Mademoiselle Lepape's great relief, the silence was broken by the opening bars of 'Volare'.

Daniel put the bowl of ice cream in front of the boy, who had closed his eyes. 'Ice-cream game,' he said. Silence. He took a spoonful of strawberry ice cream and pressed the child's nose, as he always did, and put it in his mouth. Jack tasted it, and swallowed. 'Blackbird,' he said. Daniel pressed the boy's nose again, but Jack opened his eyes. 'Daddy,' he said, 'I want to go home.'

'Soon,' said his father.

'*Il blu*,' the Italian voice crooned in the background, '*dipinto di blu*'. Daniel walked back up to the counter.

'Who chose that song?'

'I don't know,' said Lepape.

'When?' he asked.

'Last night,' she told him. To a stranger she might have looked severe; the few who had ever known her intimately would have known that her guests' peculiar behaviour had brought her to the verge of tears.

'Last night,' he repeated. He picked the boy up and left without saying goodbye. It was more than a fortnight later, when he was back in London, that he realised he had left without paying Mademoiselle Lepape. By that time, in any case, it didn't matter. By that time, she knew why.

CHAPTER 34

When he got back to Michel and Seti's house, there was a police car parked in the garden. Jack was asleep on the passenger seat of the pickup. Daniel pulled up directly outside Michel's front door, at right angles to the drop into the sheep field. Seti came out and sat with the sleeping child. In the kitchen, Daniel presented his papers to Sergeant Laval, an ill-tempered man coming to the end of his time in the force. Until Michel swore at him, Laval had seemed intent on beginning the interview with the subject of the hire car. The young officer assisting him noted down the details from Daniel's passport. At one point Laval asked why, since Linnell knew the purpose of his visit, he hadn't brought his marriage certificate with him. The sun was going down as they set off – Seti and Michel in the police car, Daniel and Jack following in the pickup – for the hospital at Millau, and the formal identification of the body.

He left the boy in reception with his friends. Two nurses led him through what looked like Casualty, then ushered him into a room off a side-ward. The atmosphere in here, Daniel noticed, was hardly in keeping with the rigidly functional character of the rest of the hospital. There were fresh flowers and magazines. There was a hot jug of filter coffee. There was even an ashtray. The window had been fitted with a double thickness of lace curtains, which were drawn.

The room fitted into a pattern that had begun with the newspaper boardroom, and continued with the chauffeured Mercedes-Benz and the Club Class air tickets. Bad news, he'd noticed, travels fast and first class.

He remembered a bad joke she'd once told him, about a Pole who wins a competition to make a parachute jump in California. The prize was a day's training with a personal free-fall instructor, a private plane for the jump, and an air-conditioned limousine that would meet the winner when he landed and drive him to a hotel suite for a champagne dinner for himself and three friends. The Pole jumps out at five thousand feet and pulls the ripcord. Nothing happens. Twenty seconds later he pulls the reserve, which also fails to open. 'The bastards,' he says. 'And I bet they've forgotten the limo as well.'

There was a faint knock on the door, a pause, and then a firmer one. A young, nervous-looking consultant appeared. Death knocks, Daniel thought. Life bursts straight on through.

'You are the husband?' he asked. Daniel nodded. Death, the young man said, had occurred between nine forty and ten that morning. Its precise causes could not be ascertained before the post mortem, 'but initial indications were of major organ failure as a consequence of multiple contusions'. Daniel looked at the man, who seemed to be taking comfort from this impersonal recital of technical data. He looked at the doctor's name badge: Eric Merle. He would have bet it was the first time he'd done it. 'Where are you from?' Daniel asked him.

'Brussels,' he said. 'Have you been there?'

'Once,' he replied.

Straying from his technical script and speaking like a human again, Merle told him that the severity of tissue damage was less than usual in such cases 'because the body' (the term sounded grotesque even if it was less appalling in these circumstances than 'your wife') 'fell into an area of dense pine forest, which would have attenuated its velocity, and because it landed in a shallow body of water.'

Not dense enough, Linnell thought. And too fucking shallow.

Merle took him into another corridor, sat him on a bench, and disappeared. To distract himself, Daniel scrutinised the line of doors opposite. Each was made of wood veneer; each had a metal kick plate at the bottom, a tall, thin window set into the right of the door frame, made of toughened glass, and a bolt that could be drawn to lock the door from the outside. A couple of nurses glanced down at him as they walked past. He could tell from their look that they knew why he was there and he wondered how. He glanced behind him and examined the door to the room he was waiting to enter. It had the wood veneer and the metal kick plate, but there was no bolt to lock people in, and there was no window.

Merle reappeared with Michel and a gendarme he hadn't seen before. 'I'll go in on my own,' Daniel said to Michel, and the two strangers led him through the door. Bracing himself, he looked ahead of him into the room. There was a chart on the far wall, he noticed, showing different forms of skin cancer, and a dispenser for surgical gloves, in various sizes. He looked around for a body, but he couldn't see one. Then he noticed that Merle and the gendarme had both positioned themselves between him and a table that was placed in an alcove immediately behind the door. The table ran along the same wall as the bench he had been sitting on. His head, leaning against the corridor wall, must have been separated from what he had learned to call 'the body' by half an inch of plasterboard. From its – from her – head, he wondered, or from her feet?

Behind the two men, he could see what might be a human shape on the table. He wondered if she had exploded on impact and whether they were preparing to catch him when he passed out. 'Ready?' asked Merle, with the fatal urgency of a hangman. He nodded.

The doctor turned back the sheet to reveal her face, down to the neck. The first thing he noticed was that he couldn't see her hair; they had wrapped a kind of plastic bandana around her head. It was a distinctive shade of pale blue that was somehow familiar, he couldn't think where from. He found himself compelled to read the tiny lettering printed on it, in navy blue. 'Regional Health Authority', he read. Item Reorder Code 7791564'. '*Il blu*,' he thought, '*dipinto di blu*.'

Finally, he looked down. Her face was lit by the same unforgiving electric light she'd grown up with round the Bedford dinner table. Her eyes were open and, though clearly lifeless, seemed undamaged. He could see the powerful overhead light reflected in her dark pupils and he tried to find an angle that would allow him to see his own reflection in her eyes, but couldn't. Curiously though, it wasn't her eyes, or her nose, also apparently intact, or the distinctive arch of her brow that drew his attention, though all identified the body – identified his wife, identified Laura – beyond possible doubt. It was the tiny V-shaped scar in her right eyebrow. 'That,' he said to Merle, forgetting to indicate which part of her face he was talking about, 'was where she was bitten by Mr Noble's dog.'

He thought how strange those words sounded as he said them in French: '*Le chien de Monsieur Noble*'. An animal, tragically commemorated in that small foreign room, that must have died twenty years ago, in Salina Kansas. An animal that had belonged to a man he would never meet. There was an uncomfortable silence. The fingernails on her right hand looked as if they'd been torn and had bled, from her frantic attempt, he assumed, to pull her reserve chute; another one of those areas of life, he reflected, where hard work alone isn't enough. He looked at the two men, who were still waiting. He still hadn't said what they needed him to. He turned to the policeman. '*C'est elle*,' he said.

CHAPTER 35

Michel gave Daniel the keys to the pickup and he helped him secure Jac
as best he could in the passenger seat, with the adult seat-belt. The bal
which Daniel had been carrying around like a mad forfeit, was on the floo
Michel walked back to Seti's car, and Daniel headed out of Millau on to th
main road south, to the Mediterranean port of Sète. As soon as the picku
was in motion, Jack fell asleep, still clutching Mr Bear by his left ear.

Sète was not, it would occur to him later, a sensible place to stay th
night, but it was here that Rosa had made his hotel reservation. The tow
was almost twenty miles south-west of Montpellier, where they woul
catch a London plane the following morning. But it never occurred to hi
to stay anywhere else: Sète, whatever its drawbacks, had the great asset o
not being Millau. It was dark when he drew into the coastal town, and h
had to stop at a bar to ask directions to the Hotel Carmet. It turned out t
be an expensive-looking establishment on the Corniche, the coast road tha
led up to the cliffs above the beaches, a couple of miles from the town'
commercial centre.

He left the car in front of the hotel entrance with the engine sti
running and carried the sleeping boy up to room 107. The staff, who ha
been forewarned of the circumstances by Whittington's assistant, wer
expecting him and handed over the plastic swipe key with none of the usu
formalities. Daniel carried the boy into the room and laid him on th
double bed. He had an irrational impulse to wrap him in his own jacke
realised he'd left it in London, and covered him instead with a spar

blanket he found in the bottom of the wardrobe. Jack's personal belongings – a carrier bag with a spare set of clothes, and his own small transparent plastic suitcase, containing a selection of plastic jungle animals – were still on the floor in the couple's spare room, where Laura had left them. 'Mr Bear,' said Jack, half waking up. Daniel went back down to the car, picked up their only two items of luggage and placed them on the bed next to the child, who had already gone back to sleep.

He opened the French windows and sat outside on the balcony. Fifteen feet below, the sea lapped against a man-made barrage of heavy rocks, placed there to stop waves eroding the building's foundations. He stared down at these boulders, and found himself listening to the music drifting up from the PA system of a nightclub in the port, away to the left. 'A little bit of Jennifer,' it boomed, 'all right. A little bit of Rita...'

He noticed a movement down on the rocks, which were tastefully lit with small but powerful exterior spotlights. It was a yellow cat, wild and on the brink of starvation, perched at the end of the wall of boulders. The animal was stretching its paw down as though fishing. At times the movement was so desperate that it almost lost its grip and fell into the sea. As his eyes grew accustomed to the light, he managed to make out the object of its interest – an apple, that was trapped on an inaccessible shelf a foot or so below the animal, just above sea-level. Occasionally a receding wave would drag it almost within range of the outstretched paw, but then it would roll back out of reach.

He walked back into the room and opened its mean-looking brown fridge. He had been looking for a brandy but, once there, for some reason picked up a mineral water. It was the kind of alcoholic volte-face he had performed, in the opposite direction, a thousand times. He looked round for an opener, couldn't find one, and cracked off the lid on a corner of the marble shelf in the bathroom, a trick she had shown him.

He went back out and sat on the balcony. He opened the bottle of tablets Rosa had given him, this time without counting them, and tipped them all on to his tongue. Instead of swallowing the pills slowly, he pressed them against the roof of his mouth, where they stuck and dissolved gently, like the fruit-flavoured aspirins he had been taught to hold against an aching tooth when he was a boy. He felt the sharp bitterness trickle down to his throat.

He stared out at the water, listening to the monotonous beat from the distant clubs, and stood up. Feeling unsteady on his feet, he walked back into the room and lay down on the bed next to the boy. He was seized by a sudden urge to get in the car and drive back to London, when he remembered that he had no papers for the vehicle. He pulled off his shoes without unlacing them. That morning in London, he remembered, he had spent a couple of minutes deciding which pair to put on.

He was on the edge of falling asleep when he heard a child call out 'Mummy'. He sat up, his heart racing. The shout had come from the corridor, he realised, when he looked across the bed to his right, where the boy was sleeping on, unconsoled. Jack's face and sleeve, he noticed, were still smeared with the chocolate ice cream from Mademoiselle Lepape's, and he had his right arm wrapped around Mr Bear. Looking at the child, he wondered if he would have understood enough to wake the next morning to the same awful recollection he himself had experienced when he came to on the plane. And, if Jack hadn't understood, how many aftershocks were in store for him in the months, or years, ahead?

Ten minutes later Monsieur Maurice, the hotel concierge, who had been given an envelope addressed to Daniel, came up to the first floor, unobserved. His colleagues, busy in reception below, would have been astonished to see that he removed his shoes as he came out of the lift, so as not to wake his bereaved foreign guests. It was the first such gesture of gentleness or consideration he had made for forty years, since professional subservience, long working hours and a savage divorce had broken his spirit.

As Monsieur Maurice slipped the message under their door, the two of them lay sleeping together on top of the brown bedspread. Out of sight on the rocks below, as the wind transmitted the dismal groove of 'La Macarena'. The cat, making a final, desperate lunge, got its claws into the apple. As it lifted it up, the fruit, which was half rotten, dropped into the water and drifted away, to be consumed by the gulls or by the ocean.

CHAPTER 36

Ie woke at six, when Jack did, and he gave the boy a drink of orange juice :om the mini-bar, then lifted him up and left for the airport. Closing the oor behind him, he picked up Monsieur Maurice's message and stuffed it ı his back pocket, unread. He collected Michel's truck, which was where e had left it, still obstructing the hotel's loading area, and headed for Iontpellier.

He left the truck in the airport car park. As he walked across the erminal foyer holding his son's hand, he was approached by a uniformed aleswoman from Peugeot, asking him if he wanted to enter a prize draw or a car. He was struck by the thought that if he took a ticket, on the alance of probabilities that had led to his being there, he'd probably win . He shook his head and they walked on. For the first time, he emembered the hire car he'd left on its roof in Michel's field. He felt in his ront pocket and found the keys. He walked over to the car rental desk and ropped them in the quick deposit box.

'Everything fine?' said the receptionist.

'Yes,' said Daniel.

He put his hand in his back pocket again and pulled out the message om Monsieur Maurice. He unscrewed the sheet of paper. It was a fax om Stewart Jardine. 'Arrive in France tomorrow,' it read, with the terse, ow unnecessary economy of words Jardine's generation still assumed to e indispensable when communicating tragedy. 'Call soonest.' There was a umber of a hotel in Millau.

His immediate thought was to get Jack further away from that fat stretch of earth in the forest and body in its hideous blue turban. It was th only when their plane was climbing away from Montpellier and he looke through the window that it dawned on him. It hadn't done him any goo to get away from Millau. The land wasn't his problem. It wasn't the lan It was the sky.

It was eleven in the morning when they got back to The Owl. H opened the door, still carrying Jack. He could see Brendan sitting at the ba with Rachel. He walked in and noticed that there were no customers; it wa only then that he remembered the café was closed for decorating. Seepin into the bar from the kitchen, there was the hiss of music from a portab radio, the noise of loud, aggressive banter from the two painters, and th smell of oil-based gloss.

When Doyle and Rachel saw him coming in, they stayed on their stoo like they would have on any day. He could see straight away that the knew, but they didn't rush forward to him. He silently thanked them for i He was trying, for some reason, to look less devastated than he was but, a he carried Jack into the bar, he could feel that his face had taken on a dea look of resolution and defeat, like a refugee. Rachel took Jack upstairs t bath him. Afterwards, she suggested, she could take him to his playgrou for the afternoon.

'No,' said Daniel.

'Yes,' said Jack.

He sat on a stool, opposite Brendan. The barman reached under th counter, pulled out Daniel's jacket and handed it to him.

'Rosa brought it up here,' he said. 'The day she took you to the airpor

'It's the one I was wearing...' Daniel said.

'I know,' said Brendan.

The workmen's radio was tuned to a classic gold station. The pai fumes made him feel empty and sick. Before he'd got into the cab a Heathrow, he'd had to buy a belt; Daniel had never been overweight, b he had noticed that, when he walked down the aisle of the plane, carryin Jack, and he couldn't keep hitching them up, his jeans had been sagging t the point where they almost fell down.

Doyle saw him looking towards the kitchen and walked down th room. 'Turn that shit off,' he shouted. He walked back to his seat. A youn man's shaven head peered round the door, and disappeared again. The hi continued. 'Now,' shouted Brendan.

'Hark at her,' said another voice, with a London accent. Brendan walked back down to the kitchen and disappeared inside. There was the noise of plastic shattering against the wall. A battery case flew loose and fell into a can of gloss that was standing in the doorway, and sank, very slowly, out of sight. The two painters were both in their early twenties and they were both bigger than Doyle, but the barman had a quality more forbidding than height or strength: the look of a man who, when it came to it, would be totally heedless of his own safety. They'd thought he was joking; they had, after all, been working for two days with their music at that same volume. As Brendan walked back to rejoin Daniel, both their heads appeared round the door to watch him go, then disappeared again.

The barman picked up an unopened bottle of Balvenie. The whisky bottle, with its long, bulbous neck and squat body, might have been designed for recycling as a petrol bomb. 'Sorry Daniel,' he said.

'Whenever I've heard my name,' Linnell replied, 'I've always known I was in trouble.'

Doyle slammed the bottle down on the bar so violently that tiny specks of white formed around the liquor at the top of the bottle. He poured a glass and went to fill a second, but Daniel shook his head. Brendan switched on the stereo behind the bar; it started to play a haunting R & B song called 'Don't Trade Me in for a New Model'. This new, loud, and different music heralded a renewed pause in the brush strokes. The bald one ventured out again, still holding his brush, and was about to say something, then turned around and went back to work.

Daniel had a coffee and went upstairs to the flat. He stood staring at the sheet of paper that was still on the wall, as it had been the first night when they met. 'I remember when you kissed me, when I kissed you, in the Parc Montsouris which is in Paris; in Paris which is in France; in France which is on the earth. On the earth, which is a star.' The place was as she'd left it, in disorder. The few clothes she hadn't taken had been strewn on the floor.

He noticed that a drawer had been taken out and turned upside down as though she'd been searching for something before she left. On the table he saw *Lament of the Border Guard*, the book she'd bought at the second-hand shop in Fowey. He opened it and found 'What Made Him Do It?', the piece he'd glanced at last time, about a man who leaps to his death from the top of an apartment block. He sat down and read the numbered stanzas at random.

'Three. Maybe he tried to fly...'

'Six. Maybe he looked out of the window and saw snow in June and small birds starving on branches made him homesick...'

'Eight. Maybe the lift was broken and he couldn't face the stairs...'

'Two. Maybe the spring was too wet, that summer too hot, and at the end of it no one came to pick his tree. He died a windfall.'

Daniel looked for the name of the author: Patrick Creagh. He wondered what had brought him to this.

He thought back to when he was a child, and he was terrified of the dentist. In the days – the weeks – before each visit, every book he read, or film he saw, seemed filled with allusions to drills and needles. He had never noticed the number of references, in daily life, to falling and death.

To coax himself back into the present, he got up and switched on the answering machine. The first message froze him where he stood.

'I'm at Michel's,' her voice said. 'I got the chance of a jump; I'm gonna see if I can go up tomorrow morning. I'll be back in the evening, whatever happens. I'll call you.'

There was another brief message from her father, one from Rosa, offering help, and another from Whittington, whose voice he could barely recognise, telling him to stay away as long as he needed to. He had an urge to listen to her message again, then resisted it, out of fear that, if he played it once, he might never stop. He took the cassette out of the machine and crushed it under his heel. He opened the main door and flung it out into the waste bins.

'Whatever happens.' The two words stuck with him, like the hook line from some teenage single. There might, it occurred to him, be some place on the earth that it was more devastatingly painful for him to be, but for the moment he couldn't quite think where that place would be.

Without quite thinking what he was doing, he called International Enquiries and got a number for Father Oakes in Bedford but when he called there was no answer. Then he rang Helen, Laura's aunt in South Wales, to ask her if she could look after Jack for a few days.

'Yes,' she said, drawing the word out over two syllables, with a rising intonation, by which she meant to show her surprise that, before he asked her, he had forgotten even to say hello, or who he was. 'How's Laura?'

He paused. He had imagined that this tragedy was so colossal that everybody in the world would already know about it. 'She's dead, Helen,' he said.

'How?' she asked. Because she had determined, in that intervening moment, to be resolute, and a source of strength, her voice was oddly devoid of shock or distress.

Mechanically, he told her how. As he spoke, he looked down again at the open book.

'Five. Maybe he dreamt he loved his neighbour and woke to find it true, and no face changed.'

'Four. Maybe he was quite sure it would end there.'

'Can you come now?' he asked Helen, 'and take him back tonight?' He tried to picture where she was, at her house in Goat Street, and only then realised he'd never been there.

'I can come,' she told him, 'but how am I going to get him back? I don't drive, remember.'

He rang Rosa and asked her to get a car to meet Helen at Paddington, bring her up to Crouch End, then take her back to St David's that evening, with Jack.

'Do they know?' Rosa asked, 'why it happened?'

He looked down at the book.

'One. Maybe he had dwelt upon the gentle farewells of falling leaves and spent his last instincts studying bitter physics.'

'I didn't ask,' he told Rosa.

At six o'clock, when he had collected Jack from Rachel's house, and brought him back to The Owl, Helen was there, sitting at the long table at the far end. It was covered with newspaper and the decorators' tools. Whatever they did to this place now, he found himself thinking, it would never be right again. Maybe if they hadn't started painting, none of this would have happened. Maybe if they put it back how it was...

''Bye, Daddy,' Jack said as he was leaving. 'Don't dream about bad ghosts.'

He went back upstairs and, without the boy to look after, he felt overtaken suddenly by weariness. He thought about going to a hotel, where he could sleep unsurrounded by symbols of her life and death. Instead, he packed all her stuff – her clothes, her make-up and her photographs, her diary, her training shoes – into eight binliners. He felt furtive, like a murderer, and he wondered, as he did it, what a psychologist would call this: displacement, perhaps? Disrespect? Denial? But it wasn't any of those things. It was just that if he woke up and found those things there, he thought he might surrender all control. He tried to lose himself in mundane things; he went over to the fridge and emptied it of the few shrivelled vegetables that were in there. There were half a dozen packets of butter that someone had brought up from the restaurant. To give himself something to do, he decided to put them in the freezer. He opened a new roll of freezer bags and, in a horrible, sickening instant, he realised what it was that the blue plastic bandaging in the hospital at Millau had reminded him of. He put the pack down and left the butter where it was, on the sink.

He went to the phone, and called Paul Jardine in Bedford.

'Hi, Daniel,' Paul said.

He had the strong impression that, if he hadn't mentioned the tragedy, Paul wouldn't have brought it up either. It was easier to let life – death – come on to you, than to confront it head on.

'I went to identify the body Paul,' he told him.

'I know,' the young man replied. 'Dad said. He's over there now. He wants to have Laura brought back here for the funeral. I said I didn't think you...'

'Paul,' said Daniel. 'Tell him it's OK. Tell him whatever he wants, it's OK.' There was a silence. 'How the hell's he going to do that?' Daniel asked then. 'He doesn't speak French, does he?'

'There's a French guy,' Paul said. 'A French guy from Paris, who went down to meet him there. There's a company that handles it.'

'Jesus,' said Daniel. 'Paul? Get Oakes.'

'OK, yes.'

'Where is he?'

'He's in Australia, Daniel.'

'Call him, and get him back.'

'Yes, Daniel,' Paul said.

He went to bed with his large atlas of the United States, which fell open at Ohio. He lay there for a few minutes contemplating the reassuring permanence of Interstate 71. Whatever else had happened in the world, Interstate 71 was still faithfully carrying the citizens of Columbus down to Cincinnati, through Bookwalter, Range and South Lebanon. It was a highway of this size, he thought, that his father had built and died on. It had taken him seventeen years to understand the reason for his obsession with the road map. He tried to picture some of the small towns in Ohio, on the tiny roads marked in yellow. They had names like Gurneyville, Modest, Sunshine and Cherry Fork – the last of which, he noticed, was within an afternoon's walk of a place called Tranquility. With his map in his hands, he fell asleep.

He woke up late the following morning. He was soaked in sweat and his heart was racing. As he drifted in and out of sleep, he had begun to be visited by dreams. He saw her jump from the plane and pull the ripcord, releasing not a parachute but a flock of doves. Other times she'd pull it and release confetti, or maypole streamers, or the canopy would appear and inflate normally, but then the ropes which connected her to it would extend endlessly as she fell, so that she hit the ground unrestrained.

There was another nightmare, in which he was lying on his back in an aromatic pine forest, by a small brook. He had been holding her, as if it was a moment after the first time he'd kissed her, and she'd walked away to fetch something, leaving him exhilarated and at ease. But she didn't reappear and then he would see her body coming towards him out of the sky; she crashed through the trees, he braced himself to break her fall, she landed on top of him. And then it was always the same. He'd say, 'Are you OK?' and she said, 'Yes', then laid her head on his shoulder, but when he tried to get up, she was cold and motionless. It recurred and it left him bereft.

He stayed in London, alone, for two days. He didn't go back into the office; he didn't know if he ever would. The time was taken up with dealing with the bank manager, the council registrar and the Home Office. He got a phone call from Mr Jardine, who was still in Millau, and reported on his dealings with the French authorities with cold civility. 'The doctors,' he said, 'told me that people...that she...would have died of heart failure before she hit the ground.'

'Yes,' said Daniel.

Who knows, both men were thinking, what goes through the human mind at such a moment? It was the first time he'd spoken to her father since the night of the explosion in Bedford, four years earlier.

Then a fax arrived from Jardine giving details of the funeral, at St David's Church in three days' time. Another fax, from Angela this time, invited Daniel to stay at Grant Street, and informed him that she had arranged a babysitter for Jack who, to use her word, 'naturally', would not be coming to the funeral. When he received it, he picked up the phone and booked a room at the Red Carpet, then called the Jardines' number. It was late afternoon – late morning in Bedford – a time when he knew Stewart would be at the golf club. 'Jack's coming too,' he told Mrs Jardine. She started to argue. 'He's coming too,' he said, gently, and without anger, 'or we're not coming.'

Through it all, it was the cruel and punishing nature of his dreams, the feeling that his imagination had turned on itself, that was the hardest thing to bear. Sometimes he would see long, detailed visions of a man preparing an aircraft for take-off. It was always an antiquated biplane, and the mechanic was an elderly, grey-haired gentleman who came out of a shed on the airfield, then poured oil into the engine and polished the wheels. Once he'd finished, he would wipe his hands on an old green rag that Daniel would recognise as material torn from her one dress.

Towards midnight on Thursday, he packed his bags: two black holdalls he'd found at the bottom of the wardrobe. He put Jack's clothes and beakers and the travel documents in one, as cabin luggage, and his own things in the other. Before he went to bed, he was making a final check to see he hadn't forgotten anything and put his hand into one of the bags' small inside pockets. He pulled out a card: it was the American taxi receipt. He turned it over. Written on the reverse, in red biro, were the words 'In Yor Bed'. He felt his legs giving way beneath him and sat down on the bed. Seeing no external source of support within reach, he gripped his left wrist, hard.

He set the alarm for eight; he had to collect Jack from Helen's around lunchtime the next day, then drive back down to Heathrow, to get a late-afternoon flight to Kansas City via New York. There was a connection that would get them to Salina tomorrow evening, a Friday. The funeral was at eleven on the Saturday morning.

He woke at five. His subconscious mind, weary, apparently, of tormenting him with orthodox drama, had branched out into the musical. He had found himself in a department store listening to 'I've Lost My Mummy', a comedy single from his childhood, performed by the Australian entertainer Rolf Harris. The song was – though he'd never noticed it in his waking hours – in waltz time, and the other customers were shuffling around, not quite dancing, to the rhythm. There was a sense of foreboding about the scene that exploited to the full the three-four time signature's inherent potential for the macabre. He'd come in to close her account at the store and he asked directions to the offices on the fifth floor.

'The fifth floor?' a uniformed salesman said. 'Oh no sir, that's not accounts, sir. That's not accounts at all.'

He got up, dressed quickly and picked up the luggage, threw it in the back of the old black Saab and headed west. It was drizzling and the streets were deserted. Even the North Circular road, seen in this calm, half-light, through the comforting strokes of the windscreen wipers, looked almost likeable. God knows, he thought, in what form his mind might represent this scene in nights to come.

By nine thirty, he was approaching the town centre of Haverfordwest in Pembrokeshire, half an hour's drive from Helen's cottage. He stopped to buy a bottle of water at a roadside café and called to tell her that he was early. When he came back to the car and glanced into the back seat, he noticed that he had forgotten one of his travel bags. He tore open the one he did have and, to his relief, found it was Jack's; he checked the passports, tickets and his credit card.

When he arrived at Helen's cottage in Goat Street, lulled by the monotony of the motorway, he saw the front door open, then felt a thud in his midriff as Jack flung himself against him. It was his normal greeting, no different this time from any other, except afterwards, when the boy took hold of Daniel's right thumb and clung to it, and wouldn't let go. Daniel went through to the lounge, sat down and tried to pick up the coffee Helen had made him, but Jack was still clinging tight to his thumb. In the end he had to peel the boy's small fingers away by force. Jack gazed up at him, with a look full of resentment, and went to stand with his back to his father, staring out of the window.

Daniel moved towards him, but then he saw Helen shake her head. He sat back on the couch and told her about the things he'd forgotten. She saw a chance to envelop him in a soothing whirl of practicality. 'You can get a razor from Mrs Mullan's in the square,' she said. 'For a suit, you'd be better stopping in Swansea.'

Entering a Welsh shop, he told Helen, was still an uneasy experience for him. Like many English visitors, he was nervous that other customers might begin to insult him, among themselves, in Welsh. It was a situation, she assured him, that occurred far more often in the English imagination than it did in the real world. 'You have to remember,' she said, 'that even here, around St David's, there are some people who are not that comfortable speaking English.'

Mrs Mullan, she told him, was born in Wolverhampton, but she was studying Welsh three evenings a week at night school. Sometimes, Helen said, you would go in and find her buried in the translation she'd been set for homework. 'What do you expect Welsh people to do?' she asked. 'Have a minute's silence while you're served?'

When they were leaving, he took Jack's hand in his again, fearing that the boy would renew his tenacious grip. But when they got to the car, Jack let go as usual and climbed obediently into his car seat. Daniel couldn't think of much worse than shopping in Swansea, especially since their schedule left him two hours to find clothes in Bedford on the Saturday morning. He stopped in the main square at St David's, lifted Jack out, and went into Mrs Mullan's small general store, where he picked up a razor, a can of shaving cream and some toothpaste.

He went up to the till. There was a notice beside it which reminded customers, in both languages, not to ask for credit. 'It's lovely to see a new face,' the middle-aged woman at the counter said to him and smiled. The only other customer, a woman in her eighties, interrupted and began to speak to the owner at length, in Welsh, a delicate language of lyrical beauty, he thought, at least as spoken by this elderly pensioner. 'Good morning,' the old lady said to him, in English, as she left.

'What did she say?' he asked the owner.

'She said,' Mrs Mullan began, 'now let me get this right – she said that, nevertheless – no, however – no, nevertheless... That nevertheless, it is tragic to see the seat of Welsh holiness reduced to the level of a weekend whore, who spends her days powdering and preening herself waiting for the next oversexed foreigner who arrives, sweating and panting with lust, to thrust his manhood between her thighs and leave her with a curse and a few foreign banknotes stuffed into her corset. There – I think that was it.'

'And a toothbrush,' said Daniel.

He'd had only four hours' sleep the night before and he was already exhausted when they arrived at Heathrow at three o'clock that afternoon. Jack was wearing a shirt his great-aunt had bought him, made out of a small Welsh flag; green and white with a red dragon. The green was very close to the bright shade of the colour that Angela Jardine hated, he thought, then realised that, for a sample of the specific tone she most thoroughly detested, she would have no further to look than the vivid emerald of his own light cotton shirt.

He drew up in the long-stay car park at Heathrow and sat staring ahead of him, motionless.

'Will Mummy be in America?' his son asked.

'No, Jack.'

'Will Grandma be there?'

'Yes.'

'And Granddad?'

'Yes.'

'And Uncle Paul?'

'Yes.'

'And Mummy?'

'No, Jack.'

Walking to the departure gate, he found he had no interest whatever in the security procedure. As the plane reached its cruising altitude, it occurred to him that he was one of the few passengers on the plane who might have been heartened to learn that there was Semtex in the hold. His thoughts kept going back to what Laura had told him about that evening in the Broad Face in Witney, when she'd met Chris, and he'd dared her to go up with him. It was that chance encounter, he thought, which had served as the lure that led her out of her old, safe life, into another, just as the capricious bounce of a football might lead a child to follow it down the garden path, across the pavement, and under the wheels of a truck.

At La Guardia Airport in New York, they had to queue for almost an hour to get through immigration. There were eight officers, each at a booth on a small raised platform, each with a line of dispirited travellers. Daniel's shirt and trousers were plastered in red and brown stains from the ice cream Jack had eaten on the plane. He handed his papers to a middle-aged woman with a greying bouffant. She glanced at his form and tossed it back at him, without speaking. He waited. The woman tapped her pen irritably against a section of the paper.

'Fill in Box Three,' she said. 'Even the Duke of England has to fill in Box Three.' He looked for Box Three and couldn't find it. 'Are you married?' snapped the officer.

'Yes,' he said. 'No. Yes.'

They landed at Salina just before eleven that night. As the plane was circling the small airport, Daniel looked down and saw the airstrip, with its points of light in the darkened landscape. Going back to parachute jumping, he remembered her saying, was like going back to a country house where you'd left a lamp on.

Paul was waiting in his car next to the tiny terminal building. Daniel got in the front seat with Jack on his knee. The boy who, like his father, hadn't rested on the planes, fell instantly into a deep sleep.

'You won't, will you?' Daniel said to Paul, glancing at the car's hi-fi. 'Not today.'

Paul shook his head, earnestly. 'No. I won't, Daniel, no.' He drove the couple of miles down the approach road, and pulled on to the Interstate. 'You know,' he added, 'Laura left an order of service.'

'She what?'

'An order of service. Dad's got it.'

'A will, you mean,' said Daniel, aware of Paul's difficulties with language.

'No,' said Paul. 'There's no will.'

They drew up in the Red Carpet parking lot. Daniel, who was too exhausted to continue this line of investigation, got out and carried his unconscious son towards the entrance.

'Hey – Daniel,' said Paul.

'Yes?'

'I won't what?'

Daniel looked at him. 'Play the music.'

'Oh,' said Paul. 'No. Of course not.' He looked a little hurt. 'I thought you were talking about...you know...Timeshift.'

'For Christ's sake, Paul,' said Daniel. He could almost have smiled. 'Everybody will be doing Timeshift tomorrow. That's what a funeral is.'

He looked across the highway. You could see St David's Church right there, forty yards away, just the other side of the I-70. He wondered if her body was there already and realised it wouldn't be. He said goodnight to Paul and carried Jack into reception. He'd made up his mind to stay at the Red Carpet, not out of anger with the Jardines, but because he felt it would be more tactful, given the nature of his last exit from their house.

There was nobody in reception. There never was, he remembered, at this hour. He carried Jack into the bar, which had its lights on, and a new country CD playing, but was also deserted. He laid the boy on one of the padded bench seats, covered him with his jacket, and leaned across the oak veneer counter. There was a storeroom at the far end of the bar to the right, and its door was open. Inside he could see a large, fair-haired woman who was bending down, fiddling with an air conditioning machine. As she stretched over, facing away from him, he could see the wide expanse of her lower back revealed in the gap between her T-shirt and the waistband of her trousers.

He raised his eyes a little, out of decency, and tried to focus on the contents of the storeroom beyond her. It was dark in there and his eyes were worn out from jet lag and grief. It was used, he guessed, as the staff wardrobe: he could see two or three coats and a handbag. On the top shelf, next to a pair of overshoes, he could just distinguish a small suitcase and, on top of it, a light brown man's hat that looked somehow familiar.

'Lucy?' he called out, tentatively.

She turned round, and stood in the storeroom doorway. At first he thought it must be her older sister. 'Hey,' she said. 'If you're gonna say hello, say it to my face, like a man.'

She was heavier, of course, and there was a new look of disillusion about her eyes; one that had become permanently embedded around the time she was shut up in a twelve by twelve cell, with two prostitutes and a crystal meth dealer, in Bedford County penitentiary. She came out front and saw the boy asleep on the seat. She put out her hand and touched his cheek. He half-woke for a second. 'No, Daddy,' he said. 'Don't prickle.'

'Oh – yeah...' she said. 'Sorry.' Daniel touched a strip of aluminium running down the side of the bar. 'Hey – Daniel,' she said, as if she knew him better than she did. 'I am so sorry.'

He looked away, and then shut his eyes for a few seconds. 'How come you're back here?' he asked.

'Yeah...' she said, 'well, they asked me. The night manager ran off one night, and I guess they were kinda desperate. Then when they saw me, they decided that I wasn't so bad as all that.'

'You're not,' he said.

She went back behind the desk, and poured a Hot Damn! for herself and a whisky, which she handed to him without asking. 'You might be right there,' she said. 'I'm not that bad, you know that?'

'What about the night school?' he asked.

'The classes? To be a...an animal nurse?'

'Yes.'

'I put my name down for this year – for October,' she said. 'I kind of need to save a little more money.'

He was gripped by an insane impulse to take her back to England to cherish her and save her. Like most such moments, it passed. But when he got back to London, and learned of a payment from a life assurance policy he didn't know Laura had, he sent the first five thousand dollars to the receptionist at the Red Carpet.

'Where's Tom?' he asked her.

'Tom's in the jailhouse,' she said. 'I don't see Tom no more.' She reached down, under the counter. 'Hey, Daniel,' she said. 'You know – they won't let me go to...you know. To the church. I have to work tomorrow. Take this there for me.' She handed him a small bunch of violets, their stems wrapped in silver paper. She led him through to the reception desk and opened the reservations book. 'You got eighteen,' she said. 'One double, one single. First floor.'

He started to walk away, then stopped. 'Eighteen's on the second,' he said.

'No,' she said, adding, in what was just recognisable as an imitation of a BBC accent, 'first floor. I'm talking English for you. That's what you call the second floor, right? In England? First floor? I've been learning stuff since you were here, you'd better look out. You know, there was a guy from England here last night; he told me all about that. He checked out. Yeah...' she said, sounding puzzled. 'He forgot a pile of his stuff here. He was kind of nuts.'

'Really?' said Daniel, who was on the edge of sleep and only half listening.

He opened the door of room eighteen and laid the boy, still fully clothed, on the smaller bed. He found a new suit of clothes for Jack, laid out on a table. They'd come from Angela, who had supposed, correctly that Daniel might not bring him along in well-pressed black. He looked at the clock; it was one in the morning. He programmed the phone to ring at eight and lifted Jack, still in his clothes, into the bed, and tucked him in. As he did this, the boy woke up and began to complain. It was small things at first – where was Mr Bear, where were his books – but it grew into an unspecified misery. He got up and lay next to his father on the big bed. For almost an hour, he whimpered quietly at nothing. At half past two, Daniel still in his clothes, finally fell asleep next to him.

When the phone rang, it took him a moment to regain consciousness and, when he did, his first thought was that he was grateful none of his nightmares had recurred. When he spoke, he was greeted not by the automated electronic voice he'd expected, but by Paul, on a cell phone.

'Daniel?' he said.

'Yes...hey – look – since you woke me up early,' Daniel said, 'can you take me out and get some clothes?'

'Yes,' said Paul. 'No problem.' He didn't sound like himself. 'Look Daniel, it's...I mean...'

'Yes?' said Daniel, hating himself for slipping into the bullying, impatient tone that Paul coaxed you into.

'It's...I mean it's just that...they're starting. It's ten to eleven.'

'What?' Daniel looked out of the window. He could see them there, in formal mourning, about to go inside. He felt suddenly alert, for the first time in days. 'Did you get Oakes?' he asked. At the end of the line, there was silence. 'Did you call Father Oakes?' he asked again, more sharply.

'No,' said Paul.

'Jesus, Paul,' he said. 'Jesus. Was it that much. . .'

The line faded, then went dead and he put the phone down.

Before he left his trailer, Paul had sat down alone at his desk. Then, solemnly, and without any enjoyment, he'd drained his novelty St Bernard.

Daniel went from shock and disappointment to anger at himself: first for having placed his trust in the Red Carpet's telephone system, then for shouting at Paul. He remembered what Laura had said: 'enterprising, courageous, masterful.' And – he could remember the inflection of her voice – 'Don't ever lose your temper with Paul.' When it came to social interaction, he realised, her brother was like a dog in a casino: he had learned, by observation and experience, to behave in a way that would not cause offence or disgrace, but he had no real understanding of, or interest in, what was going on around him.

He looked around the hotel room, hoping that his other bag might appear by magic, as things – usually with the help of Rosa and the paper's chauffeurs – had been seeming to do of late. He looked at his watch: it was seven minutes to eleven. He got up as he was – in the same green shirt he had worn in the general store at St David's and the same pair of cream linen trousers, smeared in pink and brown ice-cream stains. He hadn't shaved for two days. He picked up Jack, still asleep, still wearing the flag of Wales, and carried him down through reception. Against his skin, his own shirt had the adhesive, irritating warmth of a garment that has been slept in. He crossed the footbridge over the I-70 and went in the back gate of the church, a white-painted concrete construction from the fifties. He felt the boy begin to stir as he carried him through the cemetery, where another burial service was ending. 'Pee pee,' said Jack. He led the child round behind a gravestone. When they came out, Jack looked across the cemetery, to the place where a mourner at the previous service was throwing the first, ceremonial handful of earth into a new grave. He thought of Angela and her horror of the soil.

'Comfy earth,' said Jack.

As they drew level with the back of the church, he saw the figure of a man, leaning face-first against the back of the church building. He had raised his right forearm, and placed it between his forehead and the concrete wall, to avoid grazing his head, which was taking most of his weight.

Daniel recognised Laura's brother and approached him from behind. He seemed utterly sunk in distress.

'Paul,' he said. 'I'm sorry. It doesn't matter about Oakes.' He touched him on the shoulder. 'You know, you mustn't...'

The young man spun round; he had been urinating against the church wall, and his unexpected movement added two unmistakable streaks to the chocolate and wine that had already discoloured Daniel's trousers.

'Shit,' said Paul. It was the first time Daniel had heard him swear.

He looked at Daniel's clothes. 'Hey,' he said, sounding almost assertive, 'you know, they're not gonna like that.'

'Why?' said Daniel. 'Because they'll think that because I'm not in a suit that means I didn't care?'

Paul shook his head. 'No.'

'Why then?'

'Because it looks like you think you're someone.'

Daniel took out his handkerchief, which was already grey, spat into it and tried to clean Jack's face, which was smeared with chocolate and ice cream. He remembered how he had hated that as a child, and gave up. He picked the boy up and Paul followed them round to the front entrance of St David's. The church was full; the congregation's clothes a respectful monochrome. In the second pew from the front on the left, he could see her parents. They'd left three spaces free on the end, by the aisle. He walked quickly towards it, followed by Paul, without glancing at the backs of the other mourners. It must have been what Angela saw, he thought, when she was a bride. He sat down next to his mother-in-law, and put Jack on his right. Paul took the end seat to Jack's right, by the aisle. Daniel felt – no, not felt, was – filthy. Out of the corner of his left eye, he caught Mrs Jardine's first look, which, despite herself, was not one of condolence but of disappointed, seething reproach.

He kept his eyes forwards, facing the coffin. Laura had told everyone – even her parents – that she didn't want to be buried in pine, 'otherwise that means all furniture becomes morbid, right? That means my wardrobe's like burial chamber.' Instead they had chosen – at a cost, he discovered later, f eight thousand dollars – a casket with a polished ivory effect and gold-lated handles. It might have been modelled on some Beverly Hills pimp's retch limo. The inside, he couldn't stop himself thinking, was probably pholstered to match.

The organist, behind them, was playing a Brahms fugue out of time. To e side of the pulpit, Daniel noticed a CD player, plugged in to what he cognised as Paul's tiny black Naim amplifier and the small wooden eakers decorated with their Swiss cross. They looked innocuous enough ıt, as he knew, in a hall this size they could have powered a small rock ınd.

'What's that for?' he whispered to Laura's brother.

'The music,' he said.

'Music?'

'The music she asked for.'

'What…' Daniel began, but as he started to speak, the organ stopped aying, and the priest appeared in the raised pulpit.

Laura died, as Paul had said, without leaving a will. The brief structions she had left for her funeral consisted of a few lines she'd ritten on a single sheet of paper and left in an envelope with her brother. er notes were limited to a couple of stipulations about music and a quest that the service should be conducted by Father Oakes.

But Father Oakes was in Melbourne, ministering to his dying mother. is replacement, Father Delancey, drove in from Salina to deliver a tronising and formal sermon, in the course of which he looked bored, ver addressed the cause of her death and, at one point, referred to her as rna. When Delancey had stopped speaking, he motioned to Paul, who ached into his suit pocket and pulled out a plastic remote control unit hich he pointed at the CD machine. Nothing happened. Daniel looked on th a mixture of anger and disbelief. He shut his eyes and kept them shut, d drew in a deep breath and held it.

He would hold it, he swore to himself, as a child might swear, until his ngs burst, or he passed out. His resolve was interrupted by the sound of acoustic guitar. It was so real that he had to open his eyes and start eathing again, if only because he felt that he might already be suffering e effects of oxygen starvation and he needed to discover if he was seeing ings as well as hearing them. He didn't recognise the piece until a oman's voice began to sing with a terrible, mournful clarity: 'If you miss the train I'm on, you will know that I am gone, you can hear the whis blow a hundred miles...'

It was a slow, intense version of the song that used to wake them their room over The Owl, a recording he'd never heard before. The sing was American and she was articulating each phrase deliberately a precisely, but not with the dead meticulousness of a classical sing attempting pop music.

She sang the words as though her life depended on them. By the tir she reached the chorus: 'Lord I'm one...Lord I'm two...Lord I'm thr ...Lord I'm four...Lord I'm five hundred miles away from home' – h mind was already drifting away. 'A thousand and one, thousand and tw he found himself thinking. 'Christopher one, Christopher two.' He cou sense a feeling all round the church that Laura Jardine, who had be absent from this gathering – in spirit, if not in body – was suddenly amo them, as tangibly as if she had materialised in flesh and blood, up whe Delancey was stood in the pulpit. And the contagious emotion which mig have been generated by the absent priest was beginning to build and surge through the church and envelop it and him. For the first time sin she died, he started to be overcome by his emotions: by the way he w missing her, by his blind fury at her decision to go up that day, and by t first pangs of a naked, inconsolable grief and loneliness.

His right hand was in his front trouser pocket; in his left, he had Luc small bunch of violets, in their crumpled silver foil. Jack was still sitti motionless between Daniel and Paul. A couple of rows behind them, woman had begun to utter half-stifled sobs. He could see Delancey with h head bowed, still in the pulpit. I am not going to weep, he thought himself, in these words, in English, in front of that bastard. And yet, sensed, he was going to. Against the back of his right hand, he could f an old dry-cleaning ticket that had been pinned inside the pocket. It w held in place by a safety pin. Without removing his hand from the pock he undid the clasp and held the opened safety pin between his thumb a his right index finger, with the sharp point pressing down against the t of his thumb. He pressed hard and felt a sharp pain as the pin pricked skin, just beneath the nail. He held it there. When the recording fad away, he had a curious feeling of having survived.

There was a moment's silence. It was broken by two slowly ascend triplets of notes on a cello, followed by a deep, melancholy stroke of bow on a bass string. This sequence he did recognise, but now it seemed bypass his conscious mind and connect directly to his heart and memory. 'Summertime withers,' the voice of Elvis Costello sang, 'as the sun descends. He wants to kiss you, will you condescend...'

Without realising what he was doing, he pressed the safety pin with all his force, so that the point was driven down hard, inside the front of his right thumbnail. It went to the bottom of the nail, to the cuticle, and stayed there, embedded. He drew his breath in sharply, but he didn't cry out. 'Before you wake and find a chill within your bones; under a fine canopy of lover's dust and humerus bones...Banish all dismay, extinguish every sorrow. If I'm lost or I'm forgiven, the birds will still be singing.'

He found himself thinking of Whittington's dumb, defenceless grief in the face of the voice of Chaliapin. You couldn't quite call it crying, he thought, stupidly, to himself. It wasn't quite crying, because his tears didn't so much fall as run – constantly and in a barely perceptible stream, from his eyes. It was more as if he'd been cut and he'd started to bleed. He stared straight ahead at the blurred figure of Delancey. He could sense Angela, still impassive, next to him.

The music ended. The brief instructions left by the deceased, Delancey mentioned, said that anybody present who had known her and who wished to speak, should do. There was no response. Then Paul, in the only unprompted gesture Daniel had ever seen him make, began to pull Daniel's right sleeve. He tugged at it like a child, imperceptibly at first, then much harder.

He stepped out, past Laura's brother, and walked the few paces to the top of the aisle, where he stood for a second or two, with his back to the congregation. He glanced down at himself. His right hand was still in his pocket and, to add to the patchwork of urine, grime and chocolate that covered his trousers, a circle of crimson the size of a tennis ball had spread out in the linen material around the pocket at the top of his right leg. He turned around.

'For the people who knew her,' he said, 'and for the people here who never met her...' He resisted a temptation to glance back at the priest. 'I would like to give you an idea of how she was, in life and, through the memories she has left, in death.' He stopped. Around him there was silence: not the uneasy silence you might expect at such a public gathering, broken by a stifled cough, a creak of shoe leather, or the distant sound of a motor scooter, but total silence, as quiet, he found himself thinking, as the grave.

He was abruptly overtaken by fear, the kind of fear that Guy Montgomery used to tell him about. It occurred to him that he had spent most of his recent life in finding appropriate words to commemorate the dead and he had no idea of what he was going to say next. For the first time he began to notice faces in the congregation he recognised; first Kate, in one of the rear pews and – a couple of rows behind Paul – Jessica Lee and Brendan.

He looked at Jack. He had his face pressed into Paul's side; his uncle's left arm was around his shoulder. From the moment the music had begun, the boy had been strangely subdued, as if he had somehow finally sensed, and acknowledged, the awful presence of real tragedy.

'I'll give you an Oliver,' Daniel told them, 'for One.'

As he said this, Angela Jardine let out a deep moan, as if the sound had been physically wrenched out of her. She stepped into the aisle, walked up to him, and buried her head against his shoulder. He could feel her tears falling against his skin and her eyelashes against his neck. He was briefly unsure how he should react, as this woman leaned into him for support. He put his left arm lightly in the small of her back and spoke again.

'I'll give you an Oliver for One,' he said. 'Alive.'